I0587132

A GAME OF HORNS

A RED UNICORN ANTHOLOGY

A GAME OF HORNS

A RED UNICORN ANTHOLOGY

Edited by Lisa Mangum

WordFire Press
Colorado Springs, Colorado

A GAME OF HORNS
Copyright © 2015 WordFire Press, 2015

Additional copyright information on page 291

All rights reserved. No part of this book may be reproduced or transmitted in any form or by any electronic or mechanical means, including photocopying, recording or by any information storage and retrieval system, without the express written permission of the copyright holder, except where permitted by law. This novel is a work of fiction. Names, characters, places and incidents are either the product of the author's imagination, or, if real, used fictitiously.

ISBN: 978-1-61475-352-0

Cover painting by James A. Owen

Cover design by James A. Owen

Art Director Kevin J. Anderson

Book Design by RuneWright, LLC
www.RuneWright.com

Published by
WordFire Press, an imprint of
WordFire, Inc.
PO Box 1840
Monument CO 80132

Kevin J. Anderson & Rebecca Moesta, Publishers

WordFire Press Trade Paperback Edition September 2015
Printed in the USA
www.wordfire.com

DEDICATION

One of our most dedicated, enthusiastic, and supportive attendees of the Superstars Writing Seminars was Don Hodge—a man who got into writing late in life, but jumped in with both feet. Despite his physical difficulties, he was a light of optimism and eagerness.

Don first came to Superstars in 2012 in Las Vegas, and came to four in a row. The last we saw him was in February 2015 at the Colorado Springs seminar. Don passed away on August 15, 2015, and everyone in his Superstars Tribe misses him.

Because he was so supportive of the cause to bring more writers to the seminar, and to help those who needed an extra hand, we are proud to dedicate this *A Game of Horns* to Don's memory.

All profits from this anthology, and the previous volume, *One Horn to Rule Them All*, go into a scholarship fund to being less-fortunate students to the Superstars Writing Seminar. As of 2015, we have renamed that fund the Don Hodge Memorial Scholarship.

CONTENTS

WHEN DID UNICORNS TURN RED?

I started devouring fantasy as soon as I learned to read. Sometimes I had as many as four or five books going at a time. I left them all over the house and picked up whichever book happened to be handy. I even read in bed after lights-out. I didn't have a flashlight, so I would sneak a book under the covers and read one line at a time by the light of my electric blanket controls.

Those stories whisked me away to worlds populated by unicorns, dragons, wizards, talking beasts, knights in armor, and teens who pulled swords from stones or fought against evil on the way to becoming kings and queens.

As a child of the 1960s and 1970s, I loved all things mystical, magical, and wondrous. For me, my favorite images from that era are inextricably bound together: sunshine, puffy white clouds, peace signs, flower children, smiley faces, sparkles, rainbows—and unicorns.

In paintings and tapestries and myths, unicorns are most often portrayed as pale, ethereal creatures, so of course, I thought of them as pure and noble horse-like beings that practically glowed with magical light. They lived in forest glens and paused in their virtuous thoughts only to be petted by fair maidens in flowing dresses.

Of course, that's not the only kind of unicorn. I used to watch *Star Trek* (the original series) with my dad. In the episode "The Enemy Within" there's actually a tawny-colored unicorn *dog*. Not only wasn't it a milky color, it looked nothing like a horse. So even with unicorns the imagination can run wild.

As Kevin J. Anderson described in his introduction to *One Horn to Rule Them All: A Purple Unicorn Anthology*, he and I adopted the purple unicorn to represent a philosophy we taught: Writers should do their best work in the allotted time, no matter the writing assignment. If writers can't respect their readers enough to do a good job, they shouldn't accept the contract. Purple unicorns symbolize commitment to quality.

When our series editor, Lisa Mangum, and our managing editor, Peter Wacks, suggested that our next anthology feature *red* unicorns (complete with the perfect title from Finley Scogin), we were surprised at first and then intrigued. The color red is full of energy. Our society uses red to express so many ideas—anger, heat, love, war, danger, embarrassment, not to mention spiciness or ripe fruit—what stories would it inspire? Of *course* we wanted red unicorns.

So the following pages hold a wealth of red unicorn stories to entertain you.

Are red unicorns real? Just as real as all the other colors of unicorns. And I can't wait to see what comes after *A Game of Horns: A Red Unicorn Anthology*.

Until the next volume,

Rebecca Moesta, Publisher
WordFire Press

A Game of Horns: A Red Unicorn Anthology is the second benefit anthology to fund Superstars Writing Seminars scholarships which covers tuition for writers who have not yet had the opportunity to attend a seminar.

M.Y.T.H. Rule

Jody Lynn Nye

Gleep!" I exclaimed in surprise, as a sharp-pointed horn poked me in the back. I snaked back my long, sinuous, green-scaled neck to confront the wielder of that horn. "Why did you do that?"

Buttercup, my pet's white war unicorn, a strapping, snowy equine with a pearlescent pointed protuberance jutting nearly two feet out between his eyes, eyed me grimly over the end of the leash clenched in his teeth.

"Just keep moving, Gleep," he said. "Please."

I sighed and kept pulling forward. The appealingly atrocious scent that I had smelled at the nearest intersection of two dusty streets full of tents would have to go unresearched, at least for the moment. I continued onward into the thick of the colorful crowd.

At the sight of a green dragon, even a youthful wurm such as myself, most of the shoppers and shopkeepers in the broad expanse of boutiques, booths, tents, and kiosks that made up the Bazaar at Deva—red-skinned Deveels, magenta-hued Imps, pale Kobolds, handsome Whelfs, even a few assorted Klahds—cleared a path to put themselves out of immediate reach.

My kind has a well-deserved reputation for being dangerous. In the wild, these creatures might have been my legitimate prey. All that prevented them from running, levitating, or teleporting to safety seeing me walking free were the reputation of my pet,

Skeeve, who although a Klahd, was well-known in the Bazaar as a master magician, and the gleaming white war unicorn holding my leash. I was considered to be "under control," when that was far from being the truth. The only reason that I permitted myself to be treated as a dumb animal was for Buttercup's sake.

It had come to Skeeve's attention that Buttercup was unhappy in his enforced exile from martial action. Most bipedal creatures across the dimensions concentrate far more on safety than those with four or more limbs. For the sake of his new master, Buttercup had tried to be happy in the lap of luxury, fed only the finest mash and hay, with carrots, sugar, and apples for treats, bedded down on clean straw every night, in a palatial stable and curried daily by expert stable hands, but in truth, the unicorn longed for the days when he served as a mount to Sir Quigley. Together, they had faced terrible enemies in danger dire circumstances. That knight, who had turned out to be less than a true, honest, virtuous paladin, had at least fought in battles, the life for which Buttercup had been bred and trained.

Skeeve had no wish to put Buttercup into unnecessary danger, and therein lay the dilemma. Klahds like him, raised in small villages, away from the machinations of the great and the good, didn't understand the defense of their nations, whereas I had been educated from the egg by my mother, who was a scholar in all the martial traditions. We denizens of Draco were frequently called in by one side or often both in a conflict. War often becomes a habit. Hence, my agreement that something should be done to help Buttercup.

But Skeeve did not like to let me or the unicorn far out of his sight. I think my pet became insecure when I was away. (Thus, I never informed him when I took Pervish leave, as they say, to pursue my own interests. I always made certain to be back where he expected to see me.)

The solution, in his mind, was to occupy Buttercup within the environment that Skeeve spent most of his time: the Bazaar at Deva. It was crowded with groups who were often inimical to one another, striving for territorial or economic superiority. A great deal of underhanded negotiation and subterfuge went on here. Betrayal was commonplace. A being who was one's ally one day could be tempted into the enemy camp the next. Danger lay around every corner, whether it was an apothecary's tent that could blow up at the drop of a phial of potion, a tent full of dragons, a Pervish restaurant teeming with dishes that were still mobile and smelled like death, pickpockets, rogue magicians, merchants who might cut one another's throats if and when no one was looking, and worst of all, joke shops full of magikal prank items. In other words, the Bazaar was as close to being a war zone as any declared or undeclared hostilities anywhere in the dimensions.

The exercise usually worked splendidly. Buttercup was to take me out for walkies, usually to a point some miles distant from our primary tent, achieve a task of some ilk, then return me, himself, and the object of our trip to our tent without killing anyone or being killed ourselves along the way. If trouble arose, I had been enjoined by Skeeve not to take action on my own, but to let Buttercup handle it. I agreed, although I was always ready to lend my strength and the fearsomeness of my species' reputation should there be need. There seldom was. Even an Ogre wasn't foolish enough to take on a war unicorn in full barding and a half-grown dragon.

Usually.

On this day, however, my friend and companion seemed edgier than usual.

"What is troubling you?" I asked him as we trotted around the next corner.

"My horn is tingling," he said. "It indicates the presence of a foe."

"One?" I raised the scales over my eyes in surprise and looked around me. "The Bazaar is full of inimical entities. Why haven't you reacted before?"

"This is one of my own kind," he said, his large brown eyes solemn. "It is following us. We must be ready to defend ourselves."

I sniffed the air. The acrid soup that passed for atmosphere in the desert environ was laden with the odor of unwashed bodies, the aforementioned Pervish cooking, and numerous other stenches. Buttercup, by comparison, smelled of his plant-based diet, the leather and steel of his barding, and sweet-sour sweat exuding deliciously from his flesh.

Then, I scented a similar odor not far away. I spun on a claw, alarming a Whelf girl wearing a tiny white veil on her long golden hair. She beat me with her shopping basket and let out a loud scream.

Loud hoof beats erupted from nearby, growing louder by the moment.

"I will save you from this foul beast, fair maiden!" a stentorian voice announced.

The crowd parted suddenly, making way for a long, sharp horn. My reactions, being far faster than those of mere Deveels and Whelfs, allowed me to step to one side, permitting the oncoming equine to charge past me.

Buttercup had been correct. The newcomer was indeed a male war unicorn, though instead of pearly white, his coat was blood red. His eyes, too, gleamed red. Like Buttercup, this unicorn was well-muscled and armored as though for battle. He wheeled on a single polished ruddy hoof and came around again, his horn lowered and aiming for my heart.

I shook my head in disbelief. To challenge a dragon, in broad daylight, with the dragon's full knowledge and attention focused upon him? The creature must be insane. Better to put him out of his and everyone else's misery. I took a deep breath, preparing to envelop him in flame.

"No, Gleep!" Buttercup whinnied.

"What? Why not?" I demanded, leaping to one side as the stranger charged me again. The red unicorn thundered past, emitting a neigh of frustration. He turned in a half circle and prepared to come back at me.

"Because your safety is *my* responsibility!" Buttercup dropped my lead from his teeth and galloped into the oncoming unicorn's way. He lowered his horn and braced himself.

The red unicorn's lips drew back from his enormous square teeth in a fearsome rictus. This seemed to be exactly what he had been hoping would occur. He pounded forward, aiming for Buttercup's heart.

My friend might have been away from the field of battle for some time, but he had kept his skills, as well as his horn, honed to a fine point. As the red tine lunged inward, the white horn flicked underneath, then pushed it up and around in a perfect parry. The stranger countered the parry masterfully, then made his own riposte. Buttercup withdrew a pace, then lunged in his turn.

Parry! Riposte! Counter-parry! Disengage! Fleche! Remise! Ballestra!

The two unicorns slashed, drew back, lunged, countered, leaped, and thrust, each seeking the advantage against the other's defense. The horns nearly drew sparks as they clashed and slid against one another. Their manes and tails tossed and flew like live creatures. Their nostrils flared majestically, and their eyes gleamed in the heat of battle.

I watched with admiration. Buttercup cut red lines again and again on the other's scarlet coat. Blood, almost indistinguishable from the color, rolled down his side. The newcomer did not pay heed to his injuries, nor did he manage to draw blood even once. My friend more than held his own against the attacker, yet the red unicorn refused to retreat. I could have stepped in at any moment and ended the bout on the spot, yet I was reluctant to do so. Buttercup did not need me to intercede. Instead, I had the opportunity to observe and enjoy.

"Awright, awright!" A large Deveel, a butcher by the bloody white apron tied around his waist, stormed out of his tent and clomped on angry cloven hooves toward the fray. "Knock it off! Get out of here! You're distracting my customers!"

Distraction, indeed! If he drew Buttercup's attention away from his battle, it could prove fatal. I zipped between the Deveel and the combatants, and raised my face to confront his.

"Grrrrrrr!" I snarled, showing my pointed white teeth.

The Deveel blanched to a pale pink. I lowered my head slightly, my ears plastered low, and started to glide purposefully in his direction. The Deveel backed away, holding his hands in the air.

"Okay, I can see it's a personal disagreement. I get it! I'm going!"

By the time I turned around, the battle had moved into a narrow alleyway. Many of the Deveels and Imps watching had taken to offering bets on the outcome. The red unicorn was at bay. His rump had been backed nearly all the way against a refuse heap over which flies the size of my nose buzzed. Buttercup had scored yet another five gashes on what hide was exposed on the red unicorn's legs and breast.

"Do you surrender?" he neighed.

"No!" the newcomer insisted, executing another ballestra, which Buttercup easily evaded. "*You* surrender!"

"Me?" Buttercup asked, twisting his body into a semicircle to confront the red unicorn. "Why should I surrender?" He lowered his horn into attack position. At that range, he could not miss the stranger's exposed belly.

The red unicorn pranced this way and that, but he realized he had put himself into an indefensible position.

I sniffed. My keen nose picked up on yet another scent exuding from the newcomer: desperation.

I interposed my head and neck hastily between the two unicorns.

"We surrender!" I said. "Halt your fierce attack, stranger!"

The red unicorn stopped to-ing and fro-ing and stared at me, his mouth agape.

"You do? I mean, you surrender to me?"

"Gleep, I was about to skewer him!" Buttercup protested. "Why should we—?"

I raised a claw to silence his outburst. "May we know the name of our conqueror?"

The red unicorn raised his head proudly. Both of us could see he was exhausted. Once the fire in his eyes went out, there was little left but ashes.

"I am Donnybrook, war unicorn of Marquardt, Hero of the Mesmerance Siege, and Steed of the Gallant Lady Sir Bosena of Syrah! Whom do I have the honor to address?"

"Well," I said, "my pet calls me Gleep. That will do."

"Hail, Gleep, Dragon of the Fair, er, Garden." Donnybrook glanced over his shoulder at the rubbish heap. "And hail to thee, Buttercup, Victor of Hamakamand, Slayer of the Cyclopedian The-saurus, and Reaver of Umbulicus."

Buttercup lowered his eyes to avoid mine. I had always won-dered at the history that my companion went to so much trouble to conceal. Questions could wait. The bettors at the head of the alley looked annoyed that the fight had concluded without a clear winner. A couple of them looked as though they wanted to force the unicorns to go on with their battle. A lifted lip and a low growl from me sent them in pursuit of less hazardous amusement.

"Come with me, O our captor," I said, wrapping my tail over Donnybrook's withers. "The day is dry and hot. We would be honored to offer you refreshments."

"I have never admitted defeat in my life!" Buttercup hissed peevishly as I led the way back to our secondary quarters. Donnybrook trailed in our wake, as though shepherding his new possessions, or perhaps walking behind so as not to let us see how tired he was. "It is against my code of honor! Why did you force us to surrender?"

"I will happily claim the defeat as my own," I whispered back, keeping my head close to his twitching ear. "A dragon's honor doesn't depend on whether or not she or he has spent time in captivity. But I chose to take a leaf from my pet's book. Skeeve would see that this fellow was woefully overmatched against your skills. If his aim was to defeat you, he would not be trying to capture you. Therefore, I surmise that he requires you for some other purpose than as a chattel. As an ally, perhaps?"

Buttercup shook his head fiercely as though to dislodge a unicorn-fly. "Never! The Red-Pelted League and the White Company have never been allied."

I pushed out my lower lip thoughtfully. "Then perhaps he came to ask for your help."

"I owe him nothing. I have no reason to assist him."

I allowed a long, slow smile to touch my lips.

"I did not say we would tender our assistance for nothing. Consider my pet and his friends and allies. They demand consideration for their expertise in solving enigmas. We can do the same thing."

Buttercup emitted a scornful snort. "I do not equate being taken prisoner with being employed. Why would he not simply ask us to undertake a mission?"

"I would assume," I said, glancing back at our momentary captor and taking in the scuffed state of his barding and the piecemeal repairs done on his headstall and other accouterments, "because he has no money."

9

My assessment was further confirmed when we offered Donnybrook a bite of hay and apples in the lush garden that served as our daytime domicile. It was in a transdimensional space behind the back wall of a small and unprepossessing tent in the middle of the Bazaar. To look at it from the outside, the canvas was stained and much mended, suggesting the extreme poverty that many Deveel merchants feign in hopes of taking advantage of buyers' sympathy. On the inside, it was palatial, with a stable equal to many a king's castle in other dimensions. Skeeve saw to it that suitable food for me and Buttercup was laid out on a daily basis. Price was no object. Every item, from the oats to the fire-clams, was first-class.

I presented the sumptuous array of comestibles and was rewarded with a gleam in the red unicorn's eyes.

"We will sample these foods in your presence, if you are concerned whether or not they are fit for your consumption," I offered.

Donnybrook shouldered us aside. He knocked me sprawling, and I am no lightweight.

"I'm sure they are all fine," he said, and began to chomp his way noisily through our rations, including the choice cuts of meat that were intended for my consumption. Buttercup and I glanced at one another over his back. When at last the red unicorn crunched down the last sugar cube, he stuck his head into the broad, enameled water trough and slurped away until the level of the liquid dropped visibly. He must not have eaten for days.

When Donnybrook turned away from the depleted board, I dipped my head humbly.

"And how may we serve you, good unicorn?" I asked.

"Why would you think I need *your* help?" Donnybrook asked, his nose raised in a haughty manner. Buttercup snorted. The red unicorn sighed, and his arched neck drooped. "Is it that obvious?"

"As plain as the horn on your face," I said. I curled into a spiral on a bale of straw and tucked my tail around my feet. "Tell us about it, great and honorable master. Leave out no detail, however small."

Donnybrook met our eyes. "I have behaved abominably. I need help to undo a terrible wrong. My mistress has been taken prisoner, and it is all my fault."

"How so?"

"Do you know the dimension of Monsteros?" We nodded. Though I had not visited it myself, I knew its reputation well. "There is a long and endless war going on among many families. My mistress and I took arms on behalf of one of the clans against the tyrant, Jorjarrm."

"Gleep!" At the sound of that name, I straightened my spine. "Did you say Jorjarrm? He is still alive?"

"Yes. He is the lord of Monsteros. We fought hard, but we were greatly outnumbered. Most of the Red-Pelted League were captured or killed. Too few of them remain free to rally." He eyed me. "I was reluctant to come to ask for Buttercup's assistance, knowing that he has come to be allied not only with Klahds and Perverts, but with you. Monsteros has an army of dragons at its beck. But we need to set my mistress free. Winter is coming, and the inhabitants of Monsteros expose their prisoners to the elements—those that they do not take as slaves or slaughter outright—in order to take wagers on how long an individual captive will last. I am afraid that Lady Sir Bosena will die. She hates to be cold."

"Pray go back to the beginning," I said.

I sat back as the red unicorn unfolded his tale of woe, complete with shadow fencing to depict how he and his mistress had defeated many foes, until they were overcome.

"So," Donnybrook concluded, with a breathy sigh, "I rushed to the open spell we were to have used as an escape. That propelled me through the dimensions to Deva. I knew of Buttercup's alliance, and hoped to ... I mean, he would be a worthy conquest."

Buttercup glared at him.

I tented my claws on my belly and tapped them together one by one. I was not disinclined to assist him. Donnybrook was angry at the lord of Monsteros because of his mistress's captivity. Buttercup bitterly resented being made chattel to an old rival. I was angry, because I knew the reputation of the ruler of Monsteros. Smoke shot from my nostrils, making my companions cough at the sulfurous fumes.

"What we have here," I said, after a long and thoughtful pause to dampen my temper, "is a three-gripe problem. I believe we can solve it, but we must move swiftly."

"How?" Buttercup asked. "*We* don't have the ability to dimension-hop."

"But my pet does," I said with a smile. I went inside the cottage to the magikal safe that housed a number of valuable items that my pet wished to protect against misuse. I spun the wheel with my claws and retrieved his D-hopper. Skeeve had never mastered it, being only a young Klahd, but I knew how to operate it safely.

BAMF!

O O O

The temperature of Monsteros was not only far colder than the Bazaar, but markedly chilly when compared with the garden from which we had departed. One could not determine the color of the sky through the thick, iron-gray clouds that covered it. Snow began to fall. It settled upon the coats of my companions, but melted off my scales because of my natural heat.

"What are we going to do?" Donnybrook asked, puzzled. "There are only three of us. We cannot hope to win through to Jorjarrm's castle."

"Yes, we can," I said. "I will make sure of that." I knew my eyes glowed. Donnybrook jumped back in alarm.

"Why do you hate him so much?" Buttercup asked curiously.

"Because," I said, fire escaping my jaws, "he collects dragons. He has enslaved dozens of my kin over the decades. My mother told me of her grandsire, who went there for promised gold and disappeared. We kept his hoard warm for ages, but he never returned home. These dragons do not fight for him willingly. We will win through."

"But he is all-powerful, and he keeps an enormous army," Donnybrook said. "We can't defeat him. That's why I ... er ... retreated."

"He will admit us without question if we give him a present," I said, and smiled. "Me."

We trotted through the snow, passing checkpoints full of hairy soldiers. Denizens of Monsteros were large, ogre-like beings with thick beards and glass circles on frames made to protect their eyes, and caps made of leather that kept the endless snow off their shaggy pates. The two unicorns kept me on a tether. I pretended to pull them from side to side, rushing up to each guard post to greet the Monsters with a cheerful "Gleep!" and an affectionate lick.

Naturally, the guards let us pass. We left them wiping off the slime. I should not have favored them, but I was trying to make a good impression. I disliked being here, but we had given our word to Donnybrook to assist him.

At last, we reached the Wide Castle, the center of government, and the site on which so many of the Red-Pelted League of unicorns had fallen. The Castle itself was monstrous in scope, covering the landscape as far as the eye could see, but with only one gigantic entrance—a curtain wall protected by an iron portcullis. This would not be easily escaped.

A couple of the guards escorted us from the gate to the keep itself. A shaggy Monster herald, wearing a tabard whose charge could be described as "Per pale, dexter, on a field, gules, a flame, or; sinister, on a field azure, a snowflake, argent," led us into the great hall and announced us. It seemed they were accustomed to admitting tributes that delivered themselves

As we were ushered in to the vast vaulted room, which was supported by massive white beams that looked like the ribs of ancient dragons, I beheld dragons of every size and shape being pressed into service in the most menial of tasks. A white dragon spewed pools of water over the polished stone floor, which were then rendered into steam by small red dragons. Any scum that floated up was scorched and eaten by a flock of tiny yellow dragons no bigger than my claw. Each of them caught my eye, then looked away in embarrassment. Magnificent denizens of Draco, reduced to servants and housekeepers! I was outraged. But that was not the greatest humiliation. Other dragonkin served as messengers, flying by with scrolls clutched in their claws, as pest-catchers, or worse yet, as furniture.

At the end of the room was a massive throne made of bent swords, broken shields, crushed helms, and the skulls and bones of innumerable creatures. In this repellent seat reposed an enormous monster. I had never seen him in person, but his infamy lived on in legend and song. He was a huge, burly, ogre-like being with a massive beard that overspread the fire-and-ice device on his

13

stained, knee-length, split-skirted tunic. He brandished a huge multipart scepter in his right fist. His booted feet were propped upon the back of a slim, female copper-skinned dragon. She looked angry but was obviously unable to move.

We halted below the dais. To my horror, I began to feel that the female dragon was lucky to have the feet of the tyrant resting upon her. What was wrong with me?

"Hail, Jorjarrm, ruler of Monsteros!" Donnybrook said, through teeth clenched on my right lead. "We bring you a gift!"

"Cute!" Jorjarrm said, leaning forward and peering at me through his glass lenses. Disgusted with myself for the appeal I felt from him, I opened my eyes as wide as they would go and pranced up to him. "I could wear you for a brooch."

Suddenly, I felt as though I wanted to be petted and dandled by this Monster. I climbed up into his lap and slurped his face with my long tongue. Jorjarrm laughed and batted me away gently. He was so huge that I could curl up on his legs like a kittensnake on my pet's. I could not believe it, but I *wanted* to do just that. I gave Jorjarrm another lick, then hated myself for the compulsion. This Monster had imprisoned my grandsire, and now he had cast some kind of geas on me. I shot a look at Buttercup, pleading for help. The white unicorn pawed the floor, not knowing what to do. The closer I was to the ruler of Monsteros, the more I felt a fraternal connection to him. Could he truly be the Brother of Dragons?

"What shall I call you?" he asked. Monsteros natives were slightly akin to my dimension of Draco, so I could understand him, although he spoke with a terrible nasal accent.

"Gleep!" I exclaimed.

"Gleep, then!" Jorjarrm leaned back and laughed heartily. He brandished the massive wand. "Come here, boy! I must dub you. Come and join the Mystical Company of Monsteros."

So that was it! The wand created the compulsion. If it touched me, I would fall helpless to his command.

"But I already adore you," I said, dodging the scepter as I tried to keep my wits about me. "I do not need to be put under a spell."

In answer, he grabbed me by the neck and bopped me on the skull with the tip of the wand. The blow was cursory, but the effect was overwhelming. My head rang with a tone like a bronze bell that grew louder and louder until my senses were dazed. When it faded at last, I gazed at Jorjarrm. My heart filled with admiration. I could not think of a place I would rather be than in his lap. I crooned and turned over so he could scratch my chest. I couldn't imagine why I had ever wanted to defeat him.

"That's better," Jorjarrm said with a jovial laugh. "You are adorable, but I already have plenty of dragons. What shall I do with you? I know! I shall give you to my bride-to-be as a wedding present!" He swept the scepter to include Buttercup and Donnybrook. "All three of you!" The red unicorn visibly twitched. Buttercup nudged him and shot him a warning look. "Call for my bride!"

With a loud fanfare, the doors of the audience chamber were flung wide. Prancing female monsters clad in flowing yellow lace danced into the room. They carried baskets of scented white flowers which they scattered onto the freshly scrubbed floor. I saw the cleaner dragons, now huddled in a corner, sigh heavily.

Two Monster heralds blew lustily on trumpets. In a moment, four Monster maidens appeared, dragging between them the female that must have been Jorjarrm's bride. To my astonishment, she was not a Monster herself, but a Syrene, a race akin to Klahds. She was tall, strong and raven-haired, but dressed in a flowing white gown that was a dozen times too large for her, and her tresses had been braided clumsily around a shimmering diadem.

"Mistress!" Donnybrook whinnied, rearing eagerly. So that was Lady Sir Bosena! The ladies-in-waiting dragged her to the dais and threw her on the steps. Before she could right herself, Jorjarrm reached down and picked her up with one massive hand. He set her on his lap as he had done with me. She slapped him in the face. He only grinned.

"She's feisty," Jorjarrm said, gazing at her in adoration. "I love that. Look, my darling! I have presents for you!"

"The only present I want is to go home," Bosena said. She struggled to get down, like a toddler trapped on a great-aunt's lap. I couldn't imagine why she would want to.

"Look at them, beloved," the Monster insisted, pointing at us. "It's a dragon! Just for you."

"A dragon?" Bosena asked. "You have hundreds of them! How many dragons do you need?"

"You can never have too many dragons," Jorjarrm said, practically. "And two unicorns! A matched set, red and white. They are your wedding presents from me. The dragon is called Gleep." He gave her a hopeful look. I realized he truly wanted to please her, but it was not an easy task.

For the first time Bosena turned to look at us. When her eyes met Donnybrook's, she stopped struggling. Jorjarrm let her go. She slid off his lap and walked down the steps of the dais. When she reached Donnybrook, she grabbed him by the horn and forced his face to the floor.

"How dare you desert me!" she bellowed. Her voice echoed in the stone-roofed hall. "I would not be here if not for you!"

"I could not help it, mistress," Donnybrook said to her shoes. "I am sorry!"

"A hundred demerits, for leaving me in the hands of this imbecile!"

I giggled. I was ashamed of myself, but I giggled. She released Donnybrook and slapped me in the face. I only gazed at her. If she was the beloved of my master, Jorjarrm, she could do what she wished with me.

"Isn't she marvelous?" Jorjarrm said, beaming.

Bosena spun and glared at him. "And you! What makes you think you can marry me against my will?"

"How can you question fate?" Jorjarrm said with a shrug. "Take her away," he ordered his guards. "This woman of Syrah addles my brain! You three, go with her! Soon, my little dumpling. Soon!"

Bosena stormed out, the rest of us in her wake. I was very happy to accompany the Syrene addler from the room. She fascinated me, too.

The moment we were in her quarters, which were built on an epic scale, like most of the kingdom, the lithe woman rounded upon Donnybrook again.

"So you have returned. How will you make up for your misconduct? Desertion is punishable by death or exile!"

"I brought these wise ones with me," Donnybrook said, bowing his red horn before her. "They will figure out a way for us to escape."

"What can we do?" Bosena asked, pacing up and down. She had to hike the capacious dress up in her arms to keep from tripping on it. "Jorjarrm fears nothing."

"That is not true," Buttercup said suddenly, tossing his silky white mane. "He fears dragons."

"How can you say that, when you see that all dragonkin are his prisoners?" Bosena asked. "I have watched him humiliate wyverns, wurms, dragons, dragonets—all scaly beasts are his toys."

"My companion has the right of it, my lady," I said, nodding as the truth became evident to me. "It's the wand that gives him control." The greater the distance I achieved from Jorjarrm and his scepter, the clearer my mind became. I shook my head vigorously to rid myself of the effects. "It holds us in thrall."

"Then we must break it," Buttercup said.

"But how?" Bosena asked. Now that she had scolded Donnybrook, she stayed by his side with her arm over his withers and stroking his mane.

"Do you have any power over him?" I asked. "He said that you addle his mind."

"Oh, that? That's nothing." Bosena waved a hand. "He is not used to females who defy him. His previous seven wives were cream puffs. I have no wish to become number eight. How did you get here? Do you have an escape plan?"

I rattled my head. Her mind was so clear, it prompted me to reassert my own wits.

"We have a means of escape," I said. "We have an ancient device. A D-hopper."

"Well, use it!" Bosena said, glancing at the door. "Any minute now, the Hierarch will arrive to perform the marriage ceremony. From what the servants tell me, weddings here are bloody affairs. Jorjarrm has draped me with gems and gifted me with jewels, more than I have ever had in my life!" She gestured a table so laden with treasure that it made me long to roll upon it. "But all I want is my freedom. Let us go *now*."

I hesitated. "I don't wish to leave him."

Buttercup nudged me in the ribs with his horn. The point went right between my scales.

"Ow!"

"We are away from him now," my friend said. "You don't have to pretend to be fascinated by him. It's disgusting. Come to your senses!"

"It's not pretense." I glanced toward the iron-barred door. "The wand is very powerful. It keeps me under a certain measure of control even when I am not near it. It is the way he holds my kind prisoner. I dare not move against him as long as he holds it."

"Well, you're free enough of it now," Bosena said. "Use the D-hopper, and let's go!"

I hesitated. "I could help us escape, here and now, but I fear for the safety of my kin. So many of these would be left in thrall to the Brother of Dragons. What about the rest of them?"

"It's too bad," Donnybrook said, "but you can't really help them. *We* can get away. We can't take all of them with us in order to get them away from him."

I stared at him as if I had never seen a red unicorn before. As a matter of fact, I hadn't.

"You have a point," I said.

"I know," Donnybrook said, holding his magnificent head up with pride. "It is my greatest weapon."

Buttercup snorted in disdain.

"Not that one," I said. "We can't get them away from him." My smile spread until every one of my splendidly sharp teeth were on display. "But we can get *him* away from *them*."

"How?" Buttercup demanded.

I draped my tail companionably over Donnybrook's shoulders. "As my red friend here suggests. But we'll need a diversion. Let us confer."

O O O

A huge musical chord rang out. We had waited in the chamber as the ladies-in-waiting kirtled up Bosena's gown so it almost fit, then began to lade her with the gem-crusted bracelets, necklaces, anklets, and rings that Jorjarrm had given her.

"I will need your help," I told Buttercup. "Once I am close, I cannot act against him."

"I am ready," Buttercup said. "You have set the D-hopper to the right address?"

"I have." I took a deep breath as the ladies stepped back from Bosena. As much as a smooth-skinned biped could, she looked beautiful. Straight-backed, she picked up her bouquet—which concealed the D-hopper—and marched grim-faced out into the hall. We followed close behind.

It seemed as though every Monster in the kingdom had come to see the festivities. Guards had to make way for us through the throng of hairy faces and glass eyepieces. Several of the females were weeping into lace handkerchiefs at the sight of the wedding party. The room smelled overwhelmingly of their furry musk and gallons of perfume. I sneezed my way forward.

The carpet leading up to the dais was freshly strewn with flowers. Bosena trod over them, releasing more sickly-sweet scent. She kept a grim smile pinned on her face. It looked as though our subterfuge was going to work!

As she got close, however, a pair of guards closed in on her.

"What is this?" she asked, alarmed.

"Just a precaution," Jorjarrm said, grinning down at her from his horrible throne. "Ah, what's *this*?" One of the hairy guards had pulled the D-hopper from the center of the flowers and held it out to his master, who examined it. "A D-hopper! Primitive little thing. But why hide it, my love?"

"It's a special gift to you," Bosena insisted. She climbed up into his lap and twined one arm around his neck. With the other, she whipped off his glasses, pressed her lips against his, and planted a hard, passionate kiss on him. His arms flailed in surprise.

When his concentration broke, I regained enough of my own willpower to leap up the steps and seized the D-hopper from his limp fingers. Donnybrook and Buttercup bounded up beside me. Jorjarrm pushed Bosena away and stared at us

"It's a trap!" Jorjarrm cried, staring at us. "Guards!"

A dozen troops thundered toward us as I bit down on the controls.

BAMF!

O O O

When we could see again, we were in the middle of a wide-open, grassy plain.

"Guards, take them!" Jorjarrm ordered, retreating within their circle.

Bosena kicked the nearest Monster in the chest and took his sword. She backed away from her would-be husband and stood with us. The guards looked at the four of us disdainfully, and then charged. The unicorns lowered their heads.

Lunge! Parry! Thrust! Retreat! Counter-parry! Advance!

If I had any doubt that I had chosen worthy allies in this enterprise, they would have been dispelled on the spot. Though we were greatly outnumbered, Donnybrook repelled every attack that came his way, and remised with his horn, plunging it into a foot here, an arm there, earning howls from the guards upon whom he scored. Buttercup held forth brilliantly, showing hornsmanship that was a treat to watch. The Syrene warrior seemed to care little that she had no armor. She took on two of the largest Monster guards, swinging, slicing, and whirling like a one-woman army. I roared toward the guards, setting their fur and armor on fire with my modest flame and clawing at tender extremities.

All around us, across the broad meadows, from the burned, twisted trees, and from the puffy white clouds in the blue sky, myriad dragons of every shape, size, and color began to descend. The Monsters and their lord were so distracted by us that they didn't notice the newcomers until we were surrounded by a ring of dragons, some so large that I could have walked into their ears without ducking. The dragons seemed to sense the power contained in the wand, and they did not like it.

One of them, a magnificent silver-scaled dragon with huge blue eyes like my own, watched for a while, then reached out a massive claw and tapped Jorjarrm on the shoulder.

"Excuse me. Haven't we met?"

The lord of Monsteros spun on his heel and found himself staring upward and upward and upward to meet the giant's eyes.

"Uh, I don't believe so."

The giant dragon crouched until his chin was resting on the ground. "Oh, I think we have. You don't remember me? Smog, son of Fog, son of Grog? You kidnapped my baby sister, Cuprica?"

In Dragonspeak, Cuprica was the kind of name bestowed upon a red-scaled offspring, such as a copper-colored dragon. I fancied I knew where Cuprica had ended up.

"And what about my son, Winnower?" asked a blue-skinned matriarch with wrinkled lips around her still-sharp teeth. "We were so close, and I never hear from him, not since you lured him away."

"It's been twenty years since I heard from my beloved Mamie," a stocky bronze dragon with eight rows of terrifying white teeth said. "She would never have stayed away so long without popping back now and again for a visit. Is she even still alive? Well? What did you do with her?"

Jorjarrm turned to me in horror. Under his fur, his face had gone ghostly pale. "This is Draco. You brought me to *Draco*?"

I offered a ferocious grin. "You said you can never have too many dragons."

"Protect me!" Jorjarrm grabbed me by the neck and shoved me forward. He battered me on the back of the head with his control wand. I wanted to protest, but every blow drew me farther and farther into his thrall. "You will defend me, Gleep! Attack them! I order you to save me!"

I looked up at the gigantic winged beasts that surrounded us.

With the wand, Jorjarrm ruled my soul. For my pet, I might have lain down my life, but for this dragon-stealing Monster? I had no choice. I was under his spell. I bid a silent farewell to Skeeve. In a moment, I would die defending someone who did not deserve my sacrifice. I stepped forward, my flame pouring forth, to challenge Smog. Every eye on the plain seemed fixed upon me.

"No!" whinnied Donnybrook.

The red unicorn reared in the air and knocked the wand from Jorjarrm's hand with flailing hooves. He seized it in his teeth and ran.

"Come back here! Guards, with me!" Jorjarrm bellowed.

He thundered after Donnybrook, his enormous feet causing the ground to shake. But the red unicorn did not go far. He turned at bay, a gleam in his bright red eyes.

"I failed my lady once. I will not fail her again." He dropped the wand to the ground and brought down both front hooves upon it with all his strength.

It exploded in a ball of blue flame. Shards of it struck me in the chest like bolts of lightning.

"No!" Jorjarrm bellowed. "If you only knew how long I labored upon that wand!"

"Don't worry," Smog said, his left claw darting forward. He captured Jorjarrm and drew the struggling Monster up to his gigantic blue eye. "You will not be needing it any longer."

He rose onto his haunches, spread his broad silver wings, and leaped into the sky. Other dragons captured his Monstrous guards and flew off with them, too.

"No, let me go, let me go, pleeeeeeeeease!" Jorjarrm cried.

His voice faded into the distance. Watching him go, I felt nothing but relief. The compulsion had died with the breaking of the wand. I was free, as were all the dragons left in Monsteros. Any moment, the more sophisticated magicians among them would begin to return home to Draco. I turned to my companions.

Lady Sir Bosena stood with her back to her unicorn's flank, her borrowed sword out, her eyes wide in terror.

"My lady," I said, gently, "pray forgive the little subterfuge. You are perfectly safe here. Donnybrook has saved us all. These fine people," I indicated the remaining dragons, "have no interest in you."

"Oh, my, I just remembered!" Winnower's mother said, smacking the side of her head with her claw. "I left that sea monster only half cooked! Where is my mind?" She took off, followed by a score of smaller dragons, presumably her offspring. Others departed in her wake.

"Donnybrook deserted me!" Bosena glared at her unicorn.

"He fled only to get reinforcements," Buttercup said. "Us."

"And in so doing, he freed not only you, but hundreds of dragons," I added. "He is a hero. He adores you, my lady."

Donnybrook lowered his horn modestly. Bosena shook her head and threw her arms around his neck. I realized by her scent that she was qualified not only by courage but also by the legendary rule to have a unicorn.

"To me she is always The Woman," Donnybrook confessed. "Thank you for your help, honorable dragon and Unicorn of the White Company. I am sorry that I have no gold to reward you."

"Our fees are fixed, except where we waive them altogether," I said, after sharing a glance with Buttercup. My white-coated friend looked happier than I had ever seen him. The martial exercise and victory had done him a world of good. "In this case, naturally, they are waived."

"Oh, I can pay them," Bosena said, unhooking one of the gaudy necklaces Jorjarrm had given her. "Crom knows we don't need much. These are worth a king's ransom. Won't they do?"

"Just the one," I said, taking it delicately. I had previously noted Donnybrook's threadbare barding, and Bosena would have to buy all new armor. I looked around the empty field. "Now, where is that D-hopper? We have to get back to the Bazaar before Skeeve returns and finds us missing!"

About the Author

Jody Lynn Nye has written dozens of books and more than 120 short stories, most of them with a humorous bent. She collaborated with Robert Asprin on his famous humorous fantasy series, the Myth-Adventures of Aahz and Skeeve, and has continued it since his passing. Her latest books are *Fortunes of the Imperium* (Baen Books) and *Wishing on a Star* (Arc Manor Press). Find her on Facebook and Twitter, and on her website, www.jodylynnnye.com.

KILLING ZOMBIES IN RURAL AMERICA: A SURVIVAL GUIDE BY DOUG AND CECILIA

KRISTIN LUNA

Lesson One: Don't Get Bit

So, uh, how's your mother doing?"

Doug's old but reliable Ford F-150 rolled leisurely down Range Avenue in Colby, Kansas. With the last bit of winter thawing on the ground, it looked like the people of the small town were making every excuse to get outside and also thaw their bones.

Everybody seems pretty stiff, though, Doug thought looking at the people shambling along the sidewalks. *And what's that smell? Smells like something's rotting.*

"Fine, I guess." Fifteen-year-old Cecilia sat in the passenger's seat, fiddling with her iPhone. "Why I can't get reception? Don't they have cell towers out here?"

Cecilia was tall and skinny for her age. Her soft face was pretty, just like her mother's. Doug would've questioned if Cecilia was his if it hadn't been for those big ears peeking out of her hair and the plump Polish nose that matched his own.

"Why don't you give that contraption a break for five minutes? Talk to your old man a while." Doug tried to keep the irritation out of his voice.

"Okay, fine." Cecilia stuffed her phone in her coat pocket and turned in her seat, and her dark straight hair—another feature from her mother—whipped the cushion behind her. "Let's talk about mom. She still thinks the government is trying to poison us. That weird outbreak in Kansas City on the news? The crazy flu or whatever? Must be the government. So how's that for a mom update?"

The attitude, unfortunately, she also got from her mother.

Doug sighed, although he was thankful that Cecilia had finally said something during the four-and-a-half-hour drive from Lawrence. "Sure it is. It's always the government with her. I take it you guys are still growing your own food and whatnot?"

Doug turned the pickup truck right on College Avenue.

"Yep, and still vegetarians, you'll hate to know."

"It's just not healthy, Ceil, I'm tellin' ya. We're hunters and predators. We're meat eaters by nature." Doug hesitated, running his hand through his light brown hair, then bringing it down to itch at his orange-brown beard. He eyed the gut that had slowly grown over the last decade. "So, uh, she still with that … guy?"

"Oyibo."

"Oh-yee-boh? What kind of name is that anyway?"

"When he was in Western Africa with the Peace Corps, the people called him Oyibo. He changed his name when he got back."

Probably means dumb white man, Doug thought.

"What's he do again? Runs a communal greenhouse or something?"

"He prefers the term 'urban farmer,'" Cecilia corrected.

What a douche bag.

"Doug, don't judge him. You don't even know him."

"*Doug?* And what are you talking about? I didn't say anything!"
She might be too smart for her own good.

Cecilia rolled her eyes. "It's nice to know you're this critical of everybody, not just me," she muttered.

"What do you mean?" he asked.

Doug turned on Franklin Avenue, Colby's main downtown street, which wasn't saying much. Only a few shops lined Franklin between 3rd and 4th Street; two stores were for rent—and had been for seven years.

"Never mind," Cecilia whispered, turning away from him.

Pain seized Doug's heart. He hadn't been there for her like he should've been after the divorce. And he hadn't been to Lawrence to visit her in three years. He wasn't winning any Dad of the Year awards that was for sure.

But I'm doing something now, he reminded himself. Better late than never.

Doug bristled and tried to make his voice sound resolute. "Well, I'll, uh, work on that."

When Cecilia didn't reply, Doug looked out the window and eyed the shop to his left.

"Hey, let's grab some donuts, for old times' sake." He forced a smile, pulling into a parking space in front of Daylight Donuts.

"It's two in the afternoon. They'll be stale."

"They're still good! Marge makes one helluva bear claw. Remember how much you loved those? You could eat two in one sitting when you were nine."

"Mom doesn't let me have sugar," Cecilia said sadly. "Or gluten."

"I don't know what the hell gluten is, but no meat and no sugar? This is still *America*, isn't it?" Doug flicked the door handle impatiently. "So does this mean 'no' on the donuts?"

"No, no, no. Let's get some bear claws!"

The way her face lit up at the mention of their old favorite made Doug smile. *Maybe this trip isn't going to be hopeless after all.*

Doug opened the door to the donut shop, letting his daughter enter first.

A mechanical bell chimed. Sweet, sugary dough-smell stuck to the walls and the baby-blue padded seat cushions of the Daylight Donuts. A fluorescent light flickered just above the cash register on the counter.

"This place hasn't changed a bit," Cecilia said, somewhat unimpressed.

"You wouldn't believe how many times I've offered to change that bulb for her," Doug whispered to his daughter, nodding up to the flickering light.

He straightened, then cleared his throat. "Hello? Marge?"

After a few moments of silence, Doug shrugged, lifted the partition, and crossed the threshold to the other side of the counter.

"She must've gone out for a bit and forgot to put up the sign." He snapped a sheet of wax paper out of a box on the counter and opened the sliding glass door that guarded the donuts.

"Doug! What are you doing?" Cecilia shrieked.

He straightened and pointed the wax paper at Cecilia. "What is with this 'Doug' stuff, Ceil? Cut it out!" He hunched down and continued to look over the donuts. "Now, tell me what you want. We'll leave some money on the counter."

"This is so embarrassing." Cecilia covered her face with both hands.

"Calm down, calm down, I do this all the time. Bear claw?"

"Two, please," Cecilia whispered through her fingers.

Doug smiled and picked out the four biggest bear claws from the rack and slid them into a white paper bag. He handed the bag to his daughter, who pinched the rolled top with her thumb and forefinger, as if she hated being an accessory to his crime. *This city girl has been away from a small town for far too long.*

He pulled his wallet from his back pocket and threw a five-dollar bill on the counter. "That's more than enough. Includes a tip."

"Sure, whatever, can we get out of here now?" Cecilia begged.

Doug came around the counter and lowered the partition. "We have to stop by the movie theater. I need to grab a few things from my office."

As they walked toward the door, Doug heard a growl and looked up.

"Jesus! Marge! You damn near gave me a heart attack."

Marge stood in front of the door, blocking it. Sunlight streamed in behind her, blinding Doug and Cecilia and shadowing Marge's features.

"Uh, we just stopped by for some donuts." Doug motioned to the white bag Cecilia held. "I put a five on the counter for you."

Marge said nothing.

"You doing okay, Marge? I can't see you too well." Doug's voice was friendly, but he felt a ripple of concern under his calm demeanor.

Marge took a stumbling step forward, then another. As she lurched closer, the fluorescent lights caught her features.

"Oh, Marge, you aren't looking so good. Oh my god, is that blood on your neck?" Doug walked to the old woman's side. Her flesh sagged on her body like a wet rag on a drying line. She looked deathly pale and had dark circles under her eyes. Her movements were stilted like a body rife with arthritis.

"Doug ..." Cecilia said from behind him.

Doug turned. "Ceil! What do I have to do for you to call me 'Dad'? Huh?"

"Doug!" Cecilia screamed as Marge lunged for Doug's neck.

Doug easily avoided Marge's bite. "Whoa, Nelly!" he yelled.

The old woman threw her weight at him, gnashing her teeth in front of his face.

Doug held her back with his meaty forearms. "Marge, what the hell is wrong? What has gotten into you?"

"She's a—she's a—she's a—" Cecilia stuttered. Her eyes were wide and terrified.

"She's sick with something is what it is." Doug easily pushed Marge back, but panic starting climbing up his spine. "Maybe she has the rabies."

"That's not rabies. She's a zombie." Cecilia finally got the words out.

Keep it together, Doug. Keep calm for Cecilia. Don't panic.

"What's that even mean?" Doug's forehead wrinkled. "Zombies? Like the stuff you read in your books?"

"Vampires, Doug. I like vampires. Paranormal romance. I told you that like a million times." Cecilia's voice was harsh, as if she had temporarily forgotten about Marge.

Since when did she get so sensitive all of a sudden? About vampires, of all things!

"For heaven's sake, Ceil." Doug pushed Marge back again and gritted his teeth. "I mean, I'm sorry I forgot." He hoped he hadn't sounded too sarcastic.

Baking sheets banged to the floor in the kitchen, and a low growl followed. Doug swallowed his fear.

"Sounds like more. What do you say we blow this popsicle stand?" Doug pushed Marge back so hard she fell onto a table and rolled off to the side. "Uh, sorry, Marge," he apologized to the undead woman. He took Cecilia by the arm. "Thank Marge for the donuts."

"Thanks," Cecilia said breathlessly as they ran out the door, making the mechanical bell ring again.

Just outside, a group of people milled about in the middle of the street. As the door chimed, they stopped and turned toward the donut shop.

Doug and Cecilia hadn't paid any attention to the people before, but after Marge, they looked at the group more closely. Blood splotches smeared parts of their clothing, and their eyes were lifeless, and they quickly began running toward Doug and Cecilia with bared teeth.

Lesson Two: Do Your Research

"Quick! In here!" Doug yanked his daughter's sleeve and rushed them into the store next door to the donut shop. He slammed the glass door behind them and switched the lock. The small group of former Colby citizens attacked the glass, scratching as if they were animals separated from their prey.

"That should keep them out for a while."

"Oh my God. Is that Shanda?" Cecilia shrieked, looking at one of the zombies pounding against the door. Shanda had been Cecilia's best friend growing up, and the only person she'd remained in contact with since moving to Lawrence with her mother three years ago.

Doug looked at the zombie, then studied her riding pants and purple boots. Every Monday, Shanda would ride her horse Shelby into town in her unmistakable purple boots.

"I can't be sure," Doug lied.

"Look at her face! It's Shanda. You're just trying to make me feel better," Cecilia raged.

She's yelling at me like I was the one who turned her into a zombie!

"Well, if it is or isn't Shanda, there's nothing we can do about it right now." Doug tried to sound comforting, but it came out sounding defensive.

"Well then, what *are* we supposed to do?" Cecilia demanded.

"Okay. We have to think. They're zombies, so we need to …" Doug's eyes flashed to his daughter. *Feel free to cut in any time, dear.*

"Haven't you seen any zombie movies?" Cecilia asked.

"No. I can only play family-friendly stuff at the theater. And action movies. No horror. No zombies."

Cecilia sighed. "Well, they want to eat us, and we have to shoot them in the face, that's about all I know."

"In the face?" *Adorable.*

"Yeah, right in the face! Wait. Is this a bookstore?"

Doug huffed. "Kind of. It's Laverna's shop called Books and Sweet Things. It's more like a place people get cheap candy to sneak into my theater." Doug scowled at the thought of the empty wrappers littering the floor—candy he did not sell at the concession stand—after the movies had ended. *Damn you, Laverna.*

Cecilia rolled her eyes, then went to the seven rows of books on display. "There are some good books here," she said excitedly, touching the first few on the shelf. "They're all paranormal romance!"

Leave it to Laverna to carry the worst literature available.

"Wait. If she has these, maybe she has something about zombies. Help me look."

Cecilia quickly scanned the shelf in front of her while Doug ran to the back shelf. "We'll meet in the middle," he said.

The undead outside pounded against the glass

"Got one! No, two!" Cecilia called out, crouched by the lowest shelf.

Doug hurried to her side. "Okay, what do we got?"

"There's this one called *World War Z*, and this other one called *The Zombie Survival Guide*, both by the same guy."

"Let me see them." Doug grabbed the books and quickly flipped through them while Cecilia looked over his shoulder.

"I think we should start with this one," he said confidently, holding up *The Zombie Survival Guide*.

"I knew you were going to choose that one."

"How?"

"It's shorter and has pictures."

Before Doug could utter a rebuttal, Cecilia grabbed *The Zombie Survival Guide* by Max Brooks from his fingers.

She really is too smart for her own good.

Cecilia flipped the first few pages and began reading. "Introduction."

"Skip that, nobody reads those," Doug interrupted.

"Fine," Cecilia sighed, turning ahead. "Okay, let's see. It says it takes twenty-three hours for someone to turn into a zombie once they're bitten."

"Okay, what else?"

"They can see like us. They have excellent hearing and sense of smell. Oh, here's something: it says they can't feel anything. Their nerve receptors don't work anymore."

"How interesting," Doug said sarcastically. He winced as soon as he said it.

"Look, Doug, I'm doing my best over here!" Cecilia's eyes began welling with tears.

Doug cringed and held up his hands in front of him as a sign of surrender. "Hey, hey, I know. I'm sorry, I didn't mean to get snappy."

This moody teenager is going to be the death of me.... If the zombies aren't first, of course.

He put a hand on Cecilia's shoulder. "Why don't you skip ahead to the part about how we can help them?"

"There is no helping them," Cecilia snapped. "They're *zombies*, Doug."

Count to five. Just let it go. Maybe she's just on her period.... No, don't think about that.

Doug smiled, clenching his teeth. "Okay, then. How do we kill them?"

"Disposal," Cecilia read. "It says: 'The head in particular possesses the most serious hazard, given its concentration of the virus. Never handle an undead corpse without protective clothing. Treat it as you would any toxic, highly lethal material. Cremation is the safest, most effective way of disposal.... Any virus is unable to survive intense heat.'"

Glass shattered in the front of the store, and the zombies reached in through the shop window, completely disregarding the slashes the cut glass made on their arms.

"We have to get out of here," Doug said. He laid two twenties by the cash register. "Bring those books, and let's go out the back. We need someplace that has everything we need—True Value."

Lesson Three: Get Thee to a Hardware Store!

Much to Doug's surprise, they had no trouble slipping out of the back of the store and making their way back around to Franklin Avenue. The zombies still crowded the front of Books and Sweet Things, fumbling over each other to get inside.

"I'll tell you one thing that Max Brooks got wrong. He made those zombies sound so smart and dangerous," Doug whispered as they crossed the street and approached True Value, which was right next to his movie theater. "But these zombies seem really *stupid*."

Doug and Cecilia cringed when the front door of the hardware store creaked, then chimed. They stopped, held their breaths, looking around for any sign of the walking dead. When none showed, they let out a collective sigh.

"Which aisle?" Cecilia asked.

"Hmm. Barry doesn't carry guns, last time I checked. What did that book say, again?"

"Hammers, saws. Anything sharp."

Doug's gaze fell on a stack of firewood and liquid ethanol on the end of the first row. "And fire. Lots and lots of fire."

He piled the wood and ethanol into a shopping cart, then led them down the second aisle.

Cecilia picked up some white picket fence posts with sharp, metal spikes at the ends and put them into the cart.

Don't say anything, Doug. The kid's into vampires. Maybe it's a vampire thing.

"Hammers, here." He pointed to various hammers hanging on a pegboard.

Cecilia tentatively picked one up that had a hot pink handle.

Doug sighed.

Cecilia glared at him, as if waiting for a critical comment.

Doug quickly looked to the hammers and picked out a wood-handled Hardcore with a price tag of $79.99. "Maybe we should practice," he suggested, biting the inside of his cheek while he watched his daughter daintily swing her new makeshift weapon. "Try hitting that shelf."

"This one?" Cecilia pointed to the taupe-painted metal shelf in front of her.

"That's the one," Doug said gently.

"Like this?" Cecilia patted the shelf with the face of the hammer.

"A bit harder, sweetheart."

Tap.

"Harder."

Bang.

"For Pete's sake, Ceil, that thing's got to penetrate a skull! Smack that thing and make a dent!"

Cecilia's eyes widened as she looked past Doug's shoulder.

A guttural growl snarled behind him.

Doug felt fear shoot up his spine and tickle the back of his hair. He slowly began to turn around.

Cecilia screamed wildly and sprang onto the undead man who wore a plaid shirt and overalls. She knocked it down with her body weight, then slammed the claw of her hot pink hammer into its forehead. Over and over, Cecilia stuck the fork of the hammer into its head until blood covered the floor and the zombie stopped moving.

Cecilia looked up, horrified, at her father.

"Well, uh, I'd say you've got that down."

If it weren't for the overalls, Barry, you would've been barely recognizable. Teen angst is real, and it is real brutal.

Cecilia rose to her feet, fixing a few hairs that had gotten into her face. She wiped the blood off her cheeks with her shirtsleeve.

"We have to burn them. It'll be too hard killing them all like that," Cecilia said numbly.

"Okay, I agree." Doug nodded quickly. He bent down, took out his wallet, and tucked the last of his bills into Barry's overall pocket. "That's not quite enough, Barry. I owe you about forty dollars." Doug rose and turned back to Cecilia. "What should we do?"

"We need to draw them in with noise. Maybe some place with a loud PA system?"

Doug eyed his daughter suspiciously.

"Like … the Duplex."

The Duplex was Doug's baby, his pride and joy, his life. The only movie theater in Colby. And it was one of the two reasons Doug hadn't been to Lawrence to see his daughter in three years: He didn't trust *anyone* with the Duplex.

"Oh, no. Out of the question. No, no, no. Think again, 'cause it's never going to happen."

Lesson Four: Mind the Animals
and
Lesson Five: Kill It with Fire

Doug bit his lip while he poured liquid ethanol fuel all over the red, plush seats in theater one. The fumes burned his nose and made him feel light-headed. *The watery eyes must also be from the fumes*, he reasoned.

When he finished dousing theater one, he quickly emptied two containers into theater two, paying special attention to the red velvet curtains, which he had spent hours—no, *days*—of his life cleaning and vacuuming.

He collapsed into one of the squeaky red seats. The old springs dug into his butt, but he didn't care. He studied the horrid flower-printed carpet he never liked, but had been too busy to replace. He gingerly scraped a piece of gum off the seat in front of him with his thumbnail.

Finally, Doug got up, wiped his eyes, and exited to the lobby.

"Ceil?" He called when he didn't see his daughter.

"In here!" He heard her shout from his office.

When Doug entered his office of twenty years, he stopped, suddenly embarrassed. Cecilia sat in his chair, staring at the walls, which were covered with every letter she had ever written him, every school picture she had sent him, and every photograph of her Doug had ever taken.

Cecilia's content smile beamed right through him, and he felt his eyes grow wet again.

"I, uh, took care of the theaters. Are you ready?" Doug mumbled.

"I'm ready," Cecilia said, getting out of the chair and putting her arm around his. "Let's go trap some zombies."

Doug picked up the last bottle of ethanol from his desk and made a trail from the front door of the theater to their hiding spot in a storefront across the street, along with their cart full of True Value supplies.

"I'm going to go start the noise. Stay here," he instructed Cecilia.

Doug ran back into the office of the Duplex and switched on the audio to a movie he always had on hand. He clicked the microphone to the PA system on. He spied a picture of Cecilia on his desk. His favorite.

Might as well take this one for the road.

Doug took one last look at his office, the lobby, his beloved theater.

As Nicolas Cage's voice boomed out of the theater's lobby, Doug quickly scrambled across the street.

Cecilia eyed him as if he were crazy when he settled in next to her, out of breath.

"If anybody's voice can attract a horde of zombies, I'm betting it's Nicolas Cage's," Doug reasoned.

An hour or so passed, and the sun began to set. The streetlights flickered on. A mass of undead citizens had gathered inside the movie theater's lobby, shuffling into one another, crazed by the noise, and smacking into one another as if they were blind.

"Is that all of them?" Cecilia asked.

"Looks to be a good amount. I don't know if it's everybody, but sure looks like everyone who works downtown. Er … worked here." Doug paused, looking out over his old friends. Some of his adrenaline had worn off, and sadness began creeping in.

"Time to light it up, I guess," he said, dreading what he was about to do. "Well, ol' Duplex. It was fun while it lasted."

"You can do it," Cecilia said, encouraging him forward.

Doug fished the keys out of his pocket. "Shout if you see anything coming after me."

Cecilia nodded, gripping her bloody, hot pink hammer in one hand and a white picket fence post in the other.

Doug tried not to roll his eyes at how benign the fence post looked.

He took a deep breath, then sprinted across the street.

He unceremoniously kicked the zombies loitering outside the doors into the theater, then locked the door from the outside. The undead turned to the doors, pounding against the glass.

Doug ran to the middle of the street, knees slightly bent, ready to defend himself. He stopped, stood up, and turned to Cecilia.

"That was kind of easy."

"Surprisingly easy," said Cecilia. She stood up and joined him in the street.

"And kind of fun. We always seem to have fun, don't we, Ceil?"

Cecilia's smile faded. "Then why did you let me live with Mom? Why didn't you fight for me?"

Doug's heart dropped. "Your mom won custody, sweetheart. I tried."

"Why didn't you try harder?"

Doug sighed. "Kids need their moms. I guess I thought it would be best for you."

"Kids need their dads, too," she said. A tear rolled down her soft, white cheek.

Glass shattered behind them.

Doug and Cecilia turned to see a zombie's fist had broken through the theater doors.

"We better light this thing," Doug said, scrambling for the lighter in his pocket.

"Is that ... Shelby?"

Doug followed his daughter's finger pointing behind him.

Just under the signal lights of 4th Street was a horse.

"I thought Shelby was white," Doug said. "That horse looks ... red."

Under the streetlights, the horse stepped forward. The horse, owned by Cecilia's childhood friend, Shanda, usually had an ivory white coat, but tonight its coat was covered in some sort of dark liquid, and what looked like teeth marks.

Cecilia gulped. "Shelby?"

The horse charged, barreling down Franklin Avenue straight for them.

At the same time, the front glass of the theater fell like a sheet of ice, crashing onto the sidewalk. The zombies pushed out of the theater, angling toward Doug and Cecilia in the middle of the street.

Doug clicked the lighter frantically while eyeing the charging horse.

"Just light it, Doug!" Cecilia yelled. She dropped her hot pink hammer and held the white picket fence post with both hands. "I got Shelby."

There was no time to argue. Doug gave the flint a strong flick and held the little flame down to the street. The ethanol erupted, and a line of fire sped toward the theater.

When the horse was close enough for them to smell the metallic blood covering its snow-white coat, Cecilia angled the metal spike on the end of the fence post, aiming right for the charging horse's head.

The theater exploded in bright flames, engulfing the building and the zombies inside. Flames licked the zombies that had made it outside, and the fire quickly swallowed them.

The blast knocked Doug off his feet. His ears rang. His face stung. He wiped his eyes, searching in the smoke for his daughter.

He saw her sprawled on the ground.

"Cecilia!" Doug rushed to her. He panicked when he couldn't see her lungs move. Her arms were around her stomach. The horse must have knocked her down.

He plugged her nose and bent down to give her mouth-to-mouth.

Her eyelids flew open. "Oh god, no!" Cecilia pushed him away. She coughed, rolled onto her side, then got to her feet.

Doug threw his arms around her, then pushed her back to look her in the face. "I can't lose you, sweetheart. I'm sorry I didn't fight harder for you. I was afraid you didn't want to live with me, that you'd come to hate me like your mother did. I didn't visit because I thought you hated me." He swallowed, feeling suddenly very vulnerable.

"I don't hate you. I'm not Mom," Cecilia said.

Doug nodded, dropping his arms. "I know. I know that, sweetheart."

His eyes drifted to the dead horse on the ground a couple feet away. The bloody horse lay on its side, one white picket fence post sticking out of its forehead.

"Wow. Just an inch or two to the left and it would've been perfectly centered."

Cecilia caught Doug's eye.

Doug cleared his throat. "I, uh, I mean you did a great job. Great ... unicorning, sweetheart. You made a real fine, uh, red unicorn."

Cecilia gave him a sympathetic smile. "You're so corny, Dad."

There, in front of the bloody horse Shelby and a heap of burning zombies, Doug felt his heart expand with happiness.

She called me Dad.

Lesson Six: Help Your Neighbors

After filling up the truck bed with more supplies from True Value, Cecilia and Doug hopped into the cab.

"So what do you say, Ceil? Think this thing is spreading? Should we get to Kansas City and check on your mom? And Oh ... Ob ..."

"Oyibo."

"Yeah, him," Doug said.

Cecilia shrugged. "Eh, maybe. He's actually kind of a douche bag."

Doug swelled with pride.

"You can decide on the drive. Maybe we can help the towns along the way with their zombie problems?"

"Sure! Sounds like fun."

"You know, I'm wondering if you were ever really a pacifist." Doug put the key in the ignition.

Cecilia smiled. "Well, maybe I'm more like my father than we both thought."

Doug beamed. He started the car.

Cecilia dug *The Zombie Survival Guide* from her coat pocket. "You know, this book made it sound a lot harder than it really is. It's a pretty easy business, killing zombies."

"Maybe we should write our own survival guide," Doug suggested.

"Yeah, like start our own blog or something."

Doug's brow furrowed. "What's a blog?"

Cecilia sighed. "Never mind."

"Well, if we wrote a book, or a *blog*, whatever that is, what would we write about first?" Doug asked, heading toward Interstate 70.

"I guess we should probably warn people about the animals." Cecilia's voice became serious. "The horses, for sure."

"Zombie horses," Doug nodded emphatically. "Definitely the zombie horses."

About the Author

Kristin Luna has been making up stories and getting in trouble for them since elementary school. She writes book reviews for *Urban Fantasy Magazine*, contributes to the blog The Fictorians, her short story "The Greggs Family Zoo of Odd and Marvelous Creatures" was featured in the anthology *One Horn to Rule Them All*, and her horror story "Fog" was featured on Pseudopod in May 2015. Kristin lives in San Diego with her husband, Nic, and is working on a young adult novel.

THE DARK AMBITION OF OSWALD MARCH

TRISTAN BRAND

I arrived at Thornwood the morning after my father's sudden disappearance. The March family manor had not changed during my five-year absence. A looming stone structure studded with ivy-wreathed gargoyles, the manor lay in a deep shadow cast by the thick canopy of the surrounding wood. Hardly a welcoming place, but then, Thornwood was not a home but a castle, and Leland March its king.

My thoughts drifted back to that day, five years ago, when I'd been kicked out of the academy thanks to bad luck and a conspiracy of professors jealous of my potential. My father had met me on the driveway. "You're a disgrace, Oswald," he'd told me. "You're not worthy of my name."

"I'll show you," I'd said, even as angry tears streamed down my face. "One day, Thornwood will be mine."

He'd laughed.

Now I walked up the drive and stopped at the edge of the topiary which encircled the manor. The garden was my father's pride, a maze of poisonous hedges and grotesque fountains. Faces carved in foliage stared at me. I recognized some of them: a pair of thieves too stupid to find an easier mark, a rival tricked into arriving uninvited, a newspaper boy whom my father had simply forgotten to welcome. All victims of my father's curse protecting Thornwood from trespassers. They garnered little sympathy from me. If I'd learned anything from my father, it was that fate rewards the clever. What happened to the foolish was none of my concern.

I reached into my pocket, fingers finding the crumpled note which had been delivered to my room that morning. Thunder rumbled in the distance, and raindrops ran cold rivers down my cheeks as I read the note for the thousandth time.

It's done. Meet me at the manor at dusk.—A

I'd confirmed, of course. My father had been expected at a meeting with the Cabal the previous night and not shown up. Unthinkable. Leland March was never late. In fact, no one could recall seeing him for days. I'd asked around.

Still, I paused, my feet inches from the garden's edge. What if the whole thing was one of my father's schemes and even now he watched me, behind one of those dark windows, waiting to see me fail?

No. I wouldn't turn back now. My destiny lay within the walls of Thornwood, where I would finally take possession of the red unicorn's horn.

I closed my eyes and stepped forward.

A tingle ran up my spine. My stomach twisted, horror creeping through my thoughts, and I opened my eyes, looking down at my hands, expecting to see them growing leaves. But my skin stayed pink and when, after a moment, I remained ambulatory, I realized it had been simple adrenaline.

I smiled. Then I began to laugh. I laughed so hard I must have looked like a madman, but I did not care. I'd done it. My plan had worked.

Leland March was dead.

O O O

It had started a year ago. The endless tide of ill luck had washed me well past my last dime. The closest thing I had to a friend was a doddering necromancer who made his living resurrecting dead pets, relying on a customer base of senile old ladies dull enough in the head to mistake a putrid pile of bones for their beloved Fluffy.

I spent most evenings in a dive frequented by syndicate thugs and low-end demonologists, the type who'd be lucky to summon up even an imp. Every night I spent there I felt farther and farther away from the life I knew I deserved, the life my father had taken from me.

But then I met Ambrose.

I saw him one night sitting by himself in the corner, dark blue eyes staring defiantly out from under the rim of an out-of-fashion top hat, as if he knew he were better than his surroundings, a feeling I understood well. I walked to my usual spot in the corner, debating whether to introduce myself. He beat me to it, beckoning me over and offering a drink.

Right away, I knew I'd found a kindred spirit. His story bore parallels to mine. Once wealthy and powerful, Ambrose had it all taken away from him by the actions of a cowardly thief. To make ends meet, he'd been forced into syndicate dirty work while he searched for the thief, determined to have his vengeance.

I cared little for Ambrose's life story, but he proved to be a sympathetic listener when it came to discussing my troubles. More importantly, he proved easy to trick into paying more than his fair share of drinks and dinner.

"It's not fair," I told Ambrose one night, deep into a bottle of bad wine.

Ambrose raised an eyebrow. "Few things are."

"I shouldn't be here. I'm a March. I should be a Cabal warlock by now, working my way up the ranks."

"Like your father."

"Like my father." Every night, it all came back to my father. "He was nothing special, you know. My age, he was a nobody. He just got lucky."

"How?"

I hesitated. Drink had loosened my tongue. This was my father's greatest secret. But what did I care about his secrets? I glanced about, making sure no one was paying attention, and then leaned forward, lowering my voice. "He found the horn."

Ambrose frowned, adjusting his hat. A nervous habit of his. "What horn?"

"The horn of the red unicorn."

"I had no idea they came in the red variety."

"No doubt they're just as insipid as their white cousins."

"No doubt," Ambrose agreed, a little tersely. "What's so special about their horns?"

"It can turn any man into a slave, their will bound to the horn's owner."

Ambrose nodded. "Ah. Now that does sound impressive."

I scowled. "And yet, my father hardly uses it."

"Oh?"

"Claims it'd give away his secret. That it was better if his enemies didn't know how he did what he did. He's only taken a few slaves, and he's used them to build a network of spies and informants, gathering information in order to blackmail his enemies."

"Clever," Ambrose said.

"Pah," I said. "Shortsighted. Why bother blackmailing people when you could enslave them? If I had the horn, I'd command my own army."

"With that kind of power you could conquer the syndicates," Ambrose said.

"With that kind of power I could lead the Cabal," I said, pausing to choke down a gulp of sour wine. "But there is no point in dreaming. My father's disowned me. I will never have the horn."

Ambrose looked thoughtful. "Unicorns are of the fae. Their horns obey the laws of fae, not the laws of men. And the fae are all about inheritance."

I set down my cup. "So if he were to die, the horn would be mine, disowned or not?"

"Exactly."

I snorted. "Little chance of that. He's so full of rejuvenating potions and poultices, he'll be rattling about as a lich long after I'm in the grave."

Something strange glimmered in Ambrose's eyes. "Not if someone were to help him along."

I laughed. "Who would dare? Leland March is untouchable."

"No one's untouchable," Ambrose said.

I laughed when I saw his meaning. "You think you could kill him?" He gave a single nod. I searched his blue eyes for signs of a joke and saw only grave seriousness. "You're mad."

"Sometimes that's all it takes. A little bit of madness." He gestured toward the rest of the bar. The necromancer sat in the corner, looking sadly toward me, the stool next to him empty. "What have either of us got to lose?"

"How?"

Ambrose smiled. "That's my secret. But I'll make it like he never existed. No blood. No body." He paused and looked me straight in the eye. "Only with your permission, that is."

I nodded, his smile widened, and together, we started to scheme.

O   O   O

It was simple enough to gain entrance to the manor proper. My father never bothered locking the door, believing the garden a sufficient deterrent. The front doors led to a foyer, dimly lit and smelling of dust. When I'd lived here my father's servant, Branton, had done a passable job keeping it clean, but now cobwebs dangled from the walls. I wondered how Ambrose had dealt with him. The man had been unfailingly loyal.

Passing a pair of shadowed halls that led to long-unused wings, I instead made my way up the spiral staircase that led to the second-floor balcony. The stairs groaned as I ascended, echoing throughout the empty room like dull laughter.

I had two tasks. The first, and most pressing, was to find the horn. I had a few guesses as to where my father kept it, but the manor was vast, and I knew the search might take hours.

The second was how best to dispose of Ambrose. His choice to meet at dusk had been an unexpected boon, giving me the chance to find the horn first. However, if the search went overlong, I'd simply have to kill him when he arrived. No doubt my father had more than a few weapons tucked away. Unpleasant business, but necessary, I reminded myself. Ambrose was less a friend and more a lackey whose usefulness had ended.

At the top of the stairs I turned down a hall covered in soft red carpet that led to the main sitting room. Here was where my father greeted guests not important enough to warrant his private office. The walls were covered with hunting trophies from his youth: a harpy claw, the tip of a kraken tentacle, the gaping, sharp-toothed maw of a sand dragon.

Interspersed between ancient leather chairs stood glass domes on pedestals, each holding dark magic artifacts, the kind of defiled things that even the syndicates would execute a member for owning. Displaying them like this was my father's way of gloating.

I paused at a dome containing a gemstone that looked like an inky black emerald with a blue ember glowing faintly within. Perhaps I could suggest Ambrose take that as his reward. The demon living inside would make short work of him and save me the trouble.

"Who's there? Is that you, master?"

Startled by the voice, I stepped back, nearly knocking the demon egg off the pedestal. I quickly steadied the dome and turned toward the voice.

He was an old man, dressed in black and white servant livery and wearing a wide-brimmed hat that seemed out of place with the rest of his dress. His eyes widened when he saw me. "Thief! What are you doing here? When the master finds out—"

"I'm the master now," I said, taking a deep breath. He was only a servant. "Nothing to worry about."

The servant took a few shaky steps toward me, his hands trembling. He looked nearly eighty, face worn and ruddy, wisps of white hair trailing out from under his hat. Something about him struck me as familiar, but I couldn't quite place it. "You're his son. Oswald. I see it now. You look just like him."

I glowered at him. "My father was a bald little troll."

"I meant no offense," the servant said, voice quavering. "It's your eyes. You can see so much of a man from his eyes."

I sniffed. The old man's own eyes were a milky blue. I doubted he saw much of anything these days. "I don't know you," I said. "What happened to Branton?"

"He passed a year ago. Very unexpectedly. The master chose me as his replacement. My name is Willard."

"I don't care what your name is," I said. "Leave immediately. Your services are no longer needed."

Willard's lip quivered, and I wondered if he was about to cry. "But the master ... Your father—he—"

"He won't need anyone's services. He's dead."

Willard bowed his head, the strange hat hiding his eyes. "What happened?"

"I don't know and I don't care," I said. "I've more important things to worry about. Now leave me to them." This Willard was yet another complication. I'd have to take care of him myself. I spotted a bronze candlestick on a nearby table. Willard looked so brittle I imagined it would only take a single blow. But then I'd have a bloody mess on my hands. It'd make a poor start to the day.

An idea occurred to me as Willard turned to go. "Wait," I said, and he paused. "How closely did my father trust you?"

"Your father trusted no one," Willard said, turning back toward me.

"But you worked closely with him?"

"As closely as he allowed."

"Then you know of the horn."

Willard said nothing, but his eyes shifted. "I'm not sure what you mean."

"Don't try my patience. My father's dead. That means this house and everything it contains is mine—you and the horn included. Tell me where it is."

Willard bowed his head. "You truly are your father's son. The horn ... Your father never trusted me with where he stored it."

"But you must have some suspicions."

"His private study, perhaps?" Willard said. "Your father always said he felt safest there."

"Take me there," I said, not wanting to admit I had no idea where my father's study was. Another of his secrets that would soon be mine.

"As you wish, master," Willard said.

We left the sitting room and walked up a narrow stone staircase to the third floor. The floor was made of black wood that reflected the ghostly candles which lit up at our approach, illuminating the way like will-o'-the-wisps in the night.

Willard kept a painfully slow pace, and had I not repeatedly ordered him to move faster, I expect it would have taken us all night to reach the study.

We finally stopped at a pair of grand, brown doors which Willard unlocked with an oversized iron key. Inside was the library, a room that stretched the length of the manor's central tower, rows of bookshelves rising to a dizzying height. It smelled of vellum and mothballs. Centuries of knowledge about every type of magic was here. All mine. I smiled. Once I had the horn, I'd enslave an able scholar who could organize the collection for me, picking out the most useful tomes for my personal use.

I couldn't help but feel I was missing something. It all seemed too easy. But then, shouldn't all good plans feel easy? I shoved the worries aside.

Willard, meanwhile, had paused before a particular section of bookshelves and seemed to be carefully examining one of the shelves.

"Quit wasting time," I said. "Where's the study?"

"Apologies, master. I've never opened it myself, and your father had safeguards. If the door is triggered incorrectly, then neither of us will outlive the hour." His simpering manner of speech had been replaced by a terser tone.

"Right," I said, licking my lips. "Take your time, then."

With surprisingly steady hands, Willard picked a thin blue volume and pulled it out halfway, doing the same to its neighbor. He then crouched down and did the same thing with another half-dozen books. It seemed a pointless exercise, which I was about to comment on, when the sound of grinding stone made me turn to see a wall-panel rotating, revealing a hidden room.

"The study," Willard said.

I stepped into the shadowy room. A dozen candles lit at my presence, and I found myself face to face with my father.

O O O

The study was a cozy room, the floor covered in rich carpet. A chair of silver velvet, stately as a throne, sat before a stone hearth, above which hung my father's portrait.

It was as if my father stared at me from another world. Though not exactly photographic in quality, something about the painting perfectly captured the very essence of Leland March. The grim scowl, the haughty glare, the sense of looming power. This was a man whose shadow had consumed all who dared stand in it.

Yet there was something off about it, as well. Something in his expression. The slightest hint of surprise. Odd. My father was never surprised.

"Do you like it? I painted it myself."

I jumped, so entranced by the painting I hadn't realized Willard had been standing right behind me. "You?" I said. I had trouble imagining anything requiring this much skill could come from those shaking, ancient hands.

"I was considered quite the talent in my youth."

"We're not here to talk about painting," I said, tearing my eyes away from it. "I need to find the horn." I took stock of the rest of the room. It was remarkably sparse. Aside from the chair, the only other furniture was a simple desk that had no room for drawers, a nearly empty bookshelf, and an easel with a fresh canvas in the corner. "Help me look."

The few hiding places were quickly exhausted. I even checked behind the painting and the bookshelf for a secret safe. "It's not here," I said, wiping sweat from my brow. "You lied to me!"

"I only thought it a good place to start," Willard said.

"Useless old man. All you've done is waste my time."

Willard shrank back, as if he feared I might strike him. "Please, master. I can still help! I know things. About the horn and its history."

"What good will that do?"

"The past always tells us something of the present. Someone as clever as you could no doubt find a clue there as to where your father might have hid the horn."

It seemed a waste of time, but traipsing about the manor had left my legs a touch sore. I decided I could use a rest, if nothing else, and sat down in the silver chair, sighing slightly as I sank into the soft velvet. "Pathetic that this is all you can offer me. But fine. Tell me this history."

Willard shuffled toward the easel. "Would you mind if I painted while I talked? Your portrait would look grand, hanging next to your father's."

"Don't be daft. I've no time for posing."

Willard reached into his jacket and produced a paintbrush. I saw only a flash of something long and bone-white before it vanished behind the canvas. "Your father gifted me a special brush. With it, the painting will take no longer than it will for me to tell the story." His eyes glimmered with candlelight. "Only with your permission, of course."

I looked toward my father's portrait, its gaze somehow as penetrating in oil as it was in life. I realized as long as that painting hung this would forever remain my father's study.

"Do it," I said. But my portrait would not hang next to my father's, I decided. His I would burn.

Willard got to work, perching himself on a rickety stool, the canvas angled away from me.

"What are you waiting for?" I said. "Tell me about the horn."

Willard's eyes looked like they were gazing at something far away. The paintbrush started to move, slowly at first, but then picking up speed until it became a blur. "Master, what do you know of unicorns?"

"That they're ill-tempered fae beasts with an inflated sense of self-worth and an obsession with virgins."

From behind the canvas Willard smiled. "An apt description of most. But there as many different breeds of unicorn as there are of men. Most fearsome are the red. While their white and purple and black brethren prance about englamouring young lasses, red unicorns are warriors. They see themselves as above other living creatures, both fae and human. They meet their enemies in battle, forever enslaving the souls of any who perish by their horn."

I snorted. "If they were as powerful as that, you'd think they'd be running things."

Willard's mouth curled up in a wry smile. "Maybe they consider governance beneath them."

"Enough. I get the idea. Get back to the horn."

Willard nodded, studying the painting before him. "Your father was quite the accomplished huntsman at your age. He'd been part of a crew that took on a kraken. He traveled to Morocco in search of sand dragon eggs. Eager to take on greater challenges, he fell in with a group of fellow hunters who planned on traveling to Wales. There, they'd heard a tale of a forgotten little vale where a red unicorn made its home.

"They came to the vale, tucked deep within an ancient wood where the trees still remembered a world unsullied by men. The vale was fae land, meant to be a safe place where no mortals could tread—at least, not without permission. Had the red unicorn denied them entry, this story would have ended there. But, in truth, the red unicorn had grown bored. It had been years since its last battle. It lusted for a fight. And so it granted the hunting party entry.

"Once inside, the hunters stayed together, tracking the unicorn like wolves chasing a stag. The unicorn played their game, dancing about, revealing itself with a flash of its crimson mane and then vanishing, luring the hunters deeper and deeper into the vale. The hunters were not easily fooled and stayed vigilant, waiting for the right moment. For both parties it was to be an honorable fight.

"Leland had other plans. While the others watched for signs of hoof prints, his focus was on a small brook that seemed the sole source of water in the vale. As the day dimmed, the hunters' energy slowly flagged, and at twilight, the forest shadows spreading long and dark, the unicorn struck. The first to fall was a broad-shouldered woman who'd slain a pair of wyverns single-handedly. A single slash of the unicorn's horn, and her soul was forfeit, leaving only a husk behind. The surviving hunters squared up, determined not to be taken so easily.

"Leland, however … Well, amidst the chaos of the fight, he slipped away. No one even noticed, so intent they were on killing each other. Ah, don't scowl, young master—this was no act of cowardice. Your father knew it was useless to confront a red unicorn in battle. He had a deeper plan. He returned to the brook and followed it until he reached its source. A spring cupped in a bed of mossy rocks, its water cold and sweet, the ground around scuffed in hoof prints. There he took out a small vial and poured its contents into the spring. Then he ran out of the vale and waited.

"The hunters gave the unicorn a good fight, but in the end, all perished at the end of its horn. Bloodied and tired, the unicorn returned to the spring, deeply thirsty, and he took a long drink. The potion Leland had used was clever. Odorless, tasteless. His only mistake was he'd left his own scent near the spring. The unicorn realized too late what it meant. The potion took effect, and the unicorn slumped to the ground in a deep sleep.

"Leland waited until nightfall to return. He found the unicorn, motionless and on its side. He took out a blade of cold iron, placed it on the horn's base, and began to saw."

Willard's paintbrush seemed to take on a frenetic series of strokes, white tip flashing in the candlelight of the room. His face seemed lost and faraway, as if caught up in his own story.

I scowled. The story struck me as more fancy than reality. Likely my father had simply purchased the horn from a black market dealer and made up the story. "How, exactly, is this supposed to help me find the horn?"

"I believe the next part of the tale will be more useful in that regard."

"Then why did you not tell that part first?"

"A story must be told in the proper order," Willard said, "or it is not a story."

I was beginning to tire of the whole charade, but decided perhaps I could wait at least until he finished the portrait. "Go on, then."

"Understand this," Willard continued. "A unicorn's horn is more than a piece of bone. It is their very essence. Having it removed is like losing your manhood. The unicorn woke from its enchanted slumber consumed with shame. It had been tricked, and worse, it had allowed itself to be tricked by permitting mortals into its realm in the first place.

"The fae world had no room for a hornless unicorn, and so the red unicorn left, taking the form of a man, where at least it could hide its nub with a hat and others would not know its secret shame. A depraved being takes on depraved work, but the red unicorn still had talents and centuries of knowledge. It put them to use working as a syndicate operative. It learned how to be a thief, an extortionist, and an assassin."

"I don't understand the point of this," I said, interrupting. "How's this supposed to help me find where my father hid the horn?" I frowned. "And how could you or my father possibly know what the red unicorn did after it woke?"

"A good question," Willard said. "Things will become clear shortly." He began speaking faster. "The unicorn became very good at its work, but every morning, when it looked at its human face and the broken nub of bone on its forehead, all it could think about was the thief who had taken everything. But even if the unicorn could find the thief, it had a greater problem. Not only would it have to trick the horn back from the thief, it would need permission to act against him. Such is the cruel logic of fae law. It seemed hopeless. But the unicorn was willing to try.

"The unicorn began to learn. The skills it developed working with the syndicate, it applied to its search for the thief. The unicorn reasoned that, as the thief had used subterfuge to steal the horn, so would he be subtle with its use. The unicorn looked for people who rose unexpectedly to power, starting the year it had lost its horn. The list of suspects was long, but one by one, the unicorn whittled them down. Soon there were only a few left. The unicorn changed its tactics. It found friends of the remaining suspects. Wives. Family members. In its human guise, it befriended them. Learned about them. One by one, the unicorn discarded the remaining suspects, until there was only one name left. One with a son who hated his father as much as the unicorn did."

Something horrible clicked in my head. "Wait," I said. "Who do you mean?"

But Willard did not stop. Instead, his voice picked up speed to match the frenzied brushstrokes. "A son so pathetic his own father cast him out. A son so insipid even the dregs of humanity found him poor company. A son so naive he thought it reasonable for a friend to volunteer out of the blue to kill the most powerful warlock in the country. A son so utterly pathetic that, even as his sad little scheme turns to ash and dust, all he can do is sit and stare, mouth agape, as his vacant little brain tries to process what a fool he's been."

I forced my mouth shut. My tongue felt dry, my hands clammy. The servant stared at me over the top of the easel, blue eyes now clear and all too familiar. "Ambrose," I whispered. "No. It can't be."

"It can be, and all because of you. You permitted it all. Without your permission, I never could have presented myself to your father as a servant. I never could have spent months learning his habits. I never would have found this study, where he kept the horn sitting on the desk. Right out in the open. I never would have been able to replace it with a fake. I used the real one to fashion this paintbrush.

"Funny thing about paintbrushes made from red unicorn horns. They have the habit of imprisoning in the painting the souls of those painted. Of course, the horn was still your father's, though I held it. I never would have been able to use it against him. Not without permission, which he gave so easily. Just as you did."

"No," I said, my stomach twisting, ice creeping through my veins. "No. It isn't fair. I didn't mean it like that!"

"That's your problem, Oswald," Ambrose said, and he took off his hat, revealing a bony stub in the center of his forehead. "You think the world revolves around your whims despite a lifetime of evidence to the contrary. But this isn't your story. It's mine." He spun the easel around, and I faced my own portrait. It was a perfect likeness, with only a single spot of missing paint, right at the heart.

Too late I leaped from the chair. I tripped, pitching forward with a strangled sob, and landed on my hands and knees. "Please," I begged, reaching out toward the painting. "Don't do this."

The red unicorn laughed. "In the end," he said as he thrust the horn forward toward the painting like a dagger to my heart, "you truly were just like your father."

About the Author

Tristan Brand is a lifelong reader whose schoolbag always seemed to contain more epic fantasy novels than textbooks. After a brief detour in academia studying mathematics, he went on to work in QA and technical writing. Currently, he works as a game designer in Silicon Valley, where he lives with his dog, Locke, and cats Edgar and Sabin.

THE OLD GRAY MARE

JOHN D. PAYNE

It was a few years back, when the sign of the Gray Mare still hung over the door. Someone spilled The Ox's beer. Wasn't even good beer, mind. Grassy as green leaves. Nothing like what I've poured for you today. No, sir. A failed experiment with dry hops is what that stuff was, and I'll be the first to admit it. Always been straight and level; ask anyone.

But The Ox, he loved that grassy beer, probably on account of his being half cow. Or bull, if you take my meaning. So the first thing he does, aside from stomping his hooves and bawling like a babe ripped off his mother's teat, is look around for someone to gore.

Now, the one as did the actual spilling no one saw at the time. But if you ask anyone in town, they'll tell you it were the witch, Arilya. An elf maid, she was. Funny lass. You know the type, I'll wager. Spider webs in her hair and silver wire wound round her fingers. Drank nothing but carrot wine and perry. Talked to cats and the wind. Kept to herself, mostly.

But the one thing we all knew about her was that she hated to be touched. So much as brush her in passing, and she'd scream. "Keep your hands off me, or I'll kick your pelvis clean out of your body." Well, none of us liked the sound of that so we left her alone.

The Ox would have done well to do the same, but when he gets to seeing red, as it were, there's no reasoning with him. And on that day, when he turned around and saw her there, holding her cup of wine, he didn't even give her a breath to explain herself or apologize. He gave her a slap that sent her spinning across the room like a child's toy—and straight into a table of caravan merchants.

Well, as soon as she can shake herself loose and get to her feet, she stretches out her hands like talons and then lights up like a torch. With flames running down her arms all the way to her fingertips, she hurls a ball of eldritch fire at The Ox.

And misses.

The fireball hits a dwarf full in the face, and as you might imagine, he was not best pleased. Don't recall his name, but he'd been drinking all evening with a whole clan of gnomes. Stout for him, and plum brandy for them. Drank it in thimbles, but they'd had plenty. Enough so that when they saw sparks in the dwarf's beard, they tried to put out the fire with their brandy.

It was quite a scene. Between the flaming dwarf, the bellowing Ox, and the screaming witch, the whole place was in chaos. Most everyone was trying to get out, but that only led to a trampling mob near the door.

Where was I in all this, you might ask? Despite rumors to the contrary, I neither bolted nor cowered. Like a ship's captain at the tiller in a terrible squall, I stayed resolutely at the bar. Well, behind it at any rate.

And using my own body as a shield, I offered what meager protection I could to the little ones I had gathered up in my arms— poor, delicate things that they are. Call me a liar if you will, but I preserved every one intact, including this fiery little beauty up here. Ha ha! My little joke. Shall I fetch her down and pour you a dram? No? Just as well to save her. Her kiss gets sweeter every year, and more potent.

Where was I? Oh, yes. So the dwarf charges The Ox, beard still aflame, and with a whole pack of gnomes on his back, riding him like a war elephant. Everyone always wants to know why he attacked the seven-foot bull-man instead of the dainty elf maid. Well, I'll tell you.

I don't know.

The best I can reckon is that he simply went for the closest target, but I suppose we'll never know the truth.

In any event, the dwarf ducks under The Ox's swing and gives him a savage head-butt to the groin. Now, as you might imagine, I have a great deal of experience with both head-butts and groin attacks, so believe me when I tell you that this one was absolutely world-class.

While the great beast is staggered with pain, the gnomes all clamber up his arms and legs. In an instant, he's covered in a carpet of tiny assailants, all of them scratching and biting for all they're worth. He swats off every one he can reach, and they fly like ballista bolts. (In case you didn't know, those pointy hats the gnomes wear are steel-reinforced, so if you happen to catch the business end— believe me, you'll know it.)

Worse, everywhere one of those drunken little monsters landed, they erupted into miniature orgies of indiscriminate violence. Like rabid shrews they were. So much nose-biting. And ear-stabbing. One woman swears she saw one of the wee devils pluck out a man's eye and eat it like a pickled egg.

It was more or less at this point that the melee became, shall we say, general. Any as hadn't managed to flee the premises were part of the brouhaha. And speaking of brew, I for one find it more than a little ironical to note that many a fine ale was spilled in all this—despite the fact that the original casus belli, if you will, was in point of fact a spilled drink. A tragic waste is what it was.

The same could be said of The Ox himself, who was finally felled by a combination of witch fire, gnome bites, and chair-leg blows to the delicates. If you ask me, that's a sad commentary on the shortsightedness and futility of conflict in all its forms, but I'll leave you to find your own lesson.

The long and short of it was that the only ones left standing were the elf witch and the dwarf. Plenty of bad blood there, as I said. He seemed to have finally figured out that she was the one as set him afire, more or less. He reaches for her, and ... I don't know what he meant to do, but he never got the chance.

She'd always threatened to do it, and we'd always thought it rubbish. But as I stand before you today, she did it. Limbs alight with dancing fairy flames, she kicked that man's pelvis clean out of his body.

Well, not clean. Carried with it a considerable pile of innards. And that whole mess of steaming raw haggis flew through the room. No lie. Went straight out the door and smacked into the sign you see hanging there—the one you were pointing to when you asked your question.

It was quite a splatter, I'll tell you, when that bundle of oozing guts hit. Colored the old gray mare red (and few other, less savory colors). One particular stray entrail slapped a long red mark trailing off the head of the old nag. To all of us at the time, it looked rather like a horn. So we've been the Red Unicorn since that very day.

And in my humble opinion, a more distinctive sign you'll not see anywhere in town, nor indeed in the whole district. Catches the eye, it does. Paint it red at least once a year, with fresh blood— which is never in short supply in these parts. And that's a fact, as I'm an honest man.

o o o

"Yes," said the traveler, tapping his fingers somewhat impatiently on the bar. "A very ... thorough recounting. But what I actually asked was if there was a story behind the *mane*. On your man there."

The traveler turned to point at the thick-muscled young man standing directly below the painted sign that hung outside the entrance to the tavern. The hulking youth had a thick ruff of hair that completely surrounded his face from forehead to chin.

"Oh, that," said the bartender. "No story there. Sired by a were-lion is all. The blackhearted tom ran off and abandoned both mother and boy. Left him with nothing but that shaggy pompadour, a wicked set of claws, and a tail, poor devil."

"A tail? Truly?" the traveler asked, craning his neck.

"Aye," the bartender said. "And speaking of tails, there's quite a tale I could tell you about this wild lambic." He thumped a nearby keg. "Just got it in this morning. Sit down, sit down. I'll pour you a draft and give you the whole story."

About the Author

John D. Payne grew up on the prairie, watching the lightning flash outside his window, imagining himself as everything from a leaf in the wind to the god of thunder. Today, he lives with his wife and family near Houston, where he imagines that the clouds of mosquitoes have achieved not just sentence but malicious intent.

His debut novel, *The Crown and the Dragon*, was published in 2013 by WordFire Press. His most recently published stories can be found in *Black Denim Lit*, *The Leading Edge*, *Tides of Impossibility: A Fantasy Anthology from the Houston Writers Guild*, and *One Horn to Rule Them All: A Purple Unicorn Anthology*.

NOW I SEE YOU

JOY DAWN JOHNSON

You want me to start a what?" I feel for the plastic railing at the side of my bed and pull myself up.

"An audio journal," Dr. White says, giving her notebook a solid rap with her pen. "It's where—"

"I'm twelve. I know what it is." My hands stray to the bandages covering my eyes. I can barely deal with this. And the doctor expects me to record what I'm going through?

I hate this place. Between the unending supply of fake cherry Jell-O plopped in paper bowls, and the failed chemical attempts to mask the stench of pee and old people, the nurses make every excuse to invade my room. If I hear one more snap of latex gloves, I'm heading out the window, hospital gown and all.

"Jessi, I'm concerned that you're not accepting your condition." Dr. White shifts in the visitor's chair, the leather sighing beneath her. "Treat it like a diary. No one else ever has to listen to it. You need to remember life before the surgery and release whatever is bothering you. To find a balance between then and now."

"Is there a point to this?"

"You want to leave the hospital?"

I lean forward, knocking away one of the overstuffed pillows cocooned around me. I leave it on the floor. "Is that a real question?"

"Most kids your age don't want to be stuck in a hospital for their birthday."

"I'm not like 'most kids' anymore." The lunch cart's back wheel whines as it rolls into the room, and I think of Bernie, as I do every day before my daily dose of Jell-O and pain meds. I've missed his little barks and his shaggy hair tickling my leg as he curls against me. He's been my best friend for as long as I can remember— through Mom leaving, through my sickness.

As I lift my spoon for my first bite of Jell-O, I catch a faint glow of red as it wiggles. I say nothing. If I do, they'll start with the tests again. Dr. White is right about one thing: I want out of here. "Okay. So you want me to record Jessi's Greatest Hits. Anything else?"

"Yes. Record at least one a week. You can talk about anything as long as it's from the heart."

O O O

Jessi's log 01

For the record, I'm only doing this because the doctor told me I had to. So here goes....

I started playing lacrosse this year. I loved the rush, and sports were always my thing. Halfway through the third game, I began seeing double of everything on the field. Just as I was about to score, I saw two nets, and my shot went so wide, I hit the stands. It was embarrassing. And then there were the headaches. The pain made me want to puke and then I did.

I didn't want to worry Dad, so I kept it from him as long as I could, but that didn't last. Mom had always carried our insurance. Soon after she left, Dad's office cut back on benefits. He took me to the doctor even though I told him I didn't need one.

Dr. White used a model and Silly Putty to show the growth pushing against part of my brain. She called it the pituitary gland, but I still don't know what that is and don't really care. They shaved my head for the incision. Not having long hair doesn't always make everything feel lighter.

The doctors had hoped I wouldn't go blind from the surgery, but a cancer I can barely pronounce stole my vision.

This is so depressing. I can't do this today.

End 01

O O O

Dad places a hand on my head. "I'm sorry, honey, Mom's not coming."

"Am I supposed to act shocked or something?" I don't bother to filter the acid from my voice. Bernie rubs against my leg, like he always does when I'm upset. He's been doing it a lot lately. "It's what every nonexistent parent does in the middle of a divorce." I run my fingers along the *ABC Book of Braille.* Reading used to be fun, but this isn't exactly reading.

"*We* can do something for your birthday."

"Like what? Oh, I know. Go to the zoo or see a movie?" I lean back and wait for the tears to come. I haven't cried since Mom left.

O O O

Jessi's log 02

It's been a month since the surgery, but complications kept me in the hospital until last week. All I wanted to do back then was breathe and walk with Bernie. Dad wouldn't let me because dogs weren't allowed at hospitals.

How dumb is that? You know, if they really wanted me to get better, they would have let me see my best friend.

I'm not doing this anymore.

End 02

O O O

"So, Jessi, would you say the audio journal is helping you?" Dr. White's voice is always just a little too smooth, attempting to be that "female influence" she insists I'm lacking.

I lean against one of the dozen miniature pillows arranged on her leather couch and twist its braded fringe between my fingers.

Just for a moment, I see the red strands begin to move like a thousand tentacles reaching out for the doctor, as if trying to convince me to tell her I'm seeing things. I stuff the pillow behind the others and pretend like nothing happened.

"The podcasts? They're dumb." I wait for her to jump in and defend her precious idea, but all I get is a lungful of her mothball-meets-fruitcake perfume. "I thought they were supposed to help. I feel worse after them."

"Did you talk about something positive?"

I give her a look. Okay, I can't *really* give her the look I want to from behind my oversized glasses, but it's better than digging my nails into one of her precious pillows.

O   O   O

Jessi's log 04

I started tying Dad's ties when I turned ten. He insisted after Mom left. He said he preferred "Jessi knots" because I got the length just right. I always chose the craziest ties. It might have been silly, but all his coworkers knew he was loved.

He'd bend down, and I'd hum as I worked because that's what Mom used to do. I always tied it just a tad too tight, and he'd make funny strangling noises until Bernie started barking. I secretly knew he could do it himself, but I still did it every day before school.

As Dad showed Bernie and me out the door, he always asked, "Have you fed Bernie?"

I knew Dad loved me because every time he headed off to work, I felt him watch me leave. "Hey, sunshine. Look both ways before you cross," he'd call. He'd pretend to head to his car, but I saw him behind the hedges. His red tie bled through the openings between the branches like little ripened berries.

He never needed to watch me. It's only three straight blocks to school, and besides, I had an escort. Bernie would bark at Dad as if to say he'd never let anything happen to me. Before each cross street, Bernie and I would wait together until the signal changed. We always looked but there were never any cars. Bernie with his too-short legs stuck on an oversized body, and me with my lacrosse stick strapped to my faded green backpack that I'll probably have until the zipper falls off.

Once I'd get to school, I'd turn back and give my dad a huge wave. It was my daily revenge. Though to keep his cover, he never waved back, but I knew he smiled.

My dad has a great smile.

End 04

O   O   O

"Dr. White emailed me information about a support group."

Seriously? What is Dad thinking? "Like to talk about my feelings and what I'm going through?" Not a chance. I might let it slip that I'm seeing ... things.

"Exactly. I know you're—"

"I agreed to do the podcasts. Don't push it."

O   O   O

Jessi's log 07

I'm not able to tie Dad's tie anymore. I've tried and it comes out all wrong every time. The people he works with are going to think I don't care about him. I stopped humming. It's not like the surgery stole my voice, but everything sounds out of tune.

Dad forgets to ask me if I fed Bernie, and I remind him of our routine. I reassure Bernie that Dad still cares about him too.

Sometimes I see my dad's red ties knot themselves or the red garage door fly away, and I tell myself it's just my imagination. But there is one thing I know I see: Bernie.

When I first arrived back home, Bernie didn't rush to greet me like usual. I'd been looking forward to that moment for weeks and ... nothing. I called out to him, and for the first time since my surgery, I knew I actually saw something.

I watched Bernie trot up to me. But not the same Bernie, not exactly. He's still Bernie, of course, but I think I now see what he truly is: a unicorn. A miniature, furry unicorn. He's the one thing that comes in clearly, bleeding through the blackness like my father's tie through the bushes. It was hard to take at first, but when you go blind and your best friend is the one thing you can still see, you go with it. No matter what he looks like.

Bernie's all I need, and I tell him that every day. He nuzzles my neck, and the fine hairs of his horn tickle my cheek. I've wondered if the only reason can I see him is because he's red. Not tie red or garage door red. Bernie red.

End 07

O   O   O

I scratch behind Bernie's ear. "He just didn't see you," I whisper to him. Dad's always loved Bernie but ever since my surgery, he's so overprotective of me he doesn't even notice the little guy. He didn't say anything when he smacked Bernie with the door. Sure, his arms were full, but that doesn't matter.

"Guess what I've got?" Dad plops a grocery sack onto the kitchen table and kisses me on the forehead.

I wipe it off and turn away. "I don't care." I used to love when he did that but now it feels forced.

"I have your favorite cupcakes. But if you don't want them …"

Dad hasn't brought home double chocolate-chip cupcakes since before the surgery, before the bills. Something's up. "What do you want?" I snap.

The plastic wrapping crinkles loudly then pops open. "What do you say, honey?"

Maybe I could give him a break. "What do you want to talk about?"

"Well, I got promoted."

I lick my coated fingers. Chocolate icing has never tasted so good. "Congrats," I say as I tear off a chunk of cupcake and hold it under the table for Bernie.

"What are you doing?"

"I'm giving some to Bernie. He's been walking me to school every day." Dad doesn't say anything, and I realize he thinks Bernie can't have it because he's a dog. Well, I'm not telling him Bernie's secret, but for the record, unicorns *love* chocolate. "Don't worry he—"

"Don't worry?" Dad's voice is just a whisper. "How am I not supposed to worry?"

O   O   O

Jessi's log 09
*My morning walks have been different since the surgery.
Now Dad trails behind me to make sure I get to school. I pretend
I don't notice him, and once Bernie shows me to the school's
steps, I turn back to our house, stick out my hand and give my
great big wave, just like I used to. I wink at Bernie because we
both know my dad's only feet away.*
End 09

O   O   O

"How could you listen to my podcasts?" I can hear my recorded
voice on speaker behind Dad.

"I'm worried about you, honey."

"I'm blind, Dad." I run my fingers over the buttons, feel the
right one, and shut off the recorder. "Not helpless."

O   O   O

Jessi's log 10
*Hi, Dad. Thanks for invading my privacy. If you think you're
going to get anything more from me on here, you're wrong.*
End 10

O   O   O

"Go away, Dad." I sling my bag onto my shoulder and follow
Bernie off the school steps onto the sidewalk. He swings his horn
back to me, like he always does, to make sure I'm with him. "I know
you're there, *Dad*. I don't need your help."

He thinks he's so quiet, walking on the grass. He thinks that if
he says nothing, I'll leave him be. I speed up, and Bernie's little legs
match my pace. We'll show him. Bernie galloping, wind in my face,
I lick my lips and reach into my bag for my berry lip balm that I
can never seem to find anymore.

Sharp pain rams into my left thigh, and I stumble back from
Bernie's horn. "Bernie? What—"

I feel the electric car whir past and then Dad's solid arms grab me from behind. Dad holds me for a time, and I let him.

He would have been too late, and we both know it.

O   O   O

"You didn't see it," Dad says. "She could have been——"

Silence. Dad is on the phone with Dr. White.

"She says Bernie stopped her." My father's voice is distant. "No. I ... I haven't shown her."

Dad's footsteps sound heavy against the linoleum kitchen floor.

"It's not right to put all this on me. She's already lost too much. You want me take that from her, too? If she wants to believe——"

I lean my head against the wall. It's strange to not have my ponytail band digging into my scalp. Dad's done his best to keep the ends even, but it's not the same. I wrap my arm around Bernie, nuzzle my face into his mane, and whisper, "They can have my hair. I've got you."

Bernie rubs his horn against my leg and I laugh.

"Hey, that tickles."

"Jessi?" Dad says, and I know he's disappointed that I've been listening. He speaks into the phone again. "I'll talk to her now. I'll really tell her this time ... Yes, I'll take her to the support group on Monday, and she'll see you first thing after school on Wednesday." Dad hangs up, and I scoot over to give him enough room beside Bernie and me. He doesn't move. "It's time we get you a seeing-eye dog."

I cover Bernie's ears. "I've got Bernie." Sure he's nearly twelve and would probably lose the other half of his teeth if he ever had to sink them into someone, but he'd do that for me. And besides, maybe unicorns live longer. "I don't need some dog. Bernie is——" I feel a jab in the back of my leg, and I push Bernie's horn away. "Bernie's all I need."

Dad takes my hand. "Come with me." We walk out the back steps. I squint, expecting to see the red garage, but all I see today is Bernie. "I carved it last week ... so you could feel the letters." Dad guides my hand down to a curved piece of wood sticking out of the ground. "He loved you so much. I think he was worried about you.

He stopped eating the day of your surgery. I know you don't want to believe it ..."

The letters aren't smooth, and as I run my finger along the grooves, a tear slides down my cheek.

B. E. R. N. I. E.

I drop to my knees, and, after a moment, a red horn gently rests against my shoulder.

About the Author

Shortly after receiving her BFA and MBA, Joy Dawn Johnson worked as a project manager for more than ten years, including a stint in Baghdad, Iraq, as a government contractor. She is a member of the Society of Children's Book Writers and Illustrators and was the 2015 recipient of the Superstars Writing scholarship funded by the *One Horn to Rule Them All* anthology. This is her first publication. Visit Joy at www.joydawnjohnson.com.

SCRAPYARD PARADISE

BRANDON M. LINDSAY

It had been eighty-six days since Angelica had last seen signs of recent human habitation.

Holding the burst rifle's stock tight against her shoulder, she glanced down both paths of the T-intersection. Once satisfied she was alone, she crouched down to inspect the footprints in the mud.

They couldn't have been more than a few days old. Had the footprints been any older, rain coming through the hole in the roof—though that was a generous term, considering it was made of rebar and rusted sheets of aluminum siding—would have washed them away. The overcast sky was visible through the hole, and it gave her enough light to inspect the patch of mud for other footprints. There was only the one set.

They were small. Only a child could have made them.

Angelica stood. It was impossible that a child could survive here alone. Likely, adults were here, and the child was merely running errands, picking through the scrapyard for supplies. Damn irresponsible to let a child do that alone, unless the adults were crippled or injured.

And if there were adults here, they would likely fight to protect their supplies. Since Angelica was alone, her chances of surviving such a fight were nearly nil.

She crept back toward the entrance of the junkyard pile, wary of the various twisted cables, ripped sheets of metal, and other unidentifiable objects comprising and protruding from the walls.

Garbage had been stacked up throughout the scrapyard, forming a maze of narrow pathways between walls of refuse. Through a combination of the elements and neglect, many of the walls had collapsed, creating dead ends. There were good places to hide here in the scrapyard, sure, but there were just as many good places to get cornered. Angelica liked escape plans; this place made her nervous.

The pathway she was following, though, was different from the others. A makeshift roof of mounded trash had been built over it, creating a hallway of sorts, the walls of which had been reinforced in parts with bed frames. Some of the trash up top had shifted, though, created gaps in the roof and letting in daylight. It had the look of a permanent settlement. She had seen the mound while searching the scrapyard for a working vehicle.

From inside, however, the mound seemed far more dangerous than she had thought. Everything seemed to be fastened together by bits of wire and desperate hope. She didn't even want to think about how sturdy the roof was, as if doing so would be enough bring it all down on her head.

No way a child was living here alone. No way.

But a child *was* here. If nothing else, it meant food. And water.

Angelica returned to the entrance. Her levcart was stashed a few meters away, covered by a heat cloak as well as bits of trash to obscure it from casual observation, though it wasn't enough to withstand scrutiny. Staying in the shadow of the hallway, she glanced at the levcart, tallying the supplies on it in her mind. She had done it a dozen times today already, but it was good to have the numbers fresh in her mind before she made any decisions.

Two days. Two days until her food ran out. Four until her water did. And only if she stretched her rations more than she already had.

It was a week's hard march across the Wastes to get to the next real city, and there was no guarantee she'd find anything there that wasn't here. She'd stopped here hoping she might find something she could use without having to deal with people—at least living ones. The dead ones were easy to deal with. Just cover your nose and step over them.

She sighed. Better to die with a bullet in the brain than by starvation and dehydration. Better to die by human hands than by stumbling into a render and becoming *its* food.

As she turned to go back into the hallway, she wiped a strand of hair out of her eyes with the back of her hand and smiled grimly. At least she had lots of ammo.

O O O

Once past the T-intersection, the hallway got dark enough that Angelica needed to flip down her goggles. The cell they used was almost drained, but she figured it would last longer than she would if she let herself get surprised and shot up. She adjusted her grip on the rifle; her hands were slick with sweat.

A dim artificial light came into view as she followed a bend in the hallway, casting light on a pair of shining eyes peering out of the wall. Angelica almost opened fire until she realized it was merely the button eyes of a teddy bear jammed in a crack. She took a calming breath and flipped up her goggles, but she didn't lower her weapon as she made her way forward.

The hallway led to a cramped round room with no other exits. An electric lamp hung from the center of the ceiling. The light flickered, its power supply nearly depleted. Old toys and stuffed animals were stacked in neat piles around the edges of the room. Along the back wall was a rusted green cot, and on the cot sat a girl in a tattered dress, eyeing Angelica expectantly and swinging her short legs.

Angelica didn't aim the rifle at the girl exactly, but she didn't lower it either. She glanced around the tiny room. "Are you alone?"

The girl paused in thought for a moment, then nodded.

"No adults?"

"Nope."

Angelica watched her for any signs of a lie in her expression, then lowered her weapon. "How long have you been here?"

The girl shrugged, still swinging her legs. "A while, I guess."

"And you've been alone all this time?"

The girl lowered her large brown eyes and shook her head. "No," she said. "Hector got lost."

"Hector?"

She nodded. "He said he would keep me safe from the monsters. He said as long as he was with me, I wouldn't get hungry or sick." Tears welled in her eyes. "But I can't find him."

It had been so long since Angelica had seen tears she didn't know what to do once she saw them. Tears meant hope, and hope was something that had long been bred out of the human race. Ever since the renders had shown up, nearly forty years ago.

No one knew where they had come from. Some said the stars; others said from a rent in the earth. She'd even heard that they stepped straight out of nightmares or were a plague sent by some higher power. Angelica didn't know what to think. All she knew was that if the indicator light on her wristband flashed blue, she had to get the hell out of there or die in a render's mandibles.

The girl didn't know how lucky she was. If a render had gotten this Hector but spared her ...

Angelica set down the rifle next to the toys and sat on the cot. The girl wasted no time falling into Angelica's awkward embrace, crying loudly. Angelica brushed the girl's fine hair with her fingertips.

Minutes later, the girl quieted. Angelica thought she had fallen asleep until she sniffled and spoke. "My name's Wisteria. What's yours?"

"Angelica."

"I'm going to call you Angie."

Angelica stiffened. A nickname? The idea of one both warmed and frightened her. "Okay. That's fine, I guess."

Wisteria looked up at her, eyes pleading. "Can you find Hector for me?"

Angelica's fingers paused, but only briefly. She hadn't seen any bodies lying around, but a render wouldn't leave much behind anyway. And what if she did find something? Did she really want to show the shredded remains of a corpse to this little girl?

But it had been eighty-six days since Angelica had last seen signs of human habitation. And many, many years since someone else had needed her.

"Sure," she said with an attempt at a smile. "What does he look like?"

Wisteria leaned back and held her hands about a foot apart. "He's about this big, and red all over."

Angelica's eyes widened in shock. "What?" Had Wisteria already seen what the renders had done to him?

"And he has a horn like this." The girl placed her fist at her forehead, one finger sticking out. "And he had a tail a long time ago, but now—"

"A tail? Just what is Hector?"

Wisteria stared at Angelica as if *she* were the child. "He's a unicorn, of course."

O O O

Wind groaned over the opening in the ceiling as short sprays of rain arced into the hallway in intermittent bursts. Angelica made her way back the way she'd come, stepping over the patch of mud where she had first seen the footprints. Looking for a child's toy wasn't a complete waste of time, she told herself. Since she would be looking through the trash heap for anything she could use anyway, she might as well do what she could to help her new friend feel better. Much to her own surprise, Angelica felt no resentment at the task. If nothing else, it helped her forget her own problems, if only for a moment.

The moment didn't last long. As she turned at the T-intersection, her stomach grumbled loudly. She took a sip of the stale water in her canteen. She'd given Wisteria the piece of biscuit she had been saving. The girl said she had no food, that she hadn't needed any until Hector got lost. A nice fiction, Angelica admitted, one that had likely helped the girl deal with the horrors she had seen. Angelica knew there was no shortage of those since the renders had come.

The water helped, but only a little. She would have to collect some rainwater at some point, though it looked like there'd be time enough for that when she was on the road.

There weren't many places to look for Hector, and most were too small for her to fit. Only when she dislodged a precariously situated car hood did she find a recess, filled almost to the rim with muck. Hector the unicorn lay in it, out of reach. His red-glazed ceramic body was broken into several pieces. There was no way she could fix him, even if she could reach him. She almost wept to think how Wisteria would react, knowing that the one thing she counted on couldn't help her anymore.

She sat back on her haunches. Why was she even worrying about it? No matter what Angelica did, the girl would be dead in a few days. There was no food here, and even if she decided to take Wisteria with her, they would die on the way to the next city— either from starvation or the renders.

So why was she trying to think of a solution? Why did she insist on making this girl happy? Why did any of this matter? She didn't know. But when the solution finally came to her, she felt the beginnings of a smile form on her face as she went to work.

o   o   o

"Here. I know it's not Hector, but it's the best I could do."

Wisteria looked down at the gift in her hands. It was a piece of junk—well, actually, several pieces of junk—fastened together into an approximation of a unicorn. It was mostly bits of metal since much of the softer materials suitable for a child's toy had long ago rotted away. Angelica had been able to salvage some coarse cloth to make the mane and tail, however. In that way, this one was even better than the original.

It was much smaller than Hector had been, its corkscrew horn barely extending beyond the edge of the girl's cupped hands. Wisteria studied it for a while, brow furrowed. "I'm still hungry," she said quietly. Then she looked up. "Hector was red." The way she said this suggested the two facts were related, though if they were, Angelica couldn't see the connection. Children's logic was impenetrable.

No matter. "Here," Angelica said. The smile came easily this time. "I'll fix him up." She took the unicorn out into the hallway, rolled up her sleeve, and cut a strip of fabric from the hem of her undershirt with the bowie knife sheathed at her hip. Then she rested the edge of the blade against her bare arm and took several deep breaths. She briefly thought about the risk of infection, but then chuckled. If she lived long enough for that to matter, she was far luckier than she had any right to be.

Gritting her teeth, she drew the blade across her skin.

Once she finished painting the unicorn red, Angelica bound her wound tightly with the strip of cloth, rolled down her sleeve, and blew on the unicorn until it was dry enough. Already it was darkening, but it still looked somewhat red. She dabbed at her eyes with a clean spot on her sleeve and mastered the throbbing in her arm until her breath didn't quaver so much.

Holding the unicorn in her hands as if presenting a gift to a princess, she returned to the room where Wisteria waited.

Wisteria didn't ask where she had gotten red paint or why Angelica's arm was bandaged, but she stared at the unicorn for a long moment. "Yes," the girl whispered. "This will do."

She accepted it gingerly, and Angelica swore she saw something, a flash of light maybe, sweep over the girl. It was gone before Angelica could process it. It could've been the guttering of the lamp, but it felt like something in the air had changed the moment the girl accepted the gift Angelica had made.

"Are you going to name it?"

"Yes. Her name is Angie." Wisteria's eyes filled with tears. "I'm not hungry anymore. But I am sleepy."

She crawled onto the cot, clutching her new unicorn tightly to her chest in spite of all its sharp edges.

Angelica turned down the lamp until it was almost off and pulled the tattered bath towel up to Wisteria's chin to tuck her in.

"You'll stay, won't you?"

Angelica smiled as she brushed the girl's hair from her face. A tear rolled down her cheek, and she was grateful for the darkness. "I'll think about it."

And she would. She would think about that offer, and remember it, until her dying breath. But there was no way she could accept it.

Wisteria's eyes fluttered. She appeared on the verge of sleep, but said, "I know about Hector. Angie told me. Red unicorns are special, you know. They can see each other, even when no one else can." Her words were beginning to slur with drowsiness. "But it's okay. I have Angie now." She must have seen Hector before Angelica had even arrived, and then incorporated his disappearance into the fantasy world she had created in her mind.

Once Wisteria's eyes had closed and her breathing evened out, Angelica brushed her lips against the girl's forehead and went outside. She packed all of her food and canteen into a rucksack, which she left at the foot of Wisteria's cot. It wasn't much, but it was more than nothing. Where Angelica was going, she wouldn't need it.

She pulled up her hood against the rain and began to pull her levcart through the towers of refuse. It was still early evening, the sky gray. It was dangerous heading out on foot this late, even without the renders, but Angelica found she didn't mind. With the supplies she had left behind, she had given Wisteria a few more days of life.

And Angelica had *chosen* how she would live her own last few days. She felt as if she had finally lived a human life for a time, rather than the life of a cornered animal, and that was all she could ask for.

As she got to the edge of the scrapyard, the blue LED on her wrist wearable began flashing steadily.

She stared at it for minute, not comprehending, as terror slowly seeped into her. *Oh no.*

A render was coming.

Her instincts told her to run. She still had time. The wearables could detect renders from a couple of kilometers away, registering their presence by the unique radiation signature their bodies gave off. Angelica had at least ten minutes to get clear, fifteen if she was lucky and the render wasn't headed directly for her. The rate of flashing would tell her how likely that was, and she could change course to account for it. She had survived so far using such tactics.

And she could survive again. She could get away, head out into Wastes. Even with no food and only the rain to quench her thirst, she would survive, but only for a time.

She glanced back at the mound of trash. Imagined the render pulling it apart, finding what lay sleeping inside.

Her fingers began to shake, but she smiled grimly. Run away, and waste all this ammo?

Angelica turned around and headed back into the scrapyard, pulling her levcart and the arsenal it contained behind her.

O   O   O

Three frag grenades. An NA-8 burst rifle, with 183 armor-piercing rounds. Two pistols with six clips. A sawed-off semi-automatic shotgun of unknown design, but functional. Twenty-eight shells. A bolt-action hunting rifle with nine bullets. An M20 bazooka, one M28A2 rocket. And though she hoped it wouldn't come to it, her bowie knife.

But those were merely icing on the cake.

She had two Ballbusters—stationary weapons platforms with automated targeting. But that wasn't all. According to the water-damaged manual Angelica had found, the Ballbusters had "dynamic ammunition LOS extension." Fancy speak for bullets whose trajectories curved around corners. Good for larger targets that moved out of visible range and behind cover. The extrapolation algorithm wasn't foolproof, but it was good enough to provide a significant advantage in a tight situation. Any run-in with a render qualified as one of those.

By the change in the frequency at which her wearable flashed while she scouted, Angelica judged the render was approaching from the north—just as she had. It was unlikely, but possible, that it had followed her. Knowing that she may have led it here only strengthened her resolve to stay and fight.

She set up the Ballbusters in flanking positions, protecting them from the rain with sheets of plastic she had found. Afterward, she hunkered down in a small, covered area a hundred yards from where Wisteria slept. She hoped the girl could sleep through thunderstorms.

Her arsenal was scattered about the scrapyard. She needed to be light on her feet when the render came. The wind lashed her back as she readied the bazooka. It was devastating but inaccurate, and it worked best when there was some element of surprise. She'd use it first. She had no official combat training, but she had worked out this very scenario in her mind fifty times a day for the past five years. She was as ready as she could be.

Even so, her odds were bad. If all the human armies in the world couldn't stop the renders, she didn't have much of a chance.

But she didn't have to win. All she had to do was fight.

Angelica leaned against an old mattress, nearly prone, the weight of the bazooka against her shoulder, and waited.

Two minutes later, an ethereal glow lit the sky from behind the northern tree line. Trees fell, seemingly at random. Had her clothes not already been soaked with rain, Angelica was sure her sweat would have done the job.

A steady *thump-thump-thump* could be heard over the rain as the first of the Ballbusters engaged its target. A few moments later, the second one began firing.

The glow over the forest grew. She could see traces of white light, like the gates of heaven had been thrown open, constantly shifting beyond the trunks of the trees. She quickly calibrated her goggles' contrast ratio to prevent retinal burn.

The render stepped out of the trees, snapping branches and trunks with equal ease. Its narrow body was as long and wide as a bus, yet its long, crablike legs made it seem nimble. It scanned its surroundings, shifting its stance to avoid the armor-piercing rounds that occasionally nicked the joins in its multifaceted carapace—the render's only true weak spots. Even its four maroon, glassy eyes were heavily shielded and effectively bulletproof.

Angelica released her breath and pulled the trigger.

The thump of the rocket launching from her small shelter was deafening. She was disoriented for a split-second, but then she had the presence of mind to dump the bazooka and grab her hunting rifle.

She heard the detonation but didn't see if the rocket actually struck its target. There was no time for that. She ran for cover.

The render sped out of view. The timbre of the Ballbusters' reports cracking through the air changed slightly as the turrets swiveled to track it. One of the Ballbusters spun down; the render must have moved out of its extended LOS.

Angelica leaned against a stack of old TVs, rifle at the ready, but she wasn't looking down the sights. She had nothing to aim at yet. Her breathing was coming faster and faster. She couldn't hear the blood pumping in her ears over the rumble of the Ballbusters, but she could feel every beat of her heart like the shuddering of the cosmos.

Where are you? she wondered. *Come for me. I'm ready.*

She heard a piercing, alien scream and smiled. Probably wounded now. The render staggered into view sixty yards out, the white light from one of the joins in its leg burning hotter, almost too bright to look at, even through her goggles. Not a fatal hit, but it would slow the render down a bit. Hopefully.

She pressed the wood stock of the rifle against her cheek, squinted down the sight, exhaled, and squeezed.

The recoil jolted her. She ejected the cartridge, reloaded, fired, and was on the move again. She couldn't stay still for long without the render pinpointing her location. Even if she did keep moving, it would likely find her sooner than later. Renders had poor eyesight at long distances, but they were unnaturally clever. And once they got close, they could detect prey by other means, some sense that no one yet understood, and could even penetrate two feet of iron. If it got within five or six yards of her, she was as good as dead.

Having a chance against a render meant staying three steps ahead of it. And having more than one's fair share of luck.

After she fired off her fourth round, one of the Ballbusters powered down after spinning empty for a couple seconds. The second fired only occasionally. The render was likely picking its path to avoid the turret's LOS.

With only one turret still working, time was running out. Angelica headed up a rise to her last redoubt—the dead end where she had left the burst rifle and the sawed-off shotgun. She had booby-trapped the entrance with all three grenades. In the back was a narrow tunnel she could escape through once the render came for her.

She took up the burst rifle and shotgun, one in each hand, and stood waiting. Though it was a dead end, it was slightly elevated so she could still see the forest's edge, as well as the mound of Wisteria's room. Angelica knew that if the render closed on that mound, there was no saving the girl. She had to do what she could to draw it away.

As Angelica glanced over at the mound again, a flash of red caught her eye, but was gone before she could identify it.

White light spread across the entrance to her redoubt. One leg stepped into sight, followed by others, followed by the render's massive body.

Angelica stared into its eyes.

One leg found the trip wire. The walls of trash exploded inward, debris flying everywhere. The render screamed.

Then so did Angelica, and she opened fire with both weapons.

Liquid light sprayed as one of the render's limbs was torn free by the explosion. But now it had found her. It swept forward with the fearless, casual grace of a predator, heedless of the bullets and shot fired in its direction.

Angelica stumbled and fell to her back. The render suddenly loomed above her. Its mandibles slid apart, dripping with a viscous, paralyzing toxin. Two of its remaining legs rose up, the sharp ends poised like scorpion tails.

She tossed away the shotgun, sighted down her rifle, and fired straight into the creature's open mouth.

The legs descended.

The world blazed white for a long, long time, then slowly, everything went dark.

O O O

Angelica woke to the pitter-patter of the rain. All else was silent.

Not dead yet, she thought. She pulled off her goggles, revealing the gray clouds and the smoking, burned-out husk of the dead render in front of her.

She had killed it. She had done it.

The thrill of victory was dampened by the rising sensation that something was desperately wrong with her body.

She didn't need to look down. With her hands she felt the hard, blood-soaked surface of the render's legs, where they had pierced her just above her waist.

It didn't matter. At least she had won before she finally lost.

As she wiped her eyes, she saw a small light blinking on her wrist wearable. First blue, then purple.

Purple meant multiple signatures.

No no no! She reached for her rifle, but her fingers barely brushed the stock. Multiple signatures. Even if she weren't pinned here, dying, there was nothing she could do against more than one render. She had used up her fair share of luck already.

She watched, helpless, as a half-dozen renders strode out of the tree line, heading straight for the mound where Wisteria was, blazing white like an army of unholy angels.

Her vision began to fade. But something caught her attention: the flash of red had returned, just above the mound. For some reason, she couldn't quite force her eyes to focus on it.

Her attention was drawn back to the renders. They were moments from coming within range of finding Wisteria. She watched, unable to look away.

But then the renders walked by the mound, utterly unconcerned with the human asleep within it. They continued on without pause until they disappeared from sight.

Impossible, she thought. *They should have detected her.*

For some reason, they hadn't.

Suddenly, the red flash returned and resolved into something solid. A towering, majestic horse, its skin a roiling red like living fire. The air around it bent and shivered as if it *were* made of fire.

No, she realized. *Not a horse.* A twisting horn protruded from its forehead.

She coughed. It sounded wet. Not good. It was getting harder and harder to hold her head up. The red unicorn turned its head. Its eye, like molten steel, met hers. The horn on its head tilted slightly as it nodded once.

Relief flooded her as the implication of that nod hit her. Wisteria would be safe. Angelica smiled and whispered, "I see you, Angie." As the edges of her vision began to darken and her eyelids fluttered, she knew that Angie would be the last thing she ever saw.

Then shocking pain in her stomach forced her back into full awareness. The render's legs were drawn out of Angelica by some unseen force, and the entire creature was tossed aside like a massive ragdoll.

Angelica clutched at her middle, fearing everything would come spilling out of her wounds, but the skin was already beginning to knit together. It felt like tendrils of ice twisting inside her. Soon, both the pain and the icy sensation were gone. She pulled up her bloody shirt.

Her skin was an angry red—red, like blood and fire—but unbroken and unscarred.

Angelica looked back at Angie, tears of gratitude filling her eyes, but the red unicorn was gone.

O   O   O

The next settlement they came to was the same as the others: people peering out of hiding spots disguised with rubble, eyes wide with fear of the worst. But that only lasted a moment, until their eyes widened further with surprise.

Angelica adjusted the rifle's strap on her shoulder as she glanced down at Wisteria, holding her hand. The child clutched her little unicorn and grinned as if she hadn't a worry in the world.

And maybe she didn't. Angelica smiled back. Her followers, the men, women, and children who gathered behind her, weren't smiling. Their faces were hard, not with resignation, but with determination. Angelica nodded to them. They nodded back.

Angelica returned her attention to the residents of the new settlement. When she spoke, her voice carried clearly.

"I know you're afraid. We all were, once. But we have come to tell you of a new way to live." A few people came out of hiding, wary but curious.

Angelica continued. "You don't need to fear the renders anymore. Because we have something that protects you from them."

Behind her, the followers murmured in unison, "Angie." It was what they called Angelica, thanks to Wisteria. They didn't know about the unicorn; they thought Angelica had saved them.

Atop the settlement's tallest building, a familiar flash of red caught Angelica's gaze, hooves like flame rampant against the sky. Angelica rubbed at the red skin hidden beneath her shirt.

Perhaps the people were right. Only red unicorns could see each other, after all.

About the Author

Brandon M. Lindsay was raised in the Seattle area on a steady diet of sci-fi novels. Now he lives in Japan, where he focuses on writing epic fantasy.

VODKA DREAMS

NANCY DIMAURO

Marco swirled the vodka in his glass. The clear liquid caught the faintly yellow tinge of the deck's bug light. Sounds of the party almost drowned out the crash of the waves. He'd come outside to escape the heat and noise of their fifteenth college reunion and beach week. Tomorrow they'd all head back to the lives they'd carved out. But tonight—tonight they could still pretend they were the kids they'd been when life was new and the future was as bright as the full moon that hung over their rented beach houses.

The week had been an exercise in torture. As had the last few years. So, why did he come?

He raised the vodka bottle in salute to impossibilities, then poured more into his glass. The bottle paused on its way back down to the deck.

"No," he said to its label.

Moonlight glinted off the Red Unicorn logo. It wasn't a prissy unicorn with flowers flowing down her mane who reared to look pretty. No. This unicorn fought battles—and won. Strength vibrated from his broad chest, thick neck, and muscled legs. It reared, not to impress, but to impale challengers. His gold-tipped horn had tasted blood. The Red Unicorn took what he wanted, what he loved.

"That's a terrible idea."

The unicorn saw no reason for Marco not to do something stupid, like marching into the house, tossing Kathy over his shoulder, caveman-like, and carrying her to his room. The idea grew more appealing the more vodka slid down Marco's throat.

He stood and turned to the house. His fingers clenched around the cool glass, then he sank down into a yellow Adirondack chair.

He needed to stop drinking.

A giggling mass of women cascaded onto the deck. His unwitting torturer flittered in the middle of the pack. Her russet hair looked almost mahogany in the bug light. She wore a silver mesh cover-up, black shorts, and deep purple bikini top. Earlier in the day the group had done dramatic readings of bad romance novels on the beach.

"Delicious lassitude." He snorted. Who wrote that crap? But for a moment, when the words had fallen from Kathy's dusty rose lips, they hadn't been quite so ludicrous.

The pepper-flavored vodka burned a path down his throat.

She'd want to spend the last night on the beach. She always did. After all, it was why he was waiting out here. Even if he hadn't realized his motivation until now.

She's not yours.

He'd sent congratulations and a small silver unicorn necklace, which she'd worn all week, when she'd posted that Dustin had finally proposed. Marco hadn't expected Dustin to take the plunge even though the pair had been living together for over ten years. Proof that Dustin could get something right flashed brilliantly from Kathy's left hand.

Marco refilled his glass. Time to move on. Except …

Dustin, his once-lean features softened by too much good food and not enough exercise, stalked onto the deck. The screen door slammed behind him. The women stilled.

Laughter fell from Kathy's eyes as Dustin approached. After a short conversation, he stalked back into the house. Kathy laughed. It sounded strained. She looked through the window, then shook her head. A minute later she returned to her girlfriends, blazing as brightly as she had before Dustin interrupted.

Time to move on.

Except for the thought that Kathy might not be happy. Over the last week Marco had suspected that Kathy's calm, blissful façade was just an act, that she wasn't ecstatic over her belated engagement.

Or was it wishful thinking on his part?

"Hey."

His head jerked up as Kathy dropped onto his lap.

When had everyone gone in?

The only sound was the soft music coming from the house and the roar of the ocean. The scent of vanilla, suntan lotion, sea salt, and Kathy teased his senses.

"You're looking all glum and dire," she said.

"Trying to earn my rep." His free hand curled around her waist.

"Ah." She lifted the glass from his fingers and took a sip. Her eyes went wide. "Damn, that packs a punch. What is it?"

Reaching over the arm of the chair, he pulled up the bottle for her inspection.

She squinted in the poor light. "Red Unicorn Vodka? Did you get this in Russia?"

He grunted noncommittally.

No one at the reunion knew he was the distiller or that the Red Unicorn brand was a top seller on the West Coast and about to break into the East Coast market. He'd wanted to see his friends' reactions to the vodka before they felt obligated to say they liked it. The case he'd brought was almost gone. Good test marketing. There were three versions: White Unicorn for the unflavored, traditional style; Red Unicorn for the pepper vodka; and Purple Unicorn for the unflavored, grape-based one.

Kathy's finger traced the Red Unicorn logo. Marco stopped breathing. Silly to feel jealous about a logo he'd designed.

"There's nothing girly about this unicorn. You can tell he's male," Kathy said.

Marco's arm tightened fractionally around her waist. "I'm sure that makes him feel better."

"He's secure in his masculinity." She nodded. "You can tell." She leaned over and put the bottle on the deck.

Marco bit the inside of his cheek to suppress a groan. He should not want to toss his friend's fiancée to the deck and make love to her until she knew they belonged together. He forced his fingers to loosen.

"Looking forward to heading back to the left coast?"

Now wasn't *that* the question of the year? "Not particularly," he said. "You?"

"I live on this coast." Kathy said. "It's an easy drive from Corolla to D.C."

"Well aware. You know what I meant."

Her gaze went distant and turned toward the ocean. "I always hate when this week ends."

So did he. They had a platonic "same time next year" relationship. The end of beach week meant another year without seeing her.

"You never told me how Dustin proposed."

"Oh." She huffed out a breath. "I always figured I'd be married with kids before I was thirty. I mean Dustin and I'd been together since junior year. Why wouldn't we get married? It was probably a mistake to let him move in after he lost his job." She shrugged. "Economically it made sense. We were going to get married at some point after all. But thirty came and went. I figured he needed some time to get back on his feet."

She took another sip from his glass.

"He never seemed interested in getting another job, though. I wouldn't mind so much if he did *anything* around the house. I get up for work. He sleeps in. When I get home, he's playing a video game. Dishes in the sink, laundry baskets full, no thoughts of dinner. I'll cook or order in."

Marco's hand rose to brush her cheek, but he dropped it. Her skin radiated the warmth of the day under his palm. Yes, putting his hand on her thigh and feeling her softness was definitely the way to stop wanting her. Idiot. He pulled her closer.

"I know," she said. "Pathetic, right?"

"No."

"Don't. I know it was … is. So, last year was thirty-five. No ring. No wedding. After beach week, I decided things had to change. I told Dustin he either needed to step up, take the relationship to a new level, and propose or get out of my house. He said, 'Okay, let's get married.'"

"Romantic." Marco ground his teeth.

"Anyway, we bought the ring the next day." She held up her hand to catch the light. "For a little bit—a month, maybe two—things were fine. Good, even. He started looking for work again, picked up around the house, helped out."

"Didn't last?"

She took another sip of vodka. His hand tracked its way up her back and rested on the nape of her neck. Her lips fascinated him. Would they be as soft as her skin?

He should not rub small circles on the back of her neck. He should not think about kissing her. He should not stroke a finger down her jaw line.

"When was the last time he made you happy?"

The sound of his voice startled him. He hadn't planned on asking more about Kathy and Dustin's relationship. Seems he couldn't let it go, couldn't let *her* go.

The glass was empty. She looked down as if hoping it would magically refill. "I don't remember."

Her cheek was so soft against his palm. Gentle pressure at the nape of her neck brought her closer. The kiss began as a sharing of sympathy. A quick meeting of lips between friends. It flared into St. Elmo's fire. Her tongue darted between his lips. He gave what she wanted to take. The glass clanked to the deck.

"I can't tell you how long I've wanted to do that," he said, pausing to catch his breath.

Then he tunneled his fingers through her hair and sealed her mouth with his.

Voices spilled out from the house.

Kathy pulled away. Her eyes wide. She scrambled off his lap.

"I—I can't," she said as she backed away. She turned and jogged down the stairs to the beach.

He should not chase his friend's girl down the beach even if she was the woman of his dreams. He should not have kissed her. He should not want to do it again, or want to see the moon's glow on her skin as his hands learned all about her body.

He chuckled. It was too late to worry about *should*. He was all sorts of past *should*.

What he shouldn't do is let her get away.

He picked up the bottle and glass, then headed to the beach the way Kathy had gone. He found her leaning with her back against the retaining wall five houses away. Her head angled up toward the sky, baring the white skin of her neck to the moon; her eyes were closed.

"Kathy."

"If you say you're sorry, I'm going to kick your teeth in."

Sorry was the last thing he was.

He held out the bottle. "Drink?"

"Hell, yes."

He leaned next to her before handing her the refilled glass. They watched the tide roll in.

His fingers tangled with hers.

"Do you want to marry him?" he asked.

"I don't know." Her laugh was soft and self-deprecating. "If I don't I've wasted almost twenty years of my life on him."

Taking the glass from her hand, he asked, "What's worse? Spending the last twenty years hoping for something that never happened, or wasting the next twenty because you're unwilling to let go of something that isn't working?"

"You're one to talk."

The warmth of the vodka flowing down his throat brought a welcome calm. "Yup. Completely sucked at the marriage thing."

"What happened?"

His marriage had been a disaster. Annoyance became active dislike after a few years. His divorce had been more amicable than his marriage.

"Boring story. We'd been living together. Didn't see how a piece of paper would change anything. It did."

Her leg brushed against his, and she leaned her head on his shoulder.

Closing his eyes, he breathed in her scent. "We both changed. Or maybe I just didn't change enough. I was working to build a business. When I did come home for a few hours of sleep all she'd do was harp on me. The fun-loving girl I'd fallen for, the one I thought I'd married, was gone. So I stopped coming home." He shrugged.

"You cheated."

"Never. Not that Lilly ever believed that."

The glass never made it to his lips. Kathy's warm hand closed over his. "You're hogging that."

The warm scent of woman mixed with vanilla that was Kathy enveloped him. She pressed against him. A growl built in the back of his throat. His palms itched to lift her silver mesh top; he wanted to spread his hands across her back and settle her close to him where she belonged. He released the glass when she tugged on it.

"I have more." His voice was deep and rough. He turned to grab the bottle.

She chained him in place with the gentle caress of her finger on his cheek.

"Kathy—"

She took a gulp from the glass then pressed her cool lips against his. He opened for her. Warm vodka flowed into his mouth tasting of both the signature pepper he'd infused in the alcohol and Kathy. Her tongue speared into his mouth. His fingers dug into her hips and hauled her closer. She molded to him, her leg wrapping around his calf. Her sharp teeth pulled on his bottom lip, then nipped down his throat.

This time he didn't stop the growl. Yanking her up, he set her on the wall. Her legs wrapped around his hips and put him right where he wanted to be. He pressed into her warmth.

With a curse, he jerked back to put distance between them. Her whimper of protest went straight to his groin.

"You're engaged. We shouldn't—"

His thoughts scattered as her mouth met the juncture of his neck and shoulder.

"Kathy." His snarl was born of deep frustration. "I can't promise forever."

"You can't even promise tomorrow. You live in California."

He didn't want the one-night stand she might offer. He wanted *more*.

"I travel a lot for business. Where I'm based doesn't matter."

A hand grabbed his shoulder and spun him around. Kathy screeched as she fell off the wall. Dustin's right fist connected with Marco's jaw. He dropped to the sand.

"What the hell are you doing?"

The copper taste of blood filled Marco's mouth. He shielded his eyes as if the light reflecting off the nearby house was too bright. "H-h-heeeey, whaz up, buddy?"

"Don't 'buddy' me." Red blotches appeared on Dustin's cheeks and neck.

"Ya try the w-w-vodka?" Marco slurred. He let his legs slide out from under him to make it seem like he was trying to stand but couldn't. "Ith reeeeal gooood."

"Get up so I can knock you down again." Dustin loomed over him.

"Stop it." Kathy stepped between them.

Don't do it, Kathy. Let us work the male ego part out.

"Stay out of this." Dustin snarled.

"We're done." She held out something—Marco assumed it was her engagement ring—to Dustin.

"We're not."

She dropped the ring onto the sand.

Dustin's mouth hung open. "Do you know how much that cost?"

Kathy cocked her head. "Actually, I do. I paid for it. On second thought—" She picked up the ring and placed it on her right hand. "I'm keeping it. Get your crap out of my house."

Dustin went an alarming shade of red, his lips a tight white slash. He grabbed Kathy's arm.

Marco slowly got to his feet. "Don't," he said. "Instead, you want to walk back up to the house, get your stuff, and find someplace else to sleep tonight. Like a sofa."

The mental math was apparent on Dustin's face as he shifted his eyes between Marco and Kathy, weighing the odds of taking Marco with something other than a sucker punch.

"Bitch." Dustin spit on the beach near Kathy's feet.

Marco watched Dustin until he passed the second house, then he turned to Kathy.

"Wait," she said as she pulled her cell phone from her shorts pocket. "Hey, Jilly. Sorry to call so late but I need a favor. Can you get a locksmith out to my place? ... Yes, now. I just dumped Dustin, and—"

A high-pitched squeal from the other side of the line cut her off. At least one of Kathy's friends had despised Dustin. The woman's tone dropped low enough that Marco couldn't hear her. A minute later, Kathy pocketed her phone.

Marco raised an eyebrow.

"Can we just … sit?" Kathy asked.

They sat side by side on the beach. The gentle crash and hush susurration of the ocean told the story of eons. Kathy lay back in the sand. She grabbed the hem of his shirt and pulled him down with her.

"That wasn't because we kissed," Kathy said.

"Are you sure? I have it on pretty good authority that I'm an amazing kisser."

Kathy laughed and thumped him on the chest. Propped up on an elbow, she leaned over him. "Dustin's passive-aggressiveness was becoming less passive and more aggressive as the week approached. I think he was worried I'd press for a date while we were here. We've barely spent any time together, and what we have hasn't exactly been pleasant."

Marco had watch Kathy and Dustin throughout the week. When Dustin had reached around her to get a beer on the first night of the trip, she'd shied out of his way like she didn't want him touching her. Marco's heart had felt a traitorous stab of hope seeing that, even as his fists curled. He'd spent every minute since looking for fissures in their relationship. They hadn't been hard to see. Until now he hadn't known if they were real or his wishful thinking.

"He didn't want to marry me. He just didn't want to lose the lifestyle I've let him become accustom to." Kathy ran a finger over Marco's jaw where Dustin had hit him. "Hold on a sec."

When she lay down next to him again she had the bottle of vodka in her hand. She placed the Red Unicorn against the bruise forming on his cheek. The bottle felt cool on his hot skin.

"Why did you let him hit you?"

"It's a guy thing." He chuckled at the furrow in her brow. "Seriously, I deserved it. I kissed his fiancée. He was entitled to one. Just one."

"And the drunk act?"

"You mean the being-drunker-than-I-am act?" When she nodded, he took her free hand and brushed a kiss over it. Sea salt mingled with the taste of her. "To give you choice. If I'm drunk, the kiss is my fault. Well, mine and the Red Unicorn's. Not yours."

"Never figured you for the chivalrous type."

"I'm usually more of a rake." His fingers brushed lightly over her arm, over her shoulder, then down her back.

The small shiver that ran down her body was somewhat undercut by her bright laugh. "You really were listening during those dramatic romance readings."

"Hard not to when you're talking about throbbing breasts and heaving manhood. Wait. I think I got that backward."

The silver bell of her laughter eased something deep inside him. Kathy leaned down. The Red Unicorn bottle dropped to the sand. His hands circled her waist and drew her on top of him as their lips touched. Heat flared. Every luscious inch of her melted into him. He slid his hand under her mesh top and up her back. The firmness of her breasts pressed into his chest. He resisted the urge to pin her under him and explore every curve.

"I'll change my flight, come to D.C.," he said when they came up for air.

She rolled off him. The cooler air against his skin was a slap in the face.

"What exactly do you think is going on here?" she asked.

He propped himself up on his elbows. "I know what's not going on. I'm not your rebound guy."

She flinched.

Inching closer, Marco took her hands in his. "There's always been the possibility of *more* between us. I want that chance."

"Didn't you just say you couldn't promise me forever?"

He cupped her face in his hands. Lips brushing over her cheek, he said, "You don't want to hear about forever. You just kicked Dustin to the curb. How about just happily for now?"

Her arms wound around his neck. His finger hooked the chain holding her unicorn pendant.

Delight danced in her eyes. "Dustin hates it when I wear it."

"I'll bet." He leaned back when she leaned forward. "Do you want me to come to D.C.?"

Her gaze drifted back to the waves. Muscles tightened in Marco's neck as the pause lengthened. He clamped his teeth closed to keep from blurting out all the reasons why she should give them a chance. His hands dropped from her shoulders to her sides.

"In a month," she said.

His exhaled breath ruffled her hair.

"Can you give me a month to get everything resolved with Dustin?" she asked.

Business had him in Singapore at the end of September. He'd reschedule.

"Tell me when you want me, and I'll be there."

"How about right now?"

His body tightened in anticipation.

"No." The word coming out of his mouth shocked him.

Hurt flashed in Kathy's eyes.

He placed a kiss on her forehead and gathered her in his arms.

"Please don't take that the wrong way," he said. "I would like nothing better than to reenact *From Here to Eternity* with you right now. But you just said you needed time." He held up a hand to forestall her. "Make that offer again in a month and see how quickly I accept."

She nodded.

"Besides, as angry as Dustin was, I suspect we only have another minute or two before everyone suddenly wants to see the ocean and what we're doing."

"Sure you don't want to scandalize them?" Kathy tilted her face up to him.

"I'm sure you don't."

It took a minute to untangle where her legs had intertwined with his. By the time he heard the sound of a dozen drunks staggering up the beach, Kathy and he were sitting side by side, his arm around her, her head resting on his shoulder, watching the waves. It was something they'd done hundreds, if not thousands, of times over nearly twenty years.

"One dead unicorn." Kathy nudged the empty vodka bottle.

The top hadn't been on tight. When he'd dropped it, the remnants had leaked into the sand.

"The Red Unicorn gave his life to save a lovely maiden. What more could he ask for?"

"Happily for now, huh?" she asked.

"It's a start."

"I could get used to it."

Together, they turned to watch the waves and wait for the onslaught of their curious friends.

About the Author

Nancy is a mom, writer, speaker, and lawyer. Before being a published writer, Nancy had been a blackjack dealer, florist, tax form coder, worked in professional theatre, accidently went to law school, and passed one bar exam while recovering from a concussion. Really, the horse's headache was much worse. When she reflects that she has normal, boring life, she is often puzzled when people burst out laughing in response.

THE FALL OF WINTER

SCOTT EDER

Violet stormed through the front door and into the yard, heart thumping. Lightning slashed across a half-moon sky. Thunder detonated. Cold rain pelted her face, plastering her nightdress to her skin and her mass of blonde curls to her head in seconds. Barefoot, she squished through the mud, her glance darting across the rain-blurred courtyard to the pen, the barn, the distant hills.

She heard growls and yips and snarls buried under the steady patter in the distance.

Nonono. She'd seen the jaws, the flash of teeth, the blood in a vision. Even smelled the wet wolf fur. That, most of all, propelled her from the warmth beneath her blanket into the chill of a late autumnal deluge. *Can't have them. Can't have my babies.*

She bit her lip, standing on tiptoes. "Where?" She swallowed the dread that soured her mouth.

Bleating gray shapes flowed toward the shack like low-hanging fog.

Yelps and whines toward the hills.

Violet ran to the sound, forging a path through the sheep.

A fierce snort. An irate neigh.

Silence, but for the rainfall's steady drone.

Lightning flashed. Limned in the silvery light reared the shape of a stallion with a single horn jutting from its forehead.

The sight stopped her dead. Her breath caught. Her feet sank into the mud. Rivulets of rainfall wept down her face as she waited for another flash, proof that she hadn't imagined it. A strange burbling sensation, similar to the one she felt years ago on the day Kayden had saved her life, roiled in her belly. She felt a pull toward the hills, a call deep in her soul that ached to be answered. She took a step—

Thunder rumbled. The ground vibrated beneath her toes. She took another step.

"Violet!" Kayden called her name.

His strong hands on her shoulders tried to steer her toward the house, but she held firm.

Have to see ...

Lightning shredded the sky. The unicorn image had vanished, but the memory was seared into her brain.

"It's back, Kay," she whispered into the thunderous rumble.

Kayden squelched in the mud beside her and dropped to one knee as he draped an arm over her shoulder. He matched her stare. "I can feel it." He rubbed his shirt, touching the scar on his chest from his last encounter with a unicorn. "Where?"

Violet raised her arm and pointed to the hills.

Kayden nodded.

"Come in out of the rain you two," Kayden's wife, Winnie, called from the doorway. "You'll catch your death."

Death. The word settled into Violet's heart. After seven years, the beast had come back for her. This time, things could go differently. This time, Kayden might not be able to protect her. This time ...

A shiver wracked her thin frame.

"She's right, Vi." His arm across her shoulders tensed. "Let's get you out of the cold. We can't do anything else tonight."

Violet let her brother guide her into the house. She went through the motions of changing and climbing into bed in a daze, dreading what the morning would bring. For long moments she stared at the thin wooden walls of the room Kayden had built off the back of the shack to house their growing family.

Why now? Tears slid down her cheeks. It had taken seven years to cleanse her dreams of the purple killer who nearly stole her brother. Seven years of night terrors and screaming and wide-eyed sleepless nights. *Seven years.* She curled into a ball beneath a blanket of soft woolen heat, gripped her pillow tight, and waited for dawn.

o o o

"Vite!" Tiny, imprecise fingers poked Violet's right eye then managed to pry open her eyelid. "You 'wake, Vite?" A too-close face full of chubby red cheeks, emerald-colored eyes, pouty lips, and a shock of fire-red hair consumed Violet's limited vision. Gusts of warm, sour breath seemed to blow directly into her nostrils.

"Rose?" Violet mumbled.

"You are 'wake!" Rose mashed her nose into Violet's and batted her eyelashes.

She pushed the toddler gently out of tickling range. "I am now."

Sunlight streamed through the lone window, bathing the small room in morning. Violet sat up, careful not to dislodge her niece from her perch, and stretched. In the bright light of a new day, last night's incident seemed distant and unreal, nothing more than another bad dream.

Just another dream. She shook her head at her foolishness. She should have been used to it, but every once in a while a vivid dream intruded upon her sense of reality.

Violet sighed in relief. "Hey, Flower, should we tend to the woolly army?"

"I no flower." Rose squirmed off the cot and picked up her stuffed sheep from the floor. "Wet." She picked at a spot near its fuzzy rump.

Violet kicked off the blanket and stepped down into a puddle originating from her rain-soaked night dress piled in the corner. A chill wracked her body. Muddy footprints led from her cot to the other rooms.

Rose splashed in the thin layer of water, giggling.

It can't be. "Flower ..." Violet glanced out the window. At the edge of their farm, Kayden stood with his arms crossed, facing the hills and distant forest to the north. "Where's your ma?"

The little girl pointed toward the kitchen as she squelched in a circle, wiggling her toes with each step. Violet pulled a clean dress over her head, jammed her arms into an overcoat, grabbed the sodden garment, and followed the dirty trail into the kitchen.

Winnie stood over the washbasin, eyes closed, red hair fluttering in a chill breeze from the open window. She swayed slightly and rubbed her swollen belly.

Violet's bare heels thumped on the wooden floor. Droplets falling from the nightdress mixed with the muddy trail. She held the mess in front of her, careful not to dangle it over the small table heaped with bread and fresh vegetables.

Winnie smiled, but didn't turn or open her eyes. "Your brother's waiting for you." Her calm voice held no hint of anger or frustration at the recent desecration of her floors.

"Winnie, I—" Violet wanted to apologize for once again disrupting what should have been a tranquil, sheep-farming existence.

"Shush, hon. It's okay. Now scoot."

Rose squealed in the other room followed by a loud thump and the wail of a frustrated toddler. Winnie shook her head, and Violet hustled outside. After spreading her dress across a fence post to dry, she jogged toward her brother, sticking to the grass to avoid the swamped courtyard. The rest of the farm seemed to have survived the storm—the barn, the fence, both fine. She glanced toward the copse of aspen arcing around the head of her parents' graves. The storm had knocked hundreds of leaves from the trees, cloaking their resting place in a dragon's horde of russet and gold.

You always predicted the beast would return, Da. Wish you were here. Stupid wolves. Though other farmers had to deal with the constant danger of wolves, their farm remained impervious. Well, *had* remained impervious until a week ago when the first sheep went missing. Every night after that, more sheep disappeared, the bloody evidence clear.

The wolves had finally found their farm.

Last night was different. Weird and personal. Though the wolves invaded Violet's dream, something else had driven her into the rain, something else wanted her to bear witness.

Violet slowed to a walk as she drew close to her brother. The coiled intensity in his stance, as much as their grandfather's sword strapped to his back, gave her pause. His gaze remained fixed on the hills, jaw muscles flexing.

"What is it, Kay?"

"Nice of you to finally join me." Kayden smiled to show his comment nothing more than a tease. "We lost several last night, the most yet." He pointed to a slew of dark heaps littering the ground between two hills fifty paces off the edge of their farm. "Ready?"

Violet nodded and followed his lead, keeping close to his shoulder. Her keen gaze raked the rolling countryside, alert for signs of the hunt—a flash of gray out of the corner of her eye, the snap of a twig, the stray snarl or growl.

As they approached the killing ground, Kayden drew his grandfather's sword. Patches of rust, chips, and notches marred the once-fine blade, but its edge remained sharp and deadly. Violet was glad to see it in Kayden's strong grip. Though no swordsman, he could fell a tree with powerful strikes of a sharp ax. Wolves would fare no better.

Kayden stopped at the first gray-furred heap and jabbed the tip of the sword in the earth. "Wolves?" He rubbed his fingers through short-cropped, brown hair. "I don't get it."

Deep chunks and gouges had been torn out of the earth, the ground churned beneath a powerful force as though the setting had seen battle. Violet counted three dead wolves and two sheep beyond. She knelt over one of the wolves, searching for a wound. The rain had washed most of the blood from the fur, but she still found it—a round hole punched through the skin. She shot a look at her brother, who perked up at the attention. He walked over and knelt by her side.

"Son of a bitch." He reached for his tunic, rubbed his chest.

"Kayden?"

He stood and moved off, thoughts and vision distant. "I had hoped your vision last night nothing more than a dream, Vi, like so many before. And the throbbing of my scar the same, chalked up to the stress of a wolf attack. But now …"

A low moan sounded from near one of the sheep.

Kayden hurdled the dead animal, sword at the ready. Once on the other side, though, he tossed the sword to the ground. "Violet!"

She helped him ease a woman onto her back. Hidden by the sheep's carcass and a mud-stained cloak, they had not seen her. Her breathing was shallow, her eyes shut tight, skin sallow and drawn beneath a layer of filth. She shivered in pain and cold. Blood seeped from several deep scratches across her face, her throat. Puncture wounds dotted her hands and arms.

Kayden scanned the ground around them, brows drawn, lost in thought.

Violet stripped off her coat and laid it over the woman. "We have to save her, Kay."

He started at her statement. "Oh, uh, of course." He sheathed his sword and slid his hands under the injured woman. "We'll take her home. Winnie can tend her there." Gently, as though she were his own child, he cradled her frail body against his chest.

On the walk home, Violet watched every hill, every opening, every depression for a glimpse of gray fur, but found nothing. They moved as quickly as they could without jostling their patient.

"Did you notice the ground?" Kayden seemed unfazed by his fragile burden.

"No, why?"

"Cloven hooves. The prints surrounded her." He nodded to indicate his charge. "I think it protected her and killed the wolves. Tracks led away from the scene, into the hills to the west."

The woman gasped, face contorting in pain. Her eyes rolled beneath her lids.

They reached the edge of the farm and increased speed on the familiar turf. The milling sheep steered clear, scampering away from Kayden's determined approach.

Winnie poked her head out the door and, seeing the hurried procession, disappeared inside. Violet let Kayden enter first. Once inside, Winnie, with a curious Rose on her hip, directed him to lay the woman on Violet's cot. Within minutes, she had set out a bowl filled with steaming water, a pile of linen bandages, and dried herbs.

He eased her down. Winnie handed him Rose and pushed him out of the small room.

"Here." She dipped a linen strip in the water and handed it to Violet. "Clean the wounds on her face. I'll do her hands."

Tentative at first, not used to dealing with serious injuries, Violet dabbed at the woman's skin, removing patches of dirt and dried blood, exposing the aged skin beneath. The woman was far older than Violet had first thought. Her ancient face held an odd familiarity, as though she'd seen its shape and contours before.

"The poor dear." Winnie winced as she dug a tooth out of one of the wounds. "Thank goodness she's asleep." She fetched a mortar and pestle, ground the herbs, and mixed them with a few drops of water to form a paste, which she applied to each of the wounds.

"What will that do?" Violet asked.

"It will help prevent infection and dull the pain." She pointed to the woman's closed eyes. "See, she's relaxing a little. Come on." Rising to her feet, she held out her hand for Violet. "We'll let her sleep."

The woman gasped. Her eyes popped open and found Violet's. Recognition shocked them both. Though Violet had never met this woman before, she knew her, knew her heart, knew her soul.

"Thank the Lord of the Herd, I've found you." The woman's eyes fluttered and closed. A smile teased at her lips as she drifted back into oblivion.

O O O

Violet sat beside the cot, occasionally wiping beads of sweat from the woman's feverish brow. She pulled another twig from her tangled mass of silvery curls.

Who are you? Watching the injured woman sleep, Violet felt an odd sense of protectiveness, of kinship. The cant of her eyes, the set of her mouth, the shape of her nose. Something so familiar, so loving, lay just out of reach. And Violet very much wanted to reach out and grab it.

Whispers drifted down the hall from the kitchen, carried on the cool breeze through the open front door. Kayden and Winnie were discussing the woman. They thought their conversation private, but in a three-room shack with parchment-thin walls, nothing was private. Winnie didn't expect the woman to survive the night.

Unshed tears threatened to spill down Violet's cheeks, but she dabbed them away with the sleeve of her homespun dress. Focusing on something other than her sudden strong feelings, she dipped a cloth in the cool water and wiped the woman's face again.

"She looks like Ma." Kayden's soft, deep voice carried a hint of sadness.

Violet jumped. She hadn't heard her brother's silent approach. Heart racing, she leaned closer and found her mother behind the woman's features.

"It just hit me." He knelt by Violet's side. "But I can't ..." He shrugged, searching for the right words.

"Violet." Scratchy and weak, that single name escaped the woman's lips before her body convulsed. Head twisting from side to side, her arms and legs tensed, muscles rigid beneath the woolen coverlet. She arced off the bed.

"Pretty horsey," Rose squealed from the kitchen.

Violet's stomach rolled. Gooseflesh rushed across her skin.

Kayden rushed to the front door, but Violet knew he'd see nothing. Attuned through some cosmic meld, she sensed it approach, felt the tremor of its doomsday hoof beats, the heat of its infernal breath through the minute cracks between the planks in the walls, the strength of its conviction.

It wanted her.

But the sensation didn't fill her with dread. No. It was more of an excitement, a thrill stirring in her gut so different from the last time. A longing. A desire to explore, to gallop through the forest, to race from hilltop to hilltop to—

She placed her hand, then her cheek, on the wall, soaking in the warmth made by the creature's exhalations.

On the other side of the wall, the creature snorted and retreated.

The woman—*no, Annalise;* the name popped into Violet's head without effort—opened her eyes. With labored breath, she jerked her head toward Violet.

"Move, child," she croaked.

The drumming of hoof beats vibrated the floor.

Violet bent to Annalise's side. As she did, a pearlescent horn punched through the wall where her cheek had been. The impact split the plank. Cracks radiated from the point of entry. Violet gaped as the creature wiggled its horn.

Kayden charged in. He pulled Violet away from the struggling beast as the horn wrenched free.

A fiery red eyeball peered through the hole. The beast stamped and neighed, scanning the interior. When it spotted Annalise, it snorted and pushed against the wall, but the sight of the woman seemed to calm him.

"Help me up, child."

Keeping the red eye in sight, Kayden bent to help, but Annalise shied away.

"No! Only the girl. Only Violet."

Kayden frowned but backed away, making space for Violet. She slipped an arm behind Annalise's back, catching a whiff of the cinnamon apples her ma used to make for the Yuletide Feast, and helped her sit. The scent made her mouth water.

"Easy, easy." Annalise winced and settled into a sitting position with a heavy sigh. Violet stuffed a pillow behind her back for support. "My feet, dear." Her voice was stronger, yet little more than a rasp. She waved a bandage-wrapped hand toward the end of the cot. As if noticing the linen wraps for the first time, she flicked her wrist and let gravity unwind the rest.

Kayden opened his mouth to protest, but a stern glance stayed his words.

"Not prepared," Annalise muttered, revealing the pinkish hue of newly healed skin beneath the bandages. "Selfish girl. Up and dying before teaching her daughter."

Violet lifted the blanket and slid the woman's feet to the floor. The smell of fresh-tilled soil rose from her dirty feet. Lichen flourished between her toes.

At a loss, Kayden stood in the corner. Banished from helping, he kept a wary eye on the watching beast. "Ma'am, I—"

"Annalise," Violet and Annalise spoke at the same time. A brief smile flitted across the old woman's face. "Perhaps not all is lost." Shoulders hunched, she sat on the edge of the cot and unraveled the bandage around her neck.

"Boy!"

Kayden jumped. "Ma'am?"

Annalise skimmed her fingers across the new skin on her neck, her cheek. "Don't stand there gawking. We have much to do. They are coming." She nodded to herself as she strained to rise. "So much to do. And she no more than a slip of a girl. Tough to accept at that age without the proper instruction."

Violet jumped to her side and offered her shoulder, which the old woman grasped with an appreciative nod. At the contact, a flash of joy and contentment and righteous purpose flooded Violet's soul. She bowed under the impact, but quickly righted herself. The sensation lasted no more than a second.

"Miss Annalise, I—" Kayden hadn't moved. He wore the same calculating expression he did when the local merchants haggled over the price of wool.

"Why are you still here? Shoo. Shoo."

"Wait." Kayden stood firm. "I—we—deserve more of an explanation. What's going on? Who are you? Who is coming?"

"Kayden!" Winnie yelled from kitchen.

Shooting an accusing glance at the old woman, Kayden frowned as he strode down the hall.

Annalise closed her eyes and bowed her head. "Can you feel them?"

"Feel ... what?" But Violet knew the answer, sensed them even as the words left her mouth. "Wolves." She counted four, slinking between the trees near her parents' graves. Watching. Waiting. "They're hungry."

"The winter wolves are ravenous, my dear. Never sated, always on the hunt. Come." Annalise tottered down the hallway. "Let us see what your brother has discovered."

Arms crossed, Kayden stood in the kitchen doorway. He'd propped his grandfather's sword against the table. Winnie, with Rose on her hip, stared out the window, concern etched upon her face.

"You knew, didn't you?" Kayden turned to Annalise. "About the wolves."

She nodded. "They tracked me here. Almost got me too, the little blighters." She rubbed the freshly healed wound on her neck again. "I would have died at the edge of your land if you hadn't found me."

"You brought them to my door?" Heat filled Kayden's words. "To my family?"

"Yes. And to *my* family." She responded in kind, heat for heat. "I have protected this farm for generations. And now—" She turned away. "It's time for another to take my place."

The statement tugged at Violet's heart.

Kayden glanced at his sister, his eyes growing wide. "Not Vi. No. I won't allow it."

"Pretty horsey." Rose pointed out the window. The unicorn had come to the front of the shack and faced the trees. Massive, its blood red coat rivaled the setting sun. Its fiery mane ruffled in the gentle breeze. Its horn, a swirling mix of colors, refracted the sun's sinking light.

"He is called Equus, Lord of the Herd." Annalise's voice was filled with awe. "I bonded with him when I was young. Together we drive the winter wolves from month to month, place to place."

The unicorn's presence provoked several hunger-filled howls from within the trees. Answering howls echoed through the hills from all around the farm.

Kayden's gaze shot to Annalise. "How many?"

Annalise shook her head. "All of them."

Kayden threw up his hands. "All of them?" He glared at the ceiling. "What does that even mean?" He grasped the sword. "All of them. Okay." He kissed Rose on the top of her head and then laid his forehead against Winnie's for a long moment. "Barricade the door behind me. I'll hold them off as long as I can." He paused, turning his head to the side. "Your crimson beast better stay out of my way."

A tear glistened in Annalise's eye. "It is good to know the same strength and bravery of my son, the man who first bore that sword, courses through your veins." She smiled, a wistful curve of choices made and regrets best left unspoken.

Kayden spun. "Your son?"

Annalise nodded. "But I'm afraid even your blade and the mighty Equus together will not be enough to stem the gray-furred tide. They seek my death." She crumpled into a chair as if the weight of her years had descended upon her shoulders. "And they can have it." She looked into Violet's eyes and patted her hand. "But not quite yet."

As the old woman touched her, a strange image blossomed in Violet's mind—a herd of unicorns, a hundred strong, charged across a dying landscape, trailing hope and renewed life in their wake. At their head rode a young girl, her own mane of golden curls unbound and dancing in the wind like a golden pennant. Ahead ran the pack. Dingy, gray dogs chased the wind, the cold, the snow, devouring all in their path.

A howl rent the night. Two answered. Four. A dozen.

The sheep screamed.

"Can't you fix this?" Winnie bounced Rose on her hip, her movements harsh and jerky. "Your wounds have healed. You seem hale, your spirit strong. Take them away from here!" Her voice rose as fear took hold. She kissed Rose's cheek and pressed her to her chest, swaying in time with the lullaby she hummed.

Gray shapes slinked across the courtyard, into the pen, into the barn, their numbers growing.

"Fire," Kayden said. "Fire will drive the wolves away. I've used it before. So did my Da."

"Yes!" Winnie set Rose down and grabbed one of the kitchen chairs. She nodded for Kayden to grab another. They charged the doorway and smashed the chairs in the courtyard. The unicorn moved closer, seeming to cover their movements, stomping at any wolf brazen enough to approach.

"More wood!"

"Get the oil lamp."

They grabbed anything that would burn and threw it on the pile.

"Do you know what's coming?" Annalise asked Violet.

She nodded. "It's not going to be enough, is it? The fire?" A subtle calm gripped her heart. She opened her arms to welcome little Rose and lifted the child into her lap.

Her brother and his wife scurried about, boots scuffing, knocking over knickknacks and heirlooms in their desperate haste.

Annalise shook her head. "I'm sorry, hon. It's your legacy."

"Will it hurt?"

"Hurt?" Annalise's twinkling laugh drowned out the frantic scuffling. "No, my dear. It's glorious. Here, take my hand."

Violet hesitated, bit her lip. Heart galloping, she took her great-granddame's hand. A whole world of experiences exploded. New scents, sights, and sounds engulfed her, a riotous instant of magic.

Tears streamed down her face and into her mouth opened wide in wonder.

"Oh, my dear." Annalise cupped Violet's cheeks. "The life you'll live."

Kayden grabbed his sword and the oil lamp and joined his wife at the heap outside their front door. He ripped off his shirt. After dousing the pile in oil, he soaked his shirt and handed it to his wife. She held it out while he struck the spark. Once it had ignited, she tossed it away.

Whoosh.

The flames licked at the broken chairs, the picture frames, the drawers and tables, rising higher, crackling and popping, bathing the courtyard in fiery orange and keeping the wolves at bay.

Claws clicked across the rooftop.

Annalise glanced up. "We don't have much time. Call him. Call the Lord of your Herd."

Panic rose hard and fast. "I don't ... What?"

"Hush, child. You met him before, only he was sick and out of his mind. He came before you called. If it weren't for your brother, our legacy would have ended that day. Winter would have claimed the land forever."

Yips of pain. Snarls and growls. Kayden grunting with the effort of swinging his sword. The wind blew the heat from the pyre across the kitchen. Sweat trickled down Violet's temple.

"Close your eyes, Violet."

"Vite! Vite!" Rose planted a sloppy toddler kiss on Violet's chin.

"Picture your unicorn. His coat, his horn, the look in his eyes."

"I see him." Violet held the image of the unicorn as it was after Kayden drove the sickness out with his sacrifice—pristine white coat, glowing horn, soul-deep wisdom in its dark eyes.

"Say his name."

"I don't know hi—" A name emerged, whispered from the depth of her soul. She smiled. "Whim."

Silence.

Violet's heart thumped, strong and rhythmic.

Another beat, faint in the distance, countered her own.

"Can you feel him?" Annalise whispered.

The heartbeats synced—one beat, one purpose.

Violet breathed, "Yes," in amazement. "I can. He's coming." Excitement bubbled through her system.

"You are close, but the bond is not complete until you make physical contact."

Violet sensed Whim on the other side of the trees. He stomped through attacking wolves, kicking and spearing, fighting his way to her. She jumped to her feet, and the world around her returned.

Winnie screamed as Kayden went down. Blood seeped through several rents in her dress. She jabbed a kitchen knife at anything that moved, clenching her teeth at every yip. Kayden threw off his attacker and staggered upright. Several deep scratches scored his chest, his arms. Gasping for breath, he swung his sword at the closest gray wolf.

In front of her parents' graves, the trees parted. Another unicorn leaped into the fray.

"Whim!" Heedless of the snapping jaws and fleet attackers, Violet started for the gravesite. A low wall of fur and teeth barred her path. Snarling, heads lowered, they inched closer, forcing Violet back.

Equus charged in from the left. Knocking the wolves aside like kindling, he opened a path. Violet rushed through, sprinting for the graves and Whim, who fought for his life.

"Violet!" Kayden yelled.

Oh, Kayden, be safe. Protect your family.

A horse whinnied in pain. She spared a glance over her shoulder. Equus was buried under a mound of writhing gray.

Whim broke free and galloped toward her.

So close.

Winnie screamed, "Kayden! No!"

Violet focused on reaching Whim. She could stop the bloodshed only if she reached Whim. She could save her brother and his family only if she reached Whim. She could stop the wolves of winter only if she reached Whim.

Gotta run. Gotta, ugh! She kicked a wolf in the snout, clearing her route. Violet stretched out and touched the soft muzzle of her Lord of the Herd. Their souls fused. Within that connection she found the herd, felt their strength, their purity, their expectation. With an instinct born of magic and family and oaths honored, she called them to her.

And they came.

Pouring from the forest like an army of ghosts, the luminous herd charged across the hills, covering a mile in an instant. The thunder of their hooves, an earthquake.

Sensing their ancient foe, the wolves whimpered and melted into the shadows.

Whim was magnificent. His eyes reflected her destiny.

With the help of Winnie, Kayder limped to her side. His left arm hung useless. Blood streaked his chest.

"What have you done?" he asked, desperation in his ragged voice. "Vi, what?" He sank to the ground, exhausted, breath coming in painful gasps.

Violet knelt and stroked his cheek. "Today was my turn to save you."

"What now?" Winnie asked.

"We chase the wolves," Annalise answered. "What else?"

"Vi—"

Violet wrapped her arms around her brother. "I love you, Kay."

With surprising agility, Annalise vaulted onto Equus's back. The big red limped, favoring his right foreleg. "Time to go. I don't have much time, a season maybe, no more. I'll teach you what I can. The first lesson—can't let the wolves get too far ahead."

Violet kissed her brother's forehead and mounted Whim in a single fluid motion.

"I'll see you soon, Kay. Promise." Violet tapped Whim's flanks, and they shot off into the night, the herd on their heels, her destiny before her. "Let's find those wolves. Hyah!"

About the Author

Since he was a kid, Scott wanted to be an author. Through the years, fantastic tales of nobility and strife, honor and chaos dominated his thoughts. After twenty years mired in the corporate machine, he broke free to bring those stories to life. When he's not dragging his Knights through the fire and darkness, look for him on the bowling lanes.

Scott lives with his wife and two children on the west coast of Florida.

Look for his debut novel, *Knight of Flame*, the first book in the Chronicles of the Knights Elementalis, in most major booksellers.

CUSTOMER HOTLINE

JOSH VOGT

T hank you for calling Sinister Summonings, Inc., where we fulfill all your malicious magic needs. This is Athulizagoth, the Gibbering Horror. How may I hex you?"

"Finally! I've been waiting ages to talk to a real live person."

"Actually, sir, I'm an undead ghoul. May I ask to whom I'm speaking?"

"This is Arnol—er ... Xavius, Master of the Shadowed Cowls."

"Ah, yes. I have your account here. Looks like you're one of our Sell Your Soul lifetime members. We appreciate your business."

"Great, but I've got a problem with the hellsteed I summoned from you yesterday."

"What seems to be the issue?"

"It's a unicorn."

"You ordered from our Mythological Mounts line?"

"Yeah, and I was expecting something more, y'know, hellish. A skeletal stallion. A manticore. A giant bat. Anything but a unicorn."

"Are its eyes bursting into flame on command?"

"Sure, they've got the fire thing going on—"

"Is its coat of a crimson hue, drenched in the bloody tides of war?"

"It's nice and red, yes—"

"Are its horn and hooves formed from polished obsidian, ready to gouge and trample?"

"Well, yeah, but—"

"It sounds like the summoned hellsteed is manifesting within all acceptable parameters."

"But unicorns aren't hellsteeds! Your deal specifically promoted a beast the Devil himself would be proud to sit astride."

"Actually, sir, if you read the fine print—"

"The fine print was written in a daemonic tongue that drives mortals insane!"

"—It states that summoned steeds can manifest as anything *up to* a Prince of Darkness-endorsed mount. Actual results may vary."

"Look, I'm about to raise an army of minions to bring doom upon my twentieth-year high school reunion. I'll make those fools pay for mocking me all those years!"

"A deliciously wicked plan, sir."

"But I can hardly enact proper retribution while riding a unicorn—even one with a hot-rod makeover. I'm a master of terror and corruption. Unicorns are symbols of virtue and virginity."

"According to our records, you still qualify for that last—"

"Shut up! Can I at least upgrade my mount?"

"You could, sir, but that would double your current monthly sacrificial rate, and your summoning subscription isn't due for a free upgrade until next All Hallow's Eve. Even if you don't use the supplied steed, you'll still be charged a weekly pound of flesh to maintain its presence on the material plane. You could always purchase a secondary hellsteed—"

"Unacceptable! I'm not paying extra for a service I should've received in the first place. If you aren't going to fix this, then just cancel the summoning and give me a refund."

"Dispelling the hellsteed would invoke an early termination penalty."

"What'll that set me back?"

"Let me check your account.... Looks like we'd have to bump up your contracted death and damnation five years."

"I've been a loyal customer since childhood. I've never been late on a monthly sacrifice, and now you're telling me I have to pay even more to get out of this damn deal?"

"Company policy, sir."

"That's monstrous!"

"Thank you. We do our best."

"I want to talk to your supervisor."

"She's currently on break, I'm afraid. If you'd like, I could put you on hold until she gets back."

"Which is when?"

"Well, it's been a few centuries now ..."

"You know what? You win. I'll just keep the flaming unicorn."

"Very good, sir. As thanks for your eternal loyalty, I'd like to offer you a one-time, half-off deal on the summoning of your minion army."

"Really? That's actually pretty g—hang on. What would they manifest as?"

"To qualify for the discount, you'd need to choose either a swarm of poisonous butterflies, a flock of flesh-eating ducklings, or a horde of vampiric bunnies."

"Hell, no!"

About the Author

Josh Vogt's work includes fantasy, science fiction, horror, humor, pulp, and more. He is the author of *Pathfinder Tales: Forge of Ashes*, and an urban fantasy series, The Cleaners—*Enter the Janitor* (2015) and *The Maids of Wrath* (2016)—all published by WordFire Press. A member of SFWA as well as the International Association of Media Tie-In Writers, you can find him at JRVogt.com or on Twitter @JRVogt.

THE SHARPEST HORN

TRAVIS HEERMANN

Squirral tingled under the Queen's benevolent smile and squeezed the talisman on the leather thong around her neck, a ceramic squirrel worn smooth by her fingers.

"Do you want to stay here?" The Queen was such a kind woman, with flowing brown curls and the most warmhearted eyes Squirral had ever seen. Seated in repose behind her gilded desk, scepter in hand, the Queen's presence filled the private audience chamber like the glow of a warm lantern. Flowering vines snaked up the walls of polished alabaster, over her scrying screen, and around the filing cabinets.

"No! We forbid it!" said Mother.

The Queen's gaze flicked between Mother and Father. They had flanked poor Krystal, who could only slump under their gazes. Father clasped his hands between his knees.

Squirral clenched her teeth at how meek and deferential he appeared when others could see.

"Our daughter's place is at home," Mother said.

"What if she escapes again?" the Queen said.

"Oh, that will not happen, I assure you. Will it, Krystal?" Mother's gaze bored into her.

"I'm sorry," the Queen said, "but it's not your decision. She's twenty-three." So beautiful she was in her authority, so confident—things poor Krystal could never be.

"But she is *sick!*" Mother said. "We all know it. Even she knows it most of the time. She needs to be home where we can take care of her."

"She'll get the best care here in Narnioz. Our magical elixirs can stabilize her humors. After that, we can talk about ways to silence the demons—"

"No!" Mother said. "There are *boys* here. Boys who *fornicate.*"

The Queen swallowed as if something bitter was caught in her mouth. Why didn't she order Krystal's mother to silence? Maybe Mother had worked some sort of evil spell, sucking away the Queen's power like blood.

Squirral didn't know what "fornicate" meant, but it must be the most evil thing in the world, like biting heads off babies and puppies.

The Queen turned to Squirral. "Krystal, how is the medication working?"

Mother said, "She doesn't need your medication! Or therapy!" Her voice dripped with disdain. "Jesus is the best counselor. She needs nothing more than prayer."

The Queen's face hardened. "The magic potions I have given her are the best thing we have to make the demons go away."

You will never be free of us! the demons growled, slithering and sliding in great coils of turgid muscle through her brain.

Oh, yes, I will! Squirral snarled. *Someday, I will be free of all of you.* She opened her hand, and her mighty sword, Glamsting the Foe Pounder, flashed into existence, ready for battle.

"Krystal," the Queen said, "put down the letter opener, please."

Krystal did, and Squirral scowled inside.

"If you insist on only natural remedies," the Queen said to Mother, "I can recommend vitamins and tinctures that will benefit her general health and mood. But only the magical elixirs have an efficacy for suppressing the demon voices. They must be used with the supervision of a licensed wizard." The Queen turned to Krystal. "You look like you've lost weight. How's your appetite been? How are you sleeping?"

Mother said, "She sleeps all day and eats like a cow."

The Queen's face tightened again. "If you're not going to let her answer the questions, I must ask you to leave."

Mother's lips puckered.

"Krystal?" the Queen said.

The demons said, *You sleep a lot. And you eat enough.*

"I sleep a lot," Krystal said. "And I eat enough."

Mother straightened again. "You have no power to keep her. She's coming home."

The Queen said, "Just to be clear, I do have the authority to keep her, if she wills it. Krystal, I'll ask you again, do you want to stay here?"

She was not Krystal. She was Squirral.

Mother's face was twisted and sour, reddish-brown like a rotten apple. Father's was crumpled up like a piece of parchment. Both of them looked at her with hardened expectation.

Squirral wondered how long Krystal's parents would lock her in her room this time.

"No," Krystal said.

You fool! Squirral shouted at her.

The Queen gazed at her with infinite sadness.

Please *use your power,* Squirral cried, but Krystal's lips would not obey. *Keep me here.*

"If you're not suicidal or dangerous to others, I cannot force you to stay. I think you should, for a while, but I cannot force you."

You want to go home, the demons said, hissing in her brain like a nest of serpents, their vile, sensitive tongues licking and tasting and tickling.

"I want to go home," Krystal said.

The Queen sighed heavily. "Then we will see how you're doing next month."

O   O   O

The backseat of the carriage smelled like wet Karl. It happened every time her guardian protector, Karl the Royal Mastiff, frolicked in the afternoon rain showers in the courtyard.

Karl and Squirral had an understanding. They both wanted to get away.

"Is Karl okay?" she asked.

"I'm sure he's fine!" Mother's voice sounded like an orc's.

"Honey-baby?" Father glanced in the rearview mirror, his voice high and simpering, like talking to a tantrum-prone three-year-old. "You can't keep running off like that, sweetie. You could get hurt really bad. We only want what's best for you, you know that, right?"

She looked out the window, past all the other carriages on the great thoroughfare, toward the mountains in the distance, where strange lands awaited discovery, where rivers awaited swimming, rocks awaited climbing, and where there were unicorns to show her the way.

O O O

It was telling her mother about the unicorn that got Krystal branded as "crazy." Until then, she had just been "a pain" with an overactive imagination and an obsession for squirrels.

Mother often yearned for the day when they could find some gullible man to marry Krystal and take her off their hands. But no one from the Church wanted to marry a crazy girl. Krystal had not met any boys since her parents had pulled her out of school at twelve and vowed to homeschool her in the bosom of the Lord— and to keep her talk of squirrels and unicorns and the demons in her head from embarrassing the family.

"She's such a handful!" Mother wailed, as if mousy Krystal ever acted against her mother's wishes.

Squirral, on the other hand, was a warrior princess who could ride the unicorn out of her attic into the forested mountains, who could swan dive from sparkling waterfalls and feel the delicious caress of the water against her skin, who could raise Glamsting in defiance of tyranny wherever she found it. Squirral had her own voice, her own desires, her own feelings.

It was Krystal they wanted. They hated Squirral.

"Oh," her mother lamented, "if only we had given you a proper name like Rebecca or Sarah."

She was Squirral.

The unicorn had been so real, so vivid, so alive there in her attic room, tossing its head. A scarlet destrier, obsidian mane flowing in a wind only Squirral could feel, a glimmering pearlescent horn as thick as Krystal's wrist, a coat gleaming like fresh blood, diamond-hard hooves clomping on the creaky floorboards. The perfect war beast for Squirral the Warrior Princess.

She couldn't remember which had come first, the unicorn or the drawings plastering her walls. It was getting difficult to remember the order of things.

Mother stripped the drawings away as fast as Squirral could produce them. Entire boxes of her scribing instruments—colored quills and wax styli and sheaves of parchment—evaporated in her creative frenzy, giving life to the unicorn and the memories it imparted of the hills and forests of its home, of its friends the jabberwocks and winged monkeys and fauns and talking lions and great eagles.

When the unicorn first appeared, all Squirral could say was, "I thought unicorns were white."

"My color is chosen by the girl I visit," the unicorn replied.

"Why have you come?"

"You called me."

"But why did you answer? Why me? Why now?"

"You must answer those questions yourself."

Kill it! the demons whined and wheedled. *Take your blade and slash its throat! Cut off its horn, and you will be free of us forever!*

She stared at the unicorn for a long time as it trembled there, as if every fiber of its flesh yearned to charge into battle, its glow suffusing her, sparkles seeping into her skin like glitter. She rubbed her arms to smooth the hairs. Then she got to her feet, faced it, and touched its nose.

It was like the softest silk, and electricity tingled through every part of her, turning her skin so sensitive she could feel the weave of her pajamas.

At her touch, the unicorn's trembling ceased.

Krystal said, "May I touch your horn?"

The unicorn lowered its head. The horn was smooth, spiraled. A tingle passed into her fingers, through her body.

"Where do you want to go?" the unicorn asked.

O   O   O

Orcs caught her in the library when it opened in the morning, books piled up around her like a nest.

They kept repeating, "How did she get in here? It was locked up tight!"

They dragged Krystal away with their big, rough orc hands around her arms. She fought bravely, valiantly, but their strength was too much.

That was the first time they brought her before the Queen.

O   O   O

"What did you do while you were out there?" Mother said. "Live like a weasel?"

No, a squirrel, Squirral said.

"What did you eat for three days? We searched everywhere!"

Krystal shrugged.

Father drove into the carriage house. As always, she had to duck under the wheelbarrow and an old, rusty bicycle to get out.

"Goodness sakes, you're even dirtier in the daylight!" Mother said. "How did you get to be such a *filthy girl?* Inside and out. What man would ever want you? Get upstairs and clean up."

Krystal nodded and trudged upstairs. She got into the Waterfall of Warmth and Solitude and let the water and steam sluice over her, let it patter against her head, like a baptism, washing her clean.

Sometimes Krystal did strange things in the shower, so Squirral just let her do them and guarded the door.

Squirral watched in the steamy mirror as Krystal toweled her body—quickly, as if touching it disgusted her. She hated Krystal's hangdog expression, but she liked Krystal's hard, wiry form, the way the muscles of her arms and shoulders and between her small breasts rippled like a warrior's muscles. A lifetime of tension cranked as tight as a crossbow string did that to a person.

As she stepped out of the Grotto of Nymphs amid a boiling cloud of steam, a sharp voice made her jump.

"Put some clothes on!" Father said. "You look like a whore."

She stood in the hallway, her moist hair draping her shoulders, her face flushing red, the overlarge *Jesus Is Lord* T-shirt hanging past her knees. Mother had told her it was okay at bedtime, as long as her knees were covered and she wore underwear and a bra.

The words stung as if he had spanked her. He just stood there, looking her up and down, scowling, his mouth pinched and working.

Finally Squirral snarled at him, and he went away.

O O O

When she was twelve, her father had said, "What do you want that dog for anyway? He's just a mangy old mutt."

"He has a good heart," Krystal said. She could feel it beating as she ran her fingers through the mud-caked fur of his chest. "God sent him to me." Her parents would respond to this argument. "Why else would he keep showing up?"

The dog smiled and licked her face. *I am not a mangy, old mutt!* he said. *I am a Royal Mastiff, Karl von Woofenstein.*

She hugged him and didn't mind that his coat was full of burrs and he stank of muddy riverbed. "He says he is a Royal Mastiff. His name is Karl."

"That's no mastiff. Looks like a cross between a Saint Bernard and a Buick."

"I don't care!"

Father shoved his hands in his pockets, deep, until his arms disappeared all the way to the shoulders. "He stays in the backyard. And if you don't pick up after him, I'll shoot him."

O O O

When she was twelve, she discovered the school library. Hers was a small town, having only a small school with a small library, but there were 4,297 volumes filled with previously unimagined wonders. When she was done counting, she considered how long it would take to read every single one. Even if she read one book a day, it would take her almost twelve years to finish them all.

O O O

When she was twelve, she learned how to lose herself for hours in worlds more real than her own.

O   O   O

When she was twelve, she was reading a book on the front porch when a squirrel, plump with preparation for winter, scampered up beside her and sat down on its haunches, quick and furtive, but bold. Its deep brown eyes brimmed with wisdom.

I am your totem animal, it said. *I will be your friend.* And so it was.

O   O   O

When she was twelve, she drew a unicorn for Jimmy Owen. Her heart had been beating so loud she couldn't think straight. He had smiled, and his cheeks turned red. She wanted him to say something, but he didn't.

O   O   O

When she was twelve, her father went on a squirrel-murdering spree with his .22. He piled seven squirrel corpses on the front porch and made her look.

O   O   O

When she was twelve, she got her first period. Her mother pulled her out of school a week later.

O   O   O

In the deep of night, as Krystal lay on the floor of her room, bathed in flashlight, tongue tucked against her upper lip, the unicorn took shape on the paper under her hands. How she loved its flowing ebon mane, its eyes brimming with ferocity and wild wisdom.

A floorboard creaked in the hallway, stealthy.

Squirral froze. Her heart hammered impossibly fast, her mouth suddenly dry as fallen leaves.

Something outside her door, breathing heavy, husky. It was an orc, maybe the chieftain himself. For long minutes, the breathing lingered, close, as if a face leaned against the wood.

The doorknob twitched, but it did not turn.

Suddenly, her muscles free, she flung herself up and across the room and snatched a wooden chair.

The doorknob began to turn.

Squirral jammed the chair under the doorknob and threw her weight against it.

One last jerk and the doorknob stilled. Footsteps retreated quickly.

The orc had never gotten in, and it never would. Squirral was too alert, too wary, always on the lookout for danger.

She could not imagine what the orc would do if he got in—maybe *fornicate* her—but it wouldn't be good.

o   o   o

Are you not weary of being poor little Krystal In The Attic? Squirral said. Locked up and beaten down, with your hair all combed and braided like a kid's, wardrobe of nothing but pajamas!

Some days, when Mother allowed her downstairs after she vowed to behave herself, Krystal sat in the backyard brushing burrs out of Karl's coat. He flinched as she dragged out the most deeply embedded ones and then licked her face.

"Where do you go at night?" she asked him.

I leap the castle wall and patrol the countryside for orc spies, of course.

"I want to go with you," Squirral said. "We'll run away together."

No, milady, Karl said.

Oh, YES, do! DO! the demons hissed and burbled, rising half out of their lava pools. Do *run away again! Run away where that foul queen with her vile "medicines" can never find you!*

The words chewed away tiny pieces of her every time the demons spoke.

You are so fat and ugly, people will mistake you for an ogre. They will kill you, and oh, will not that be fun to watch! the demons sneered.

"Shut up!" Krystal whimpered, clutching her ears, a gesture which only contained the demons more tightly in her head.

And let's not forget stupid! No school in thirteen years! Still in the seventh grade! Why, you don't even know what "fornicate" means! Stupid, stupid Krystal ...

Squirral rose, Glamsting coalescing in her hand, "Silence, you foul, calumnious knaves!" She stabbed the point of sword into the floor. "One more word and I shall send you back to hell!"

The demons laughed, knowing Squirral was powerless to hurt them, but they went away for a while anyway, jeering.

The Orc Chieftain's voice roared up the stairs, "What the hell are you doing up there? Cut out that racket!"

The noise so startled her, Glamsting clattered to the floor like a yardstick.

Quivering with anger, Squirral spat at the closed door.

How had Squirral and Krystal gotten upstairs? Where was Karl? Darkness had already fallen; he must be on patrol.

The yearning to go with him ached behind her breastbone.

Grabbing up her quills and styli, she wondered if perhaps she could.

O   O   O

"Karl's gone!" Krystal cried. "I can't find him!"

Her father glanced at her from his easy chair. "Stupid mutt probably ran off again." The television blared with some news program full of loud, angry, frightened people.

"We have to find him! Mom!"

"I'm sorry, dear." Her mother kept crocheting on the couch.

Neither of them would meet her gaze.

The sobs turned her words into a slurry. "How long has he been gone?"

Her father shrugged. "Must have run off while we were looking for you. The whole world's going to hell, and you're worried about a stupid dog. Sumbitch growled at me all the time anyway."

Krystal expected her mother to chastise him for foul language, but instead she said, "It's the End Times." A flash of sullen guilt crossed her face.

"Now, go on. You're making me miss my show," her father said.

O   O   O

The unicorn charged into her room, skidding on the carpet of drawings, a swirl of crimson glitter settling upon Squirral's bare arms like droplets of gore.

She stood, Glamsting in one hand and bag full of walnuts and acorns in the other. She said to the unicorn, "Take me to Karl."

"Alas, I cannot."

"Why?"

"I cannot find him."

"Then let's search for him!"

"I can only touch points of this world like pearls in a necklace."

Anguish shuddered through her. Karl, her only friend in the world, was gone. "Then take me out of here."

"Where do you wish to go?"

"Away."

The unicorn tossed its head, and its mane settled around its muscled neck like liquid charcoal. "The cost is too high."

"What is the cost?"

"I cannot tell you until you are ready to pay it. But I am bound to you, thus I will take you where you wish, in your own world, and watch over you until sunrise, when I must return to my own."

"Show me your world."

"Touch my horn."

Squirral touched its horn and fell into a vortex of images. A world of vast forests and impossibly green pastures festooned with moss and veils of rainbow blossoms, rolling hills and ice-cold waterfalls, tiny winged things darting in bursts of pixie dust, verdant fields and cultivated gardens, modest dwellings that seemed to grow from the land itself, filled with families that laughed instead of scowled. And this powerful beast was its protector.

With a gasp she was back. As the vision tore away, it left an ache so profound she could scarcely catch her breath.

For a long time, she thought. The unicorn waited.

A demon snarled, *Stab it! Gut it! Cut off its horn! Its magic will heal you.*

Ix-nay on the orn-hay! another demon said.

Another whined, *Don't tell her that! We'll lose her!*

We must be good to our hostess, or she will no longer believe us.

"I don't believe you now," Krystal whispered.

See what I mean? the demon said to its cohorts. *We must win back her trust! Only the truth.*

The other demons gnashed their teeth and chewed on silence.

So, the first demon said, *if you kill this unicorn, grind its horn into powder, bake the powder into bread, and eat it, you will be free of us forever.*

Squirral's heart clenched. *There must be another way.*

It is the only way. The Queen's elixirs will never be more than temporary.

Squirral gripped Glamsting with anguished indecision. The unicorn was right there, no way for it to escape a single quick thrust.

"Why are you telling us this?" she said.

No reply came.

The unicorn still waited patiently, and Krystal thought hard about where she wanted to go—somewhere no one would look for her, somewhere she wouldn't have to worry about Karl.

O O O

This time, Squirral made a nest in the deepest, darkest corner of the Great Library of Alexandria, thinking that it would be days before anyone found her, but it only took about half an hour for a bespectacled caretaker to discover her, surrounded by books and the cracked shells of her provisions.

The caretaker had a pleasant enough demeanor at first, but quailed before Squirral's ferocious refusal to "vacate the premises."

Then the orcs had come again with their manacles and brought her to this towering fortress. With its warm bed and delicious food, it wasn't so bad for an orc fortress.

They asked her name a hundred times, and after a hundred refusals, they started calling her "Jane Doe." Squirral just snickered. She was no deer. No matter what they said, she wouldn't tell them her name, because once she did, they would call Krystal's mother and father.

Krystal spent three quiet days in a hospital in the city, where her only companions were nurses and orderlies and the soothing hiss of the vents. She enjoyed it more than anything in recent memory. The nurses were kind and gentle and wore such pretty pajamas. One of them even let her borrow a book she had just finished.

The book was named *The Forbidden Embrace*, and the cover showed a half-naked man and woman. There were a lot of words and strange phrases she could not understand, but she finished the book in an afternoon. When she put it down, her fingers were cramped, her eyes scratchy from having blinked precisely three times while reading it, and her entire body trembled with yearning and loneliness. The book lay against her chest and jumped with the beat of her heart, as if it were a trapdoor beneath which some ravenous creature struggled for freedom.

And then one day, her mother and father stood in the door of her room.

Krystal hid while Squirral defied them.

"How on earth did you get a hundred and fifty miles from home?" they asked. "Do you have any idea how much trouble this is?"

Squirral just smiled.

Later that day, the Queen appeared, offered a smile, and asked Krystal how she was doing.

Krystal said, "Fine."

"How did they find me?" Squirral asked.

"They filed a writ of missing person. The hospital told the police about an unidentified woman camped out in a locked library. It took a few days, but someone put two and two together."

"Four," Krystal said.

"What?"

"Two and two is four," Krystal said.

The doctor smiled. "Do you want to stay here, just for a little while, get some rest, until we can stabilize you? They can help you here, better than the hospital back home."

The demons screamed, *No!*

Squirral nodded. *Yes.*

"Yes," Krystal said.

O O O

"No," Mother said.

"I'm afraid at this point you don't have a say," the doctor said. "Krystal has voluntarily committed herself. She is free to go when she wishes, but she has expressed to me her desire to stay. According to the law, you cannot remove her without her consent."

Squirral cheered.

"Nonsense!" Mother said. "She is *sick*. She belongs at home, close to the bosom of Jesus."

The doctor took a deep breath as if struggling to compose herself.

"You cannot keep her in a ward where there are *men*," Mother said. "They might damage her fragile nature!"

"I'm inclined to think she is in more danger at home," the doctor said.

Mother stiffened as if slapped, her cheeks reddening. "You'll be hearing from our attorney."

"I'll look forward to it."

Mother and Father stormed out.

The doctor shook her head with a sigh, then smiled at Krystal. "You're going to be fine." She offered her hand, and Krystal took it, and it was warm and soft and kind. Then the doctor departed.

Krystal peeked through the window blinds, and even from this distance, several floors up, she could see her mother trembling with rage as she crossed the parking lot. Father ambled behind, arms swallowed by his pockets to hide his orc-claws.

o o o

"Your parents are petitioning the court for guardianship of you," the doctor said. "Do you know what this means?"

"Aren't they already my guardians?"

"Actually, no, since you're no longer a minor."

"Oh."

"If the judge agrees, they'll be able to make *all* decisions for you. You'll be declared incompetent, stripped of your civil rights, and relegated to the status of a child for the rest of your life. Your wishes will no longer matter."

Squirral jumped up. "No! She—I mean, I'm feeling better now!"

The doctor patted her hand and smiled. "I know. I can tell. There are programs—charities—that can help you get your own place when you choose to leave here. You don't have to go home if you don't want to. The medication seems to be working. The voices ..."

"I haven't heard them for a while."

"That's wonderful!" the doctor said. "Pretty soon, you can get out of here and start up on your own. Get your GED, meet someone special. You're so pretty, Krystal, and kind. Once you learn how to manage your illness, with medication, therapy, and lifestyle choices, you can have a fabulous life. Doesn't that sound good?"

Squirral's heart melted. "It does." She almost sobbed, but warriors didn't cry.

O O O

Herds of crimson war-unicorns plastered the walls of her room, creatures of ferocious majesty and regal bearing.

Many of them had guardian protectors. Royal mastiffs, all.

At mealtimes and med checks, the nurses complemented her on her talent. She just smiled, tucked her tongue into the corner of her mouth, and kept drawing.

Occasionally a voice would whisper to her, as if from the bottom of a deep well. *Gut it! Grind its horn for bread! You will never need the hospital again! You will never hear us again!*

All she could do at those times was sit in the corner and wring her hands.

O O O

The doctor's eyes were wet. "I'm so sorry, Krystal."

The sadness on her face was so profound Krystal wanted to comfort her. "They won, didn't they."

"I did everything I could, but the judge ..."

"It's okay," Krystal said. "I'm ready." She sat up straighter on the floor and placed her colored pencils calmly on the paper.

The unicorn would come tonight.

"You're so talented, you should be illustrating children's books or drawing graphic novels or something."

Krystal's eyes wandered over the hand-drawn wallpaper. Could she aspire to such a thing?

No! the demons roared, with her parents' voices.

"They're coming to get you tonight," the doctor said.

○ ○ ○

With frenzied abandon, Krystal scribbled, shaded, outlined. The harder she scribbled, the more she could hear distant galloping hoof beats, as if echoing under a verdant canopy, where life mattered and everything was part of something else, alive with verve and hunger for laughter and not locked away in a dusty attic where orcs lurked at the bottom of the stairs.

As the minutes ticked by, Squirral left Krystal drawing on the floor and paced the room.

Silhouettes appeared on the blinds. The door swung open and her parents held papers in hand, expectant, smug, self-righteous, flanked by orc guards.

Glamsting burst into Squirral's hand. She raised it in a two-handed grip, teeth clenched.

The unicorn burst into the room in a shower of stardust and crimson mist, skidding to a halt between them. It snorted, brandishing its horn.

Her parents stood agape in the doorway.

"Do you still want to come away with me?" the unicorn said.

"Yes," Squirral said.

"Forever?"

"Forever."

"Are you willing to pay the cost?"

"What is the cost?"

The unicorn said, "Blood."

I will pay it, Squirral said.

"I won't!" Krystal said. "I'll never see Karl again. I'll never see my room again!"

Karl is dead! Squirral cried, snatching at Krystal's hospital robe. *And your room is a prison!*

Kill it NOW! the demons raged. *Be free!*

No. Squirral faced the demons but kept her hold on Krystal's robe. *Never.*

Krystal stammered, "I …"

Listen to me! Squirral said. *I'm the only one in this room who loves you, all of you.*

Krystal saw the truth. "Will Karl be there?"

I don't know, perhaps, Squirral said. *But we both know he is no longer here.*

"Then okay."

Together, they slung their leg over the unicorn's back. The unicorn snorted and tossed its exquisite mane.

"Krystal!" Her mother's voice shrilled to the precipice of a strangled shriek. "What are you doing?"

Glamsting was sharp. Squirral wouldn't be taken alive by the orcs again. She twisted her fingers in the unicorn's mane.

The unicorn reared, cleaving the air with its hooves, slicing the boundaries between worlds with its horn.

And then, they were gone.

About the Author

Freelance writer, novelist, award-winning screenwriter, editor, poker player, poet, biker, and roustabout, Travis Heermann is a graduate of the Odyssey Writing Workshop and the author of *Death Wind, The Ronin Trilogy, The Wild Boys,* and *Rogues of the Black Fury,* plus several short fiction pieces in anthologies and magazines and a metric ton of role-playing game material (both in print and online).

He enjoys cycling, martial arts, torturing young minds with otherworldly ideas, and zombies. He has three long-cherished dreams: a produced screenplay, a NYT bestseller, and a seat in the World Series of Poker.

THE SETTING SUN

VICTORIA D. MORRIS

 *eep within the ancient trees,*
where no one ventures but a breeze.
The branches dance to an age-old rhyme,
whispering words: once upon a time.

Inside the glen, beneath their shield,
a magic lives in an open field.
There all creatures of the wood,
are free to frolic under nature's hood.

But in all of these, the protected host,
even there—there is a ghost.
For none still walk out with the sun;
the barrier fell, the only one.

She once paced freely through their gaze,
and in her wake, rose a crimson haze.
She held the balance of dark and light,
though never once did she choose to fight.

Her mighty heart held strong and true,
the world's emotion, within her view.

She gave to each and every soul,
just what they'd need or what they'd hold.

She took it in, all that black and hate,
the emotional strife, the damaged fate.
She held it fast within her sight;
no creature's hurt could give her fright.

But when the world turned darker still,
the human condition broke through her will.
She traveled long through every night.
Her walks grew slower; she gave less light.

But tarry on, she did her best.
She could not leave, not like the rest.
The creatures closest to that glen,
they watched her close—they remember when.

They sadly mention to this very day,
how once the unicorn was there to stay.
How she graced the wood with sentient peace,
but could ne'er find a path for her own release.

Then one twilight, lit in gorgeous hue,
she stumbled into their shocked review.
She fell on broken legs and cried;
the world's growing rage had turned the tide.

She tried to stand, but her body could not.
Then beneath her frame, the ground grew hot.
The creatures there say a tear slid free.
Down her muzzle now came two—then three.

The last fell free—touched forest floor,
and there the magic opened a door.
She rose within a brightly lit wave.
The earth now holds no unicorn grave.

For when she died, beneath ancient wood,
the magic proved her heart so good.
Instead of death, she changed anew.
And we still see her, in all our view.

On special days, she's with us still,
and those that believe can see her will.
Her brilliance flashes as the day is done.
She is the red in each setting sun.

Remember then, when the world goes dark,
that you—a believer—carry her spark.
Though you may be but one in a crowd,
every voice is special—every heart is loud.

Speak your truth, and live life well.
Defeat the dark, and ring light's bell.
For on those days when hate hasn't won;
the Red Unicorn dances in the setting sun.

About the Author

Victoria lives on the edge of a misty forest in the Pacific NorthWest with her husband and two daughters, a big white dog, and a bald eagle that likes to circle over her house when she brings in the groceries. A lifelong artist and not quite as long writer, Victoria is working on a six-book fantasy series, with a middle-grade trilogy on the side. She also draws portraits to relax. Find out more at: www.VictoriaDMorris.com.

THE WHOLE OF ME

GREGORY D. LITTLE

Mother and Father were fighting again.

Millie scarce went a day without waking up to the sound. Daylight brought respite from the nightmares, but her parents' constant arguments, delivered in the strained hush of ropes pulled taut unto snapping, had become a form of waking nightmares. At least the nightmares that existed only in her head were Righteous.

Today the argument sounded more like a set of rapids hissing through a narrow canyon than a creaking rope. Though they never raised their voices, even after ten years her parents failed to realize just how sharp their only child's hearing was.

Too focused on your eyes to notice your ears. Millie's eyes were what everyone focused on. Or, rather, refused to. As wide and pale as the glacier just visible at the horizon line from where their little house lay nestled, no one Millie had ever met could meet her gaze without flinching.

But all her senses were sharp, the better to judge Righteous sensations from unworthy ones. With her ears, she'd heard the whispers about her that flitted around the valley. *Uncanny. Unnatural.* Righteousness did not make for many friends.

Millie rose from the bed in her cozy room. White-walled and wood-trimmed, the room glowed as the morning sunlight streamed in between window slats, setting dust motes alight. Making the bed, washing up, and getting dressed afforded Millie plenty of time to listen to her parents.

"The war's at our doorstep. The peddler told me the Southern Covenant's front lines will be here in a week. They march as if none oppose them," Mother said, her voice muted with strain. For a name spoken in these parts primarily as a synonym for "monsters," talk of the Southern Covenant always blossomed as warmth in Millie's breast.

Mother wanted to flee. Unworthy, but understandable.

"We've built too much here to just pull up stakes," Father said. "This valley isn't on the way anywhere." His words curdled with desperation. Refusing to abandon their home? Righteous, but misguided.

It was an old argument. Only the details and the timetable changed. It awoke little feeling in Millie. She'd spent years watching other children throw tantrums or dance with joy, never understanding what she was seeing. Strong emotions had no claim on her. Yet another reason she was shunned.

Millie paused in her ablutions. Something in the structure of the argument, so rigid Millie could almost have repeated it word for word, changed. A silence of hesitation descended, and then came Father's voice, so low even Millie could barely hear it through her closed door.

"There might be another way," he said with the gravity of the first mass of snow that presaged the avalanche. His words were mysterious, but his tone was Righteous.

Mother's answering silence held a thrumming quality of confusion eroding to horror.

"No!" Her whisper was fierce, thick ice cracking deep. "What possible good could that do?"

"He's part of the very covenant that marches against us! He can mark us as friends if we allow Him. He can help us!"

Righteous fire bloomed in Millie's breast at his words. She barely stifled delirious laughter.

"He is *not* the god of the south, whatever you might believe, Garald. Even if he was, I would never pray to that *thing!*"

Millie found herself pressed to the door, one ear resting against cool, smooth wood that smelled of hickory as she flared her nostrils. Her heart raced in her chest. She had never felt so strongly about … *anything*. What was happening to her?

"Again, you mean, Bethany?" Father said, his voice full of scorn. "You'll never pray to Him *again*? You prayed to Him the same as me. Not quite eleven years ago, if I recall."

Something as cold and certain as a grave opened within Millie. The people of the valley always whispered about those times. How badly her parents had wanted a child. How long they'd been trying, how desperate they'd grown.

How a freak storm the year before Millie's birth had smashed flat every field save her parents'.

"Don't you throw that back in my face," Mother snapped, barely keeping her voice in check. "I may have gone along for our family's sake, but it was all you. I was never happy about it. I never imagined for a moment it would work."

"But it *did* work," Father said, his voice conciliatory, reasonable. "It could work again."

"You swore to me never again, Garald. You swore." Millie heard actual tears in her mother's words, and Bethany Carver was not a woman given to emotional display.

"All right, all right," Father relented. "We'll think of something else. You'll see. It'll be all right."

His words were unworthy, as was his intent. But his desire …

It was so very Righteous.

O O O

The days of Mother's predicted week passed. Father's frown-lines deepened. Mother's clenched jaw tightened beneath the pallor of her face. The house divided into armed camps, a mummery of the war coming to their doorstep.

They no longer pretended peace for Millie's sake.

"The Covenant soldiers pillage every place they pass," Father remarked once over steaming honeycake desserts turned bitter from the poison in the air.

"All the better not to trust in any god of such men," Mother replied, as if to stop his heart with sweetness.

"It worked once before," Father said a different time, while stacking wood on the hearth for a fire. It was his lone defense, the only one he required, Millie knew.

"Yes, my love," Mother said, looking up from mending a tear in Father's coveralls. She had spent the days mending, gathering, and bundling their possessions. The ones she said they couldn't leave behind. The ultimatum was clear in her actions even if she never spoke it in Millie's hearing. "But you did not have to endure the fruit of that aid. Let the old stones sleep where we found them."

Millie was forced to stop judging her parents' words and tones, so fraught with contradictions they had become.

On the fifth night of Mother's predicted seven, Millie was sent to bed early, a rare accord between her parents. She had to thread her way between the bundles strewn throughout the little house's back hallway. Those would be tied to the mules come morning if Mother had her way. Millie entered her room, but after letting the door shut with an audible thump, she pulled it open again on freshly oiled hinges. A wedge of firelight was visible through the crack.

There she listened as the same arguments were spun again, once, twice, thrice. At last Mother stalked off in disgust, and Father took up a vigil at the kitchen table, clutching his face with knotted fingers. After a time he stood, disappearing from Millie's view for several minutes. When he returned, he added fresh logs to the fire and brought a kettle of water to a boil. He was going to make tea for Mother.

A peace offering, or so Millie thought. But Father added a dash of powder to the steaming, amber liquid in the mug. Millie's nose caught the barest hint of acrid stain in the air wafting from that mug. Smiling with satisfaction, Father carried the tainted tea toward Mother, sitting in her favorite chair. Millie heard murmured words of thanks and a strained sort of reconciliation. Father indicating that he had given in.

Sometime later he emerged into view again, this time cradling Mother's limp form across his chest as he passed Millie's room and headed for his own. Millie noted with a dry relief that Mother's chest still rose and fell.

Alive. Asleep. Quite without realizing it, Millie soon followed suit.

She woke from a dreadful nightmare of beating drums filled with rippling blood to an assortment of pains in her neck and back. Whispers filled the air around her. The whispering wall was talkative tonight.

It had always drawn her, the panel along the back hallway where the plaster was brightest and thickest. It never ceased its murmurings. Mother and Father never commented on it, though she caught Father's gaze drifting toward it every now and again when he was feeling his most Righteous. But the whispers, though enticing, had always been wordless before, even to Millie's keen ears.

She emerged from her room and froze. Even in the dim, pre-dawn light, she could see the newly formed, ragged, man-sized hole occupying the whispering wall's center, beyond which lay some deeper darkness. In addition to the whispers, she heard other words rising up from the darkness.

Words spoken in her father's voice, but in no language Millie had ever heard.

o o o

A narrow tunnel lay behind the wall, a rough-cut, spiral stairway leading downward through the rich, black soil and into the bedrock beyond. The passageway must be far older than her parents' little house.

With every step, the hairs of Millie's arms and neck stood more at attention, only partly because of the cold. The whispers grew louder, and the voice of her father as well, both speaking words in the same impossible language.

Millie emerged into a dank, roughly spherical chamber carved from the slate gray of living rock. It was outlined in the flickering light of candles set into hollows in the chamber walls. A smell of mold and rot permeated the air.

A strange altar of stone occupied the chamber's rear. The statue atop it was of a shape Millie could neither describe nor truly understand—all wide eyes and spiraling horns protruding from a mass that seemed to defy creation. To look upon it disturbed Millie, made her nauseous. It filled her with a Righteous ecstasy so powerful she sagged to her knees.

Father knelt already, shirtless and sweating despite the cold, his forehead pressed against the stone of the idol, which glowed with red light where his skin touched it. His strange, muttered words filled the air, the stone chamber somehow catching and magnifying his whispers.

At some sound Millie could have sworn she didn't make, Father turned from his crouch and regarded her with mute horror. Millie stared unblinking into the sudden intensity of his gaze. They stood there, their faces frozen mirrors of one another. Then, slowly and without speaking to Millie, Father turned back to his altar and continued his prayer. Millie's heart swelled with pride.

Father concluded his prayer, voice rising in a crescendo, then he stood and brushed past Millie without a word. He refused to meet her eyes as he passed, but his brimmed with unworthy shame and relief. He retreated back up the stairs; Millie heard his footsteps mounting the stone steps then pausing.

"It was here when we built the house," he said from above. "When we dug the foundation. Waiting for us. I wish ..." He trailed off. Then his feet squeaked on the wooden planks of the hallway floor, and he was gone.

Millie turned to regard the idol.

The thing they prayed to for me.

She had a sudden, staggering sense that every aspect of her life had possessed a hole in it that she'd never before seen. A million pieces of her life, a million moments, yet all the holes were the same shape, like the missing piece of a puzzle.

Staring at the little stone idol, Millie thought she could guess the shape of the missing piece.

Above her the house creaked in a sudden, stiff breeze. Millie couldn't say how, but the sound reminded her of a smile, the parting of wooden lips around gritted stone teeth.

"What are you?" she asked, her voice croaking from disuse. She spoke so seldom that she forgot how seldom she spoke.

The wooden pilings of the house groaned anew from above as wind howled through the house's eaves. Dust rained from the chamber's ceiling, tickling Millie's throat as she breathed. These things were not words, yet they layered slivers of meaning atop one another to form ideas that she somehow understood.

She was asking the wrong question.

"What am I?" She felt the warmth radiating from the stone even as the last syllable left her throat. The little idol with its many eyes and horns was pleased. The house squalled, the wind shrieked, and the stone beneath her feet vibrated.

"I am a piece of you," she said, giving voice to the voiceless. "But what am I to do?" She wasn't sure how she meant the question. Soldiers were coming to burn their lands and raze their home. Her father had drugged her mother. And Millie apparently owed her existence to prayers offered to some dark, twisting form that peered out from a stone idol deep beneath her home.

An orifice opened in a nook between two of the idol's eyes, forming so gradually Millie couldn't be certain it hadn't been there all along. At first she thought the hole was bleeding before realizing it was disgorging something long and spiraling and red as blood.

It emerged straight and rigid, first as long as her palm, then as long as her forearm, and finally nearly the full length of her arm. She dashed forward and plucked it up before it could fall. It was a horn. Narrow and tapered and delicate, it looked to be made of some cross between ivory and marble, but was a uniform blood red color, even looking wet though it was dry to the touch.

The world shifted around her as she gazed at her prize, speaking in its wordless voice.

"This is for me," she said. "And I am to take it to the capital."

O O O

Millie shifted her pack from one shoulder to the other, trying to relieve the pressure on the growing knot at the base of her neck. The bloody point in the air hovered at the upper left of her vision. She'd gotten used to it easily enough, noticing it only when the world wept a drop of blood at her horn's intrusion.

The howling winds and booming thunder had taught her how to press the horn's tip against the skin of the world, which lay everywhere, even in the air itself. Once pierced, the horn slid into the world's meat easily and stuck there, always in her sight yet invisible but for the dribble of blood it exacted in payment for its touch.

She had emerged from the hidden shrine back into the house and made directly for her parents' room. There she had found her mother locked in the tortured sleep of some drug, the older woman's face pinched and pale, her teeth bared in a rictus. Pity had overwhelmed Millie.

Her mother was unworthy to her bones. Millie was more certain of that than ever. But Mother had once withstood the weight of Righteous seed and born Righteous fruit. A single touch of the horn upon her mother's brow had eased her slumber, relaxing taut muscles and adding peaceful rhythms back into her breathing.

Millie found her father cowering in the corner opposite the bed. Righteous in desire but weak in deed. The touch of the horn to his skin had produced decidedly *different* results.

The road out of the valley was crowded now, and growing more so by the hour with wagons dragged by mismatched teams of horses and soldiers walking in small clumps, their packs and weapons hefted over shoulders slumped with exhaustion. They came in two flavors, some uniforms the color of rust and others a white soiled to gray.

Only the once-whites had weapons, and they watched the rusts with hands twitching about hafts. The once-whites' baleful eyes brimmed with hope and suspicion, as if they could not believe their good fortune. The rusts carried only supplies, though their shoulders slumped all the more despite their lighter burdens.

The two warring armies, marching north toward the capital and not killing one another. Millie avoided both sides, needing no outside urging to do so. Their hollow stares sparked something close to fear in her. Once she risked drifting close to a family riding a ramshackle, two-wheeled wagon pulled by a stinking nag of a horse. Millie was on the verge of speaking, but they read the question in her face.

"It's peace," the mother called down hoarsely from her perch. She indicated a clump of rusts with a jerk of the shoulder. "Them of the Southern Covenant surrendered last night."

Odd. Millie had thought they were winning only the day before. She nearly said as much, but the world around her shifted, grasses and clouds swirling in previously unfelt winds, providing her the answer.

Father had prayed for peace.

Millie kept asking questions inside her mind, and the world kept providing her with answers, but it wasn't *really* the world. It was the little idol, or the greater something the idol represented. And the further Millie got from that moment of contact with the cold, writhing stone, the more its wishes seemed indistinguishable from her own.

Soon enough a pleasing weight settled upon her mind, bearing down with a pressure that comforted like swaddling. She stopped asking questions, as the answers were already waiting inside.

O O O

Millie came upon the herd two days later, the valley well behind her. Despite the awesome sight of so many horses, she felt no surprise. Indeed, she found she'd been expecting it.

Hundreds of horses moved in a great, seething mass headed north. Huge warhorses, piebalds and chestnuts, blacks and bays, duns and roans and palominos. Some were bareback, some still bore saddle and bridle, but all those of the herd were riderless. A loose ring of soldiers, once-whites riding chargers of their own, surrounded the horses, keeping them pointed unerringly north.

They are bound for queen and capital. One side will call them a gift of good faith, the other the spoils of war.

Millie shadowed the herd's left flank for hours, the effort of keeping up with the horses leaving her legs loose and shaking. At last a halt was called from somewhere toward the front of the mass.

Millie waited until dusk to approach the nearest soldier, who was maintaining his solitary vigil upon this sector of the herd, a lonely cook fire banishing a small swatch of the night. Almost gagging at the overpowering stench of horseflesh, Millie made her approach obvious, angling so that he could easily see her coming in the light of the small fire. She still appeared to be a young girl.

No man with any spine would see a true threat.

The once-white's slump stiffened to alertness, and he stood at her approach. That too was good. He would fear her less if he could loom.

"You there, girl," the once-white said, lowering the nicked and notched tip of his spear just enough so that firelight played hypnotically along its length. "Are you alone? What possessed you to wander about at night?" His brows twitched, furrowing and straightening, unable to decide how Millie should be treated.

Pinching the bloody welt in the air to the left side of her vision, Millie withdrew her horn, allowing the man to see it appear seemingly from nowhere. The once-white blinked and scrubbed a gauntleted hand across his eyes, as if to clear them.

"I found this," Millie said. The red horn shone with false wetness, looking freshly bathed in blood though it was dry and roughly textured to the touch. "See?" She proffered it to the man, cradled upon her palms. Firelight sent flickering orange highlights dancing across the wet red surface, and for just an instant, Millie could smell the iron tang of the blood the horn promised.

Ignoring the alarm that revealed itself upon his face, the man leaned in, trying to see what it was she held. In a smooth motion, Millie gripped the horn's wider end and flowed forward, drawing its tip from the bottom of the man's left eye down his cheek, leaving a red line of blood in its wake.

Millie turned away as the horn did its work.

After a heartbeat, the once-white began to scream, but it cut off quickly once the mechanisms required for screaming no longer fit together. Millie burned what remained of his body upon his own fire, sitting so the wind carried the caustic smoke away from her.

She adopted his small camp for her own, stuffing his food stores into her pack atop her dwindling ones and touching the horn's tip primly to anything she didn't want to keep. Once the camp had been set in order to her satisfaction, it was time to see to the horses.

The first was sleeping, and the prick of the horn against its flank did nothing more than make it grunt, as if it knew this was both its destiny and for the best. Red rushed outward from the wound in all directions, hugging the creature's flank as it transformed the hide from dun to the same scarlet of the horn.

Moments later, a horn identical to hers erupted from the red horse's forehead with the sound of cracking bone. The animal turned to regard her briefly with an eye the same ice-blue of her own, and she felt a swell of mutual understanding and kinship pass between them.

Now you and I are one, each said to the other. Then the horse—unicorn now—turned and lowered its head so that its horn pricked its neighbor.

Smiling with satisfaction, Millie found her way to the soldier's blankets and fell into deep sleep.

O   O   O

Millie dreamed of breaking bones and tearing muscles. Pain lanced through her joints, as if they were being pulled apart, as if her very body was being reshaped in sleep. When she woke to the light of dawn, she discovered it had been.

Her feet were both longer than she remembered and further away by nearly a pace. Her shoulders had broadened, and the straight lines of her body had bent themselves into the curves of womanhood, filling in the flesh between.

The fingertips Millie ran along her face found terrain familiar yet not. Her raven hair hung to her waist. She had crossed through adolescence in the span between midnight and dawn. She rose, wincing and aching. Confusion gripped her before understanding pried its fingers away.

For what was coming, looking helpless would be a detriment.

Her clothes were a ruin. Fortunately it did not take her long to find a fresh corpse from which to borrow clothing. The horses, now unicorns all, had followed her example and turned upon their handlers in the night, and the once-white uniform on a nearby body had escaped the worst of what had been visited upon its owner. Pulling tunic and trousers on over her now adult frame, Millie noted with a pleased sense of irony that the once-white cloth now had its own rust-colored stains.

The herd followed her lead as if they shared a single mind. Each animal seemed to seek her out and lock eyes with her, each piece of the whole wanting to be acknowledged in its own small way. *Reporting for duty.*

So it was that Millie reached the capital leading an army of blood red unicorns only to find the gates barred to her.

"I would speak with the queen," Millie's voice, backed by the herd, was the full-throated roar of a woman in her prime. "I bring her the spoils of her war!" She made sure the guards could see the stolen uniform she wore, and she brandished her horn high. She had not grown up in a single night for naught. She would need to fight soon.

The gates cracked open, and spear-hefting soldiers in true white uniforms spilled out in ranks, moving to encircle Millie and the herd. Though the soldiers' fabric gleamed blindingly in the sun and they stood proud and tall to a person, Millie could still see the artifice. *Too young in some places, too old in others.*

The cream of the queen's ranks had either perished on the field or were still staggering back, bloodied and wearied by war. But it mattered not. Millie would not fight these soldiers. They were here to take possession of the herd, which they watched with a mixture of wariness and awe. Unicorns were seldom seen in lands trod by human feet—red unicorns the rarest of all. This was a gift beyond price.

The ranks completed their circle but for a space immediately before Millie, where only a single warrior stood. She wore shining plate and held a sword and shield, each gleaming mirror bright. The woman's hair was a river of gold tamed into a braid that wound about her head.

"Who are you?" The warrior's voice rang out like the pealing of a great bell. A woman used to declamation, to having her words transmuted into law. Millie's newfound awareness muttered within her, guiding her eyes to the golden circlet beneath that coiled braid.

"My name is Millie Carver, Highness," Millie said to the queen. She recalled the stories of the warrior queen who had quite literally won the throne on the edge of her sword. The queen fairly burned with passionate fire, but she had pointed it in entirely the wrong direction. She must be dealt with here and now. Matters had always bent to this.

I will take her throne for my own, Millie thought in the voice that had supplanted hers.

"I was told to expect a gift of horses, delivered by my own soldiers. Instead *unicorns* arrive, delivered by a young woman wearing a bloodstained, ill-fitting uniform. Are you a soldier of mine?" The queen sounded incredulous.

"No, Highness," Millie said. "I murdered the soldier whose clothes I now wear." It would be sad to destroy the queen. So much Righteous potential, but her certainty had been hardened into the wrong shape long ago. In another life she and Millie might have been sisters, pieces of the same whole.

"By your own lips you condemn yourself," the queen said, eyes alight with anger. "The beasts are uncanny and unnatural. But they will fetch high enough prices outside my kingdom to rebuild what your Covenant has destroyed. Let those with a lust for such oddities risk whatever malefic secrets they hide."

At the queen's gesture, the soldiers lowered their spears, turning their circle into a razor-toothed mouth, ready to close lest the creatures try anything. The unicorns watched them placidly, eerily still.

"You, though," the queen said, "you I will see dead for the sake of justice." She drew her sword. "I honor you by giving you death by combat. I will see that you are armed—"

"I have my weapon," Millie said, brandishing her horn.

The queen squinted, but finally nodded. "Don't think to trick me with some magic toy, girl. I am warded against such by armor, clothing, and skin. If it is your wish to die behind that bit of bloody ivory, so be it."

So certain. The part of Millie that was still Millie felt a fear as strong as any in her life, but the enormity of that which occupied her mind and body steadied her. All was as it should be. All would be well. Renewed, Millie smiled and stepped toward the queen, the other woman mirroring the action.

They held blade and horn before their faces then swept them down and outward in salute. In an eye blink, Millie visualized the battle, how she would rend the world's fabric, severing the queen's sword arm, shield arm, and head in quick succession. It would all be over with her first strike. She raised the horn to deflect the queen's swing, already bunching her muscles to deal merciful death in three subsequent motions.

The blade sheared through the horn as though it did not exist, burying its icy edge into Millie's shoulder and carving cruelly deep.

Millie fell, shock overwhelming the freezing burn of the pain. A cloudy sense of betrayal rose up as her heart beat out her life upon the cobbled avenue.

"Madwoman," the queen said, shaking her head in wonder and disgust. "Now you know justice."

Why? Millie asked the question over and over in her head, timed with the beats of her treacherous heart. *Why? Why? Why?* The answers that had once come to her so readily, so easily, drew away, like village lights receding into the foggy night. *Have I not done well?*

But a last niggling mote of understanding drew her vision, shrinking now to a tunnel, toward the queen as she cleaned her blade of Millie's blood on Millie's own stolen cloak.

The queen had so much Righteous potential. It was only pointed the wrong way. Millie watched as a tiny bead of blood evaded the queen's efforts, sliding up the runnel on the bottom side of the blade.

You were but a part of me, the thing within her whispered with startling clarity. *For a time, the most important part. But only the whole of me matters. And for true victory, they must believe they have won. Now, their very hero will invest me within her nation and her people.*

The bead of blood slipped undetected up the queen's sleeve, leaving no stain to mark its passage.

And they will welcome it.

About the Author

Rocket scientist by day and fantasy and science fiction author by night, Gregory D. Little's short fiction can also be found in *The Colored Lens*. His debut YA fantasy novel, *Unwilling Souls*, will be released in 2015. He lives in Virginia with his wife and their yellow Lab.

ODIN'S EYE

FRANK MORIN

agnar Narwhal stood at the tail end of a half-circle of better men. He scanned the younger, stronger faces of mighty warriors, already veterans of many seasons of violent struggle in the harsh northland.

By Idun's wrath, they were barely more than children to him. He was the last of the old warriors. The most blessed of his brothers in arms had fallen in glorious battle. The unlucky had succumbed to festering battle wounds, and a few had suffered ignoble deaths by dying in their sleep.

Ragnar had outlived them all. He'd been a great warrior. Too great.

Now he suppressed a grimace as he struggled to stand tall without the aid of his crutch. He rubbed his hands across his best leathers and the concealed pockets inside. He had never resorted to subterfuge before, but today he faced his last and greatest challenge. Even if he outlived the coming winter snows, his last chance of a glorious death in battle had passed years ago. Today would be his final opportunity to earn a place with the blessed einherjar in Valhalla's halls of glory.

The warriors stood in the center of the village before a roaring bonfire that held at bay the last of the autumn night's chill. The heat felt good on his bad leg. Outside of the circle of heat, the rest of the villagers hovered in the fading shadows.

"She comes," cried Horik Vermundson, clan chief and the primary contender in today's contest.

Ragnar stiffened, bringing his thoughts to the present while his companions straightened, hands tightening on axe handles worn smooth from long use. He followed Horik's gaze into the northern sky, gray with the coming of dawn, and spotted the approaching figure.

The Valkyrie descended from the cloud-laden sky astride a mighty red unicorn. The eight-legged creature was a wonder, the pride of Odin's stables. Ragnar had seen it once before, the last time the Valkyries had come to the village to honor their clan with a choosing. The unicorn was longer than a mortal stallion, but only a little broader. As the other warriors gaped in wonder, having been too young to remember the last Valkyrie visit, Ragnar glanced to the left where the maidens waited.

Dressed in their finest, the girls whispered among themselves as the magnificent unicorn galloped from the sky. His own Nora, one of the eldest of the candidates at sixteen, reassured Unfrin, the twelve-year-old daughter of mighty Ref-Nose Gimrson. Nora was always helping, and he smiled to see her acting true to her nature even today, when others might have suppressed qualities often deemed weak or undesirable. She was dressed in a fine linen dress with an elaborately worked leather vest and covered in a snowy white bear pelt she had helped him cure. As the village tanner, he had saved the finest pelt for her.

The unicorn came to ground with a sound like the striking of Thor's hammer, stirring up a cloud of dust. By the time the air cleared, the Valkyrie had dismounted. She stood tall for a woman, her thick, blonde hair falling loose about her shoulders, unlike the maidens who wore theirs in complex braids. She wore black leathers with a crimson cloak. Her face glowed, her cheeks pale as ice, her lips blood red, and her eyes a glittering gold. Only dim vestiges remained of Olga, the little girl she had been before being taken from the village so long ago.

He took it as a good sign that she had been the one sent to choose the next maiden to join the Valkyrie ranks. Again he glanced at his beloved daughter. Nora would honor the village and his legacy. Today he would settle both of their fates.

Horik approached Olga the Valkyrie and saluted with his axe. "Welcome, daughter of the skies." He might have been young, but he had taken to the pomp and long-winded speeches of chieftain with the ease of a seal slipping into the icy North Sea.

As Horik launched into his speech and the other contestants gathered closer to Olga, Ragnar slowly circled around the gathering. All eyes were glued to the beautiful Valkyrie, so he took the chance of approaching the mighty unicorn that hovered some paces behind her.

The creature towered over him, its shoulder a solid seven feet from the frozen turf. It looked down upon him with brilliant sapphire eyes that sparkled with intelligence. Hopefully he hadn't underestimated its cleverness.

Too late to change plans now. Wrapping himself in remembered honor, he approached the beast and extended a hand, proffering a cluster of his best carrots.

The unicorn smelled of cinders and snowfields after a battle. It snorted once, softly, and dipped its head toward his hand. Its glittering golden horn was long enough to spear him and a friend together.

Ragnar stood perfectly still as it sniffed his offering. Its breath washed over him like an icy breeze, filling him with the fiery thrill of battle, the likes of which he had not felt since his youthful berserking days.

In a single inhalation, the unicorn sucked the carrots right out of his hand and lifted its head away. For a second, its piercing gaze lingered on his face. Then with regal grace, it winked at him.

How was he supposed to respond to that?

The unicorn glanced to the side where the Valkyrie stood silently listening to Horik's ongoing monologue, as if checking to make sure she hadn't noticed it snacking while on the job.

Ragnar retreated before anyone noticed. He had hoped to talk with the creature, but that would have to wait. The first skirmish had proven successful. Only with careful increments would he win this battle.

The Valkyrie who had been Olga Gaukrsdottir inclined her head, accepting the honor Horik bestowed upon her. Without bothering with additional formalities, she surveyed the gathered warriors. "You, the fathers of the maiden candidates, will meet in a contest of arms to determine which family will win the honor of dedicating their daughter to Odin's service."

Ragnar joined the others in a mighty cheer, which was taken up by the rest of the villagers. Dawn had lifted the cloak of night from the village and the nearby fjord. Soon Sol would ride her blazing chariot into the eastern sky and begin the long journey across the heavens for another day.

"Today we will see which of you is blessed of Thor and of Loki," Olga continued.

She explained that the contestants would face five challenges. Four would be selected by lucky competitors who won the initial toss of the bones and the final by whoever led in the standings by that time.

The initial game of chance wasn't such a simple thing. As the men stepped up to a thick table made of hewn oak to cast the bones that would decide the game of chance, most of the men purposefully threw badly, knocking the bones from the table and thus disqualifying themselves. They weren't clumsy. They were ceding the honor to the greatest warriors, those everyone knew would most likely win the day.

Ragnar could no longer afford such high standards. He broke from the unspoken agreement and threw the stones true. A couple of the younger men grumbled at the breach of etiquette, but since they were all technically cheating, how could they complain that Ragnar didn't cheat right?

Ragnar earned the fourth spot, behind the clan chief Horik and two others, both great warriors with daughters old enough to stand in the candidates' circle. Ref-Nose Gimrson stood as tall as Ragnar himself had in his youth. Arnlaugr Anlafson was half again as broad as any of the other men and as strong as an ox. If not for Ragnar's dire need, he too would have rooted for one of the three mighty men to win the competition.

No one gave Ragnar a second thought. He was allowed to compete because his precious Nora was a jewel of the village and she had to stand with the other maidens. Ragnar's days of glory had passed so long ago, villagers avoided looking him in the eye for fear that his looming dishonor might rub off on them.

Before this day ended, they'd chant his name one last time.

Horik chose first, as was his right. "First, we drink to honor Odin!"

The choice was greeted with loud cheering and enthusiasm as the contestants led Olga to the great hall. Casks of the clan's best ale were produced and the men assembled for the most popular drinking game.

Ragnar downed his first mug in time with the others, silently saluting Horik for the crafty choice. No man ever wanted to admit another could out-drink him, so the contestants cheered each other on as they drank mug after clay mug. They eagerly honored their fathers, but forgot that today's drinking wouldn't end in drunken brawling.

Ragnar only drained three pints before spilling one. Horik dropped out at five. He gave Ragnar a knowing smile when he rose from the table amidst good-natured jeering from the other men.

Most of the others managed at least eight mugs. The winner, Ref-Nose, drained fourteen before collapsing under the table. They staggered out of the great hall, chanting Ref-Nose's name. Two of the more stable contestants dragged Ref-Nose out from under the table and carried him along.

Nora rushed to Ragnar when he limped out of the hall. He leaned on her, smiling at how lovely she looked, how she walked with the confidence of a woman years her senior. With her older siblings all married with families of their own, she worked with him and Alf, his only apprentice, as good a man as any still living.

Nora was as strong as her elder brothers, but possessed a grace and a skill of hand none of them had ever matched. With her help, his furs had never turned out better. No doubt Odin himself would commission a new winter coat from her once he saw the quality of her work.

It took several minutes before Ref-Nose could croak out his choice for the next round. "Axe throwing."

Ragnar smiled. The day was working in his favor.

They took turns throwing axes at a series of ever-shrinking targets set at ever-increasing distances. Most of the men, still unsteady from their heavy drinking, barely scored hits on the first two.

Ragnar clove nine.

Men who had accepted him into the company only for Nora's sake or because he'd once been mighty looked on him with new respect. Only Arnlaugr Anlafson tied Ragnar, and he was the second-best axe thrower in the village. Ref-Nose usually was first, but he'd drunk so much he placed a distant fourth.

"By Thor," Horik exclaimed when he missed his seventh target, landing him in third place, "Ragnar, how did you do that?"

"I have Thor's blessing today," Ragnar said, waving at the cheering crowds.

He didn't add that ever since he'd injured his leg, he'd mastered the art. He'd brought down hares, a deer, and even a couple of his neighbor's sheep that had wandered into his yard.

He shared a triumphantly raised fist with Nora when she came to check on him. She kissed his cheek and hugged him tight, even though it might diminish his image of a fierce warrior. Under the guise of tending his wounded leg, she slipped him a small ceramic jar. He rubbed the contents across the back of his leather leggings when no one was looking.

"You did wonderful," Nora exclaimed. "I knew you could."

He cupped her face in his hand. She looked so much like her mother. On nights when he missed his beloved Ellen the most, Nora would remind him of younger days when Ellen still walked beside him. Now he stood on the verge of lifting Nora into the ranks of the Valkyrie. No greater honor could be attained by a maiden of the village and, if he succeeded, she in turn could guarantee his place in Odin's hall.

"We're on our way, my dear," he laughed, catching her in a tight embrace.

His glory was short-lived. Arnlaugr's roll of the bones had earned him the next choice, and he shouted his decision with meaty arms thrown into the air. "Solo long-boat rowing!"

Ragnar groaned. His days of wielding any oar besides the paddle he used to stir his tanning vats were long gone. Worse, he dare not sit down and risk the solution he had so carefully applied to his pants. So as they all prepared to board the waiting long boats on the north end of the harbor, he focused on the next phase of his strange and unusual plan. It used to hurt to think crafty thoughts, but what else was an aging man to do while younger men went to war?

While the others chanted battle cries and leaped aboard their boats with favorite oars in hand, Ragnar limped aboard his boat with a small iron brazier of hot coals. While younger men raced back and forth across their boats, paddling with all their might, Ragnar allowed the current to drift his boat slowly toward the finish line on the far side of the harbor. He spent the tedious half hour carefully roasting half a dozen fine apples.

Eventually they sent a small rowboat to tow him in. He was met with jeers and laughter by men who had respected him only an hour ago. He ignored them all and limped through the crowd, leading the way slowly up the bank to the waiting Valkyrie.

"May I offer a gift to your magnificent steed?" he asked, gesturing with his burden of apples. They filled the air with a wonderful aroma. He tried not to look anxious as Olga studied him and his gift. He needed her to say yes, but couldn't give away the reason why.

"You may," she said finally.

He had been afraid for a moment that she would claim the apples for herself. As a girl she had always loved apple pie.

Despite rising calls from the other contestants to make his choice known, Ragnar approached the immense unicorn and bowed stiff muscles before its crimson bulk. "Will you accept this simple gift?"

Again it inclined its head toward him. This time it touched his shoulder with its horn. He gasped as every happy memory he'd ever had flashed through his mind. Images of battles won and glorious victories made up part of the flood, but fewer than he would have expected. He was surprised to note the majority of his happiest moments were quiet ones with his Ellen or Nora, teaching his children or telling stories around the fire.

He blinked as the rush of memories faded. Already the apples were gone, and the eight-legged unicorn had lifted its head away.

"Make your choice known," the Valkyrie ordered.

He hesitated and a hush fell over the crowd. This was the critical moment of his plan, but he still found it difficult to speak it aloud. Finally he took a deep breath and made his choice.

"Bareback unicorn riding."

A universal gasp rippled through the contestants, the maidens, and the gathered villagers. Even the Valkyrie looked startled, showing more emotion than she had all morning. He doubted anyone had ever dared make such a choice.

Ragnar turned toward the towering unicorn and added, "If you consent, of course."

It huffed a breath over him, smelling of polar ice. If he didn't know better, he'd have sworn for a moment it looked amused.

The Valkyrie didn't. She approached until they stood nose to nose. He hadn't realized Olga had grown quite so tall. Her eyes flashed and he felt real danger in her presence for the first time. He forced himself to hold his ground.

"This is unusual," she said finally. "And likely to prove painful for you. Nevertheless, I grant your request."

When she turned to remove the complex saddle strapped to the unicorn's back, he helped undo some of the buckles between the second and third sets of legs. That gave him the chance to slide his hands across both sides of the unicorn's torso, rubbing in some of the clear liquid held in his secret pocket.

"Show us how it's done, Ragnar," Ref-Nose laughed, having regained some of his equilibrium during the long-boat row.

"I chose," Ragnar said. "And I go last. You go first."

Ref-Nose was still drunk enough that he accepted the challenge.

The lingering effects of his drunkenness probably helped ease the pain of a broken ankle and cracked ribs when the unicorn bucked him over the great hall.

The others fared no better. Each one leaped astride the unicorn from a short stepladder, shouted their readiness, and was just as quickly launched soaring into the air.

"Did you want us all to end up as crippled as you, old man?" Volund Smidkelson demanded as his young wife tended his bruised knee.

"You're never too old to learn something new," Ragnar retorted as he prepared to climb up the stepladder. He paused, rubbing his hands across his pants to ease his aching leg—and to apply the last coat of his special solution.

He couldn't quite manage to mount the magnificent animal on his own, so Nora helped him into position. That elicited more jeers from the injured contestants, but the presence of young Alf cowed the villagers from joining in and insulting Nora by association. Ragnar paid them no heed, shifting back and forth to settle into position and to allow the special coating on his pants to bond with the solution he had applied to the unicorn's flanks.

As a tanner, he knew glues and solvents and had spent the last long winter working out this special formula. This was his life's greatest work, his last chance to reach Valhalla. This was his moment.

Nora shared a knowing smile with him, kissed his cheek, and retreated.

He gripped the unicorn's flowing mane and raised his other fist high. "I am ready."

The unicorn hesitated, and that alone guaranteed he'd win the contest, as it allowed him to stay upon its back a critical second longer. Then the weight of thanks it owed him for the carrots and apples was spent and the unicorn erupted underneath him just as it had with the others. The speed of its bucking movement snapped Ragnar's neck back, straining muscles. The world lurched around him, and his teeth clacked together. His free hand waved wildly over his head, and he felt a wrenching pain in his legs.

If he hadn't been so used to dealing with aching muscles and unexpected pains, he might have been undone. The world righted itself, and he realized he was still seated astride the mighty unicorn. He tried to hide his surprise and his groans, instead soaking in the looks of astonishment of everyone present, including the Valkyrie.

The unicorn glanced over its shoulder, and its glorious eyes widened to see him still sitting there.

It no longer looked amused.

It bucked and jumped and twisted and reared, crossing the entire central square in its wild antics, sending villagers fleeing for safety. Its golden horn blazed with anger as it strove to dislodge him. It snorted and orange flames flickered out its nostrils. Its anger smelled of charnel pits and the wild freedom of berserker madness.

The wild gyrations twisted Ragnar into painful knots. His neck burned, and every muscle in his body felt strained. The repeated crashing against the unicorn's back sent searing agony coursing down his legs, worse than the time Ref-Nose's father had kicked him in the sweets. He screamed with fear and agony, but closed his eyes and hung on with all his strength, drawing upon the indomitable will that had seen him through battles that had claimed the lives of many chosen men.

Then the wild bucking stopped. The Valkyrie stood at the head of her steed, a calming hand on its glittering horn. Wonderstruck villagers peeked out from behind nearby buildings, only daring to come out when it appeared the danger was past.

"I have never seen such a feat," the Valkyrie said. "Even among my sisters. You are indeed blessed of Odin this day!"

Villagers gathered around, cheering Ragnar's name, and he basked in the glory of the moment. Not for years upon years had he felt such universal respect, enjoyed such honor.

Nora rushed up to help him dismount. Disguising her movements as helping to ease his aching muscles, she rubbed the solvent on his legs that would release him from his mount. Before allowing her to pull him from the unicorn's back, where he would surely collapse, he had to make his final choice.

Ragnar looked out over the crowd of cheering villagers, gloried in the respect shining in the Valkyrie's eyes. This was a fitting end to an honorable life. His own daughter would soon become a daughter of the sky, ready to welcome him to Valhalla's halls as a chosen one.

He turned to the beautiful Valkyrie. Her father had won eternal glory this same way. Ragnar wanted to share this moment, to help the others understand what old Gaukr had achieved.

"Olga," he cried to the Valkyrie. "Tell me, how is your father?"

The cheering subsided as everyone leaned in, eager to hear.

"I have no father," the Valkyrie said, no emotion on her face.

"The man who was once your father, Olga Gaukrsdottir," Ragnar repeated. "He who won you this great honor in your youth and who you led to Odin's halls months ago!"

"You are mistaken," Olga said, her golden eyes unblinking. "That name no longer belongs to me, and the man you speak of is no einharjer. He was not worthy."

The silence deepened as those words drove levity from every

heart. Ragnar leaned forward, his limbs quivering with pain and horror. "But he was your father. You must have chosen him."

"He died in his sleep," she said coldly. "He was an old man. Odin needs great warriors at his table, not cripples."

The truth struck Ragnar like a thrown axe, and he swayed where he sat. Gaukr had often spoken of his beloved Olga, of his pride in her choosing, of the honor he expected her to pay him in return. Only in quiet moments had he ever admitted to Ragnar how much he had missed her.

Ragnar glanced at his own beloved Nora. This was the moment, the moment the two of them had worked toward in secret for the past year. All he had to do was choose the final contest, the one he knew he could win. He could secure for her the greatest honor any maiden could enjoy.

He glanced to where Alf waited expectantly with the rest of the villagers, then at Nora again. Her cheeks were flushed with excitement, her eyes shining with joy at his victory. His heart should be singing with her, but it felt cold in his chest. Every ache, every pain he'd endured to reach this moment dragged against his will. He'd suffered so much. He clutched the sweaty mane of the majestic unicorn. Eternity rested in his palms.

For the first time, he understood the price.

He made his choice.

After Horik won the final challenge and the clan celebrated the choosing of his lovely Unfrin Horiksdottir, Ragnar limped home, every muscle complaining about the abuse. He might never recover from today's contest.

Nora walked on one side of him, Alf on the other, supporting him like he was his own father. Nora kept glancing back at the celebration. He could see she yearned to stay, to bask in the glory Unfrin enjoyed, the glory that should have been hers.

"Oh, Father," she finally said with a sigh. "I'm so sorry."

"Don't be, my dear," he said, hugging her tighter.

"But you worked so hard for this," she protested. "All of your dreams are lost."

"No, dear one," he said. "Today I was truly blessed by Odin. He granted me a glimpse through his all-seeing eye, and I saw truth for the first time."

"What truth?" she asked, turning to face him.

He kissed her cheek. "It is one you will see for yourself - in time. I promise you."

After they eased him into his favorite chair by the fire, he placed Nora's hand in Alf's. "Now go. You children enjoy the party."

They left together hand in hand.

Ragnar stared into the fire, his thoughts no longer on the fleeting glory of the battlefield, but on a different kind of glory. Of Ellen and Nora, of his children and grandchildren to be. He closed his eyes, content.

About the Author

Frank Morin loves good stories in every form. When not writing or trying to keep up with his active family, he's often found hiking, camping, SCUBA diving, or enjoying other outdoor activities. For updates on writing, including his popular YA fantasy novel, *Set in Stone*, visit: www.frankmorin.org.

QUEEN OF THE HIDDEN WAY

MARY PLETSCH

I want you," the Pharaoh proclaimed, "to bring me a karkadann. *Alive*."

The entire court's attention fell on Wepwawet, the captain of the guard, who was on his knees before the Pharaoh.

Anpu, all of fourteen years old, knew this moment was an opportunity. She noted who among the court appeared scandalized, who nodded in approval, and who had been awed by the Pharaoh's audacity.

Only her cousin Kau seemed unsurprised by the proclamation. Anpu had not realized the Pharaoh shared confidences with Kau. A knowing smile curved Kau's handsome lips as he gestured to the foreign magicians, who, as of late, were his constant companions. He turned his gaze to Anpu, and his smile broadened. Ashamed at being caught staring, Anpu hurriedly looked back toward the center of the drama.

Wepwawet kept his features impassive as stone. He, like Anpu, knew a death sentence when he heard one. The new Pharaoh, Anpu's great-uncle Akhteset, clearly wanted to rid himself of everyone who had been loyal to his predecessor—Nitocris, Anpu's mother.

"Yes, my Pharaoh," Wepwawet said, bowing his head to the inevitable.

Anpu hated Akhteset, but she had to admire his cunning. It had been barely a month since Nitocris's untimely death, and Akhteset's hold on power was not yet consolidated. He would lose support if he were seen to slaughter Wepwawet without cause, but it would be another thing entirely if the captain lost his life trying to capture one of the lethal beasts known as the lords of the desert. Wepwawet would be eliminated, and Akhteset's hands would remain unsullied.

Anpu's mother had taught her to recognize and interpret the webs of intrigue that infested the royal court. Though the land of Kumat had prospered under Pharaoh Nitocris, some of the old priests and advisors had mumbled to themselves that, as the God of the Sun was a man, so too should be the Pharaoh, His avatar among the people. Akhteset had claimed the cobra which had killed the Pharaoh and her consort had been sent to their bedchamber by the gods to restore the natural order of things.

Anpu did not agree. She had encountered cobras many times in the desert as she played far beyond the shadows of the city walls. The holy snakes, though deadly, preferred to be left alone. More tellingly, the cobra had no sooner killed the Pharaoh and her consort than it had slithered its way towards Anpu's chamber. She had no doubt that it would have bitten her too had not Wepwawet and his blade intervened. She was convinced the snake had been charmed by sorcery and brought to the palace.

When Wepwawet was dead, who would protect the rightful ruler of Kumat, the child who was the greatest challenger to Akhteset's rule? Anpu was smart enough to know that she was running out of time, but her stomach sank as she examined the members of the court again. She was reluctant to trust any of them. Even those who were not fond of Akhteset might prefer themselves, or their candidates of choice, above a second female pharaoh who was still but a child.

If she were wise, perhaps she would accept her cousin Kau's offer to marry.

Kau had been busy the past month, insinuating himself into the favor of the merchants' guilds. Akhteset was known as a military campaigner, and much of the standing army was on his side, but the wealthy merchants had powerful mercenaries of their own. If she married Kau, she would exalt his power base above Akhteset's, legitimize his claim on the throne—and give up her own title as Pharaoh forever.

No. Anpu would not surrender her own power solely to avenge herself on Akhteset. That retribution, however well deserved, would come at too high a price.

Anpu had only one chance. The myths suggested the mighty karkadann might deign to lie down in the lap of an innocent maiden. Anpu was not certain if that innocence was an inexperience of body or a purity of spirit, but Wepwawet, old soldier that he was, was neither innocent nor maiden. If Anpu wished to save his life, to rescue her faithful defender and in so doing, save herself, it was up to her to find a karkadann first.

O   O   O

For most of her life, Anpu had dressed in commoners' clothing and walked unknown among the people. At first, Wepwawet had worn similar clothes and taken her to the temple or the market. Later, she had traveled on her own beyond the city walls. Her father had worried, but her mother insisted that a future Pharaoh needed to learn independence, self-reliance, and the ability to weigh risk. Anpu had met, and learned to love, the people she had been destined to rule.

Now Anpu was grateful that she knew how to slip out of the holy city through the palace drains. As she traveled from the stone sewers into the natural caverns that stretched westward toward the City of the Dead, Anpu wondered if perhaps she ought not return home again. Having transformed into the aspect of a commoner, she could shed her former identity as easily as a cobra sheds its skin.

But it was one thing to hide beneath a dusty cloak for a time, and quite another to live in its shadow. Anpu was not truly a street child. She did not know how to find food, where to sleep, or who, in the bazaar and the alleyways, might do a young girl harm. Yet she knew all too well that the palace was no safer. Sooner or later she would find another cobra in her bedroom, or an asp in her bath. Without Wepwawet, there would be no one to rescue her.

If she could only see Wepwawet safely through this coming day, then together, they could come up with a plan to flee. But first,

Anpu had to find a domesticated karkadann, and quickly.

Surely there had to be someone out in the nomad camps who knew how to trap a karkadann. Anpu had often insinuated herself into a blanket-wrapped crowd gathered around a campfire, listening to storytellers spin wondrous tales. Her favorite stories had been those about a group of warriors who rode atop one-horned beasts, bringing justice to the oppressed, healing to the sick, wisdom to the ignorant, freedom to the enslaved, and retribution to the guilty. Surely those tales had some truth to them.

Anpu turned to her left, emerging from the mouth of a cave. She hurried over the hot dunes toward a nearby wadi known as the Thieves' Market. Anpu knew that some of the goods she saw there were stolen. Others, though, belonged to poor craftsmen who could not afford the city's market fees, or to foreign smugglers who wanted to avoid taxation. The Thieves' Market was dangerous, but it was a good place to begin her search—far better than wandering the desert hoping to chance across a nomad camp.

Anpu ambled through the cacophonous crowd inspecting a clutter of goods displayed on wagons, blankets, ropes suspended between the oases' trees, and sometimes even on the ground. Farmers hawked fresh vegetables, chefs cooked over sizzling braziers, and craftspeople displayed handmade goods for sale. On the far side of the market, Anpu glimpsed an animal tamer exhibiting a collared lion. His wagon also featured caged birds, tamed rodents, and trained dogs. Such a trader might also have a karkadann, or know where to catch one.

To reach the animal tamer's wagon, Anpu had to weave her way through a knot of people listening to a musician. The performer's lilting tune showed off his skill, but Anpu found his song unpleasant in a way she could not easily describe. There were so many notes, ascending and descending without warning in an uneven rhythm. The effect was confusing and strange. It made Anpu's head hurt, but it also drove her to think on it further. She found herself urged to concentrate, to listen until she could find meaning in it, or until meaning was given to her ...

The crowd parted ahead of her. Anpu realized, belatedly, that she had shoved her way through the spectators, drawn to the sound like a moth to a flame. Consciousness returned like a slap of cold water when she saw the great equine form on its knees before the crowd.

She had never imagined to be so close to one of the lords of the desert. Even on its knees, the karkadann's head towered over hers. Its hide gleamed like burnished gold, save for the area along its spine that was slashed with brilliant lazuli stripes. Its horn thrust skyward like an obelisk, and its eyeteeth were long and jagged.

The only thing more shocking than the karkadann was the identity of the musician. He bowed his head to a long reed flute, finishing his song with a relentless barrage of notes. Laughing, he bowed to receive the adulation of the crowd.

"Kau?" she demanded. Anpu had thought her cousin a creature of the court; she had never imagined she would see him in the Thieves' Market dressed in a nomad's cloak. Her stunned brain registered that the men nearest to him were the same foreign magicians who had accompanied him that morning in the Pharaoh's hall.

"Anpu," he said, his formal nod utterly incongruous with their surroundings. She expected him to sneer at her, or perhaps even to pretend he didn't recognize her in her worn, dusty clothing. She did not expect the cold smile that curled his lips. "Look at what I have procured for our Pharaoh."

The rest of the crowd began to wander away now that the show had ended. Kau's companions stepped forward menacingly, as though to grab her, but Kau waved them off. He lifted the flute and pursed his lips, steering his breath into a tune. The karkadann obediently lurched to its feet, swayed once as though drunk, and then rose onto its hind legs like an ornately carved statue. From this angle, Anpu could see that the lord of the desert was, in fact, a lady. Her body was magnificent, but her eyes were strangely dull.

"The karkadann … she is terrifying," she breathed. "How are you this creature's master?"

Kau raised the flute. "Have you ever seen the entertainers who charm snakes with the sorcery of music?"

Anpu had. "A karkadann is not a snake."

Kau's smile widened. "It is only a matter of knowing the right song." He played a quick series of notes, and the karkadann obediently returned to all fours. Anpu realized that Kau's discordant song held the creature's mind in thrall.

Kau winked at her, his face so strikingly handsome, his eyes so bewitching. "Think of it," Kau coaxed. "You and I, riding to our coronation, mounted on a karkadann."

"Our … coronation?" Anpu whispered.

Kau's grin broadened. "I am a generous man, and my offer of marriage still stands. Join with me. Together we will stand at the Pharaoh's right and left hand—and when the Sun sets, we will rise."

Perhaps she should reconsider Kau's offer. Perhaps this was her best opportunity to overthrow Akhteset. Even those who had mourned Nitocris's passing had found comfort in the presence of a man on the throne once more. Anpu represented more uncertainty and confusion; Akhteset was a new stability. Kau could be a new stability as well.

And yet.

Her eyes fell on the flute in Kau's hand, and it crossed her mind that while Akhteset had powerful allies in the form of the northern army, he also possessed all the subtlety of a cudgel. Upon Nitocris's death, he had taken the palace by display of force. It was beyond Akhteset's skill to charm anyone.

But, apparently, not beyond Kau's.

Anpu looked at her cousin through narrowed eyes, remembering the entertainers in the Thieves' Market who charmed snakes for coins, and she wondered just who was responsible for the deaths of her parents.

Kau's smile faded. Anpu knew he would be quick to wrath if she were to reject him, and if she were to voice her suspicions, well, she would be the first to die beneath the karkadann's hooves. The flute in his hands held the power to take her life, or worse, to shackle her soul. She was in danger, right now.

She needed to play along with Kau. She had learned the basics of music in childhood; she would listen, and she would learn the karkadann's song. Then, someday, when Kau's back was turned, she would steal the flute and play the notes that would incite the karkadann to kill.

And then she would be no better than Kau. Anpu thought of the snake that had been set upon her parents—an innocent creature transformed into a weapon to do a human's will.

"I …" she began, stepping near, bowing her head, holding out her hand.

Kau smiled in triumph, switching the flute to his left hand so he could reach out and take her offered hand with his right.

Anpu stretched out her arm like a striking cobra and snatched the flute out of Kau's grasp. Gripping each end of the reed in her hands, she snapped it in two over her knee.

Kau staggered backward, staring at her in horror. "What have you done?"

"I have avenged my parents," Anpu retorted, hoping she sounded braver than she felt, for she realized her own life might well be forfeit.

The karkadann awoke, shaking her head as though waking from a dream. She caught sight of her, and her eye rolled in her head until Anpu could see the white. It was too late for Anpu to hide the damning evidence in her hands.

The karkadann fixed on Kau and bared its dagger teeth.

Kau pursed his lips and tried to whistle that mesmerizing song. Fear dried his mouth. He managed a few notes before he choked. Kau gagged, licked his lips, puckered in vain. By then the karkadann was upon him, lowering her head, thrusting her horn through his heart in an executioner's coup de grâce.

All but one of Kau's foreign allies turned tail and ran for their lives. The bravest dared draw his scimitar. He launched himself at the karkadann, slashing at the great artery on its neck. Even through her fear, Anpu observed and analyzed, noting that the magician waited for the karkadann to skewer Kau before pressing his attack.

His strategy did not save him. The karkadann reared up, hoisting Kau on her horn while she lashed out with her forelegs, knocking the scimitar from the man's hands. Kau's lifeblood streamed down onto the karkadann like the summer rains and mingled with the fluid pouring from the cut on the karkadann's neck, staining its coat a gory red. The unicorn tossed her head, and Anpu could not tell if Kau were still conscious and struggling or whether the karkadann's movements were sufficient to send his limbs flailing.

Anpu closed her eyes and looked away, but her mind's eye was not so easily blinded. Her memory replayed what it had seen in the instant before her eyelids had closed: Kau's body thrown off the karkadann's bloody horn, impacting the magician who had held the scimitar; the swordsman and Kau trampled into meat under the unicorn's hooves; the other magicians fleeing even as the bloodstained karkadann pursued them. Anpu had no doubt that the creature would catch them.

Even with her eyes shut, she could hear the panicked shouts and cries from the crowd. She was jostled, thrown to her knees by unseen people rushing past her. If Wepwawet were here, he would carry her away from the rampaging karkadann. If she were wise, she would at least try to run.

But running had not saved the magicians. When the clattering and screams around her turned to silence, Anpu took a deep breath, climbed to her feet, and opened her eyes.

She stood alone in the wreckage of the Thieves' Market, facing a red unicorn. The karkadann watched her from across a field of gore, her entire coat now stained russet with the blood of her kills. She flared her nostrils and curled her lip, baring teeth like ceremonial blades. Anpu was thunderstruck when she spoke.

"Name yourself."

"Anpu." She hated the quaver in her voice. Would this creature attack if she perceived her as weak? She steeled herself to speak the way her mother had taught her. "Rightful Pharaoh of Kumat."

"You wear no crown, Anpu-who-claims-the-throne." The karkadann tilted her head and stepped closer, peering at her as though she could see through her flesh and bone into her very soul.

Anpu's heart quailed. A stammering retraction was on its way up her throat to her lips when she saw something in the karkadann's eye. Her own reflection looking back at her was that of a craven child.

Her reflection was a *lie*.

Anpu stood up straight and strong, raising her chin and meeting the karkadann's gaze head-on. "My rival, Akhteset, thinks force alone can make a ruler. That one"—she gestured to Kau's trampled body—"sought to win the throne by guile. But only integrity can turn a queen into a true Pharaoh. Only those whose highest goals are the service of wisdom, courage, love, and abundance can ever reflect the glory of the Gods."

The karkadann whuffled. She sounded amused. "You say you would be queen so that you may serve?"

"To rule my people *is* to serve them, for if it were not, why would they need a Pharaoh in the first place? The nomads of the desert have no Pharaoh, and they survive according to their own customs. They travel under the wings of their Shaykhs, and this lifestyle serves them well. But for those of us who farm the rich lands of the holy river, we have done better with a government that can protect our borders, support our merchants and offer praises to our Gods, whose blessings are reflected all around us."

The karkadann nodded. "You are wise beyond your years, Anpu of Kumat. May the blessings of the Guardian Jackal be upon you."

Anpu bit her lip, surprised to hear an animal speaking of the Gods. But the karkadann was no dumb creature, and, of course, the Gods were not prisoners in their temples, but manifest in the natural world. How easy it was to forget that truth in a culture where worship was focused in particular places via age-old rituals. Anpu had rarely spoken to the Gods herself when she had priestesses to speak on her behalf.

She would need to rectify that shortcoming.

The karkadann continued, "I am known as Samiel, the Poison Wind. I am the wrath of the desert, the scouring grains of the sandstorm, and the retribution of the Goddess. I bring the punishment due to those who would enslave the Goddess's creatures—those whom I have slain here, and those whose deaths are yet to come." Samiel rose up on her hind legs, screaming her battle cry to the sun, and leaped away in a gallop to the east.

Anpu felt her heart clench. "No! Stop! You can't go that way!"

Samiel drew up sharply, her hindquarters bunching as her back hooves slid forward to touch her front hooves. The sun illuminated her coat, stained with blood, and Anpu imagined the karkadann becoming redder still, tail and mane soaked with gore, and Wepwawet and his guards crumpled beneath her feet like the bodies that littered the wadi.

Samiel turned her head and spoke in a voice that both chuckled at Anpu's audacity and threatened her with an undertone of warning. "You are bold, Anpu-who-would-be-Pharaoh, but your queenship has no claim on me."

"There is danger that way," Anpu insisted.

The karkadann raised her head, listening.

"Akhteset has demanded my mother's Royal Guard bring to him a karkadann. This morning Captain Wepwawet called his men and ventured to the eastern oasis where rumor says a karkadann has been seen. If you go in that direction, you are sure to cross their paths."

"You would not see me recaptured?"

"I mean no insult," Anpu responded. "No, I would not see you captured, but I would also not see my last ally killed."

"Not your last ally," the karkadann responded. "The wind brings to me a message. My pairmate, Azazel, has followed my tracks since I first fell under the bewitchment of that treacherous flute. She has come to rescue me, and I will not flee this place and leave her alone, not when the breeze murmurs to me of men and horses, the dry threat of rope and the tangy metal of chains. I would see your city in ruins before I would leave my pairmate behind."

Pairmate. What did that mean? It seemed more than *friend*, more than *family*; whatever the translation, it was clear that Samiel would defend Azazel with her life.

"Wait," Anpu pleaded. "Akhteset—the false Pharaoh—has schemed to set your pairmate against my old defender. Wepwawet has no choice: he will be put to death for disobeying royal orders, or he will die on your friend's sharp horn. I do not want to see your pairmate harmed, but I cannot stand by while Wepwawet is made to suffer for his loyalty to me."

"And how would you defend Wepwawet, Anpu-who-would-be-queen? Azazel and I have sharp teeth and strong limbs, horns like sabers and hooves like hammers. What weapon do you have against us? If Akhteset did not have soldiers more numerous than your Royal Guard, you would already have removed him from your throne."

"You may kill Wepwawet, and half the city besides, but do you think Akhteset would permit two wild animals to run amok in his territory? If he cannot ride you, he would gladly see you dead. How do you propose to live with every citizen of Kumat hunting for you?"

Samiel's eyes narrowed. "Have you any alternative?"

Anpu placed her hands on her hips. "You have said it yourself, Samiel the Poison Wind. I am blessed by the Guardian Jackal, protector and defender, Opener of the Hidden Way. I can guide you, Azazel, and the Royal Guards out to the desert beyond the City of the Dead, following the underground caverns, if you only agree to spare my guards' lives."

Samiel picked at the turf, considering, then slung her head in a gesture toward her back. "Climb on and hold fast."

O   O   O

Anpu had learned to ride on her mother's horses, but to travel on a bloody karkadann was a different matter altogether. Anpu wound her hands into Samiel's matted mane, pressed her body to the karkadann's neck, and held on with all her might. People on the road threw themselves out of the way. It was hard for her to see through tear-blurred eyes, but she thought she glimpsed the people falling to their knees in her wake. Over the clatter of Samiel's hooves, she might have heard the people's voices entreating the Gods to tell them if Anpu and her gory mount were their deliverance or their destruction.

Samiel, following the scent of her pairmate, vaulted to the top of a dune and looked down into the oasis below. Feeling the karkadann grow still, Anpu lifted her head. Near the shore of the oasis, the royal guardsmen held their spears in a defensive formation while a purple karkadann menaced them with lowered head and bared teeth.

"We're not too late," Anpu gasped.

Samiel threw back her bloody head and bugled her war cry. The other karkadann whistled back. The nervous guards clustered closer together as they turned to look. Wepwawet shoved his way through the formation to protect his soldiers against this new threat, holding his sword at the ready.

"Samiel?" Azazel's voice was gruff thunder. "What is the meaning of this—that you suffer a girl to ride you like a common horse?"

"Anpu!" Wepwawet's eyes widened as Anpu approached him atop a bloody karkadann. He tried to sound authoritative, but terror tainted his words. "Come down from there, come clear!"

"No," Anpu said, speaking like the queen she was destined to become. She and Samiel circled the guards until they stood between the men and Azazel. "We will not allow you to harm one another."

"My lady, you must understand," Wepwawet pleaded. "The Pharaoh has given me no choice. I must bring him a karkadann or forfeit my own life."

Anpu felt her throat close, because she too had seen only two choices until Samiel reminded her that she was a child of the Guardian Jackal, god of hidden wisdom. "There is a third path," she said, "revealed to me by Samiel, the karkadann who carries me. We will go to the river, where the sewer drain empties into the water, where the tunnels are large enough for horses. We will follow the underground caverns to the Jackal God's kingdom, the tombs beneath the City of the Dead. From there we will make our way into the desert to freedom, and no one will see where we have gone. We can leave this city behind, and I can show us the way."

"That karkadann," Wepwawet said warily, "is covered in blood."

"And I," Anpu retorted, "have had my fill of blood today."

O   O   O

Anpu clung to Samiel's mane as she led the Royal Guards through the darkened caverns of the City of the Dead. Wepwawet walked at her right side, carrying a torch, while the karkadann Azazel moved riderless at her left. The Royal Guards followed behind. Even in the dark where Anpu could not see the red stains, she could still smell the coppery tang of blood.

"We will assemble a mercenary army," Wepwawet said as they walked. "We will promise them a reward from the treasury after we return, overthrow Akhteset, and install you on the throne."

Anpu bit her lip. She was the Pharaoh's only child, but there was a difference between protecting the innocent and engulfing her entire nation in war. Blood already coated her hands. The more she thought of it, the more she realized that her destiny was not as simple as Wepwawet would have it seem.

"I am sorry," Anpu said quietly. "I will not join you in this."

"But you are the destined Pharaoh!" Wepwawet protested. "Akhteset tried to kill us both."

"Akhteset tried to kill you," Anpu replied, "and I understand why you are angry. But it was Kau who killed my parents, and he is dead now. Justice has been served for his crimes."

"Kau," Wepwawet breathed.

"And in killing Kau and his allies," Anpu persisted, "others also paid the price. Innocent bystanders in the Thieves' Market. Merchants whose goods were destroyed. People who were injured, even killed, in the stampede to escape Samiel's wrath. If I declare war, it is not just Akhteset who suffers. It is us, and the people of Kumat, as well. I do not know what kind of Pharaoh Akhteset will be, but if he is a good one, I will not bring down ruin upon Kumat solely for the sake of vengeance."

Wepwawet stared at her. "Then what will you do?"

"Samiel," Anpu asked softly, "the nomads speak of a band of heroes who travel the world with their unicorn companions, bringing justice to the oppressed, healing to the sick, wisdom to the ignorant, freedom to the enslaved, and retribution to the guilty. Is this story true?"

"I do not know," Samiel began, but Azazel interrupted.

"I have heard of such people," the purple unicorn said. "One is from a country far to the east, and she has skin like plate armor. Her rider is called the justice-bringer. Another is native to the north, and her rider is known as both warrior and holy woman. But these two travel alone. If there is a herd of such riders outside the tales, I have not met them."

"Then this is what I will do," Anpu said. "This is why I was born to lead. Not to start a war in my homeland, but to find these riders and bring them together. That is, assuming my companion will help me." She touched Samiel's shoulder.

The karkadann snorted. "Azazel? What were your plans upon freeing me?"

Azazel whickered. "A return to our previous existence of running down invaders in our desert?"

"Just so." Samiel tossed her head. "If Azazel is willing, Anpu-who-would-be-leader, I will travel with you."

The purple karkadann nudged Wepwawet's shoulder. "I am willing if this one is."

"You would suffer me to ride you?" the captain asked.

"If Anpu wishes to gather the unicorn riders, she needs to learn the ways of sword and spear. I am to understand you might teach her?"

Wepwawet stared at the karkadann, then at Anpu.

Anpu bit her lip, wondering if the old captain would be able to accept such a radical change from the world he had known, if he could ever come to view his little princess as a warrior.

Then Wepwawet nodded. "I swore to protect Anpu when she was only a dream in her mother's womb. Teaching her the arts of battle will be the best way to defend her when I am gone."

"Then get on," the purple unicorn said, dropping to her knees so Wepwawet could ride.

Moments later, Anpu and Samiel, Wepwawet and Azazel, and the Royal Guards, completed their passage through the tunnels of the City of the Dead, and were reborn into the light of a desert sunrise.

About the Author

Mary Pletsch attended Superstars Writing Seminars in 2010 and has since published multiple short stories in a variety of genres, including science fiction, fantasy, and horror. As a collector of vintage My Little Pony and FashionStar Fillies, she takes her unicorns (red and otherwise) seriously! Mary is also a glider pilot, Transformers enthusiast, and graduate of the Royal Military College of Canada. She lives in New Brunswick with Dylan Blacquiere and their four cats. Visit her online at www.fictorians.com.

THE RED UNICORN CANDY STORE

KATIE CROSS

T he magical Red Unicorn Candy Store was no ordinary candy store.

It had lollipop trees and barrels of chocolate chips and star-shaped jellies, just like any respectable candy store. Piped frosting decorated the windowsills, and sprinkles covered the ceiling in a dizzying array of colors. The Red Unicorn Candy Store soared ten stories into the sky. Anyone who wanted to could go inside and lick the walls; they tasted like sour apple suckers. Caramel held it all together, of course, as nothing held candy together better than hardened caramel.

But the Red Unicorn Candy Store had something no other candy store in the land had: the Red Unicorn Horn.

It hovered above Marshmallow Mountain—which is exactly what it sounds like: a monstrous pile of marshmallows held together by white fondant—rotating and swiveling without ceasing. Rumors about the horn swirled around town like wisps of cotton candy. Most people thought the Red Unicorn Horn was just a big piece of candy made of sugar and spice and everything nice. Which would have been fine, except for the other rumor.

The Red Unicorn Horn is powerful, they said. *Filled with magic, unpredictable. And it never stops moving.*

Mr. Thomas took care of the Red Unicorn Candy Store, but in truth, the candy store ran itself. No one could own such a place, so Mr. Thomas simply made sure the cogs worked smoothly, the children didn't get sour tummies from too much candy, and the gold coins were kept safe from thieves. But he had nothing to do with the constantly full vat of jelly beans, or the coconut grass that grew bright green and fresh every morning.

Despite working in a world of sweets and sugar, Mr. Thomas looked skeletal. His knobby elbows stuck out of his skin, and his spindly fingers moved like the legs of a spider, but he had a head of bushy white hair, a jolly face, and a deep laugh. All the children adored Mr. Thomas, which is why the Red Unicorn Candy Store permitted him to stay.

Mr. Thomas loved living in the massive house of sours and sprinkles. The Red Unicorn Candy Store provided him with warm meals and a cozy bed to sleep in at night. Everything would have been perfect—except for one naughty child.

Jeremiah Reed.

Jeremiah Reed had cheeks so round that his face seemed stuffed with bowls of sweet jelly, the red color seeping through his skin in a permanent blush. Mr. Thomas had never seen a more sluggardly, peevish boy in all his long life. Unfortunately, Jeremiah's mother was a sickly woman, and, fearing her son would have a willowy, bendable frame like her, she gave him all the pastries and muffins he wanted.

Of all the bad children in all the candy stores in all the world, none were as greedy or mischievous as plump Jeremiah Reed.

"Clean it up!" Jeremiah would command after knocking over gummy worm farms—glass jars filled with crumbled cookies that looked like dirt.

Sometimes the floor would absorb the candy and the jars would refill immediately, but other times the spilled goodies remained for Mr. Thomas to clean up and then charge Jeremiah's weepy mother, who never seemed to notice her son's mischievous antics.

Sometimes Jeremiah would squash chocolate-covered strawberries and sword fight with pastel candy sticks until they shattered. No matter how much Mr. Thomas pled and implored, Jeremiah insisted on swimming in the steaming river of hot chocolate, drawing rude pictures on the walls with strawberry sauce, and sculpting houses out of blocks of fudge. He would finish eating his way through the store, waddle out plump, sticky, and satisfied, and his mother would leave a handful of gold coins on the gumdrop desk.

One particularly bleak winter day, when the snow fell with the kind of fat flakes that stick to your eyelashes like powdered sugar, Mr. Thomas looked up from his desk made from stacks of penny candy (the store often changed the flavor of the desk in the middle of the night) to find a little boy crying in the middle of the candy cane path.

"Hush, now," Mr. Thomas said, rushing to soothe the lost child. "There, there. The store knows where your mother is. It will find her. You just have to tell me your favorite candy."

"P-peanut b-b-butter c-cups!"

"A wise choice. Look!" Mr. Thomas said, pointing to the red-and-white striped path. "Follow the cups, and you'll find your mama. You won't get lost here, poor child."

A peanut butter cup appeared on the candy cane path ahead of the little boy, and then a second cup. A trail sprang up that led to the left. It wound around the field of gummy bears, the small city of taffy buildings, through the twirling display of bubble gum suckers, and headed toward the window. A woman with bright red hair just like the child's stood at a display of chocolate-covered cherries.

"Mama!" the boy cried, and, plucking up a cup or ten, he scampered to her side.

Mr. Thomas straightened with a smile that quickly turned dark for Jeremiah Reed had just toddled into the Red Unicorn Candy Store and shoved a little girl into a display of sugar wafers.

"Oh, dear," Mr. Thomas muttered, and a nearby cup of black licorice sticks began to shake. He glanced at them and sighed. "I agree. This won't be pretty. He seems to be in a very bad mood."

To say Jeremiah Reed was in a surly mood that day would have been like describing the sour powder tubes as sweet treats. He'd eaten an entire gingerbread house for breakfast—which is what nasty, wolfish children like to eat—but he'd wanted to eat a plate of cashew brittle instead.

"I'm thirsty!" Jeremiah bellowed and stormed over to the steaming river of hot chocolate. When he reached for a cup off the wall, the cup moved to the side, narrowly avoiding his fat fingers. He tried again, but the cup disappeared in a poof of cocoa powder. Turning bright red, Jeremiah slammed both hands into the wall, hoping to grab at least *one* cup, but all of them scattered and flew away like porcelain birds.

"Fine!" he yelled. "I shall just drink it with my face!"

Then piggish Jeremiah Reed plunged his face into the river of hot chocolate and gulped until his stomach hurt.

Mr. Thomas ran over to stop Jeremiah, but he arrived too late. "Jeremiah!" he called. "Now the entire river of hot chocolate will have to be replaced. No one will drink if it's had your face in it. What a terrible little boy."

"It doesn't taste like peppermint!" Jeremiah screamed, his face reddening beneath the hot chocolate oozing off his skin. "I want peppermint!"

Many customers lately had complained that the rare, sweet taste of peppermint hot chocolate they couldn't find anywhere else had disappeared from the store. It was a *special* peppermint flavor, of course. A super-secret Red Unicorn Candy Store trademark. Mr. Thomas couldn't figure out how to fix it, and the store didn't seem inclined to change, so he simply had to reassure people that it would return when it was supposed to return.

"Well, too bad," Mr. Thomas said to Jeremiah, setting his hands on his hips. "You can't have everything you want. The store won't let you."

A tower of bright yellow cupcakes hopped up and down in agreement.

"Then I want the Red Unicorn Horn!" Jeremiah cried in his nasally, high-pitched voice. Mr. Thomas grimaced and stuck his fingers in his ears to muffle the horrid sound. Jeremiah pointed into the air. "Give me the horn."

"No. The store will not let you have it."

"Yes, it will! I *always* get what I want!"

"You certainly will not have it," Mr. Thomas replied with exaggerated force. "The store does not like greedy children."

Jeremiah glared at Mr. Thomas with beady eyes. "I deserve it! None of your other candy is good. I've eaten it all. Who cares about you, anyway? I'll just get it myself."

"The last little boy to go after the Red Unicorn Horn said the same thing, but what he found was not what he expected."

Jeremiah set his chubby fists on his hips. "I'm better than him!"

"He died."

"I won't! Now give it to me!" he bellowed, the collar of his shirt sticking to his second chin, which still dripped with hot chocolate.

Mr. Thomas glanced to the top of the store, past Fudge Hall on level three and the Powder Room on level seven, until he saw the bright red horn at the very, very, very top of Marshmallow Mountain. It seemed to wink and wave, beckoning Jeremiah to come closer.

"Are you determined?"

"Yes."

"Then you may go after it, Jeremiah," Mr. Thomas said, hanging his head. "But you must heed this warning: the Red Unicorn Horn is not a candy. Going after it will put your very life in jeopardy."

Jeremiah glared at him.

"I'm going!" he declared, all three of his chins wobbling. "And no candy store is going to stop me!"

Tall tubes of red bubble gum balls suddenly opened, spilling the treats all over the floor around Jeremiah's feet.

Mr. Thomas sighed. "Yes," he agreed out loud. "This *is* going to be a mess."

O O O

Mr. Thomas watched Jeremiah begin his ascent of Marshmallow Mountain from the balcony of the second floor, where the Cookie Room displayed thousands of the scrumptious desserts. From red velvet to chocolate chip, from peanut butter to macadamia nut, every single cookie stayed warm.

"He'll never make it," Mr. Thomas said sadly, watching as Jeremiah tried to struggle over a particularly sprawling marshmallow boulder below. He'd been climbing for twenty minutes and had only made it ten feet. A warm chocolate cookie floated to Mr. Thomas's side. He took it with a grateful smile. "Thank you. This *does* make me feel better."

Just then, a puff of powdered sugar exploded from the crack between two marshmallow rocks, temporarily blinding Jeremiah. Startled by the unexpected explosion, he rolled backward and bounced down two more boulders.

"Oh, dear," Mr. Thomas said, chewing through the delicious cookie. "It'll take him ten more minutes to climb back up."

Because of Jeremiah's short, squishy legs, most of the boulders were too big for him to climb, but he still managed to cut a gradual upward path around the mountain.

Mr. Thomas walked the path beside the caramel apple wall, which curved upward along Marshmallow Mountain, following greedy Jeremiah's slow progress. A crowd of children followed Mr. Thomas, as they usually did.

"He can't do it!" declared a little girl through her last mouthful of cake-batter fudge. Another square of fudge appeared in her hands—the Candy Store agreed with her sentiments—and she squealed in delight.

"Much too big," agreed another boy before stuffing a chocolate-covered cinnamon bear in his mouth.

Jeremiah's sweaty hands on the sugary boulders created a white, sticky film that covered his wrists and arms as he grappled up the mountain. By the time Jeremiah reached Fudge Hall, the crowd of children had doubled. Mr. Thomas followed dutifully along, mumbling sad exclamations to himself with every step Jeremiah took.

"It won't end well," he'd say, then pat a child on the head and keep walking up the spiral candy wall.

"Look!" called a little boy. "The fudge is melting!"

Indeed, the fudge rocks on Marshmallow Mountain *were* melting. And the small stream of caramel that trickled through the rock field had become stickier than ever. Boulders of fudge melted as soon as Jeremiah approached, and soon he had to wade through a thick mire of chocolate sludge that was occasionally filled with nuts.

"He'll never make it to the fifth level," Mr. Thomas told a nearby parent. "The pretzels are just too difficult, I think."

Two chocolate-dipped pretzel sticks appeared to both Mr. Thomas and the parent in reassurance.

This Jeremiah Reed was a *sad* business, indeed.

Jeremiah, however, surprised everyone by not only wading through the thick sludge, but eating it along the way as well. Even *he* had to keep up his energy, after all.

But by the time he made it to the Pretzel Maze on Marshmallow Mountain, he collapsed to his knees in exhaustion.

"He's going to quit!" the parent said, waving the pretzel stick. "Look! He can't go on!"

"Give it up, Jeremiah!" Mr. Thomas called through cupped hands. "The Candy Store won't let you win! You continue at your own peril, silly boy!"

Jeremiah's face scrunched into a determined frown. He slowly pushed to his feet again and started to clamber over, between, and through the pretzel maze. Hiking through crumbling pretzels is awkward enough when you're healthy, but when you're Jeremiah Reed, it's downright *dangerous.*

"Well," Mr. Thomas said to himself, slowly walking past Pretzel Village on level six and up the ramp to the next level, "he'll certainly never make it through the Peppermint Stick Forest on level nine."

A nearby tree of peanut brittle branches gave a little shake in agreement.

Jeremiah Reed trudged onward until he stepped into the red-and-white swirls of the Peppermint Stick Forest and began his final ascent of Marshmallow Mountain. By this time, Mr. Thomas stood on level nine, very near to the Red Unicorn Horn. It sparkled and twinkled and shone in a very becoming way.

"No," he sighed, his hands folded behind his back. "This is bad."

This time, the Candy Store had no comfort to give him, and it rained black sugar crystals instead.

Unfortunately for Jeremiah Reed, the red-and-white pillars of the Peppermint Stick Forest stood very close together, forcing him to push past each stick with his hands until peppermint sludge covered his shoulders, arms, and very dimpled elbows.

"Stop now!" Mr. Thomas called. "The Candy Store will not let a human boy touch the horn!"

"I will not stop!" Jeremiah cried weakly. His legs were covered with so much candy that he couldn't bend his knees. "I will have the Red Unicorn Horn!"

"No, Jeremiah. You shall not."

Jeremiah reached out, but his arms had turned into literal sticks of peppermint. He kicked and sidestepped and danced his way through the Peppermint Stick Forest until his legs stuck together. Then he hopped, nudging each striped peppermint candy aside with his head.

By the time he reached the top, Jeremiah had nearly turned into the fattest peppermint stick ever seen. Except for his eyes, mouth, what little brain he used, and the weak pulse of his fading heart, Jeremiah had become a massive piece of hard, stubborn candy.

"Cherry!" Jeremiah shouted, half-mad with fatigue and sugar and desperation. "It's going to taste like cherry. No! Strawberry. It'll taste like strawberries."

Inch after miserable inch he hopped until finally he reached the top. With the last of his energy, Jeremiah leaped for the Red Unicorn Horn. But it was too late. His brain hardened to sugar, his eyes faded into stripes, and his heart gave a final minty beat.

The gargantuan piece of peppermint that had once been Jeremiah fell into a pool of hot chocolate that bubbled and gurgled at the very top of the mountain. The peppermint stick rolled and tumbled and turned in the hot chocolate, leaving a milky white foam. Since it was too big to roll down the river of hot chocolate, it remained in the pool, bobbing in place, flavoring the chocolate liquid with the sweet taste of peppermint.

Mr. Thomas shook his head.

"It happens every time. Their greed is always greater than their common sense."

A bright red cherry sucker appeared in the air next to Mr. Thomas. "Yes," he agreed. "Things will be better around here from now on. Now I shall have to go comfort Mrs. Reed."

In the meantime, the Red Unicorn Horn continued its constant vigilance atop Marshmallow Mountain, never ceasing, never stopping.

About the Author

Katie Cross is a big fan of cookies and running in the mountains. When she's not writing stories about girls with swords who don't need a man to save them, she's probably hiking with her husband and two vizslas. Find more of her work and her best-selling YA fantasy series, The Network Series, at www.missmabels.com.

VENGEANCE FOR DINNER

EMILY GODHAND AND J.S. BENNETT

Crawford slammed her coffee mug on the diner counter and set her pistol beside it.

"Ladies, we're taking down Guerrero."

The chintzy novelty clock above the chalkboard menu chimed six in the evening and summer heat blistered through the picture windows on the far wall. A *CLOSED* sign hung on one. Beetles the size of penny candy battered the glass, leaving behind yellowish smears.

August in Rutherford County.

Three women sat shoulder-to-shoulder at the counter, hunched over coffee and untouched menus.

A waitress with wrinkles made of smiles refilled Crawford's mug, a thin crust of sweat lining the collar of her shirt as she eyed the gun. A few droplets of coffee dribbled onto the countertop, and she hastily wiped them away with the corner of her once-white apron, now a study of Pollock in mustard and A1.

"Ya'll sure you don't want nothin'? Sweet tea? We've got raspberry. Made fresh."

Crawford stared over her sunglasses at the waitress. "My dear lady, sweet tea should be nothing but caffeine and unholy amounts of sugar like the good Lord intended."

The old woman puttered back to the register and disappeared into the kitchen for a smoke.

Crawford faced the wall and tapped her dark fingers on the rim of her mug, a martial rat-a-tat in the silence of the diner. A ceiling fan turned lazily overhead, pushing stale air down around her shoulders. "If Guerrero wants to go into business for herself, we'll consider her a competitor." She wiped a cherry-red lipstick smudge from her mug. "Any objections?"

"Not from me, honeybunch," said Zelenko, gaunt-faced and resplendent in her eggshell-colored pantsuit and pillbox hat. "I, for one, think this is long overdue."

In the high-backed stool to Crawford's left, Nightingale, swallowed by a camouflage jacket three sizes too large, shrugged and scratched at her neck, where a sizable boil had taken up residence. "Would it change your mind if I said I objected?"

Zelenko rolled her eyes and muttered something under her breath.

Nightingale turned, lifted a hand to her face, gave two exaggerated sniffs, and sneezed toward Zelenko.

Crawford rolled her eyes at Zelenko's undignified squeal and leaned back on her stool. "Well?"

Nightingale scratched at her shaggy hair. "All I'm sayin' is maybe we should give the accused a chance to defend herself."

Zelenko sneered and crossed her delicate, bony legs at the knee, bumping the underside of the counter. "Oh, don't be a bleeding heart. She dug her own grave—no pun intended, of course."

Crawford raised her brows over the rim of her sunglasses.

Zelenko looked to her employer and pursed her painted lips, dragging a gloved finger along the scratched Formica countertop.

"It was only a matter of time. Ever since the Great War, she's had this notion in her head that she's some lone cowgirl on a crusade. Nuh-uh, sister. She wouldn't have gotten anywhere without us, and now she wants to cut us out?" she said with a scoff.

Crawford set her hand on Zelenko's bony shoulder.

"You're right," she replied. "Who supplied Guerrero with some of her best weapons, huh?"

She leaned in and whispered in the woman's ear, "You."

Crawford turned to Nightingale.

"And you. If they managed to survive Guerrero and Zelenko, who did they meet next? Who birthed Yellow Fever, the Spanish Influenza, and the Black Plague?"

Crawford slid her hands along the other women's backs and pulled them close. "Guerrero's managed to exceed my expectations, sure. But my coffers are getting empty, and frankly, I'm a little annoyed."

Nightingale sighed and wiped her nose with her sleeve. "Let's be realistic. This has been a rough century for everyone but Guerrero. Penicillin, blood transfusions—hell, surgery with friggin' *robots*. And don't get me started on vaccines."

Zelenko fluttered a silk kerchief out of her breast pocket and dabbed at the sweat around her neck. "And GMOs, and irrigation systems, and preservatives—just spit it out, dear. You think she's asking too much of us."

Crawford slapped both of them on the back of their heads. Zelenko's hat slid over her eyes. She pushed it back on her blonde pin curls with an incensed harrumph.

"Oh, spare me," said Crawford. "So it's gotten a little hard. You adapt and overcome like you always have. What about those resistant strains you were working on, Nightingale, eh? Or climate change, Zelenko? Brilliant, ladies. Brilliant."

She glanced at both of them, then adjusted her sunglasses and toasted them with her coffee.

"You all have served me well these past few millennia. We've always worked together, and I'm not about to see that fall apart because some humans discovered a little *science*. It's just their new mysticism, and we've used that against them before."

"So, what?" Nightingale said. "What are we gonna do, kill her? It's not like that'll up our numbers any."

"Oh, come now," said Crawford, grinning. "Like all of my judgments end in death."

Zelenko coughed pointedly into her handkerchief.

"Besides, we need her. We need each other," Crawford said. She straightened her coat by the lapels and holstered her pistol. "Let's go remind her of that."

They rose as one from the counter.

"Hey!" cried the waitress as she caught them at the door. "Ya'll ready for your check, then?"

Crawford stopped. "Who handled the check last time?" she asked.

Zelenko raised her hand, and Crawford sighed. "Fine, I'll get it." She gently took the waitress by the elbow. "Your coffee was good. Always worth a few points in my book."

The waitress frowned, then staggered back. The left side of her face slowly drooped into a flaccid frown. Her legs gave out from underneath her, and she fell onto Crawford's chest, her hands first grasping, then clinging, to the woman's jacket. Her lips sputtered gibberish until her knees gave out, and she collapsed.

Outside, the first of the evening's crickets gave a merry chirp.

"That was nice of you," Nightingale commented, opening the door for the others, the bell tinkling good-bye.

Crawford stepped over the corpse. "You're covering the bill next time," she said to Nightingale as she exited the diner.

O O O

Evening fell heavy and fast, blanketing the sea of wheat that lined the stretch of empty highway. The setting sun lit the horizon on fire, sending a suffocating, smoky darkness over the Southern countryside. Above the occasional pool of standing water from the last summer shower, thick swarms of mosquitoes fogged the air.

Crawford's Dodge Magnum, sleek and black, pulled into a driveway flanked by overgrown dogwoods and rhododendrons. Gravel sprayed up from the tires in time to the thwack of limbs against the windows.

Zelenko covered her nose with her handkerchief.

"What *is* that smell?" she snapped.

Nightingale chewed on a lock of her shaggy, dark hair. "Oink oink."

Zelenko narrowed her eyes. "Wh—"

"Pigs," Crawford interrupted before Zelenko's righteous indignation could blossom. She jerked her chin. "Hear that?"

Zelenko frowned and tilted her head. There it was, the snuffles and keening squeals of hogs. She kept her kerchief at her nose but remained quiet until the Magnum rolled to a stop in front of the old ranch house and barn.

The house was old but in good shape, painted cornflower blue, ringed by a wraparound porch and flower garden.

The three women stepped out into the heat, the slam of the doors punctuating the evening's symphony—croaking frogs in C minor—and waited in silence by the wooden fence enclosing the property. Crawford slipped her hands into the pockets of her trench coat as she circled the house. Her boots kicked up hordes of gnats.

Under a bay window overlooking the road, a woman in a plaid shirt over a filthy white tank top uprooted earthy bundles of weeds from a patch of butter-yellow petunias.

"Guerrero!" Crawford called.

Guerrero, pinch-faced and glistening with sweat, tipped back the brim of her oversized sun hat. Her skin was a palette of blotchy purples and sunburned reds. She rolled her shoulders and cracked her neck as she stood to greet them.

"Ladies!" Guerrero said, mopping her face with her shirt. "To what do I owe the pleasure?" She tugged off her ratty gardening gloves and dropped them over the porch railing.

Crawford crossed her arms. "Just stopping by to chat, doll. Got some business to discuss."

"Ya'll stayin' the night? I got a stable for your iron horse there," she said with a smile.

Their faces, cold and gaunt, stared back at her with dead eyes.

Guerrero rubbed her arms.

"Brrr." Her grin never wavered. "An ambush? Boss, c'mon now, I invented that."

"If I wanted to ambush you, Guerrero, you wouldn't see me coming," Crawford replied.

She moved back, toward the sagging wooden fence, and yanked a sickle out of a slat, where it had likely been collecting rust for decades. She turned it over in one hand and ran her finger down the blade with the other. Dull, but usable.

Crawford tapped the blade. "I'm wondering where your share is at this decade. You got time to plant poppies—"

"Petunias," Guerrero corrected.

Crawford scowled. "Whatever. You got time to play house but not to get your job done?"

Guerrero didn't answer at first. She yanked off her sun hat and dug around in her pocket for a half-empty can of chew, then popped a glob in one cheek and shook the can in Zelenko's direction. "Want some?"

"No," Zelenko said with a sniff. "That's filthy, you degenerate."

Guerrero shrugged and closed the tin. "Look, don't get me wrong, boss," she said as she carefully peeled away the strands of hair glued to her forehead by sweat. "I like my job. I've been doing it for over fifteen thousand years, so don't jump on me because it's been an off few years. I had World War II, all right? Nukes? Vietnam? Agent Orange? Come on, that was good. I'm doing a lot better than these two numbskulls," she said as she fluttered her dirt-stained fingers at Nightingale and Zelenko.

"Now, wait just a *minute*—" Zelenko started to say.

Guerrero held up a hand to cut her off. "Don't worry your pretty little head, toots. Wouldn't want you to hurt yourself," she said. She spat her chew out the side of her mouth, rust-brown liquid sluicing down her chin. "Get real. Except for a few old farts kickin' it from pneumonia and some real bad cases of drought, these two combined have barely been pulling in half of my load."

Zelenko's powdered face pulled into a snarl.

Nightingale stepped between the two women, her hands raised in a placatory gesture. "Well, you certainly know how to cause strife, honey, no one's doubtin' that."

Crawford sauntered closer to Guerrero, who stood stock-still and hooked her thumbs into her belt loops. She pointed the sickle at the center of Guerrero's chest. "You're very, very wrong about those numbers, kid."

With deliberate slowness, she trailed the tip of the blade down Guerrero's sweaty cheek. Guerrero flinched but didn't pull away. A fly landed on her shoulder.

"I meet every last person who comes to me." Crawford's tongue dashed across her lips. "I know their life, time of death, and, of course, the cause."

The sickle hovered over the cleft of Guerrero's clavicle. Crawford tugged gently at the collar of her shirt, then pointed the blade toward Nightingale and Zelenko.

Nightingale thumbed her chest. "Heart disease? Respiratory infection? Hello?"

"And," Zelenko interjected hotly, "don't forget the Holodomor and the Great Leap Forward."

Crawford chuckled and scratched her chin with the tip of the blade. "See? You're not even in the top ten, Guerrero. People are more likely to crap themselves to death than ever see you. Now you did good with religion. Great idea, there. But you forget that the only reason you've been so successful for millennia are these two right here. And now they tell me you aren't full of—what do you call it?—*esprit de corps* anymore. And I'm paying the price for it."

Guerrero shooed the fly away, adjusted her shirt, and shrugged. "We *were* close. But you guys are stuck in the past." She pointed to Nightingale. "When was the last time you had a proper epidemic, huh? Whatever happened to Ebola?"

Nightingale sighed. "That was barely an outbreak, moron."

Guerrero's finger swung to Zelenko. "And you! There's a whole country of fat-asses just begging for a good famine, and you can't even give them that!"

Zelenko adjusted her hat and patted at her curls, silent.

"Young lady, you watch your tone with me," Crawford said. "You are *strictly* a human invention. However well you've done in the past half-century, you would have never gotten anywhere without the rest of us."

Guerrero rolled her eyes and brushed past Crawford. Tiny puffs of dust marked her trail as she walked up the driveway. "Yeah, two hundred years ago, maybe." She whirled around and gestured to the massive barn behind her. "But me, I've got something you'll *really* like. Long-term plan, if you will."

Crawford looked to her comrades then slammed the sickle back into the wooden fence, sending splinters into the grass. "You didn't think to let me know about this?"

Guerrero wrinkled her nose. "What was I supposed to say, boss? Your 'Suggestion Box' sits on top of a shredder."

Crawford regarded her for a long moment, then raised her arms in defeat. "Fine. Show me."

Guerrero grinned and slid open the wooden door.

Inside, the barn was a museum of warfare, coated in a thick layer of dust and pig-stench. Spears and swords and battle-axes lined the walls. In the wooden cabinet by the door, hand cannons and derringers and flintlock pistols hung above automatic rifles; a Stinger missile was festively wrapped in Christmas lights. Nailed above bags of feed were tapestries and oil paintings and woodblock prints detailing battles from centuries past. A pinup calendar showed a blonde in fatigues perched atop a V2 ballistic missile.

But the centerpiece, the only display that was clean and well-used, was a massive red tank in the middle of the barn. The white-washed cannon barrel barely cleared the barn doors.

Guerrero waved her arm. "Like my warhorse? Much improved, right?" she said.

"Warhorse?" said Crawford under her breath. "It looks more like a unicorn."

Guerrero ignored her and stared up at the tank with her hands on her hips. She tapped its steel hull fondly. "Good old T-90. Got a 125mm smoothbore 2A46."

Nightingale and Zelenko exchanged glances. "S'nice," Nightingale mumbled.

Guerrero continued on, oblivious. "But that's not the best part. You see that grain silo over there?" She motioned toward a seemingly harmless metal tower, no different than the dozen other hulking silos that dotted the stretch of farmland. "Twenty-two tons of divine fury. You can take out a whole country in time for breakfast. Ta-da!"

Nightingale whistled, then ducked her head when Zelenko slapped her arm.

"That's your master plan?" Zelenko snapped. "Nuclear warfare? Gee, I don't know, sweetie, wasn't there an entire Cold War dedicated to learning how much those things accomplished? What was the number of nukes deployed, again? Oh, was it—was it zero?"

Guerrero shook her head. "Philistine."

Crawford kept her eyes on the tank, inspecting every last detail of what was a truly custom job. She chuckled to herself when she noticed the decal on one side: a fiery-eyed red unicorn rearing up on its hind legs, its several rows of teeth stained with blood. She kept her hand on the metal as she sauntered around the tank, until her fingers trailed across the letters "Death Machine" on the other side. A twitch started at her left eye, then spread to the corners of her mouth.

"You think you can become Death?" she asked, looking over her shoulder at the taller woman.

Guerrero flipped her hair over her shoulder and smiled.

Crawford's hands shook, then slowly pulled into fists. "And you're stupid enough to think a few fancy weapons can pull that off?"

Guerrero chuckled. "Not stupid. Just good enough."

Zelenko scoffed as she tugged on her white gloves. "Sugar," she drawled, "'good enough' only counts in horseshoes."

Guerrero's lips curved into a nasty smile. "And hand grenades!" she added brightly. Her hand shot out to open a tackle box propped up on a plastic chair. "Catch!"

The dummy grenade, a shiny steel M69, landed at Zelenko's feet. Nightingale let out an aborted squeal and stumbled back into a display of maces. Zelenko shrieked and kicked the sphere away with one sand-colored pump. It skidded onto a patch of straw. A few seconds later, the M69 erupted with a stream of white smoke and a deafening pop.

Nightingale flinched.

Zelenko, pale and quivering, pointed a finger at Guerrero. "Bitch!"

Crawford snatched up the still-smoking husk. It rusted under her fingers then crumbled to dust. Her glare withered Guerrero's smirk.

"You think you're special because mankind created you on their own?" Crawford shouted. Her voice was as ragged as sandpaper. She looked down at her hand, as if weighing it, then strode forward and struck Guerrero hard. The smack was louder than Guerrero's soft gasp. With her free hand, Crawford caught the other woman by the chin and stroked the rapidly pinkening mark on her cheek.

"It's always the same with you," she cooed. Her hands dug into Guerrero's lapels. She jerked the other woman forward until the crown of her head rammed into Guerrero's jaw.

Guerrero yelped and stumbled back, covering her mouth. "Ow! I think you knocked out a tooth." She spat a mouthful of pink onto the straw scattered across the floor.

Zelenko swallowed a giggle.

Guerrero glowered at her and took a moment to catch her breath, then tipped her head mockingly. "Aw, baby, don't be like that. You've been gettin' awful greedy lately. Even Tweedledee and Tweedledum over there think so, don't you?"

She winked at Nightingale, who scuffed the toe of her boot in the straw.

"Well, I mean ..." Nightingale mumbled.

Guerrero chuckled, dry and raspy. Her swelling lip obscured her words like a blob of cotton beneath the tongue.

"I know ya'll don't appreciate my efforts, but *some* of us like to make sure there's enough of a generation left to cull for the next century, you know? That's the beauty of war. You can't have just one."

Nightingale tossed her hand out. "So you're a bag of Lay's? Man, that's not justification for working on your own. Your job was to keep the humans in line so they didn't wise up."

"I got more people coming to me willingly after they've met you. You think I like cleaning up your messes?" Crawford added.

Guerrero sighed and dabbed at her busted lip. "I thought you'd appreciate those."

She glanced out the open barn door.

"'Scuse me, ya'll—gotta feed the pigs." She hefted a pitchfork off the wall before stomping out to the yard with the others trailing behind, and kept talking.

"Look, people are always going to kill each other. They don't need disease and hunger, and neither do I. I'm doing fine on my own these days. So maybe I skimmed a little off the top. So what? The stronger I am, the more returns you get, you shortsighted asshole. You're starving us out—"

"Hey!" Zelenko protested.

"—leaving us the crap at the bottom of the barrel. Well, I'm tired of it. You want a good harvest, you either let me take what I need or you start withering away, too," she finished. The hogs perked up at her arrival, crowding the fence.

"Oh, shut it. *I* don't think long-term? The end goal is all I *can* see. It's kind of my thing, in case you forgot," Crawford said, raising her arms. "I've taken every man, king, and god since time immemorial. What makes you think you can stand against me?"

"Against *us?*" Zelenko added.

Nightingale shook her head sadly. "We used to be friends, man. Symbiosis and all that."

Guerrero whirled around, her black eyes flashing in the last light of day. "Well, maybe I'm friggin' tired of it."

She stuck two fingers past her lips and let out a shrill whistle. In their pen, the hogs snorted and vibrated with nervous energy.

With a grunt, Guerrero swung around and skewered the pitchfork's rusty tines in Zelenko's concave gut. A shock of red stained the woman's white blazer. Zelenko screeched, her hands immediately going to her stomach, fingers fluttering uselessly around the wound.

Tendons straining like bridge cables in her neck, Guerrero pushed Zelenko back against the chicken-wire pigpen. Zelenko's hat sailed off her head as Guerrero gave one final heave, and the other woman toppled into the squealing, teeming mass of hogs.

The ravenous swine descended upon her. Zelenko swatted and shoved one pig away from her delicate face while forcing her heeled pump into the gut of another. Two more pigs chomped their teeth into her other calf while a third pig ripped away her shoe and worried at it like a dog. But if Zelenko knew one thing, it was all-consuming hunger. Gristle and bone were as appetizing as a five-course banquet to the starving.

And yet it was all she knew. Each slap to the hogs shriveled their muscles until their hide clung to their bones, but nothing she did could abate their hunger. The weaker and more gaunt they became, the more they wanted, and the more they took from her.

Crawford's eyes widened, and her dark skin turned ashen. With an inhuman growl, she leaped over the fence into the pigpen and landed with her hands in the mud. The filth turned black as pitch, then boiled and popped in a wave of desecrating decay that spread over the swine from their trotters to their snouts. The swine squealed in horror as their hide sloughed off from the creeping rot that melted the flesh from their bones and tore open their insides.

The dying remains of Zelenko lay a mangled mess of gnawed bone and half-eaten flesh in the putrid muck. Crawford picked her way past the liquefied corpses of pigs to her comrade, who reached out with a shaking, skeletal hand. Her lipless mouth opened to speak, but she only managed a creaking groan. Crawford grasped Zelenko's hand in her own and stared down at her friend, her face emotionless as Zelenko's fingers slipped away.

In the chaos, Nightingale stood frozen, her lips parted soundlessly.

Guerrero stumbled back with the pitchfork in hand, and that, if nothing else, shook Nightingale into action. She lifted her arms just as Guerrero swung the pitchfork and grabbed the splintered wood, twisting to throw Guerrero off balance.

"Guerrero! What are you *doing*?" she shouted. "We were friends. We went everywhere together."

Guerrero shifted her grip until the pitchfork hung between them. She pushed forward, slamming the handle into Nightingale's chest and shoving her back. "Should've thought of that before you decided to take me on!"

Nightingale caught herself. Her face twisted into a scowl as she raised her hand.

Guerrero yelped as the skin on her forearms began to swell into angry red boils, scabbed and heavy with pus. She doubled over and dropped to one knee, gasping for air as the infection spread to her lungs.

Blood dribbled between her lips and leaked from her eyes and ears. She spat out the blood and gritted her teeth. She scooped up a clod of dirt and threw it at Nightingale's face, obscuring the woman's vision for just a blink—enough time to slam her into the pile of hay behind them.

Nightingale grabbed her arm, but Guerrero shoved her aside and rammed the pitchfork deep into her chest, pinning her to the pile.

Guerrero wasted no time while Nightingale struggled against the pitchfork. She felt her insides churning to mush while her body consumed itself with fever. She scrambled to the barn and snatched a mason jar filled with yellowish jelly off the wall.

There was one sure way to fight pestilence. She slammed the napalm into the straw. The glass shattered on impact. Guerrero fumbled with the lighter in her pocket then tossed it into the hay.

White-hot flames exploded outward, throwing Guerrero onto her back. The fire devoured the fabric of Nightingale's jacket, then the woman herself. Guerrero gulped down air and smiled as the other woman's screams harmonized with the roar of the fire.

On the other side of the pigpen, Crawford looked up from Zelenko's ragged corpse. With a wave of her hand, the flames subsided into thick, foul-smelling smoke, but Nightingale still burned. What little skin remained was nothing but weeping char.

Crawford and Guerrero exchanged glances. Guerrero grinned with bloody teeth and darted into the barn. Crawford slipped over the fence, but paused as an ungodly rumble shook the ground under her feet. She shielded her eyes with one hand. A beat later, the barn doors splintered like cheap plywood beneath the treads of Guerrero's T-90.

The tank rolled by, kicking up a spray of mud that splattered Crawford's black coat. Crawford rushed forward, but not in time to stop the T-90 from tearing down the driveway and crunching Crawford's Magnum. The screech of metal on metal rent the evening, and a moment later the T-90 doubled back, trailed by a cloud of dust.

Crawford stared at the wreckage.

The sight of her mangled car, illuminated by the fading light of day, stirred something in her. Her lips twitched at one corner as she stared ahead, until they pulled into a wide grin.

"Well, praise the Lord and pass the ammunition."

The T-90's cannon groaned as it rotated. Crawford's gun had yet to clear its leather before there was a flash of light. An earsplitting boom knocked her to her knees as a shell rocketed from the turret. The pigpen behind her went up a blast of smoke and mud. A moment later, the machine gun started up.

Crawford covered her head as the rounds rained destruction around her, shredding the fence of the pigpen into scrap. Crawford gritted her teeth, and with each blink, she disappeared and materialized closer and closer, until she was dangling from the white cannon and staring into the gun.

The barrel rusted and crumbled underneath her hands. "Hey," said Crawford. "I broke your unicorn."

Guerrero didn't hesitate to fire again.

The round ripped past Crawford's face just as she dropped to the ground. First the skin, then the muscle, flayed from her cheek to reveal grinning white teeth. Crawford scrambled to her feet and up the side of the hull as the tank rushed over her. The hatch warped and cracked at her touch, dropping pieces on Guerrero's head.

Crawford reached into the cab of the tank and grasped the woman by her neck. She lifted Guerrero out and heaved her to the ground.

"I'm not done with you yet," she said, joining the woman in the dust.

Guerrero slammed her boot into Crawford's shin, pulled herself to her feet, staggered into the barn, and snatched a rusty old rifle off the wall.

Crawford ducked and rushed Guerrero before the woman could adjust her aim. A quick hook of her arm had both woman and gun in a lock, and a kick deep into the back of her knee brought them to the ground.

Guerrero reversed the hold and tossed her boss over her shoulder into the dusty straw. The rifle clattered to the floor in the struggle.

Guerrero let it go and scampered to her old, trusty standbys mounted on the wall: a heater shield and long sword. She whirled. Crawford met her thrust with a parry from a flanged mace. The head of the mace smashed into her shield, knocking it to the floor.

"Dammit!" Guerrero spat. She moved to slice between Crawford's ribs, but Crawford danced out of the way and grabbed Guerrero's forearm, yanking her forward and twisting her wrist until the sword dropped to the floor. She kicked it aside.

Guerrero retaliated with an elbow to the jaw, pushing Crawford away. She didn't give the woman a chance to recover before she charged her, knocking them both to the straw-covered wooden floor. Guerrero straddled the other woman and pounded her palm into Crawford's windpipe once before Crawford caught Guerrero's fist in her own.

Crawford bucked her hips, throwing Guerrero on her back. Guerrero sprawled out gracelessly, her plaid shirt spreading around her.

Crawford was on top of her. She grabbed a fistful of dark hair and yanked the other woman's head forward. Their lips met in a crushing kiss. Guerrero gasped as the older woman pulled the last bit of precious air from her lungs and held her thrashing body in place. It was always a struggle with Guerrero. Eventually, she stilled.

Crawford rolled off the corpse and landed on her back in the dust.

Time passed. The sun sank lower until the air cooled and the insects slowed to a sleepy buzz.

Crawford sighed and drank deeply from a flask off her hip. She exhaled with a grimace, then sat up and surveyed the destruction that smoldered around her. She smiled with grim pleasure, then chuckled to herself and staggered to her feet. Her boots dragged in the dust as she made a circle around the impromptu battlefield to each of her fallen comrades, offering a few drops of liquor to their ruins to revive them.

Zelenko and Nightingale found each other and huddled together in the smoldering hay, their faces streaked with ash and grime, hands clutched tight.

Finally, Crawford came to Guerrero's corpse and emptied the rest of the bottle over the woman's face.

"Get up, ladies," she said. "There's no rest for the wicked. We've got work to do."

About the Authors

Emily Godhand is a supernatural thriller author whose works tend to focus on an exploration of violence, immortality, and human consciousness. She lives in Denver with her seven rats, who revere her as their divine queen.

JS Bennett is a Tennessee native and romantic suspense author. In her spare time, she catches up on her history and watches bad movies with her two dogs.

THE TRADE

RAPHYEL M. JORDAN

It was always cold in the caves, and even worse on the dark side of Europa. Almost forty degrees Kelvin at the poles. At least acclimating body temp is one of the perks bioengineered humans have. It's decent enough, I guess, though I think the scientists should've implemented more uni traits in us when colonizing the moon proved more difficult than anticipated. I, for one, would've preferred having a single horn that fired laser beams. That could've been helpful right about now, but that might be the soldier in me talking.

I looked through the icicle prison bars of my cage, noting a subtle presence on the other side. I was trained to take note of slight ripples against the ice that seemed … off. Sure sign of a uni's camo. The tales moms once told daughters on Earth concerning unicorns is a far cry from the truth—a uni's camouflage being one of key items never mentioned. Knowing the monsters were capable of that trick could've saved a lot of lives during their initial strike twenty years ago.

I scooted closer to my sister, Amy, when another coughing attack interrupted her sleep. I rubbed her back, hoping it would ease the episode. It did, a little. Her wheezing was getting worse. Unis had raided our town during my leave a while back, and she had leaped in front of me when one of them had me in its sights. She took the beam in the right shoulder, not far from the lung.

I moved Amy as gently as I could onto her side. The wound had cauterized, but keeping it clean in a prison cell, even one made of ice, was hard to do. If she had been any younger than twelve, I doubt she would've held out this long, though I now feared she didn't have much fight left.

Please, just hold on.

I brushed back the blue hair streaked on her face, rubbing the thick strands between my fingers. Her head was still oily, of course—just another way to keep the body from wasting too much heat. Amy used to imagine having brown curly hair and olive skin, like the lady we descended from did centuries ago. Mom had a hologram of her in our hut before the unicorns attacked.

The creature opposite of our bars publicized its presence with a sniff. Steam fumed from its nostrils, forming crystals. I'd heard that Earthlings called it pixie dust, the fools.

I arose and stood in front of Amy. If it didn't leave her alone, honest to God, I'd kill it with my bare hands. I'm a soldier. I killed my first uni two years ago when I was fifteen.

The unicorn unveiled itself. Like me, its silvered skin glistened as ice; we'd altered ours to account for radiation two centuries ago. It leaned against the cage, a spiraling pearl horn half a meter long piercing between one of the openings. The bars creaked as he applied more pressure.

"Timmy?"

Dammit. Why couldn't she be allowed to dream a bit longer?

Amy went from being in a daze to eyes the size of fists in less than a second.

"Don't move, Amy," I told her. "It's okay."

The uni's blackened stare shot through me as if I were nothing. It snorted as it backed up and lowered its head. *Mind your place, human.*

I eased away from the bars. The uni's mental projection of a voice sounded male. Telepaths. I still found it weird, their lips not having to move in order to communicate. They must've thought us so inferior. And to think we thought it a great idea to experiment on them after first contact.

The uni fired two blue beams from his horn, melting the bottom of three bars before he swatted the rest away. *I am Zupho. The Alpha wants to see you.*

Amy grabbed my right leg with her one good arm and shook her head. Her grip was so weak.

"I won't leave my sister," I told the monster. "Her wound is draining her."

You don't make demands. The Alpha says to move, and you will do so. Now, come.

I wouldn't be any good to Amy if the uni dropped me, so I turned and crouched down to her. "I have to see what this is about."

"Timmy—please—don't leave me here! You—" Her coughing cut her off. The attack was so fierce, it made her eyes water.

I eased her onto her back and tossed my old jacket over her. I turned to leave, and she took my hand. They were so cold, even for us. A shiver ran down my spine. If I left now, would she still be alive upon my return?

I turned around and cupped her face. "I will be right back. Understand?" I placed her head onto my chest. She better not leave me. God, she better not.

The unicorn shoved my back with his snout. *I will not repeat myself.*

Zupho didn't say anything else as I followed him to what I assumed was some sort of council chamber. Nearby geysers vibrated the walls, and the cave brightened as we neared the surface. I wished Amy had been with me. She would've gone on one of her typical rants attempting to explain what caused the moon's eruptions and quakes.

She was the smart one. She wanted to be a leading scientist, while I would've been fine working the mines or drilling like everyone else. Too bad for the unis, I turned out to be a better shot instead.

The creature led me deeper into the uncharted caves on the moon; no one I knew had ventured this far behind enemy lines. We came upon an opening where the ground had smoothed. My eyes adjusted accordingly, given Europa had the brightest surface of any celestial body in the solar system besides the sun. The area where I stood looked like a stage. Jupiter was probably peeking over the mountains outside. I hadn't seen it since being captured, so the kid in me wanted to ask the tour guide if we could take a quick glimpse, though I knew better.

We're here, Zupho said as we stopped at the center of the stage.

Twenty-four unicorns appeared from the shadows around me. They stood silently in formation, their front left legs bent ever so slightly. It gave me chills.

A uni larger than Zupho trotted up to me, sniffing as it rested its red-stained horn on my shoulder. There was no telling how many soldiers it had killed. I kept my hands to my side, though my trigger finger twitched.

Five agonized minutes of silence passed as the two dozen animals studied me. Something needed to happen; I was wasting too much time. Amy needed me. Maybe this was a test, or I was supposed to speak first. Only one way to find out.

"I was told the Alpha wanted to speak with me. Is he here?"

Three of the unis leapt onto the stage. They dragged their horns across the ground as they approached me.

I dropped to my knees and eyed the floor. "I had to leave my sister for this. She's dying." I swallowed the lump in my throat. "She doesn't deserve that. I am the soldier. Not her. I don't know how capable your people are, but she needs medical attention." I lifted my gaze to the nearest uni. "She's only twelve years old. I hope you can at least understand the concept of innocence."

We do appreciate such notions, human. The questions is, can you?

I spun around, and froze. Before me stood a creature far larger than any of the other unis, being the size of what was once called a Clydesdale. How had something so enormous sneaked up on me?

The unicorn looked down on me, eyes the color of pearls. The protrusion from its head faded to ebony at the tip. The hue of its skin was that of a flower Amy had shown me in one of her old notes; I think it was called a rose. The color on this creature seemed unnatural, however. It was too—dare I say it—beautiful.

It circled me, its hooves not making a sound. So large, yet so elegant. No one had laid eyes on an Alpha before, or if they had, they never had the chance to tell anyone about it.

The red unicorn sniffed the top of my head. *Your scent is fresh. You speak well for one so young, human. Which are you? Male or female?*

"Um, male ... ma'am." Now that the shock had worn off, I sensed a feminine tone from the Alpha.

*A boy, you say. Shame. And the tiny one that stays with you … * She snorted. *Its scent is similar to your own. A female, hmm? A "sister," I believe you call it.* The Alpha sniffed again. *Strong, though I doubt she realizes it yet.*

The unicorn shimmied back, shaking her head wildly. *You also have the blood of my brethren on you, boy. For that alone, you should be left to rot in the cell with the rest of your comrades. But fortune has fallen upon you. My herd faces a dilemma, and you will help us resolve it.*

The unicorns needed my help? With what? Why me? Weren't there other prisoners with better credentials, other soldiers older and stronger?

"What do you need me to do?" I asked warily.

Your people kidnapped my son, and you are going to retrieve him.

I assumed my ears weren't working too well until I remembered the unicorn wasn't speaking to me at all. "When was the colt taken?"

He was abducted two days ago, based on your silly calendar. The Alpha approached me. *I know your scientists will examine him to the point of death. To study a rare crimson alpha, of course they would seize the opportunity without hesitation.*

That last part was certainly true, but humans venturing this deep into the lower layers didn't make sense. Then again, a dispatched recon unit might slip behind lines if given enough reason. Maybe they had a lead on the location of our prison and a group had been ordered to scout and confirm.

And what if the said recon team was in the middle of the operation when they lucked out and found a baby red unicorn more than likely grazing on some fresh hexagon crystals? How could they pass up learning additional information about what made the enemy tick, especially if the foal had the potential of leading forces when it grew up?

We kill them out of curiosity. They kill us out of anger. What a stupid cycle.

"Where was your colt last seen?"

He is not allowed to travel beyond the northern layers. He would have stayed near my den, as he always does. The other prisoners either lack your ability to track us, or are far too weak to undertake a journey beyond these borders and survive. I have no further options.

Either I was delirious, or I sensed a crack in the Alpha's voice. She might have been the leader of this herd of unicorns, but today, she seemed to be a mother who just wanted her kidnapped child returned to her. Anyone could empathize with that ... I guess, including me.

I straightened. "What do I get in return?"

The Alpha stared me down. *You get to live.*

My life wasn't the one on the brink of ending.

"For years, our races have suffered because of our differences, but I think there's one thing we both seem to appreciate."

Really.

"It's family. My parents have been without knowledge of their children's well-being for what would be three months to an Earthy. That's hundreds of cycles here. Surely you can appreciate such a loss now, even with your case being a mere two days. Maybe we can come to an equal exchange on that note?"

Zupho snorted as he reared. *Enough, human. You dare make bargains with the Alpha?*

Silence, Zupho, the Alpha ordered. She swung her head side to side and fluttered her long lashes. I could see the perplexity in her eyes as she pondered. Moments later, she pointed her horn at my chest. *State your proposal.*

"Release my sister."

Alpha—, Zupho objected.

She charged the tip of her horn and aimed it at the silver unicorn.

Zupho lowered his head and backed away.

The Alpha returned her attention to me. *Just her?*

Including the remaining prisoners into the bargain wasn't possible. It had to be a fair trade, as much as I hated it. "Just her. An innocent for an innocent."

Very well. Take your leave, then. The longer you remain here, the longer your sister will be without your care.

I paused. "Can I explain the situation to her?"

The red unicorn trotted away, not saying another word. Zupho and the other three on stage placed themselves between us.

"Let me at least tell her good-bye. I told her I'd come right back."

Then you best not make the same mistake in breaking your promises with me as you have with her, the Alpha answered back as she left. *Otherwise, your people will be the ones to face the consequences of your failure, starting with her.*

Five unicorns would bring a good fight, and twenty-six would bring a massacre. I couldn't let that happen. The unis on post broke their formation once the Alpha was out of sight and disappeared into the shadows.

Zupho and the others faded as their camo enveloped them.

You best hurry, human. It seems time is not on either of our sides.

o o o

Four days on the surface, and I understood why the unis had been unable to track down the recon unit. We had not only learned about the unicorn's camo capabilities, but like any good human, we had improved it for ourselves. Given infrared was obsolete, the local unis didn't know what signs a soldier like me would look for. Subtle dips in the iced sheets indicating where a human-sized body had taken a nap. Parts of walls covered with an extra layer of ice to hide evidence of a colt scraping its hooves against the ridges as it struggled to break free. The subtle hints were there.

The moon's defining feature, a series of crevices and thin ridges a few meters high, might have slowed someone else down on this journey, but I leaped over them with minimal effort. They said our ancestors could jump higher, given how much stronger they were than us. I at least remembered a teacher telling me Earth's Luna was about the same size as Europa, making gravity a close equivalent.

To live on a planet that had such a strong gravitational pull? Earthies had no idea how amazing they were, until it was too late. Even so, I figured we had our benefits too. Nana and Grampi were first-generation, genetically altered people to be naturally born. No suits. No space bubbles. No living underneath the ice to avoid Jupiter's radiation. No need for terraforming. We were too good to be true. All we had to do was learn how the locals managed to do it, via a couple of dissections here and there. Look where that got us. Look where that got my sister. I'd never forgive the unicorns, or us, if I lost her.

I stopped and slid against an iced wall as I covered my face. Amy had been half-dead when I left her days ago, and now she didn't have anyone to care for her. She had to be gone by now. I didn't even get to see Amy during her last moments. My heartbeat raced as the truth came upon me. It was too late. I had failed her.

I opened my eyes, and what I saw stopped my thoughts from spiraling into deeper despair. Four pairs of human footprints adjoined by four tiny hooves were in front of me. The Special Ops team was getting sloppy, and so was I. No, the Alpha was right. Amy was strong. She was a fighter. She was still hanging in there. God, she had to be. I scrambled to my feet and picked up the pace.

The recon team was still a decent ways out by the looks of the prints, and there was no telling how close they were to reaching a forward operating base or drop zone. Explaining to four soldiers why a unicorn needed to be returned to its herd would be tough enough. Having to tell that to a CO and a room filled with scientists and military advisors would be near impossible.

Reaching the team and reasoning with them before a worse situation came up was my only option. Anything less would result in the red unicorn and her herd seeking vengeance for the lost colt. And if Amy wasn't already dead by then, she and whatever remaining captives wouldn't have to wait very long.

An echoing, high-pitched neigh pumped my adrenaline. I was gaining on them, but as I gazed across a vast plain of ice, all I saw were smooth ridges. So, why didn't I see the team?

Wait. Oh, no.

"Don't move."

I froze. Stupid me. Of course the team had realized someone was tailing them and left bread crumbs. Two scouts appeared in front of me, disengaging their camo and lowering their blasters. One of them tapped my shoulder.

"Looks like we got an escapee, Sarge," the young woman said as she examined my top, puzzled. "Army. Rank?"

"Private Timothy Miles of the 532nd infantry unit," I recited. "I was on leave when my home was raided by a uni squad. My parents are Renae—"

"Did you say the 532nd?" the other soldier said. "We thought we lost all of you guys!"

Before I could say anything else, I was bombarded by pats on the back and handshakes. The sergeant phased into sight as he approached me. He held a halter tied to a pink unicorn trembling behind him. The foal didn't even have the hint of a horn yet. Give him another Earth year or two and his skin would be as radiant as his mother's.

The sergeant handed the rope to the third soldier then faced me. "Good to have you back with us, Private Miles. We weren't sure what was following us, otherwise we would've stopped sooner. You have perfect timing. We're a day out from the FOB, but we've got plenty to spare. Hungry? I bet you have a story to tell over dinner."

I eyed the tiny unicorn, his big black eyes darting left to right. I wondered if he was even old enough to speak telepathically. I honestly felt sorry for him—just another victim caught in the middle a war, like Amy.

He snuffled suddenly, startling the soldiers so much that they drew their weapons on him. That was a bit random of the uni … Or was it?

"Can I touch him, sir?" I asked the sergeant.

"Go ahead. You probably won't get another chance once the brainiacs are done with it."

I approached the frightened unicorn and extended my palm to his nose. He sniffed again. The foal's breath was warm. His ears pricked forward as he rubbed my palm with the tiny hairs on his snout. Just as I thought. He probably smelled his mother. I leaned over to his ear as I rubbed his forehead. The one soldier still within my eyesight watched me carefully.

"Can you understand me?" I whispered to the foal. "If so, we're going to help each other. I hope."

O O O

The sergeant's last name was Yukimura. The guy who first spotted me was Khalaf, their lead scout. The rifle on his back could drop something from two klicks away, easy. The woman who had asked for my rank was the main gunner, Pashkov, and Mellis was the team's technician.

I explained the situation the instant they completed the pleasantries. I needed to hurry. The FOB would wonder why the team hadn't radioed in and send people to investigate.

Sarge took off his helmet and rubbed his buzzed head after I finished. "You want me to return this thing"—Yukimura thumped the colt's ear—"and in return, we get your sister back but lose you in the process?" He shook his head. "Now that we know the enemy's position, we can launch a full op and get your sister out— plus anyone else who might still be in the caves. Don't you want to see your folks again, Miles?"

"I was out of options, sir."

"And you still are, I'm afraid. With this red uni, we can save more lives beyond those in the cave. This doesn't seem like a tough decision."

I got up, and Khalaf stood too.

"What I'm offering might end further bloodshed even sooner," I insisted. "Way sooner."

"Yes, it *might*," Khalaf pointed out. "This uni is a guarantee, though."

"It's a guarantee to a quick burial. They're ready to respond if anything happens to the colt."

Yukimura tugged the uni closer to him and rubbed his mane. "We'll just have to respond before they realize anything's happened, then." He stood up and rested his hands on my shoulders. "You obviously made some sort of connection with these creatures while you were with them, but we don't have that luxury. The answer is no. I'm sorry."

I couldn't blame them. Their arguments made sense. From where they stood, I was looking through a tiny visor, where only Amy was in sight. Not only were they good soldiers, but they were good people.

Attempting to reason with unicorns sounded insane, even to me. Still, the look in the Alpha's eyes had to account for something. I hated having to admit it, but maybe they weren't the monsters I thought them to be.

I groaned, realizing I wanted to save the unicorns almost as much as I wanted to save Amy.

"Are you okay, son?" Yukimura asked.

I glanced at Mellis' sidearm too hard, evaluating if I could force them to hand over the foal. Yeah, right. Four highly trained Special Ops personnel against me.

"You don't want to do that," Mellis told me, shaking his head. "Just relax, okay? We're on the same side, remember?"

I sat down, my foot tapping the ground. "We're making a mistake."

The colt started to buck as he tried to shake the muzzle off his mouth. Something had excited him. Every soldier stood, weapons drawn.

"They're close," Sarge said. "Check for ripples."

"There!" Pashkov cried as she raised her rifle and fired. Blue plasma spat out of the barrel.

Mellis and Khalaf forced me down and shielded me with their own bodies while they fired. I hollered for them to stop, but the rounds were too loud.

Blue unibeams zipped from every direction. Despite their tech, Special Ops could only do so much when ambushed and fully exposed.

I rolled onto my back and covered my ears. As I did, I noticed the visual displacement behind Yukimura's back.

"Sarge," I cried. "On your six!"

A horn erupted through his left shoulder before he could move. His yell made the others turn around as the unicorn pinned him to the ground. The unicorn lifted his camo, withdrew his horn, and looked at me. It was Zupho. He placed a hoof on top of the sergeant's neck, keeping him down.

Everyone, including the unis, stopped firing.

"What the hell are you doing?" I asked as I stood up.

What you cannot. The Alpha may have placed her faith in you, but not I. Her colt will be returned to us, one way or another.

Pashkov had her sights on Zupho, while Mellis and Khalaf kept their weapons drawn on the other four unicorns. A standoff. Great.

The gunner edged her crosshairs between Zupho's eyes. "I guess we have something in common, Miles. You."

The unicorns had used me the same way the team had used the colt. I had led them straight to us.

I placed myself between Pashkov's barrel and Zupho. "Let's all calm down. We can sort this out!"

"It looks a little late for that," Mellis said over his shoulder.

Yukimura groaned, still on the ground.

I stepped back. "Zupho, listen to me. I know you're trying to protect your leader's baby. That's noble of you, but these people have made an oath to defend our own people—our own children—by any means necessary too. Don't you get it? We're more alike than you think!"

You manipulate with words, but I believe in the value of actions. We watched you from afar, and your deeds proved useless. You had your chance.

"You know what?" Pashkov said. "Miles forgot to mention one other thing about us: We're sore losers. If this is where it ends for us, fine, but you won't get what you want either, uni."

I knew what she would do next in an instant. I leaped in front of the colt as Pashkov aimed and fired.

The blast struck my stomach like an icicle launched from a tiny catapult. The impact spun me around. The heat was so spectacular, it felt cold. I couldn't move. And then, the pain was gone—along with the sensation in my legs.

"Miles!" I heard Khalaf cry.

I watched Zupho take his hoof off Yukimura and back away. The two stared at one another, as if sharing momentary mental exchange of some sort before the sergeant sat up.

"Everybody stand down," Yukimura ordered as he placed a hand over his wound.

Zupho moved away even more, and the other unicorns did the same.

Pashkov slid to my side and rested my head in her lap. She spoke what sounded like Russian, repeating the same words over and over. I assumed she was apologizing.

Zupho trotted over to me. His black eyes were as sharp as ever, though hints of confusion shone through.

You leaped in front of our young when he is not your own. Explain.

I chuckled through my cough; I sounded like Amy. "Blame it on stupid muscle memory."

The unicorn examined me. He didn't seem to understand what the shot had done to me as he nudged my body with his horn.

The colt, freed of the sergeant's grip, hurried over to Zupho's side. The two nuzzled each other momentarily before Zupho nudged the colt to the rest of his group. One of them escorted him away while the other three returned. The remaining four stood together. The tips of their horns sparked and glowed as they charged up.

"Zupho," I managed to beg.

He glanced at me, and then lifted his head. The glow from his horn dimmed away, and the others followed his lead.

Fine. Your actions are the only reason these "good soldiers" will be spared. He turned to Yukimura, glaring. *Tell your people this: You face us with aggression, and we respond with aggression. We witness compassion, and we respond with compassion. Whatever our next course will be is up to you.*

Zupho walked away, and the others followed.

Mellis raised his weapon; he had a clear shot. Khalaf, however, placed his hand on the barrel and lowered the weapon.

The Alpha will remember your agreement, Timothy Miles, Zupho whispered into our heads. *Your people can make preparations for your sister's retrieval at this location. And, sergeant, do not bother telling anyone where we are. We will be gone by the time you arrive.*

They disappeared. Now that the excitement had worn off, I realized the rest of my body had gone numb. I thought I had been paralyzed, but now all my other senses were beginning to fade too.

"Mellis, call for a medic dispatch, now!" Yukimura said over my limp body. "You're going to be fine, Miles. Just hold on."

A comforting lie.

I'm so sorry, Amy, I thought, wishing I had the unicorn's gift of telepathy. *I meant to say good-bye. Still, you were worth it. And so was the baby red unicorn. An innocent for an innocent. A good trade. Maybe this will lead to something greater.*

About the Author

When drawing fanfic graphic novels was no longer fulfilling enough as a teen, Raphyel Jordan ventured to greater adventures in storytelling. Now, when he isn't busy saving the world through his trusty video games, he spends time writing about exciting worlds untouched by man.

Jordan writes young adult science fiction and fantasy. For more details on characters and art, visit: RaphyelMJordan.com.

HIS MOST VIOLENT FRIEND

GREGORY D. LITTLE

With a groan and a thud, the superweapon broke down. Again.

"Blood and flame," Del swore, blowing out his cheeks in a sigh. His father had taught him that artificer work was ninety percent repair and maintenance. Del had naively thought the finest of the Imperial Army's technology might have been an exception.

The vast weapon stood before and above him, blocking out the sky with a blood-hued bulk battered and scarred from five years of conquest. The men called the mechanism "the red unicorn," but despite its crimson armor plate, four-legged locomotion, and the single void-black, hraxite horn protruding from its head, it was far too stocky to truly look like a horse.

It was also inert as a rock. The trapezoidal fueling pylon connecting the unicorn's underbelly with the ground offered some stability, but the autumn winds were stiff. A nasty gust had set the unicorn swaying, making it far more dangerous to the army on whose side it fought than to the city it was tasked with conquering.

Out of foolish hope, Del gave the crank protruding from the pylon one last turn. He told himself it would work this time. The red unicorn would launch itself forward from the pylon, gallop across earth already ruined from its previous passages, and smash its way through the city wall beyond. Holding his breath, Del toggled an activation lever the length of his arm.

There wasn't even the groan and thud.

In the distance, Strathryen's wall peeked through the great arched hole in the side of the mountain within which the city lay. A short tunnel provided the only exterior access to the mountain's hollow core, and the latest alabaster section of wall remained stubbornly unblemished. A single pearl set in the mottled oyster-gray of the mountain's stone.

Even if the damned thing worked, the twice-damned moles would only rotate a fresh section of wall into position, and we'd be at it again tomorrow. Del quashed his frustration, embarrassed at his mental use of the slur. *Your mother taught you better. Remember, you're here to earn enough to support her and Aubri.* Since Father's death, Del's mother and sister depended on him. It was easy to forget after five years apart.

Strathryen was unique. With only one entrance into the mountain, the Thryens had built their city wall atop a massive gear buried beneath the mountain. Whenever the unicorn demolished a section of wall, the masters of the city rotated the gear before the army could pour into the breach, moving the ruined section of wall out of the way and presenting a fresh one through the narrow mountain aperture.

In the beginning, soldiers had tried to rush the breach the moment it was formed, only to be smashed between debris and mountain as the great gear turned. Wall and unicorn were evenly matched. The horned battering ram took almost as much damage as it gave in each attack. It was all the army could do to drag their wounded superweapon away each time before it was crushed forever as the early soldiers had been.

There was no way to starve out the city. The Thryens grew fungal food in tunnels too deep to reach. There had always been rumors of secret tunnels leading from city to countryside, but if they existed, no human had ever found them. Smashing Strathryen's entire wall bit by bit was the only option. And the sole weapon the army possessed capable of such destruction might as well have been a statue.

Sweating despite the chill, Del resisted the urge to kick the pylon as the scarlet glow of the runes running up its side began to fade, their magic dissipating unspent. He glanced around, sensing the eager tension of the army slipping into disappointment and even anger. Tradition dictated that every on-duty soldier stand in formal ranks to watch each charge of the red unicorn, ready in case this was the day the last of Strathryen's accursed wall fell and the city was opened to the army's assault.

Waiting to go home, in other words.

Sighing again, Del replaced the red flag in the pylon's receptacle with a black one. No attack today. *Please let there be one tomorrow.*

O O O

While the winch teams worked to lower the unicorn back to the ground, Del moved off to prep the service area. Even a month ago, he'd have had several helpers, but casualties of all kinds struck the men and women who worked the unicorn at a far greater rate than they did the soldiery. Del was all that remained, his fellows whittled away until the unicorn, his last, most violent friend, was all he had left.

Two men Del had never seen before approached from the edge of the wide ring of stones designating the servicing area. One was haughty, his black, flinty eyes scowling above the perfect circle of mustache and beard which ringed his mouth as if drawn in by charcoal pencil. He wore his black hair close-cropped, a style that imitated that of military officers, but even the most arrogant of officers would never dress as this man did, in silks and brushed velvets.

As he drew close, the overwhelming smell of roses wafted from him. It was a scent Del associated with his mother and her garden, but it was layered on so thick it threatened to curdle the memory and make Del gag. Despite the scent's strength, the perfumed man carried himself like the entire world emitted a distinctly unpleasant odor.

His companion wore plate armor that protruded at odd angles and was covered in cracked enamel. It clinked as he drew to a halt, his face covered by a strange helm of many faceted angles. A wide, scarred leather belt encircled his waist, and a ribbon of segmented steel links wound around the belt.

The steel ribbon, edged on two sides and sporting hooked barbs at intervals along the flats, was connected to a hilt and cross guard carried in the man's right hand. A whipsword. Supremely difficult to master, too few people could manage the weapon to make it worth employing in massed combat.

It was a weapon for sadists and torturers. Del felt his stomach drop and splash into something oily and icy by turns.

"Such a pity," the haughty man said by way of greeting. "I'd so hoped to see the mechanism in action."

Del had to suppress a grunt at the term. It was tough to send the unicorn into battle day after day and not think of it as a living thing.

"I understand there have been more and more problems with the mechanism of late," the haughty man continued. "That it's even begun to slow the war effort."

His words carried an air of authority that Del didn't like. He'd mistakenly assumed the man was some visiting dignitary from the capital, there to acquire a plausible basis for the various war stories he would tell to impress his friends later.

"I am Inquisitor Imris," the haughty man said, and the oily, icy sensation in Del's stomach shot outward along all his nerves. "I have been sent by His Most Gloried Radiance to root out the cause of the war's stalled progress and guide it back to the path of expediency. Our emperor suspects foul play may be at work."

"I can assure you that's not the case, Inquisitor." Del forced himself to stand upright. Conspiracies of spies and saboteurs were easy fodder for suspicious minds. "The truth is far more mundane." He hesitated, not wanting to make excuses, but having begun, he had to continue. "We've been out here a long time. Even great works such as the ... the mechanism wear out."

After five years of constant war and thrice as many cities captured, the siege had become a race to see which side's technological marvel would permanently fail first. All to sate an emperor whose lust for conquest and expansion Del now saw was insatiable. It had not felt so at first. It had seemed a good living, something that could keep Del's family fed after his father's death.

"Come with me, Artisan Lieutenant," Imris said.

A slight shuffle of the armored whipswordsman's feet put Del's thoughts of disobedience to rest.

"We are going to have a chat in the general's tent."

O   O   O

The general's gloomy pavilion seemed to eat the daylight, doubling down on the pall the inquisitor's presence cast. Del stood before General Ober, his commanding officer as ashen as the tent walls, and flanked by Imris and the whipswordsman.

What happened? What news did this inquisitor bring that could age the general another five years in a day?

Del had trouble meeting the general's eyes even as the man weakly dressed him down, parroting Imris's words about how important the unicorn was to the war effort. Never mind that Ober had only yesterday reminded Del that equipment—or men—left in the field for five years could never be expected to do what he was now ordering Del to do.

The whipswordsman fiddled with the coils around his waist with one gauntleted fist, loosening them slightly before pulling them taut again with a tug of the hilt. The paired actions shifted the coils over time, and Del found himself following the stop-and-start path of one particular barb, damaged in some previous use, as it wended its way along the man's leather-clad waist.

"I do hope you are paying attention," Imris said to Del. "And, General Ober, I would think a man with so much at stake could muster more conviction when demanding a higher quality of performance from his men." He clucked his tongue. "I find overt displays of leverage distasteful, but they are sometimes warranted. Need I remind you of the state I left your family in upon my departure from the capital?"

The hairs on Del's arms and neck rose at the same rate as the remaining blood drained from Ober's bearded face.

"No need to remind," the general said, his voice as faint as if it came from his deathbed. "'Unharmed for the nonce,' you said, 'but unharmed is far from comfortable.'"

"Yes, indeed," Imris responded, his words emphasized by the slinking sound of the whipswordsman toying with his coils. Imris's lips twisted as he spoke, as though he did indeed find the words distasteful. "The emperor grows impatient and will press on any levers available to him. And do not think," Imris said, turning slithery eyes back to Del, "that his levers stop at the capital. I had long leagues to study your records, Artificer Lieutenant Del Trayvin. General Ober's family is in our grasp, yet perhaps their distance removes some of the impact. But you grew up very near here, didn't you?"

The last of the inquisitor's words reached Del as though through a long tunnel, fuzzy with distance. His body went numb.

"I suggest," Imris said, "that you get the mechanism operational with all haste."

o o o

Strathryen's pristine wall silently mocked Del from its crevice in the mountain. Beneath the bright autumn sky, he directed the winch teams to lay the unicorn on its side. He emptied it of parts as quickly as he dared, carefully documenting each action so he might reverse it once he'd found the problem.

Imris and his pet torturer were seldom far.

"Have you found the time to visit your dear mother and sister?" the inquisitor asked once, almost casually. "How nice it must be to find yourself so close to home after so long away. I confess to some concern when I learned this fact." He turned his gaze back toward the general's pavilion, eyes disappointed. "How could our good general allow sole control of our greatest strategic asset to fall to a man who may very well harbor *sympathies* for the enemy? It positively reeks of conspiracy."

Anger flashed in Del, only partly from the guilt of *not* having visited his family, but he quashed it. "I assure you I'm a loyal soldier of the Imperium, Inquisitor Imris," he said. *What more do you want me to say? There's no one else qualified to work on the unicorn.* "I'm loyal *because* of my family. It's my wartime salary that supports them."

The Imperium's wars had begun shortly after Del's father had died. Without those wars, Del could have done as his father had done, supporting the family by plying his trade as an artificer on well pumps and mills in his own village, a half-day's ride from the army's current camp. But wars brought price spikes, forcing Del to search for more lucrative use of his skills.

Imris fixed him with an unreadable expression before blessedly moving on, giving the unicorn's hraxite horn a wide berth where it came nearest to touching the ground. Del's thoughts slipped crazily. He imagined himself running up behind Imris and shoving the man into the horn. But with the unicorn's magic drained away, save for the last dregs pooling in its heart, the horn of black crystal would do no more than render a man unconscious at a touch.

Anger made work difficult, and Del lost another hour before regaining his concentration.

At midafternoon on the second day, in the midst of a delightfully Imris-free stretch of time, Del dug out a gear stripped of half its teeth, probably during the last attack. It took him two hours to replace it and the rest of the evening to reassemble everything. His hands throbbed and ached, and all he could smell or taste was the sweet tang of oil, but it was done.

Relief washed through him, dragging exhaustion in its wake, but he sent a runner bearing news of his success before allowing himself to sit. His limbs shook with weariness and hunger, but the former won out. He passed out beneath the rising moons.

O O O

Del had worked with machinery for too long not to recognize the feeling of cold steel against his skin, though he had never woken to the sensation against his throat.

Moving nothing else, he opened his eyes.

His first thought was he had slept away the rest of the month, seeing five moons in the sky where there should have been only two. Then he realized his mistake.

Three pale, round faces stared down at him with large, blank eyes that were all pupil. The sight would have unnerved anyone who hadn't grown up near the area. The Thryens had risked much, coming on a night with the two largest moons bright and waxing.

Their black-shrouded bodies were oddly lanky for subterranean dwelling, and they carried a cold, earthy smell from the depths with them on the rare occasions when they ventured beyond their walls. To outsiders, Thryens were indistinguishable from one another, so it was entirely possible that Del had known one or all of these individuals growing up.

"Speak not!" the one holding the knife commanded, and the choppy syntax and clipped accent awoke an unexpected wash of nostalgia and homesickness in Del, despite the threat of death. "You are the device's last master. We have seen to that. Yet still you send it against us without hesitation."

Sorrow warred with fear and anger in Del's heart. He kept his breathing shallow, the better to avoid tempting the knife's edge. If he understood them correctly, they were admitting responsibility for at least some of the "misfortunes" that had befallen his fellow artificers.

So unlike them. For a subterranean race, many thought subterfuge was their natural state, but that was not the case. They detested trickery or spycraft. For them to kill or kidnap his fellow artificers ...

It means they've done the math, and they know we will win unless they take drastic action. Some in the army had despaired that the Thryens must be simply rebuilding the wall within the mountain as they rotated fresh sections into place. If so, the assaults would never end. This revelation suggested otherwise.

The realization woke nausea in Del's gut. The injustice of it cramped within him. The Thryens were the peaceful denizens of a peaceful city. But making war against them was how his family ate. Not to mention what would happen to him if he failed to uphold his duty.

"You must not allow this injustice to proceed," the Thryen holding the knife said. "Sabotage the device beyond repair!"

Del tried to speak, and the knife eased back a bit as the apple of his throat worked. He thought he felt wetness where the blade's edge had rested. The pressure remained, though, a warning not to speak too loudly.

"I can't do that," Del said. "They are already suspicious. They are watching for sabotage."

"Then turn the device against your own!" one of the other Thryens said. "Break them. Make it seem a malfunction."

The thought made Del dizzy with horror.

"If your people surrender," he said, speaking with a voice that seemed not his own, "you'll be spared the worst of the emperor's wrath." Disgust welled in him, threatening to choke off his speech, all the more because he couldn't be certain he was telling the truth.

"Disappointing," the lead Thryen hissed. "You were better when young, Del Trayvin."

Del darted his eyes away, feeling heat in his cheeks. He almost called out the names of Thryens he could remember, but the knife's promise remained.

"You shame us," the lead Thryen said. "You force us to choose for you. You will ensure the device can no longer harm us before the next moonrise, or your kin will bear your shame into their graves."

One of them bent and set something at his feet. Then, like wraiths, they were gone. After a solid minute of waiting and breathing as little as possible, Del rose to see what they'd left him, dread dragging at his joints.

He recognized the small circle of metal even by the light of only two moons. So far as he knew, his mother had never removed her wedding ring once in all the time since his father had died.

Del rose, fighting through exhaustion, hunger, and fear. He had work to do yet.

O   O   O

"And yet here I was to understand that you had finished your task." Imris's voice rang out of the thinning darkness like a death knell.

Del froze where he was, bent over the red unicorn's attack pattern gearbox, freshly removed and lit by torch, moon, and starlight. *Lie. Tell him you were mistaken, that you found something else wrong.* But Del's faculties were spent. What little remained was focused on the modifications he had to make in such haste.

"No matter how many opportunities I give you," the inquisitor said, "you continue to disappoint."

Belatedly, Del opened his mouth to respond that this wasn't what it looked like. But, of course, it was exactly what it looked like. His good reasons would never satisfy the inquisitor.

Out of the darkness from which Imris's voice emerged, Del heard the sound of rustling metal links.

"Do you know how I spent my night, Artisan Lieutenant?"

Del pinched his eyes shut and gritted his teeth. His weariness with Imris's self-infatuation was almost enough to drown out his fear.

"No, Inquisitor Imris, I don't."

"Your repairs were proceeding so very slowly, so I took it upon myself to visit your family homestead," he said mildly.

A jag of fear pulsed through Del, so palpably familiar that at first his memory was confused. Then the pieces fell together.

He tried to kidnap them, but found the homestead abandoned.

But of course, Del's family had already been kidnapped. And say what you will about the unpleasantness of your family being kidnapped, at least it could only happen once at a time.

It was almost funny. *Imris threatened to do the same thing. The Thryens just beat him to the punch.*

He wondered if the place had been ransacked. He imagined flatware shattered and smears of blood. *No. No, the Thryens wouldn't be violent.* He swallowed around a lump in his throat. *Not before their deadline.* Del had no such confidence in Imris's tender care. *Perhaps the Thryens did me a favor.*

"You think I evacuated my family to keep them safe from you." Del turned and saw Imris and his pet sadist stepping into the torchlight emanating from the posts near the unicorn's great snout. "And you're here to arrest me. But I didn't rescue my family. As a matter of fact, I'm here trying to do that right now." No point in hiding it anymore.

His heart hammered so hard he wondered if they could see the vibrations in his chest wall. Imris was not stupid. The light of understanding dawned on his face.

"Ah, I see. Your childhood … neighbors, as it were, were quicker than I." Imris laughed, a rich, rolling sound like thunder off canyon walls.

That laugh smothered Del's last hesitation.

"You have my sympathies, Artisan Lieutenant, but of course, you see the bind this puts me in. Whereas before I merely suspected wrongdoing on your part, now you confess it." His features drew down, as if the false sadness was a set of hooks pulling them into the ground.

"Sergeant Kedri," Imris said, "take him into custody. But first, make certain he is unable to run."

With one fluid movement of Kedri's arm, the coiled whipsword spiraled into the air, glittering mirrors of torchlight chained together in a grand arc. The edges of that blade would sever both flesh and bone, while the barbed flats would merely strip skin from sinew.

Cursing, Del lunged for the unicorn's nearest foot. The whip came down, trailing a line of fire along his leg though his rugged work leathers. Del bit back a shriek, hand outstretched toward the unicorn's kill switch, which would purge any pooled energy still lurking within the mechanism without resulting in dangerous movement. At least, that was how the safety interlocks had been designed to function. But those interlocks were housed in the attack pattern gearbox, which now lay strewn across the dewy grass and mud.

Kedri was in no hurry. With a casual twist of one shoulder, he tugged the end of his whipsword back into the air to arc above him, letting it gather energy for its next dreadful strike.

His leg throbbing and barely able to support him, Del reached the kill switch and fell against the lever with all his weight until he felt it snap into place. Instead of harmlessly releasing magical force through concealed vents all along the unicorn's body, the great mechanism expended the dregs of its energy, fulfilling remembered orders from its last activation.

The hraxite horn flared black, pushing out ribbons of darkness that deepened the night around it. As the whipsword sliced a hissing trajectory through the air, its tip ventured too close to one of those ribbons.

The glittering links vaporized in a blink. The trickle of energy remaining in the horn was enough to slither down the steel whip's length and evaporate Kedri's arm in the bargain. The maimed man yelped in shock then began to scream as Del dove free of the unicorn's foot. He landed hard. The pain of his leg blinded his vision for a few moments.

When Del's sight returned, he saw Imris watching the unicorn in stunned silence. The metal beast was trying to run lying on its side. Then one-armed Kedri, mad with pain and apparently unaware of what he was doing, barreled into Imris, knocking both himself and the inquisitor to the ground.

As the men fell, the last pools of magic within the unicorn reached its open mouth. Dutifully executing the chewing motion intended to tear through stone during an attack, the unicorn's head gouged a furrow into the earth, sweeping toward Imris and Kedri. The great jaws began to close.

Del tried not to hear the sound that came when those steel teeth met, heedless of the bodies of the men they had to travel through.

It was fortunate that all that steel was already lacquered red.

o o o

Sandy-eyed from worry and lack of sleep, Del watched his most violent friend embark on its most important attack.

As always, the army stood in ranks to watch, weapons at the ready. General Ober had mounted his warhorse at the front of the ranks. If he wondered at the absence of the inquisitor and his whipswordsman, the general said nothing to Del of it.

The earth shook. The red unicorn's thunderous passage sent clods of soil and ruined vegetation skyward.

Del grew tenser with every step. How long would the Thryens stay their hand upon his mother and sister once they saw the unicorn headed their way?

This is the only way, Del thought. *The only way that I can save everybody.*

The emperor's hunger for conquest would never be sated.

The men were silent as the unicorn shook the world on its approach, but Del heard an audible intake of breath when his new commands for the beast took hold. Despite drawing ever closer to the pristine wall, the unicorn didn't accelerate. When its cantering legs should have sped to a gallop, they bunched instead. The gasps among the onlookers became cries and a sea of pointing fingers.

In the city too, I'll bet. Are you watching, Mother? Aubri?

Ignoring the wall, the unicorn skidded almost to a halt, then drove upward from its hind legs and speared its hraxite horn into the peak of the rock aperture in the mountain's outer face.

Every good artificer knew the weakness of any arch was its keystone.

Cracks formed quickly amid the thunder and spread outward like jagged, black lightning bolts, following flaws in the mountain stone. The collapse began with a sheeting wall of rock that cascaded down like a cataract onto the unicorn.

Del winced every time a sharp spear of stone pierced his friend's steel hide. But his heart leaped with hope as well. *I can't save you from the emperor's hunger,* he thought at the city and his family, *but I can make it so you can't be reached from the outside.* It was the best he could do, though he knew it meant never seeing his mother and sister again. The thought left a freely bleeding wound in him. *Be kind to them,* he thought at the Thryens.

The moment the red unicorn's hraxite heart was breached was obvious. The roar vibrated through Del's skull like the blow of a maul. Soldiers dropped their weapons to cover their ears; some men fell to the ground entirely.

Black blossoms erupted from every seam in the unicorn, and for an instant, it looked like disparate pieces of red steel floating in common orbit against the void of the night sky. Then another section of mountain gave way, and whatever remained of the red unicorn was buried beneath it without a trace.

The only way into the city was blocked, perhaps forever.

I'm sorry, my friend. Thank you. The rumbling subsided, and soldiers picked themselves off the ground in stunned silence. To Del's shock, a ragged cheer rose up from the ranks. It was wordless, a spontaneous explosion of long-repressed emotions. The men, at least, understood the meaning of what had happened. With no siege weapon, there could be no more siege.

General Ober, his face unreadable, turned his mount and moved through the dissolving ranks, back toward the tents.

o o o

The army marched with renewed vigor. General Ober had not sent to the capital for instructions. His order had gone out at once.

The forces of the Imperium were homeward bound.

Del did not leave with them. The general had listened to his request, then simply turned and stared off in the opposite direction toward the assembling columns, giving Del his tacit permission to leave.

He knew it was foolish to do so, a last, vain hope, but Del returned to his family's homestead. He only stayed a day before setting out again, unable to bear the emptiness.

It was a slog to catch up with the army on his injured leg, but there was nowhere else to go. The great columns had slowed to a crawl. Local refugees transformed into camp followers now clogged the army's flanks.

As days passed, Del shed his leathers and uniform bit by bit, trading them for clothes more befitting a civilian. He found himself mending wagon wheels and tent poles in exchange for meals and safe places to bed down. He tried not to think of his family's fate. He had vague notions of returning to find a way into the buried city. Perhaps his mother and sister would forgive him.

More than a week into the slow march, he was scanning the camp for work that needed doing when his eyes picked out two female figures from perhaps a dozen others washing and mending tent canvas. Del's gaze latched onto them with a familiarity that went deeper than bone despite the hooded cloaks they wore.

Tunnels. The thought came unbidden. *Secret tunnels from the city to the countryside ...*

The younger of the two women noticed Del's scrutiny first and turned to face him. His sister had always had sharp eyes, and they widened as they met Del's own. Aubri's face split into the sunny smile he'd been missing for years.

About the Author

Rocket scientist by day and fantasy and science fiction author by night, Gregory D. Little's short fiction can also be found in *The Colored Lens*. His debut YA fantasy novel, *Unwilling Souls*, will be released in 2015. He lives in Virginia with his wife and their yellow Lab.

LAURA'S MAGIC CLOCK

ROBERT J. MCCARTER

The *tick-tick-tick* of the old clock greets me as I slowly emerge from unconsciousness, my bladder full, my head thick, wisps of dreams circling my mind. I want to go back to sleep. I *need* to go back to sleep, but the *tick-tick-tick* won't let me submerge into the darkness I crave.

I roll over on the smooth, silk sheets and pull the pillow under my chest. I hate silk sheets, how my body slips around on them, but she had loved them, so I keep them. Just like she had been so excited when she found that damn old tick-tock clock at the flea market. The old man that sold it to us told her it was magic, that it had a gypsy spell and would "grant a great boon to its owner at their darkest hour."

It's an odd thing. A rearing unicorn about a foot tall made of polished redwood with a brass horn and hooves, a round clock under the creature's belly.

"It's hideous," I told her, the old man giving me the stink eye.

"I love it, and I love you." Her face lit up like an eight-year-old on Christmas morning. I bought it for her—if you had seen her smile, you would have bought it too. She smiled with her whole face, her cheeks full, her blue eyes scrunching like upside-down crescent moons. She hugged me hard, my nose filling with her delicious scent, my heart overflowing with love. I didn't say a word when she put it in our bedroom, despite the fact that I hated the sound of it.

Tick-tick-tick. It's the same every morning. That damn clock brings me back to the world, makes me think of her.

She's a pronoun now. It's always "her" or "she" these days. I don't speak her name. I don't think her name. Pronoun she may be, but I can't let go of her. I can't even move that damn clock into the living room.

The cold air on my skin wakes me up a bit more as I get out from under the covers, my bare feet taking me to that damn clock as if of their own volition—and it's "damn clock" in my mind now. It wakes me up. It reminds me of her. Her smile, her scent, those crescent-moon eyes, come flooding back to me.

I lay one hand on the back of the unicorn, feeling the raised grain of the wood, smelling the pungent polish she had lavished it with when we got home. With my other hand I turn the cool brass fob on the back and wind up the clock, a clickity-click-clack sound briefly overwhelming the tick-tick.

I can't let it wind down either. This used to be her ritual, winding the clock first thing in the morning before doing the bladder's or the stomach's bidding. "Gotta wind it to keep the magic going," she would say. But she's not here to do it, so I do it.

It's almost like the clock is talking to me. *Tick-tick.* It's time to wake up. *Tick-tick.* Don't forget to wind me. *Tick-tick.* She's gone, but I can help you remember her. *Tick-tick.* You know you want to remember her. *Tick-tick.* She's dead because of you. *Tick-tick.* The guilt is tearing you apart.

I wish the clock had really been magic. Maybe then she would have lived.

O O O

Out of the bedroom and away from the damn unicorn clock, my life seems almost normal. I shower, dress, grab coffee and a bagel on the way to the subway, and sit in the rhythmically bouncing car as it takes me to Wall Street.

The subway is all about smells. Dirt tracked in from the last rainstorm. Bodies and their sweat and perfume concentrated by proximity. And something else—it smells old. As if the decades have permeated the worn steel poles and drab plastic seats with its own scent. As if time itself has a smell—not a very pleasant one, I might add.

All the other senses get tuned out there. Everyone's got head-phones on, their heads down, fiddling with their phones, trying to pretend they're not in a little metal car zipping along under the towering skyscrapers above. Everyone's bodies are closed in tight, although you can feel the touch of your neighbor's hip if you're sitting, or an elbow swaying into yours if you're standing.

But you tune all of that out. Scroll through Facebook. Tap on your laptop. Blast your ears with music. Then, all that's left is that smell. Dirt, sweat, perfume, time, desperation.

That morning, I'm standing and wasting time on Facebook. I don't want to waste time on Facebook, with its endless pictures of food and self-congratulatory posts from people I barely know. I should be reading a book, for God's sake. But I don't have the will.

I flick past one of those annoying link-bait articles a girl I had dated briefly in high school liked—and being glad I had only dated her briefly—the *clack-clack* of the subway sounding like the *tick-tick* of that clock, and I smell her.

Maybe my nose is just overloaded by the subway. Maybe my mind is playing tricks on me. But it's *her*. I'm sure of it. Perfume in the bottle is not the same as perfume on the skin. A good perfume changes with each person, transforms into something unique.

This scent is sweet, like roses, with something distinctly sharp, like aged Parmesan cheese, plus something a little sour and lemony. Her scent.

My heart starts *thump-thump-thumping* in my chest and prickly sweat forms on the small of my back. I don't move fast. I am hoping she's there, but knowing it's impossible. I want so desperately to see her face, but not wanting the inevitable disappointment.

The subway slows down for the Fulton Station stop. I look up from my phone and see a woman with long brown hair and a dark coat stepping out of the car. I can't see her face, but the hair, with its chestnut hue and gentle wave at the tips, is hers. The scent is hers.

I feel her name form on my tongue. No longer a pronoun, I mumble, "Laura?"

My hand, still gripping the steel rail, shakes. I let go, reflexively rubbing my sweaty palm on my pants before stepping off the subway car into the cavelike station.

I can't see her anymore. She's lost in the crowd. The train whooshes away behind me and the crowd departs, and I just stand there.

It smelled like Laura. What I saw of her looked like Laura. But it can't be her. Laura's dead.

O   O   O

Some people believe in ghosts, think any little oddity—like the flickering of a light—is their loved one communicating with them. I don't buy it. I don't believe in ghosts, but I do believe that most of us are haunted. Not by some literal, ethereal spirit but by our pasts and our regrets and our guilt.

She has been haunting me since her death. And it's no surprise. I'm to blame. How could I not be haunted by it?

My nose is still full of her as my feet carry me up out of the claustrophobia of the subway into a crisp New York morning. The sounds of the city descend on me. Honking cars, a distant ambulance—its siren bouncing off the high-rises of Broadway—the shuffling of pedestrians, the murmur of conversation.

I pull my leather jacket tight around me and look for her. But it's no use. If it had been her—even though it couldn't have been her—she would be lost in the crowd by now.

I join the throng and head south towards Rector Street and my job at Larry's Downtown Deli. I'd gotten off the subway too soon, but I don't feel like going back down. I breathe deeply of the smell of New York City hoping to get another whiff of her, but all I smell is exhaust, old grease, coffee from a street vendor, and odor de Dumpster. If you live in a big city, you know what I'm talking about. The scent is not pleasant, but familiar. It's so strong you can actually taste it.

At work, I tick-tick through my day with a rhythm almost as regular as that redwood clock. Running frozen pizzas through the little oven, stocking the salad bar, checking people out, my feet always moving across the worn linoleum.

After her death, I quit my job as a claims adjuster. The pressure was too much. I've been running one of those little ubiquitous Big Apple delis for the last six months. Not that there isn't any pressure at the deli, there's plenty, but because I'm always dealing with customers and I'm always moving, my mind has a harder time wandering back. Back to when Laura became a pronoun in my vocabulary.

O O O

There is surprisingly little to the story of her death. A Wednesday night out in the city. Too much to drink—way too much—she more than I. Distraction. Tragedy.

She was also a claims adjustor and had just received a "stern talking to" from her supervisor over some of the claims she had handled. She was, honestly, too kind for the job.

It wasn't much, really. Not in the long view, but that night it was a big deal—thus the excessive drinking after work.

We had decided to walk home. Thirty blocks didn't seem that far in our inebriated state. Besides, I think going home right away would have felt like a return to reality, the last thing she wanted.

It was the end of summer, an almost full moon throwing silvery light down the high-rise canyons as we walked, a little unsteadily, and talked. She smiled a lot, widely and with her teeth showing, but her eyes never did that upside-down crescent moon thing, so even in my altered state I knew it wasn't a real smile.

We held hands. I kept squeezing hers, trying to let her know it was okay, that I loved her. I wore a gray suit, she a brown skirt with heels and a sweater. It was our work clothing; we had decided to drink our dinner as soon as we got off work.

"Oh," she said, her speech less slurred than it had been. "*This* is why you wanted to walk."

I didn't recall being the one wanting to walk. "What?"

We were on Columbus Circle, almost to Time Warner Center. She let go of my hand and pointed. A Tesla Model S was parked in front of the towering, glass-walled entrance. It was Batmobile-black and beautifully lit, looking like Bruce Wayne was about to step out wearing a tux with a supermodel in a red evening dress on his arm.

I'm not from New York. I grew up in California where everyone drives all the time, and truth be told, I miss owning a car and driving.

I stared, gape jawed. I smelled the city, dirt and exhaust and rotting trash. I heard the cars honking, tires humming, brakes squealing. I felt the warmth that had once been her hand in mine. But none of that mattered. It was just me and the beautifully designed electric car.

"I'm tired of ... of ..." she said, moving away from me, but I didn't turn. "Walking!" she added with a laugh once she had finally pulled the word out of her sodden consciousness.

I heard her heels scraping over the sidewalk. "Cabby!" she yelled.

Then horns blared, brakes screeched, and there was a sickening crunch, a scream, and a thud.

o   o   o

Dead is dead. The dead stay dead, except in my dreams.

I often dream of that night in front of Time Warner Center, the broken body of my Laura in my arms. After her last rattling breath and the last beat of her heart, she suddenly seemed light, somehow insubstantial. It was no longer Laura, just a body that looked like Laura. The demarcation was so sudden, so final.

In my dreams it's worse.

Sometimes she struggles to get up, but her broken limbs won't support her and she collapses with a wet thump. Other times I pull her into my arms and her blue eyes open, except they're not blue, they're all bloody and she says, "You did this," as coagulating blood pours out her mouth.

I did do wrong by her in the past. A brief moment of drunken infidelity cost us most of six months. The time I forgot her birthday. When she opened up to me about problems she was having with a coworker and I accidentally laughed.

Each time we would talk it out—much longer than I ever wanted—with the *tick-tick* of her clock in the background. I just wanted to apologize and move on, but she needed to talk about things. A lot.

But this we can't talk out. I can't tell her how sorry I am for getting so drunk. It was her bad day; I should have been taking care of her. I can't tell her how awful I feel for letting go of her hand. How horrified I am that a stupid car distracted me at the single moment in our history together when she needed me the most. If only I could apologize.

After the funeral, I quit my job and started working at the deli. I almost left New York, but it's all I have left of her. She is New York to me. We met the day I got to the city, after all, and we spent nearly every day after that together.

O   O   O

She is on the subway with me again today. That sweet, sharp, sour smell again alerts me to her presence. I glimpse a woman from behind that could be her. Long brown hair with a bit of curl at the bottom. Tall and willowy. A purposeful stride.

I get out a stop early and try to follow her. I push through the crowd as fast as I can, but when I come up into the bright sunlight of an April day, I can't find her. People everywhere, but not her.

My heart thumps in my chest the whole time, my mouth sour from the adrenaline playing in my veins. My head doesn't believe it can be her, but my body does.

The Fulton Station subway stop comes out near Zuccotti Park. It's not very big, just a paved area with cement benches and lots of trees. I find myself standing on the Broadway side, my legs shaky, watching, hoping, praying.

I feel like I'm a boy again, the time I broke the delicate porcelain vase my mother had loved. I held the sharp shards in my hands wishing I could take it back, praying that it hadn't really happened. But I couldn't do anything about the broken vase, just like I couldn't do anything about my broken Laura.

Broken is broken. Dead is dead.

The rhythmic honking on Broadway, for a moment, sounds like the *tick-tick* of the unicorn clock.

"Are you okay?" a woman asks.

I'm slumped against a streetlight, my head in my hands.

The woman's voice sounds young and sweet. It has a melodic lilt to it and a trace of a New England accent. My heart starts pounding again. *She* had a voice like that.

I look up but can't see much, the morning sun haloed behind her hair.

"Do you need me to call somebody?"

I blink against the sunlight, her name dancing on my lips, when I see the woman clearly—a ragged homeless lady with a grocery cart full of junk behind her.

She thinks I needed help. All the people in this park and she thinks I'm so bad off that she can help me.

"No. No, thank you," I mumble, getting up and walking toward the deli.

O   O   O

Laura and I never got married, officially. She had issues with her family and couldn't bear the thought of them all coming together—and the drama that would ensue—for her wedding.

I remember the night I asked her. We sat on the floor of our little apartment playing Scrabble.

"We should get married, you know," I said as I tried to figure out a word with two *T*s, an *S*, and an *I* that wasn't a dirty word.

I wasn't looking at her, but I heard her suck in air through her nose and hold it. I could feel her eyes on me, the tick-tick of that unicorn clock in our bedroom counting down the seconds.

Tick-tick. No answer yet.

Tick-tick. I couldn't look at her. What if she hated the idea? What if she was just staying with me until she found someone better? Although, after five years, I should have given up that irrational insecurity.

Tick-tick. Did she just sniff?

I finally looked up, and she was crying, but there was a smile on her face and her blue eyes were squished into those upside-down crescent moons. The tears freaked me out. Asking her freaked me out. I had thought about it for a long time, but didn't plan the asking.

"Are you okay?" I finally asked.

She nodded, swept the Scrabble board out of the way, the tiles clattering everywhere, and then she was in my arms. I tasted the salt of her tears and the perfumed waxiness of her lipstick. She was warm and so alive that night.

Later, after we made love, she told me she couldn't stand inviting her family to her wedding, and she couldn't get married without inviting her family. I mean, Vegas would have been fine with me, but she couldn't do it. She was caught in this familial paradox.

Hours later we were still on the floor, our backs up against the couch, drinking wine. I was frustrated that I couldn't figure out a way to meet her needs. Excited that she had said yes—although not directly in words. And tired from the glorious physical expression of her "yes."

I shrugged and smiled. "What do we do?"

She was quiet for a long time. The *tick-tick* of the clock and the honking of horns twenty floors below the only sounds. "I got it!" she said, her smile wide. She pulled a blanket around her nude body and sat right in front of me. "We don't need a priest, and we certainly don't need my family. Right here, right now, we are married. I am your wife, and you are my husband."

I studied her face, her beautiful face. High cheekbones, sparkling blue eyes, lovely full lips. She was always too good for me. Not just in terms of beauty, but the kind of person she was. She would carry granola bars in her purse and give them to homeless people. "They'll just drink any money," she told me once. "This way they can at least eat something." She always thought of others more than herself.

The declaration wasn't exactly what I wanted, but I wanted her even more. "Umm ... I do," I said.

She was on me again, her lips brushing at my ear. "I do, too. And I expect a ring."

O   O   O

I hate the salad bar most of all. People slop food all over, and I have to clean it up. Constantly. Bacon bits in the beets, hard-boiled eggs in the carrots, lettuce absolutely everywhere. It's disgusting.

It feels a little bit like of my own version of hell. A menial task that I keep doing—wiping, picking, refilling from the bins in the back. It goes on and on. It never ends. It seems like I can never catch up. Sometimes, though, I consider it my penance for what happened to her. Then I don't really mind it.

The deli is on the ground floor of old high-rise on Rector, just off Broadway. The walls are white and the fluorescent lights whiter. It isn't very big, just enough room for the little salad bar, the deli case, the baked goods, a small pizza oven, and the checkout area. One long counter with tables on the other side.

I'm on the night shift and actually making progress on the damn salad bar. I don't usually work nights—I'm the manager, after all—but some recent personnel turnover has me working doubles. During the day we've got at least two people. At night it's just one person from 10:00 p.m. to 2:00 a.m.

And then I smell her. Sweet like a flower, sharp like cheese, sour like citrus. That smell is in my soul. All our years together she used the same perfume. No one else ever smells that way.

I'm wiping between the round containers of the salad bar, my heart suddenly thumping in my head like a two-year-old with his first drum. I don't look up. I don't want to look up. What if I don't see anything? What if it is a woman walking away from me again or a homeless lady?

I read once that the sense of smell is hardwired directly into the brain. It's not like the eyes and the ears where you can see and hear things that aren't real. If you are smelling something, it's because those nerves are stimulated. There is a cause. There has to be.

I freeze, gripping the white rag as hard as I can. That smell doesn't go away. It gets stronger. It's coming from the person standing on the other side of the salad bar. I stare at the sliced cucumbers, but out of my peripheral vision I can see a dark skirt and a white blouse. The same thing she wore that night I failed her, the night she died.

"I'm sorry," I whisper as I close my eyes tight against the tears. "I'm so sorry."

That night came back, like it always did. I let go of her hand, just for a moment. The squeal of tires. A sickening crash. A scream.

Holding her in my arms, the metallic smell of blood mixing with her normal flowery scent. Feeling her life ebb away.

"Are you okay?" she asks.

"I'm sorry. I'm sorry. I'm sorry." I slide down to the floor, sitting among discarded bacon bits and shredded carrots.

I hear the clicking of high heels on linoleum, reminding me of the *tick-tick* of the clock in my bedroom. My arms around my knees, I rock back and forth chanting, "I'm sorry. I'm sorry. I'm sorry."

"Mister, are you okay?"

I hear her voice, but it's distant. That smell, sweet and sharp and sour, fills my nose. Images of that night fill my eyes as tears leak out.

I don't look. I can't look. It can't be her. But while my eyes are closed there is still the tiniest chance that it is.

The beeps of a dialing phone. "Yes, I'm at Larry's Downtown Deli on Rector, right off Broadway. Send an ambulance. Someone here needs help."

I feel a hand on my shoulder as I continue to rock. "It's going to be okay. You're going to be okay."

I don't believe her. I can't believe her. I keep my eyes closed.

O O O

Laura was smart, much smarter than me. I was a little better with numbers, but she was a lot better with people. She understood people in a way that always baffled me. She quickly seemed to "get" them and could say just the right thing.

That woman in the deli seems more and more like Laura.

"I'm right here," she says after I've been loaded into the ambulance. My eyes are still shut tight. She slips her warm hand into mine and squeezes. "I'm not going anywhere."

It's the kind of thing Laura would do.

Who is she, this late-night salad bar patron? She smells like Laura. Her voice is a lot like Laura's. She acts like Laura.

"I'm sorry," I whisper, probably for the hundredth time. The ambulance is on the move, the siren loud, the rumble of tires on pavement and the ever-present honking of cars making it hard to hear. I don't expect her to hear me.

"It's okay," she whispers back, her face close to mine, her Laura-smell filling my senses. "I forgive you."

There's a paramedic in the ambulance with us. I can smell his sweat and hear him move, but I don't care. It's like it's just me and Laura and no one else.

I hold my breath. Did she say that she forgave me? "You do?"

"Of course," she says with the smallest of chuckles. "You didn't mean to."

I squeeze her hand, and she squeezes back. It's her. It has to be her. Somehow she has come back to me. Somehow she is here. I think about the redwood unicorn clock and the gypsy spell. Can it be?

"I was so careless," I say. "I shouldn't have let go."

She gently squeezes my hand again. "It's okay, really it is."

My eyes are still closed. I don't dare look. I don't want to take the chance that the illusion, or spell, or whatever it is, will shatter.

"But how are you here?" I ask. "You can't be here."

"I'm … I'm here for you," she says, and I can hear something in her voice. It sounds thicker than it had and is tinged with sadness. Is she crying?

"I miss you, Laura," I say. "God, how I miss you."

We don't speak the rest of the trip, we just hold hands. It takes everything I have, but I keep my eyes closed. If this is a spell, if this is magic, I'm not willing to do anything that might disturb it.

When they open the ambulance doors and pull out the gurney, she says, "Give us a moment, will you?" She must be talking to the paramedics.

"I have to go," she says to me.

I take a deep breath of her scent, trying to fill myself up with it. "I miss you already."

She sniffs, and I feel a single tear fall onto my cheek. "I forgive you. You know that, don't you?"

I nod. I haven't cried much since Laura died, and I feel a tsunami of tears coming. "Yes. Thank you."

She squeezes my hand one last time. "I love you," she says.

"I love you too."

She leaves and I so miss the warmth of her hand. I hear her heels as they *click-click* on the pavement as she walks away.

O   O   O

I sit and stare at that garish old unicorn clock as it does its tick-tick thing on the dresser of our bedroom. No, of *my* bedroom. I have decided. It is time. But still I wait.

It's been three months since my breakdown in the deli, since the woman that smelled and sounded and acted like Laura said she forgave me. I've thought a lot about what happened that night and what happened afterwards. A few days in the hospital getting a psych evaluation, then into daily counseling for a while, now down to once a week.

I'm doing better, much better. I still miss Laura, I still feel guilty about what happened, but it is no longer tearing me apart and defining my every moment.

Tick-tick, the clock tells me. One step at a time is the way through this. One day at a time. One hour at a time. One *tick* at a time.

I never went back to the deli, I just couldn't return. I took some real time off and have tried to get my life together. I started back at the firm, staring at insurance claims all day.

Tick-tick. I still wish I hadn't let go of her hand, but I'm not perfect. I'm human. I make mistakes.

It's late, 11:00 p.m., and I should be sleeping, but I stare at the clock just a little longer.

Maybe that woman was just a Good Samaritan somehow playing the part of Laura. Maybe the clock is magic and it was really Laura coming back from the dead to help me. Maybe it doesn't matter.

I carefully pick up the clock and carry it out to the living room and place it on the mantel over the little gas fireplace. The unicorn looks good there. It doesn't seem so garish to me anymore.

This is Laura's magic clock, and I love it because of that, but I'm ready to sleep without that *tick-tick* in my ear.

About the Author

Robert J. McCarter lives in the mountains of Arizona with his beautiful wife and his ridiculously adorable dog, pounding away at the keyboard producing software (to make a living) and stories (to fill his soul and hopefully yours). He has written a series of first person ghost novels (starting with *Shuffled Off: A Ghost's Memoir*) and a superhero / love story series (*Neutrinoman and Lightningirl: A Love Story*). Find out more at: RobertJMcCarter.com.

THE CORRELATION EFFECT

NANCY DIMAURO

Dozens of eyes turned as I entered the gym. A wash of colors, from the violet of disbelief to sun-kissed yellow amusement, swept over their auras and mingled with the smell of old sweat in the room. I understood the amusement. Psyonics didn't train with the D.C. Metro Police, but my partner, Rick Muller, insisted.

"Vonna," Muller shouted from the other side of the gymnasium. Sure enough, his aura flashed buttercup in delight. "What're you wearing?"

I'd traded my leathers, a psy's first layer of armor, for fabric that wouldn't overheat or snag as I sparred. Animal-based materials like leather and silk protected my psionic senses from the stray emotions insens—humans without psychic abilities—unconsciously threw off. My navy blue silk workout clothes were a sharp contrast to Muller's cotton T-shirt and sweats. His dark brown hair, cut military short, made his square jaw seem more angular. Lines of muscles delineated his arms, abs, and thighs. A faint white line etched a scar on his left cheek and drew attention to his hazel eyes.

Cops moved out of my way.

"Tell me why am I doing this, again?" I planted my hands on my hips.

Muller's glee tipped to a brighter shade. He had none of an insens' fear of psyonics. Touching a psychic was the equivalent of offering your throat to a hungry vampire, yet Muller didn't hesitate to put a hand on my arm or shoulder. Occasionally, he'd even pat me on the back. I never told him how much his small signs of affection meant to me, but they did.

"Not every opponent's psy," he said.

Muller knew my psychic abilities were non-offensive. My education had, therefore, involved extensive unarmed combat training.

"Three minutes before you're on your back," I warned him.

"Can't wait, Spooky."

Bills passed between the officers who were presumably wagering on the outcome.

Muller tugged on my shirtsleeve and exposed a thin line of skin between it and my silk glove. He leveled a flat stare at me.

"Where's your comm?"

I was supposed to wear the tiny transmitter at all times.

"In my jacket. What? I'm with you."

He pointed to the unit attached to the back of his hand. "Use the damn thing."

We stalked to opposite sides of the training mats. "I'm going to come at you."

Two minutes later, Muller stared at the ceiling. Money changed hands on the sidelines.

"Guess Johnny Boy hasn't completely botched your training."

"Johnny Boy" was Muller's pejorative for Jonathan, the Director of the Psyonics Corporation and the most powerful man on the planet. My relationship with Jonathan was beyond complicated; he was my part-nemesis, part-mentor, part-something else. Growling at Muller's nickname only encouraged him.

He stood with a grunt. He wiped his hands on his smoke-gray sweats. His chest rose and fell in an easy rhythm. Our short bout hadn't tired him.

"Enough going easy on you," he said.

He took a ready position. Whispers rose. More money changed hands. My psychic abilities would announce his next move as soon as he knew it, and the extra milliseconds that gave me to react would allow me to put him on his back. Again. I smiled. The dusty opal of mischief enveloped him.

A laugh rippled through me. "Should I give you five minutes before I take you down?"

"Pride goeth."

His comm chirped.

Groans rose from the spectators.

The gray of December sleet obscured Muller's features. His lips tightened. His grim determination manifested in his aura as the color of a dirty Band-Aid. There'd been another murder in this city of killers.

"Be there in fifteen." He closed his eyes. "Another Red Unicorn victim has been found."

My gut clenched. The media dubbed the serial killer's murders "the Red Unicorn Killings" since he left a stuffed unicorn at crime scenes. What the press didn't know was that the unicorns started white until the killer soaked them in his victims' blood.

"You've got five to shower," Muller said as he took a wad of bills from Officer Williams. He riffled through them, grunted, then handed half to me. "Your cut."

"I don't understand you." I walked toward the showers.

Muller kept pace. "I'm not complicated."

"I meant you—cops."

"Ah. They bet to blow off steam. They liked how you dropped me on my ass." He shrugged. "We get a cut."

I yanked open the door to the women's locker room. "The Band of Brothers thing?"

Muller held the door, his hip against its side. "More like … tribe. Not the same blood but one, down to the marrow." He leaned closer, his face inches from mine. The light spicy scent of aftershave tickled my nose. "Who's got your back, Vonna?"

My gaze flickered toward the gym, then away. "That should be obvious."

"Should it?" The plum of curiosity twined around him. He grunted as he released the door. "Four minutes."

O O O

We rolled up on the scene, a warehouse off Martin Luther King Boulevard in South East, fifteen minutes later. Muller toggled the blue duty light in his unmarked cruiser.

Officers have rituals. Muller's was almost psychic. The colors in his aura marking the emotions that swirled around the insens dimmed to an almost nonexistence wash. He'd drained away his surface emotions.

He opened the car door. The city's sounds flooded in. The hush of tires on damp pavement underscored the muted voice of officers and the sharper trill of the reporters who listened to the police band. The recent rain's scent muted the city's stink. The door thunked closed.

When the trunk also slammed shut I slid from the car. Muller stood at the rear of the vehicle. His eyes closed. His face tilted upward. Ten breaths later, his eyes snapped open. He rapped his knuckles three times on the trunk in his final ritual.

Muller kept his silence both physical and psychic. He cop-walked—more than a brisk walk but less than a rushed stride—to the building. The grimy color of dirty Band-Aids covered the officers' auras. A few newer recruits twinned ashes of roses showing revulsion. One, fresh enough to look like he'd just graduated from the Academy, radiated the cranberry of shock.

"Can I do my job?" I asked.

Muller's eyes narrowed, then he gripped my arm and pulled me out of the flow of officers. After the first sexual homicide I'd handled for him, he'd grown reluctant to let me relive the victim's memories.

"Basic empathic readings—" His voice was a near growl.

"Aren't enough. Rick, the Red Unicorn's escalating."

I dropped my voice so it didn't carry on the spring breeze. "I'm no good to you unless you let me use my abilities." His aura flashed his protest. "We're not going to catch him before he kills again unless you let me see him."

He rubbed the nonexistent stubble on his jaw. "I don't like how much it hurts you."

I waited.

"It's likely a sexual homicide," he said.

Silence stretched.

He breathed my name out. "He'll make a mistake."

"How many women will die first?"

Flickers in his aura declared my arrow hit home. The pressure from a red-ball—a murder with lots of media attention—and a mounting body count weighed heavily against his protectiveness of me.

He shook a finger in my face. "I won't have you reliving their deaths when you fit his victim profile."

Silent, he stalked into the warehouse. The sticky sweet scent of decaying flesh and blood hit like a wall. The low hum of flies was audible over the hushed whispers of techs. I tasted the Red Unicorn's fury. He hadn't coldly dispatched this woman. This murder felt ... personal.

His previous kills hadn't used enough energy for me to be certain the monster was psy. But now I knew. The sour tang of a large psychic energy burst filled the warehouse. Even the insens felt it. Officers rubbed their arms as if to ward off a sudden chill. Hairs stood on the back of necks in the ionized air.

The Red Unicorn was psychic.

Which was a problem.

For me.

Officers and technicians fell back. Muller met the victim alone. Theirs was a private moment of communion. Of promises given and received. I felt like a Peeping Tom as the dirty Band-Aid color of Muller's aura deepened. A moment later, he nodded for me.

A stuffed unicorn, the color of dried blood, perched in what was left of a rib cage. A small patch of white remained on its muzzle. He'd put the unicorn in the body cavity because the woman's blood had been spread too thin over the room. Another deviation from the pattern. Another sign of psychic deterioration.

Chunks of flesh scattered over dozens of feet made it look like something had crawled *Alien*-like out of her, tearing and rending. A real possibility with a psy attack. The other victims had been hacked with something our medical examiner Deva thought was a thin, spiraled blade. But they were looking for a nonexistent weapon. Raw power had mutilated his victims.

"Impressions?" Muller asked, his tone gruff.

"He knew her. Have we found enough of the brain to do a time of death? I think she might be the fourth, not fifth, victim."

Muller waved Deva forward. The small Indian woman in a medical coat stepped away from her colleagues. Her black hair ran like rain down her back and framed a dark brown face with liquid brown eyes. She wore a pair of faded blue jeans and a bright purple tank top. Her gold aura displayed a rainbow of emotion. Her disgust sharpened the closer she came to the torso.

"Preliminary," he snapped.

Deva's aura flashed, but she wasn't insulted. Muller got brusque when he fact-collected.

"Elita Girard, age twenty-four—"

"Time of death?"

She ran her hands over her face. "Not enough tissue for a TOD scan, but I'd estimate six days."

"Damn it." Muller's voice was soft.

We had the Red Unicorn's timeline wrong. Josefa, the women we'd assumed was his fourth victim, had died two days ago. We'd projected a nine-day cool down period where the Red Unicorn selected, and then stalked, his next kill. But someone would die tomorrow—the day after, at the latest.

"All right, Vonna." Resignation and defeat wreathed Muller. "You get what you wanted. We need a death reading."

My stomach clenched. I never *wanted* to ride those final moments to death.

O   O   O

Sunset beams of crimson slashed through the high warehouse windows as the last few officers departed. Deva wheeled Elita's remains away from the point of death and lowered the stretcher. Experience had taught us the shorter distance I fell when the memories took me the better. I sat cross-legged on the floor next to the gurney.

My eyes closed. I drew in long even breaths and formed a mental doppelganger to hold my emotions. I dumped my fear and revulsion into my doppelganger. Let it dither.

I pulled off my glove, touched the remains.

O   O   O

I can't move.

Why are you doing this?

A shadow moves across my vision. No features. The world has an oddly filtered feel as if I'm high.

I don't know what you want. Pure? I don't understand. Wha—?

Pain lances through me. Blue velvet light fills me. I'm coming apart. Oh God, it hurts.

The world vanishes in a flash of white agony.

O   O   O

Muller pulled in front of the Psyonics Corporation. Before the psychics took over the world, the five-sided building stood as the United States' military headquarters. We kept it when we gave the government back as a symbol of what we could do if we needed to.

His gaze went to the Pentagon. "If you get anything from Elita's memories, give me a call."

I couldn't tell him the Red Unicorn was psychic. We had strict rules on rogues. Where Muller wanted the Red Unicorn caged, we wanted him dead. Our failure to stop the Red Unicorn before he killed, if known, would make governments reconsider the global power structure. Jonathan wouldn't allow that.

But how could I withhold the knowledge from my partner?

How could I justify letting the police department look for a killer they'd never catch without psy intervention? How could I let the Red Unicorn select his next victim while I hindered the investigation?

I scrubbed my hands over my face. "You headed in?"

Muller nodded. "I'm missing something."

I opened the car door so Muller wouldn't see my guilt. If he realized I was holding out he'd interrogate me until one of us broke. Right now, he had a better chance of surviving whole than I did.

"Pick me up in six hours."

"That's not enough recovery time." He faced me as I slid out. "You need twice that."

"It's enough. We're on his timeline."

Cornflower blue pride shot through the rainbow that was Rick Muller.

How could I lie to him? I bit my lower lip and dashed for the doors.

The building engulfed me. Minutes later I stood in front of Jonathan's private river-view quarters on the fifth floor. I sent a gentle mental touch. His door opened.

Jonathan stood by the window. Raw silk emerald lounging pants encased his runner's legs. His lightweight black silk top highlighted the paleness of his skin and his white-blond hair. Sharp cheekbones complimented his strong jaw line. Jonathan wore the role of most powerful being in the world with a grace I'd never match.

"Problem?" he asked as I entered his sitting room.

"The Red Unicorn." I paused for his nod of recognition. I allowed my certainty to seep past my shields. "Is ours."

Emotions flared and were gone from his aura quicker than I could catalogue. Dealing with other psy was easier than with insens. Psy didn't waste time with pointless questions.

"Details."

I laid out what I'd learned. "He's near the top of the strength spectrum. Burster or Tugger."

Jonathan was a strong Burster and affected people on a cellular level. A Tugger, or Brain in street-slang, could take control of a person. The designations explained how the Red Unicorn restrained Elita.

"Or a mix of both," Jonathan said. "I'll track it from my end." He paused. "Did you tell Muller?"

"No."

"Good."

I wasn't so sure.

"You're ready to drop. Unless you want to spend time in Silence you should rest."

"I will."

As I crossed the threshold, Jonathan said, "And Vonna? You're confined until this beast is caught."

I whirled and almost fell as I overbalanced. "What?"

He placed his hand on my shoulder. "You missed his message."

"What message?"

"He altered her memories as she was dying to prevent you from seeing him. He knows what you are," he said.

Muller thought I fit the victim profile too.

My mouth went dry. Darkness edged my vision. That couldn't be right. I clung to the door and tried to remember how to breathe. Jonathan moved deeper into the room, then returned.

"Keep this on you."

He held out a stickpin approximately an inch long.

"A tracker?"

"Just in case. Keep it in the lining of your jacket or underwear or someplace he's unlikely to find it right away."

I reached for the device. Jonathan's free hand closed over mine.

"For once, be smart. Turn the tracker on. Stay safe."

The oranges and reds of worry and distress leaked past his shields.

"I'll do what I can."

"Not reassured," he said, but he released my hand.

Neither was I.

O O O

A figure looms. I strain trying to see him.

Vonna, his voice ices through me.

The world shatters in a scream of blue velvet light.

O O O

I bolted upright in bed. Sweat prickled my skin. My breath, loud in the near silence of my room, came in harsh gasps. The Red Unicorn had said my name. A copper-penny scent tickled my nose.

"Lights!"

A unicorn, its coat the color of fresh blood, perched at the foot of my bed. I forced back a scream. I gripped the toy in my shaking hand. The unicorn was sticky with something pinned under its horn.

A picture of Muller.

I fumbled for my phone, then punched Muller's number. Cradling the phone between my neck and shoulder I balanced on one leg as I pulled on the nearest set of leathers. The call tripped over to voice mail. I sat on the edge of my bed to zip up my boots. I snatched the comm and Jonathan's tracker off the nightstand.

The Pentagon wasn't safe.

"Dispatch. Please locate Detective Muller."

I raced down the hall to the elevators.

"One moment," a mechanized voice responded. "Detective Muller is 10-10A." Off duty—home.

I toggled off the comm and dropped it into my pocket. The elevator dinged open. An eternal ride later, the doors opened on ground level.

Air heavy with the scent of cherry blossoms slapped me as I burst from the building. Jonathan would lock down any car I requisitioned. If I waited for a cab, security would stop me. Not happening when Muller was in danger. He was my partner, my only friend. And ... and I had his back.

There was a twenty-four-hour diner down Columbia Pike. I could get a cab there. My boots clunked against the pavement as I ran. I fumbled my phone from my pocket.

"Deva," I half-screamed. "Tell me Rick is with you."

"He went home to sleep. What's wrong?"

I debated for a nanosecond. "The Red Unicorn left a calling card with Rick's picture on my bed."

"Oh, God," Deva breathed. "Was it—"

"Fresh? Yeah. I'm headed to Rick's now. Let whoever needs to know he's in trouble know."

"Done." Fear had driven the drowsiness from her voice.

"Deva? Tell them ... Red's psy." I hung up before she could reply.

The lights from the diner beckoned from four blocks away. My fingers closed around the tracker. I pushed it into the lining of my pants pocket. I made a second call.

"He's got Rick," I said without preamble.

"Where are you?" Tension snapped in Jonathan's voice.

I babbled my bedside discovery.

Jonathan cursed in the background. Presumably, he'd verified I was gone and the tracker was off.

"Rick's bait."

Obviously. But Jonathan would sacrifice Rick to protect me.
Not happening.

Two blocks to the diner.

"I won't let him die."

"Vonna, listen!"

A wave of power slapped me off my feet. Blue velvet lightning
enveloped me. The phone slid through my limp fingers. My cheek
bounced across the pavement. Layers of flesh scraped off. Blue
flashes of lights became black spots. Jonathan's voice was so very
far away and small as he screamed my name.

o o o

Dim light streamed down from the empty warehouse's ceiling-level
windows. Panic scattered my thoughts. I closed my eyes. My
doppelganger sprang Athena-like from my head. With a push, it
assumed my fears. I had to focus.

The tracker!

Where was it?

I wore only a light pink chemise and matching underwear. The
Red Unicorn had stripped away my first layer of protection. The
emotional residue of living in a city with millions of humans
hampered a psyonic's responses. But ambient emotions didn't
affect me as strongly as other psy did. Empathy didn't let me *feel*
emotion. It let me *see* it. If he'd wanted to overwhelm me, he should
have packed the room with people.

My hand was stiff. Streaks of red-brown coated my fingers. No
memories had come when I'd touched the blood. No memories
meant nothing sentient had died. I'd been stupid. I'd been triggered
into panic like an *insen*.

I pushed upright.

A shadow unfolded into a man, a head taller and nearly twice
as broad in the shoulders as me. He wore dark blue jeans and a
black cotton T-shirt. No barriers. A riot of colors swirled around
him: greens for desire; yellows of joy; the deep reds and purples of
scorn; the blanched almond of disappointment. The last grew in
intensity.

My head throbbed, and stomach threatened revolt from the visual kaleidoscope. I put out my hand to catch my balance against a nonexistent wall. My doppelganger curled into a fetal position. She recognized death.

"Lies." His voice was high and soft.

Power crashed into me. I dropped to a knee. My shields held. For now. I drew in a shuddering breath.

I met his eyes. My world pitched and disorientation took me. A hand of power yanked me off my feet. Phantom restraints pulled my arms from my sides. I hung crucified in the air. The Red Unicorn stalked forward.

My clothes lay in a heap behind him. A white unicorn similar to those we'd taken from his crime scenes rested on top.

His languid pace and aura showed no fear of discovery. Our best estimate was that he kept the women alive for two to eight hours. How long had I been unconscious? I swallowed despite the dryness of my mouth. Was I out of time?

The Red Unicorn paced a slow circle around me. I braced for a touch that never came. He stepped in front of me. I fixed my gaze on the edge of his aura to avoid being pulled into his emotional miasma.

"I had hoped." He shook his head. "But no. Just like the rest. Not pure."

A flick of his wrist sent me flying across the room. Air whooshed out of my lungs. Lights danced before my eyes. The concrete floor scraped my left shoulder and back. Blue velvet lightning smashed into me. Small fissures appeared in my shields. I pushed back. The assault stopped.

The tracker felt miles away. I lurched to my feet. The Red Unicorn cocked his head.

I lunged. Silver surprise and cranberry shock dominated his aura. Training rather than conscious thought had him deflecting my punch. Instead of breaking his nose, my fist slammed into his cheekbone. The shock of impact reverberated up my arm. Then my weight crashed into him and he staggered. I hopped back to regain my balance. The dark violet of his outrage grew bright.

He didn't like prey that fought back?

Good.

I stepped into his jab and took it on my ribs. Something snapped. I twisted and backed closer to my clothes. His hand-to-hand combat training was better than mine, and he significantly outweighed me. Staying in a slugfest with him was suicidal. But I needed him down for a second so I could activate the tracker. I'd trust Jonathan to get here, wherever here was, quickly.

The Red Unicorn planted his feet and lowered his head like his namesake beast, ready to charge. Energy pricked my skin.

I'd last longer in a fistfight than deflecting psychic attacks.

Stepping into him, I punched his unguarded torso. The building energy wave dissipated. Dark violet turned to dark magenta anger. I backed out of his reach. He sprang. The floor scored my back like a cheese grater. My right hand stabbed toward his throat. He deflected the blow. The nails of my left hand raked his face. He screamed and reared back. I crawled from under him.

The Red Unicorn knelt on hands and knees. "You were supposed to be pure."

Pure? My glance fell on the unicorn. Unicorns came to maidens! Ah, hell. I edged closer to my clothes.

"I've never—"

Roaring, the Red Unicorn leaped and caught my thigh. I kicked with my free foot and caught him on the temple. His grip loosened. Vids made knocking someone out look easy, but my bare foot didn't have enough force. His fingers dug into my ankle. We wrestled. I was pinned. His eyes, a muddy green, drilled into mine. Pressure built against my shields.

"You're wrong," I panted.

"I smell the sex."

My neck muscles tightened as I pushed back. "Not. My. Memories."

The pressure lessened. I'd caught his attention.

"You know about me," I said, keeping my voice level. "I take memories from the dead."

Peach-puff interest and Alice-blue insecurity masked his features. Slowly, hope blurred into the mix.

My body went slack in relief. I had him.

"They aren't mine."

Praying I wasn't making a fatal mistake, I lowered a section of shield. If the bet paid off, I'd win precious seconds. If not, I was dead. The blue velvet of his power snaked into my mind. I fought to stay myself as the world dissolved into someone else's memory.

O O O

I can't believe she's mine.

I look across the bridal suite at my new wife. Anticipation of her soft white skin under my hand makes me hard.

The Red Unicorn seizes the vision, wrestles away from reality, turns to the mirror over the dresser. Sees the blond man in the rented tuxedo looking back at him.

The vision snaps.

O O O

I hammered my shields closed.

The Red Unicorn reared from psychic blowback. I pushed him away and raced to my clothes. I snatched up my pants and toggled on the tracker. I grabbed my boot.

The Red Unicorn shook his head.

I took four quick steps and slammed the steel-reinforced boot heel into his head. This time the Unicorn fell.

I fished the comm out of my jacket and backed away from the killer on the floor.

"Dispatch," I said.

"Vonna?" Muller's voice broke through the mechanized response.

"Rick." Relief swamped me.

"We're outside," he said, talking over me. "A psychic shield's over the building. Johnny Boy didn't know if you were connected to the Red Unicorn and didn't want to hurt you by breaking it. You okay?"

The Red Unicorn groaned. Standing on one leg like a flamingo, I pulled on my boot.

"Vonna?"

I took uneven strides to the Red Unicorn. I kicked him in the head again with my booted foot. He collapsed.

"The shield should be gone now," I said

Something heavy hit a door I hadn't noticed to my left.

Adrenaline flowed out of me. My legs shook. I was on the ground. Rick reached me a heartbeat before Jonathan did.

"Don't touch her," Jonathan ordered. "Bare skin contact will send her further into shock."

Muller moved back. Jonathan's silk-clad arms lifted me.

"Is that *thing* dead?" Jonathan asked.

A team of black-clad psi enforcers, all Bursters, circled the Red Unicorn. Behind them stood a row of D.C. Metro officers, weapons trained on the Red Unicorn's still figure.

"No, sir," an Enforcer answered. "Needs medical."

"The med facilities at Pentagon are closest, and we know how to restrain a psychic," Jonathan said.

"He needs to stand trial," Muller said.

Colors danced before my eyes. Flashes peppered my vision. My world went dark.

O O C

A circle of ten silver stasis tubes stood in the center of the Medical Bay. Psyonics with damaged shields or fracturing minds were placed in Silence—virtual sensory deprivation—to let them either heal or be humanely put down. Medical equipment beeped with vital readings. Tubes flowed from IV stands and machines into the chambers and the individuals imprisoned in them.

The Red Unicorn lay sedated in the closest tube. Jonathan deemed the man unsalvageable. I owed those other women; I owed Muller to witness this. I nodded.

"Go ahead," Jonathan told the medical staff.

The fluids flowing into the Red Unicorn's chamber changed from clear to a milky pink. Dark turquoise and deep burgundy, agony and panic, flared from the observation window on the tube.

He was conscious?

Terminations occurred once the psionic was comatose. It was supposed to be the humane alternative. Thumps and screams came from inside the tube.

My stomach roiled. "Jonathan?"

"He tried to kill you." His voice had a frozen edge. "I didn't take him apart cell by cell. It's more mercy than he deserves." The purple stone of vengeance and magenta of wrath smothered his image.

"I ..."

Jonathan put his hand on my back and steered me out of the room. The door closed behind us and cut off the screams.

O O O

Maize and light blue leaped around Muller when we walked into the reception area. Modern black and silver furniture was tastefully arranged around the former military checkpoint. Muller paced the space, then he saw me. He hugged me gently and tried to avoid my cracked ribs. I winced.

"The Red Unicorn died trying to escape," Jonathan said.

I closed my eyes, but not before I saw the flash of emotion. Muller knew Jonathan had executed the man and accepted that something closer to the law of the jungle rather than men's law prevailed.

He kept a hand on my good arm. "Can I take you to the station? Lots of people want to see you."

Jonathan sighed. "Just watch her concussion. Make her take it easy."

Muller's aura indicated his amusement at making me "take it easy."

O O O

"Spooky's back," Officer Williams yelled when we entered the squad room.

Her flash of joy stopped me. Officer Williams hated psyonics; "Spooky" was the nicest thing she'd ever called me.

I turned to Muller. "What?"

He smirked. "You got hurt protecting me. Makes you cop. Welcome to the Tribe."

Plainclothes and uniformed officers closed around us, all wishing me well. All gently touching an arm, a shoulder, as if verifying I was all right. The rainbow of emotions verified Muller's assessment. Their acceptance, finally, after years of working with them, brought tears to my eyes.

Muller's hand snaked into my pocket.

"Hey!"

A swirl of colors was his only response. He held up my comm. "Wear it."

I took the device. Sharp needles pricked my skin as the device adhered to the inside of my wrist. Muller grunted. His hand rested on my shoulder. Cornflower blue pride, the green of sentimentality, and the light sky blue of acceptance bloomed in his aura. Around the room officers radiated the same light sky blue.

Tribe.

No longer torn between worlds, I was home.

About the Author

Nancy is a mom, writer, speaker, and lawyer. Before being a published writer, Nancy had been a blackjack dealer, florist, tax form coder, worked in professional theatre, and accidently went to law school and passed one bar exam while recovering from a concussion. Really, the horse's headache was much worse. When she reflects that she has normal, boring life, she is often puzzled when people burst out laughing in response.

FEEDING THE FERAL CHILDREN

DAVID FARLAND

Yan woke in the predawn, sweat making her blouse cling to the hollow of her chest. She lay on her bed, unwilling to move, lest she waken her three-year-old sister who curled into her, her face close to Yan's breast. The little girl would be hungry when she woke; this one was always hungry, and Yan did not want to have to get up and steam the rice.

Lightning snarled softly in the distance, like a hunting tiger, and just outside the window the bamboo rustled in the wind.

Yan had dreamt of Huang Fa. Only a few years before, the Silk Road had been opened to Persia, and Huang Fa had dared take it for her last spring. Winter was coming, and snow would soon fill the Himalayas. If Huang Fa did not return soon, the trails would be blocked until next year.

In Yan's dream, she'd seen his startlingly clear eyes under the moonlight, while the crickets sang their nightly hymns of longing and the carp finned in the pond beside her cottage. "When I return," he'd said, "I will have much silver. Your father will surely agree to the match when he sees what I bring." Huang Fa was but a lowly merchant from a fishmonger's family, and he dared to hope to marry a landowner's daughter. He would have to rise much higher in station to do so; he would need to buy land himself.

His voice, soft and husky, seemed preternaturally clear in the dream, as if he stood over her bed. His image had left her feeling over-warm, with a soft fluttering in her womb. At fifteen, Yan was young and in love, and she felt all of the longing and guilt and confusion that went with it. Her mother had once told her, "A girl's first love is always the most treasured. If you are fortunate, he will also be your last love."

Yan inhaled deeply, hoping that perhaps Huang Fa really had come in the night, that she might catch his scent. But the early morning sky outside smelled only of thunder. She wondered where Huang Fa might be, and as she did, she whispered a prayer to the Sun God. "Wherever he is, may he greet the morning with pleasant thoughts of me."

O   O   O

The land was black in the Altai Mountains, black stone upon black stone, with only the sparest of grasses and shrubs cropping up here and there.

Huang Fa stalked through the cold predawn in a sullen rage, and for a moment he tried to conjure an image of Yan. Walking a hundred li in a single night can drive the humanity from a man, make him hard and cold. Fatigue had left him reeling, and the icy winds wafting down from the Altai Mountains over the barren gray stones had drained the warmth from him. He had only one sandal, and so he hobbled as best he could. In a jest of fate, his sandaled foot had developed blisters that bled, and so hurt more than his naked foot.

Before the sun was even a sullen smudge on the smoke-gray sky, he spotted his roan horse, gazing down in a desultory stare at the barren rocks, its long dark mane and tail gusting in the wind. The barbarians that had stolen her had left her tied to the only tree within three li, and they'd fallen asleep under it. For ten hours Huang Fa had been wondering how best to kill them.

Huang Fa felt a touch on his elbow. "Are you sure you want to do this?" whispered the monk with no name.

Huang Fa paused and turned toward the monk, who was but a shadow in the darkness, with a bit of moonlight shining upon his clean-shaven head. The monk had no name, for he had renounced it. He whispered urgently, "These men are not killers. They were kind enough to merely sneak off with all your belongings, sparing your life. To take theirs would be to return compassion with brutality."

Huang Fa argued, "The barbarians only stole the horse before, but they won't make the same mistake again. Once they open my bags and find the dragon's tooth ..."

The monk did not argue. He knew the barbarians would never relinquish such a great treasure. Yet the dragon's tooth meant little to Huang Fa. He had to save his mare. The barbarians could not guess the worth of such a fine mount. These men consumed horses as if they were chickens. Even if they did not butcher her, they would likely only wait until she bore her foal and then harvest her mare's milk to make liquor.

Huang Fa was determined to get his mare back at any cost, and he could not let them live.

Dread clenched his stomach. He wasn't sure how many men he might have to face. He was determined to use the wizard warrior Jiang Ziya's wolf strategy of battle—to attack when least expected, at the weakest point.

Stepping carefully, Huang Fa strode over the sparse prairie, with only the barest of grass. There was no rustling of feet, no brush of his pants woven from silky China grass as he rushed into the camp.

One barbarian, wearing a hairy vest of musk ox hide and a fur cap, sat on guard, but had fallen asleep with his back to a nearly leafless saxaul tree. Another lay nearby rolled in a blanket. The two had camped without a fire.

In the gloom, Huang Fa heard a sound and dully registered that a snow pheasant was already up, thundering down from a rocky summit to take cover in the rocks. To the south, in the hills beyond a glacial river, a wolf howled.

Huang Fa strode angrily to the young barbarian on guard duty, grabbed his own bronze battle-ax from the young man's sleeping hands, and smashed the man's face before he had even a chance to rouse. Blood blackened the man's chin, and he choked out a "Gah!" as he tried to hold himself upright. Huang Fa struck another blow to the skull to finish him.

The thief's bowlegged friend must have heard the skirmish, for he gave a yelp of warning and hopped out of his blanket, then leaped over the stones like a jerboa.

Want to race? Huang Fa thought. He hurled his ax. A blow to the right lung knocked the barbarian to the ground, and there was no fight left in him. Huang Fa went to the man. "You think it funny to steal a man's horse and his sandal too? Laugh now." He split the man's skull with his bronze ax.

The deed would haunt him. He might make a joke while killing another, but it was a foul thing to do. Damn the horse thieves.

He flipped the man over to make sure that he was not breathing. What he saw sickened him. It was not a man, but a boy— barely thirteen, just gaining his adult size. He lay back, gazing blankly at the gray sky, and his eyes were fixed. His teeth had all been filed down to points, and a tattoo upon his chin showed the trunk of a tree in black, rising up to his forehead. Branches from it spread out upon either side of his cheeks and forehead, creating the holy symbol of the Tree of Life.

Huang Fa wished he had never seen that face. He wondered if the boy was a shaman. He went to the other barbarian, found that he too was no older than a child, and that his teeth had been filed to points, and that he bore the same tribal markings.

Only five years ago, Huang Fa thought, *I was their age.*

No words could adequately describe how much their faces disturbed him. Though his stomach was empty, he lurched away from camp and did not return until his heart quit pounding. He avoided peering into the faces of the dead.

"Bojing," Huang Fa softly called to his mare. "Are you all right?" He stepped close to let her catch his scent. She nuzzled the hollow beneath his chin, and he stroked her neck gratefully. She was the finest horse he'd ever seen. He had bought her from an Arab band, and now he stroked her side fondly. For weeks now he had only walked her over the mountains, afraid that the hard journey might cause her to lose the foal.

It would have been a shame to let the barbarians eat such a majestic horse.

Huang Fa checked his saddlebags, where he retrieved his left sandal. "Ha, ha," he said to the dead barbarians.

His paltry supplies were intact, except that the boys had eaten the last of his wrinkled apples. But the silver was there, with precious ointments of frankincense for Yan, opium tar, and a single dragon's fang to sell to the apothecaries.

The Taoist crept up to the camp at last. "May I fix us some beans?" he asked humbly.

Huang Fa fumed. The monk was not a coward. He was heading back from Persia, where Emperor Qin would likely cut out his tongue because of his religious views. The emperor hated Taoists and Buddhists.

But the monk had refused to fight the barbarians. A man who would not kill animals, who would not even eat meat, could not be counted on in a fight. Right now, Huang Fa did not feel any more tolerant of the Taoist than the emperor did. Damn the Taoist and his compassion.

"No, you may not," Huang Fa said.

The monk merely bowed in acquiescence.

Satisfied at last, Huang Fa built a small fire. Fuel was scarce, so he settled on dried dung from a wild ass that had ranged this far north in the spring. Soon the fire blazed like a gem. The skull of a giant ox, bleached by the sun, lay in the golden grass beneath the tree, its broad black horns faded like ash. A poem was scrawled on it in charcoal.

A cold moon sets
below these holy mountains.
My hands are so cold.
Is this where the gods
come to die?

Huang Fa glanced down toward the skirts of the mountain and saw that, indeed, from here the full moon was setting far below him in the southwest, so that it seemed he looked upon it as if he were a god in the clouds. It floated in the lavender dawn like a glowing pearl beneath the water, slowly descending into the mists. The mountainside was covered in black and barren stone for many li. Huang Fa hoped to glimpse lights—the twinkling of campfires. He and the monk had been chasing the season's last caravan; it could not be more than a few days ahead.

As weary as the dead, Huang Fa rolled himself in the barbarian boy's blanket and tried to sleep. But the faces of the dead boys haunted him, and in a fitful but troubled sleep, he dreamt of young boys that circled his camp, laughing cruelly as they prepared their vengeance.

O O O

The Altair Mountains were black, but the desert at their feet was red. Red rocks and red sand. Even the sparse grasses were coated with red dust.

Huang Fa and the monk led the mare into a small fortress with adobe walls at a trading village called Arumchee on the border of the Taklamakan Desert.

For two days, Huang Fa had not slept. At night he dreamt of vengeful spirits circling in the grass, and by day he felt dazed and exhausted.

Every soul embodies both the yin and yang, he told himself. *Each is balanced between darkness and light. I gave into the darkness for a moment, and now I must seek balance again.*

The thought soothed him. Still, it felt comforting to hear the crow of chickens, to see silk garments hanging upon bushes outside of the adobe huts, and to smell fresh beans and chicken cooking in the houses. It felt even better to be inside the strong walls of a fortress, even if those walls were as red as the desert.

Huang Fa needed to report the killings. Slaying raiders wasn't a simple matter, even if it was just a pair of young horse thieves. This had been a righteous kill, and everyone needed to know that— otherwise there could be reprisals.

Huang Fa wasn't worried for himself. He was just passing through. Six weeks from now, he'd be home, safe in his cabin on the lake. He'd have a fine horse for his stables and a dowry to give Yan's father.

But the traders and settlers here had to live among the barbarians. Mostly, the settlers were jade carvers who worked the stone gathered near Black Mountain, but every year there were more and more caravans heading for Persia and Greece. The caravanserais paid good bribes and hefty tolls to the barbarians for safe passage; these people needed to know that the barbarian raiders had failed to keep their bargain—and so paid with their lives.

Huang Fa reported to the garrison commander, a wealthy fellow named Chong Deming who wore a wide golden belt of office over armor made from layers of red silk. He sat on a stool outside a weathered manor house while sipping porridge from a red ceramic bowl. He had white hair and a beard so long he must have thought himself the equal to one of the emperor's counselors.

A barbarian woman in bright blue silks squatted on the ground next to him, as if she was his wife. Huang Fa humbly kowtowed, joining his fists together and bowing solemnly, and then approached and bore his news upon further invitation.

Alarm grew evident on the commander's face on hearing Huang Fa's news.

"You killed two barbarian boys?" Chong Deming asked, his penetrating gaze spearing Huang Fa. "Which tribe?"

Huang Fa shrugged. He had come across so many barbarians the past few months that he no longer knew or cared what tribe they came from.

"What did they look like?"

"They were merely youths," Huang Fa answered frankly. "They wore bright pants of purple, and their teeth were filed down like fangs. Their faces were tattooed with the symbol of the Holy Tree. One had this hunting spear," he said, holding up a javelin with a dark-green jade tip, "and the other had a bow made from the horn of an aurochs."

Chong Deming pulled at his beard thoughtfully. "Oroqin barbarians," he said. "As I thought. Normally they are peaceful people, eating sheep and goats from their flocks, and hunting for wild asses in the mountains. But their animals have been hit hard by a plague of anthrax, and so the barbarians have been starving for the past few seasons.

"Some of their men tried to rob a caravan last spring. The caravan guards made quick work of these unskilled barbarians, and my men hunted those that escaped. We tracked them for five days and caught them in their yurts in the mountains. We hunted them

271

from chariots and finished off the men with our long-handled halberds. But we spared the women and children. We did not have the heart ..."

The old general fell silent, and Huang Fa looked to the monk for his reaction. The young man shook his bald head sadly and asked the general, "Did your compassion gain them nothing?"

The general mourned, "I'd hoped they would find their way back into the mountains, that their own people would feed them, but I fear that they are doomed." He looked to Huang Fa. "Did these two young men have any distinguishing features?"

"One was a runty kid that squinted, with bowed legs. The other was clean and handsome. He wore a necklace made of jade and bear's teeth."

At that, Chong Deming's face fell, and he peered down into his bowl of morning porridge thoughtfully. Steam curled up from it. At long last, he blew over the wide lip of the clay bowl, but did not sip from it. "That would be Battarsaikhan's son, Chuluun." His voice became soft, frightened. "You've heard of Battarsaikhan?"

The name stirred at the back of Huang Fa's brain, like a rat in its burrow. "I think ..."

"It means 'hero who wins without battle.' He is a hunchback, a powerful sorcerer who kills with magic rather than ax or bow. He is the most dangerous man in all these mountains. His oldest sons died in our attack at White Ox River last summer."

"Gah," the monk muttered. The news was terrible.

"Battarsaikhan was in the mountains then, training the boy that you killed," Chong Deming said. His voice came hoarse, bitter with sorrow. "Now, the sorcerer has no children left. Couldn't you have let those boys live? They were just trying to feed their starving tribe. You could have just taken your horse ..."

Huang Fa stared at the old commander wordlessly, shame thick in his throat. "I did not know of their need. I did not want them coming for me again. You, as a general, know that only a fool spares an enemy."

"Then because you were afraid of retribution, I fear you shall suffer retribution," Chong Deming said. "If I were you, I'd run from here as fast as I could. The last caravan of the season passed the fortress only two days ago. There was a wizard traveling with it.

He might be able to protect you. You can catch them if you hurry—but you should leave now. Battarsaikhan will be reeling from rage, and his spells can reach far."

"I am sorry," Huang Fa said. "I ..." He got an idea. The traders paid tolls every year, and among the barbarians, it was said that the life of a man was worth little. "Can we send a gift to this sorcerer? A peace offering?"

"Do you think anything in the world will be enough to assuage his wrath?" the monk asked.

There was little in Huang Fa's saddlebags that might be worth the life of a man's last son. The silver was a soft metal, of less value than bronze to the barbarians. The spices ... were questionable. Huang Fa answered, "I have a dragon's tooth that was dug from out of the stone in Persia. It is worth the price of many horses."

He went to his saddle packs and pulled out the tooth—eight inches long, serrated, and curved like a dagger. Huang Fa had seen the giant dragon skull encased in stone that it had been pulled from. It had been polished by its previous owner so that the ancient bone glowed like amber.

"Perhaps," Chong Deming said thoughtfully, "it will please. Perhaps to a sorcerer it will be worth enough."

O O O

For four days, Huang Fa traveled with the monk and led his mare, skirting the grasslands at the edge of the desert, chasing the wizard's caravan. Here there had once been wild asses, giant wild bulls, and red deer in abundance, and cheetahs to hunt them. But over the past twenty years the rising number of caravans had driven many herds away, and the plague of anthrax had killed most other animals. Some said that the caravans themselves spread the disease. It was well-known that one could catch it from handling the skins of animals that had died from the plague.

Now, the red plains seemed barren, almost lifeless. In two days Huang Fa saw only a few wild ostriches and a couple of giant elephants that the emperor's men sometimes harnessed and trained for war. Such beasts were difficult for the barbarians to hunt, he knew. The swift ostriches were a temptation, forever running just out of the bow's range. The elephants, masters of the plains, were four times the weight of the smaller Indus elephants, and had rust-colored tusks that could grow to over twelve feet in length. The bull elephants sometimes became mad and attacked even caravans.

For Huang Fa to travel past such a herd in a caravan was a bold deed. To creep past them with only a monk at his side, pulling his mare on a rope, was terrifying. Yet to his surprise, the larger bulls only sniffed the air with their trunks and flapped their ears in agitation. They did not stomp the grass or throw hay in the air. They did not charge.

Still, the young men kept a respectful distance and traveled as long as they could. Such was Huang Fa's urgency to find the caravan, to get home to Yan, that he did not want to camp until well after dark.

The monk spoke little as they traveled. He plodded along, staring ahead evenly, whispering poems that he composed in his head.

Huang Fa was bumbling along, eyes growing heavy, imagining what it would be like to take Yan into his arms at last when he dreamed of the feral children.

There were dozens of them, circling a campfire in a large cavern. They were thin creatures with protruding bellies and skin clinging tightly over their ribs. Their bare backs had been tattooed with images of snake-headed lizards. Their gaunt faces were just flesh-colored bones, and their teeth had all been filed.

There were children of all ages in the group, from toddlers to the ages of ten or eleven. They were practically naked, all bare flesh.

Now, a couple of the nearest turned, peered at him hungrily, and jostled their neighbors. They too turned to search for him, but many of the children seemed unable to spot him, as if he were far away.

Suddenly, in the midst of the bonfire, a sorcerer appeared, as if bursting up from the flames. He wore a mask of red jade, a demon's face, and he wore a cloak made of tiger hide. He danced among the flames, hopping among the coals without apparent harm. He carried a huge rattle made from a giant cobra's skull in his right hand and held the dragon's tooth in his left. He sang as he danced, his voice rising and falling in the quavering melody of grief.

The children around the fire chanted words that Huang Fa could not quite understand. They pounded their right fists into their left hands, and one by one it seemed that all of the children became more aware of him. They began turning and peering at him with greater eagerness. Huang Fa spotted saliva dripping down the chin of one starving girl toddler, her mouth full of fangs.

Suddenly the sorcerer snarled a curse, almost spitting his words, and hurled the dragon tooth through the darkness. Huang Fa jerked, as one sometimes will in sleep, as he tried to dodge. The fang hit Huang Fa in the chest.

His eyes sprang open.

He stood, heart pounding in fear at the terrible dream. *It is just my guilt that haunts me,* he reassured himself. *Someday I will forget it.*

The sun cast immeasurable shadows. He glanced behind and saw it sailing over the edge of the world, hanging beneath the clouds like a red, staring eye.

"Ai!" he whispered to the Taoist monk, still wrestling his fear. "I had a terrible dream."

"Tell me what you saw, and perhaps I can divine the meaning," the monk suggested.

It had been so vivid, Huang Fa could still feel where the dragon's tooth had hit him. He reached down to touch the spot—and found the dragon's tooth lodged in the hair of his sheepskin vest.

The monk gaped at the tooth.

Huang Fa peered around the plains, to see if someone could have thrown it, but all he could see was rippling fields of grass.

That's when he knew. The sorcerer had thrown the tooth at him—a distance of more than three hundred li.

"It does not take a divine scholar," the monk said, "to know that the sorcerer has rejected your apology."

O O O

Darkness came, and with it the howling of wolves and the cries of hunting cats in the desert. Huang Fa and the monk loped up a hill, and far in the distance, miles away, they spotted the bright-colored silk pavilions of the caravan. The pavilions, made in the peaked

Arab style, had lamps and campfires lit within, and each glowed a different color like radiant gems in the desert, shades of ruby and tourmaline, diamond and sapphire. The pavilions beckoned, but Huang Fa's legs felt like lead.

"A march of a single night would bring us to the wizard's caravan."

"I cannot go on," the monk begged, panting. "The stars are strangely dark tonight." He leaned over and grabbed his knees, trying to catch his breath.

It was true. There was a cloudy haze across the heavens, obscuring the River of Stars. Huang Fa had a star chart, painted upon a silken map, that could help guide a man across the desert at night, but tonight it would be of no use. "We should camp," the monk suggested. "A man who races headlong in the night is sure to fall in a hole."

Huang Fa considered lighting a knot of grass and using it as a torch, but felt reluctant to do so. It might attract unwanted eyes. He glanced behind him, with an uncanny certainty that he was being watched.

O   O   O

In his dream that night, the feral children stalked him.

He dreamt first that the moon was up, as bright as a mirror of beaten silver, and by its light he saw a strange creature—grand and majestic. It was an elk, he thought, or something like an elk. Its hair was as pale as cotton, and it stood taller than two men; its antlers had many tines and were so broad that a man could have lain between them. At first he thought there were cobwebs between the tines, but then he realized it was a thickening of the horn, unlike any that he had seen upon an elk before.

The creature mesmerized him. Never had he seen such a regal animal, so full of power and strength.

Then he heard a rustling behind him and realized that something was creeping toward him through deep grass. He whirled and glimpsed pale bodies, naked children sneaking on all fours, like wolves on the trail of a wounded ibex. He was not sure if they were after him or the majestic elk.

In his dream, he knotted a clump of dry grass and struck a flint with his knife, igniting it. He raised his makeshift torch in the cold air, hoping that it would frighten the feral children away, but they only growled low in their throats, crawling ever closer. Their eyes glowed strangely in the night, the color of blood sapphires, and they were close enough so he could see their teeth filed down to fangs and the glint of the green jade daggers in their hands.

Some were nearly men in size, others mere toddlers.

In that dream, the monk was not beside him, and Huang Fa called out in terror, "Where are you, my friend?"

Lost in the distance, the monk called back, "I have chosen to take the Way. You should have, too."

O   O   O

Dawn came with muddled results. Huang Fa awoke, the monk shaking him insistently. "Something is wrong," he whispered. Huang Fa sensed it even before he opened his eyes. The air felt stifled, dead, and for a moment he lay in his blankets, imagining that dawn was hours off.

"The sun is up," the monk warned, "but it is a day unlike any I have ever seen. A storm comes."

Huang Fa squinted. The whole world had gone red, from heaven above to the earth beneath. On the horizon was a red cloud, a wall of filth, filling the air, rising incredibly high, taller than thunderheads. The sun could not pierce through the cloud, and so it seemed more like night than morning. Indeed, the sun was less than a sooty smudge, and the grim light that filtered through was the color of a poor ruby.

"My friend," Huang Fa shouted, leaping to his feet, "the Yellow Wind is coming!"

"Yellow Wind?" the monk asked.

"Yes, a dust storm out of the Gobi! One blew over our village when I was but a child, but it will be worse here! Quick, grab our blankets. I will get the horse. We must find shelter!"

The fine mare was tied to a small tree, peering east with her ears slanted forward and her eyes dull with terror and fatigue. Her right knee was bent forward, as if her hoof was sore. She wheezed, and muscles in her shoulder spasmed. She lost her balance and stumbled a bit.

Resting a palm on her snout, Huang Fa found that she was feverish. She did not respond to his touch. She did not lean in for affection or shy away nervously. It was as if he didn't exist, as if he were a ghost.

She coughed lightly, trying to clear phlegm from her lungs, and then just stood, wheezing.

"Don't touch her," the monk warned. "She has anthrax. I have seen it before."

Huang Fa peered at the coming storm. He'd never heard of one so immense. It came like the night, a grim shade. The dust rose higher than the tallest cloud, blotting out the sun. The storm did not ride on a great gust of wind. Indeed, the air felt sullen, still, almost dead. The storm only crept toward them.

"Cover your nose," Huang Fa said. "The dust will clog your throat. When it hits, don't stop moving. If you lie down, the dust might bury you."

The monk, a thin young man, looked terrified.

"Can we run from it?" the monk asked. "It moves slowly."

"We cannot run faster than the storm," Huang Fa said. "Even if we could for a time, it would catch us when we tired. The only shelter is ahead of us—at the caravan."

The monk peered back down the trail, glanced at a mound of rocks not five hundred yards off. It might provide some shelter from the coming wind, but not much.

"Let us hurry, then," the monk urged.

Huang Fa patted his horse, quickly untied her.

"Leave her," the monk whispered. "She will only slow us, and she does not have long to live. Besides, if we reach the caravan, she might infect the other animals."

"I can't leave her," Huang Fa said. She was his future. The silver might be a dowry, but the mare was worth far more. "She might get better. The anthrax does not always kill."

The monk shrugged, leaving the decision to him.

Huang Fa pulled at the mare's rope, but she would not follow. He wrapped an arm around her neck. "Come, Bojing," he whispered, "please ..."

The mare stood, ears flicking forward. She knew what he wanted. She staggered a step, but then stopped.

"It is a curse," Huang Fa wailed, wringing his hands.

The monk tried to calm him. "Sometimes a storm is just a storm," he said. "Sometimes a sickness is just a sickness. I think these things are beyond the powers of even a famed sorcerer like Battarsaikhan."

Huang Fa hung his head, thinking furiously. He remembered the dragon's tooth. The sorcerer had thrown it hundreds of li.

He covered his head with a straw hat from his pack, wrapped a rag across his face, then strode toward the storm.

"Try to remember where we last saw the lights of the caravan," the monk suggested. "We should make straight for it."

Huang Fa gazed toward the horizon but could not be sure of the direction. He followed the monk. Grimly, the curtain of red dust rolled toward them until it swallowed them whole.

O   O   O

All through the morning, Huang Fa and the monk pushed through the dust storm. The gritty dust stung Huang Fa's eyes, and he kept them narrowed to slits. Even then, his eyes soon streamed from tears.

The dust filled his sinuses until sludge ran from his nose, and when he tried to breathe from his mouth, mud clogged his throat and left him gasping. He'd never imagined such a hell.

The dust was incredibly fine, and it coated everything, gritting up his skin, filling every orifice.

It was all he could do to keep plodding, placing one foot in front of another. Time and again, the monk would reach back and grab Huang Fa, who was trying to pull the mare. She grew more headstrong as her sickness worsened.

The only thing that kept Huang Fa moving was the thought of Yan at the end of his trail.

The tracks of the caravan would normally have been easy to follow, but dust was rapidly settling over everything, creating a red carpet that filled the hoof prints. Dust infiltrated his lungs, so that they felt heavy, as if he carried stones in them.

They had not gone far into the cloud when the mare simply stopped.

"What's wrong?" the monk called.

Huang Fa looked but could not see the monk, until the fellow suddenly materialized out of the dust not ten feet ahead.

"Bojing!" Huang Fa cried.

The monk tugged at the rope and cursed, but it did no good. Bojing merely stood, coughing and wheezing. Huang Fa leaned his head against her chest to listen to her lungs, and Bojing seemed to take that as a sign. She dropped to her front knees, and then lay down to die.

Huang Fa did not want to leave her in such misery. He put his coat over her face, hoping it would keep the dust from her lungs. Then he knelt beside her for several long minutes, just stroking her.

"Leave her," the monk begged. "Don't touch her. The anthrax might spread to you!"

"I can't leave her," Huang Fa shouted.

He realized now that it was hopeless. He only wanted to comfort the precious beast as she died. "I'm sorry, my princess," Huang Fa whispered again and again as he stroked her gritty hide.

Between the dusty air and the anthrax, she died within an hour.

When she was gone, Huang Fa removed her saddle packs, filled with what was left of his treasure, and stumbled on.

He closed his eyes against the storm and let the monk guide him.

The world seemed darker, and when Huang Fa looked up, he wondered if he had lost track of time, for it seemed that night had fallen. Then he realized his mistake: he'd stood at the edge of the storm and marveled at how terrible it was, but standing upon the brink of it was nothing compared to what he saw now. The wind that had seemed gentle, subdued, was beginning to gust stronger, and as it did, the dust belted them in waves. The haze that had hidden the sun an hour earlier now thickened and threatened to blot it out entirely.

Surely I am cursed, Huang Fa thought. *I wanted so badly to save my mare. Now the sorcerer has ripped her from my grasp. Battarsaikhan is fierce indeed!*

He staggered forward blindly, led by the monk, whose ability to negotiate through the storm felt nothing less than mystical. Huang Fa could not breathe, could not get air into his lungs, and he began to fear that, despite his best efforts, he would suffocate in the storm.

Coughing, his face hidden beneath his robes, he dropped to his knees to crawl, holding on to the cuff of the monk's robe. At last his hand bumped something that yielded. They had found a tent.

The monk knelt and untied some fastenings, and they lunged into a pavilion where several merchants wearing their finest wares—multicolored silks as bright as songbirds and butterflies—sat on cushions around a single golden lantern, drinking tea. Even in here the air was thick with dust. A courtly scholar in dark blue robes peered at Huang Fa knowingly and announced, "And here, good sirs, are the visitors that I promised: one man who is holy, and another who is damned."

The silk merchants gaped at Huang Fa and the monk in astonishment. "Incredible!" one of them cried. "In the midst of a killer storm!" another shouted. Two of the men actually clapped in delight at such a spectacle.

O   O   O

That night, as wind prowled outside the pavilion like a demon spirit and dust filtered through the air in a dense fog, Huang Fa peered through gritty eyes at the wizard, a eunuch with a face that was somehow regal despite the fact that he had no beard.

"You should not have given Battarsaikhan the dragon's tooth," the wizard warned after he had heard Huang Fa's tale. It had been hours since he'd entered the pavilion, but only now was he able to breathe well enough to plead for help. The day was dying, the sun descending into a bland orange haze, and the silk merchants lay about in a strange lethargy, weary of breathing, so that only the wizard, Huang Fa, and the monk were up.

"If a sorcerer has something that you have touched and owned," the wizard continued, "it can give him power over you."

"I only hoped to gain his forgiveness, Master Wong," Huang Fa apologized.

"There shall be none," the wizard intoned. He peered down into his lap.

"Is there nothing we can do?" the monk begged. "How will the sorcerer attack?"

"I am an expert in divination," Master Wong replied. "I am not an expert in all sorceries, but I have traveled the Earth, and I know something of these barbarians. He will send an animal spirit to possess Huang Fa, one that will fill him with animal desires and lead him to ruin."

"What kind of spirit?" the monk asked.

The wizard shook his head. "I cannot be sure. A fox spirit would fill him with lust, a wolf with a thirst for blood. A boar will turn him into a glutton. An ape spirit would make him act like a fool, but we are far from the land of apes. It will be … an animal close to the sorcerer."

Master Wong clapped his hands and asked a young boy, his assistant, to bring his "special trunk." The boy hurried to another pavilion and returned moments later. Master Wong had Huang Fa lie down; he took a bottle of henna dye and a calligraphy brush and began to write spells of warding upon Huang Fa's face. As he worked, he explained, "Animal spirits cannot take control of you unless you welcome them in. You can fight them. You must fight them. The spells that I am writing will help. The spirits will seek to enter through an orifice. Your nostrils or mouth are the weakest points, and so I will surround them with spells."

"You told the others I was damned," Huang Fa said. "How did you know?"

Master Wong hesitated in his brushstroke. "I cast the yarrow stalks this morning and formed a trigram, then read from the I-Ching."

Huang Fa was skeptical at this. The I-Ching, or Book of Changes, suggested that all of life was in a flux. Every person's situation was always about to change, and by casting the yarrow stalks, one could then consult the book and learn direction for the future. But it was not as simple as that. In part, one had to rely upon the abilities of the wizard who did the divination. One had to trust his insights.

"So you learned that I was damned from the I-Ching?"

"I have felt your coming for days," replied Master Wong. "'A stranger is coming,' the yarrow stalks foretold, 'one with blood on his hands and a curse on his soul. He has an enemy more powerful than this storm.'"

"You divined all of this?"

The wizard nodded solemnly, then set down his brush and folded his hands. "I could learn little more—except for the hour of your coming."

"Is there any hope for me?"

Master Wong frowned. "This Battarsaikhan has powers far beyond mine. He sent this storm to slow you down—or kill you—and that is no small feat. Yet this I also know: the human heart has a magic of its own, as powerful as any spell. Perhaps if we understood his powers better ..."

Huang Fa's heart hammered, filling him with hope. "Is there a surer form of divination than the I-Ching?"

Master Wong leaned over Huang Fa and gave an inscrutable expression, as if he might be annoyed. "You are a skeptic? You don't trust me? I do my own readings twice a day. I would not have survived for a hundred and twelve years without them! If the stalks tell me to eat an apricot today, I eat it. If they tell me to stay out of the rain—"

The monk's mouth dropped in surprise. "You are a hundred and twelve years old?"

The wizard did not look a day over fifty. He kept a straight face for a moment before bursting out laughing at his own jest. "If you want a surer form of divination," he suggested to Huang Fa, "we can consult the turtle's oracle bones."

That was a form of divination Huang Fa could trust. The turtle was the most blessed creature under heaven. Because of this, the gods had granted the turtle long life and great wisdom, and it held a special place close to the gods as one of the four holy animals. Indeed, Huang Fa sometimes prayed to turtles, for they could act as intermediaries to the gods.

To consult oracle bones, the wizard carved a question into the shell of a turtle that had been ritually sacrificed. Then he would drill small holes in the shell, insert a stick of incense into each hole, and light the incense. When the stick burned down, the heat would weaken the shell, causing it to crack. If the bone cracked inward, toward the center of the shell, then the answer to the question was "yes." If it cracked toward the outer part of the shell, then the answer was "no."

This form of divination limited the wizard to asking yes-or-no questions, which was its weakness, but the virtue of this method was that heaven left no ambiguity in the answer.

"Suggest a question," Master Wong offered, "and I will consult the oracle bones tonight."

Huang Fa blew his nose. The air was so dusty that the mucus came out black. He felt dirty down to his lungs, in every pore of his skin, to the very core of his soul.

Huang Fa formed his question for the gods: "Can I escape the Sorcerer Battarsaikhan's curse?"

O   O   O

The wind shrieked outside the tent, drumming at the silk and tugging at the pegs and stays. Inside the pavilion, all was dark and strangely cold. The only light came from eight sticks of incense that rose from holes in the turtle shell. The sweet scent of jasmine curled up from the cherry coals until the dusty room bore a cloying air.

Huang Fa lay in a troubled dream, shaking from chills. He dreamt of children crawling stealthily through the storm, faces bared to the wind. They dragged something large and bulky behind them as they crawled, something with hair, though the dim light defeated Huang Fa's vision.

It is the mare's head, Huang Fa thought unreasonably, and whimpered in horror.

But the children came on—toddlers with knives in their hands, and young girls in nothing but loin clothes. There were fierce boys with sharpened teeth and eyes that shone with their own inner light, as if stars might burst from them.

They reached the door flap of the pavilion and crept inside, dragging their hairy burden. Huang Fa felt vaguely detached as they neared his bed, even though he expected them to plunge their daggers into his flesh.

"I meant no harm," he apologized. "I did not know your need."

The feral children gave no answer.

A chill swept over him, as if an icy wind blew up from the caverns of hell and rippled up his spine. His muscles felt as rubbery as dead eels.

A half a dozen children stood above the hairy thing. By the light from the incense, Huang Fa could see an animal hide rolled up and tied into a bundle.

It is the hide from my horse, he thought. *They will put it upon me so that I catch the anthrax.*

He felt torn between the desire to run, to fight, or simply to lie still and accept whatever fate the feral children deemed fit.

Three children uncut the strings that bound the hide and unrolled it, almost celebrating with excitement. Even in the dim light Huang Fa could see that it was not the hide of his fine red mare. This skin was a deeper red, like the bark of red pines in the mountain.

Four waifs spread the great hide over him with great ceremony, and Huang Fa breathed in the luxurious scent of a well-tanned hide. The fur upon it was like heaven, like a banked fire that warmed him through and through.

The children turned to leave; Huang Fa suddenly roused to a sense of danger. His eyes flew open, and he stilled his breathing to listen for the sound of stealthy motion.

The room was dark, the dead air heavy with dust. Outside, the storm had quieted. Nothing moved in the pavilion. The only sound was the soft snoring of a trader on the far side of the tent, hidden beneath a sheepskin.

Droplets of sweat stood out on Huang Fa's forehead and made his shirt cling to his chest. Briefly he worried that he had caught anthrax, but then realized that he had been lost in a fever dream and that his fever had broken.

For days he had been sick with worry, and now he felt suddenly released. He leaned up on one elbow, peered around the room. There were no feral children here.

He touched the pelt spread upon him, a fine animal hide unlike any that he could recall seeing. The fur was thick, luxurious, and the animal was huge.

Perhaps it is from some kind of yak, he wondered, and then realized that someone must have discerned just how chilly the night had become and laid the hide over him. His fever had turned a kindness into a nightmare.

Huang Fa pulled the hide over his head and wished that he could lie beneath it forever, smell the clean scent of the leather, fall into the embrace of its everlasting warmth.

○ ○ ○

At dawn, Huang Fa woke to the scent of tea brewing. Sunlight streamed through the tent. Someone had gone outside and was using a branch from a bush to sweep dust from the walls of the pavilion.

"Good news," the monk said. "The storm blew out last night, and the bad air is clearing. The sun came up as red as a phoenix this morning, but all is well."

The merchants were up and bustling about in their colorful silks, packing kegs of precious oils and spices outside. Master Wong merely sat drinking his tea, his face looking drawn and hard.

Huang Fa got up and stretched, pulling the deep-red hide up to him. He then looked upon a small trunk to where the turtle shell lay. The brown lines upon its curved back looked like cracks in the mud after a river dries. The stubs of eight incense sticks poked out from it.

Huang Fa felt good, full of light and hope. He nodded to the shell and begged the wizard, "Have you checked the oracle bones?"

Master Wong gazed at him for a long moment, his face stoic. He finally nodded a bit and said evenly. "You cannot escape your fate. I'm sorry. We cannot always escape the consequences of our errors, no matter how bitterly we regret our deeds."

At that moment, Huang Fa felt a strange sensation. His face was growing numb, and he noted that the skin on his forehead itched. He reached up and touched the side of his head—and felt a distinct nub protruding sharply up, stretching his skin taut.

"What?" he asked, fear lurching in his stomach. He noted something odd about his hand. A fine soft fur had begun to grow out of it, as dark red as the darkest cedar wood.

Huang Fa screamed in wordless terror and leaped out from under the hide.

"The animal spirit has entered you," the wizard said apologetically. "Battarsaikhan's spell is more powerful than I could have dreamed. It is not just your nature that will change."

Huang Fa scrambled away from his bed, shoving the great red hide away. He peered at the luxurious fur.

"In the land of the Kazakhs," Master Wong explained, "the animal that wore that skin is called a 'giant deer,' and its meat is treasured as the sweetest of all venison. Its hide is as dark at the trunks of the red pines in the mountains where it lives, and its wide antlers are valued by all, but it is so rare that some believe it to be only a myth. Here near the Altai Mountains, a few still survive, but even in our tales it is hardly more than a myth—the Xie Chai. Though it has two horns, some insist that it is a type of unicorn."

Huang Fa felt a sudden excruciating pain in his ankles as bones twisted. He fought against a strange compulsion to stand on all fours. He knew the name of the Xie Chai, of course. It was said that the unicorn could smell good and evil and was attracted by the scent of righteous men while it punished the evil. The Buddhists said that it often carried the book of law in its antlers.

"Haaaawlp!" Huang Fa cried, but the words twisted in his mouth, and only an animal's mewling cry escaped his lips.

"This is your fate—the fate that Battarsaikhan, the peaceful sorcerer, has placed upon you," the wizard said sadly. "You shall roam the land upon four hooves and be doomed to paw beneath the snow for lichens and grass at the feet of the Altai Mountains. You shall never know the love of a woman, for you are among the last of your kind.

"You shall be hunted all the days of your life, by both barbarians and by true men, by wolves and snow leopards in the mountains, by cheetahs on the plains. There is no escape for you, oh man with a gentle soul, nowhere that you may hide. I fear you will not last the winter, for most of all you shall be hunted by the feral children, from whose mouths you have taken their livelihood, and it is the will of the sorcerer that you shall be found.

"At the very last, you shall feed the feral children with your own flesh."

An image of Yan flashed before Huang Fa. He saw her at the foot of a screen, painting an image of a phoenix upon black silk. She looked up toward sunlight streaming in through a window.

Huang Fa lunged toward the flap of the tent and lurched through it into the dusty air. His new animal instincts made him yearn for freedom, to run under the open sky, and he clattered the last few steps upon hooves that slipped upon the silk beneath him. His growing antlers caught in the flaps of the tent and threatened to break his neck before he tore free. The sky outside was filled with dust and had a surreal glow to it, as red as if lit by the Sun God's fires.

Yan, he thought.

Huang Fa snorted and whirled, his feet kicking up dust, and peered into the tall grass near camp. There he saw tiny figures— the sprawling bodies of half-starved children, hiding in the grass, teeth filed sharper than daggers.

He turned and bounded away, his tail raised high like a flag of warning, his feet exploding with power as he ascended into the air, dipped to the earth, and then soared upward again.

O   O   O

In late winter, Yan woke one night. The lunar New Year had just begun, and it was the night of the lantern festival. A great red lantern hung from the rafters on her porch, streaming a little light through her window.

She'd dreamt of Huang Fa again, and the excitement of the holidays was dulled by a sense of loss. He had never come home. She feared that he was trapped in the snowy mountains, or that he had died while crossing the desert.

Yet tonight her heart told her that he still lived, and she imagined that he had come to her bed.

She inhaled deeply, trying to catch the scent of him. She tried to remember the light in his eyes, his broad handsome smile, but the memory had faded.

Yan untangled herself from her bedsheets, from the arms of her little sister whom she feared might waken and beg for breakfast.

She went to the door. The red lantern hung above her head, burning gaily in the night.

She gazed out across the wooden bridge in front of her house, toward the bamboo grove whose leaves rustled in a light wind.

A beast stood there—huge and dark, its fur a deep red. It was so large that at first she thought it was a horse. Then she saw that it dwarfed even a stallion. Its broad antlers were like those of an enormous elk, yet webbing stretched between the tines, as if to catch the light of the full moon.

It tiptoed toward her, into the circle of light by the door, and she knew it for what it was—a Xie Chai unicorn.

It extended its snout, as if to catch her scent, and she put forth her hand, hoping that it might enjoy the allure of the rosewater perfume she wore. Such animals could discern a man's heart. It would tell her if she was good or evil.

She longed to be good, but she knew her love for Huang Fa was too great.

The unicorn stepped near, and she was astonished at how huge it was. She saw its eyes, shining in the light of the lantern, filled with some unimaginable desire.

Suddenly she could smell the musky scent of a young man that often haunted her dreams. She knew that scent intimately, knew the young man's clean limbs and sweet breath.

"Huang Fa?" she wondered aloud.

The beast looked startled. The muscles in its shoulders began to bunch, as if it would leap away.

She knew then what had happened. Huang Fa had turned into this magical beast, and, yearning for her, he had come to her at last.

But *how* had this happened?

Inside the house, her little sister woke in the night. "Yan?" she cried. "Yan, I'm hungry!"

In that instant the unicorn grew afraid. There was no more coherent thought in its head, only nameless animal fear that took over.

The proud beast whirled and bounded, leaping through the stream.

"Huang Fa!" Yan called, rushing to the edge of the porch.

A low fog covered the ground, and the unicorn bounded through it, as if leaping upon clouds, until it disappeared into the plum orchard, lost under a silver moon.

About the Author

David Farland is an award-winning, bestselling author with more than fifty novels in print. He has won the Philip K. Dick Award for his novel *On My Way to Paradise* and over seven awards for his novel *Nightingale*. He is best known for his *New York Times* bestselling series The Runelords.

ADDITIONAL
COPYRIGHT INFORMATION

"M.Y.T.H. Rule"
Copyright © 2015 Jody Lynn Nye

"Killing Zombies in Rural America:
A Survival Guide by Doug and Cecilia"
Copyright © 2015 Kristin Luna

"The Dark Ambition of Oswald March"
Copyright © 2015 Tristan Brand

"The Old Gray Mare"
Copyright © 2015 John D. Payne

"Now I See You"
Copyright © 2015 Joy Dawn Johnson

"Scrapyard Paradise"
Copyright © 2015 Brandon M. Lindsay

"Vodka Dreams"
Copyright © 2015 Falcon's Fables LLC

"The Fall of Winter"
Copyright © 2015 Scott Elder

"Customer Hotline"
Copyright © 2015 Josh Vogt

"The Sharpest Horn"
Copyright © 2015 Travis Heermann

"The Setting Sun"
Copyright © 2015 Victoria D. Morris

"The Whole of Me"
Copyright © 2015 Gregory D. Little

"Odin's Eye"
Copyright © 2015 Frank Morin

"Queen of the Hidden Way"
Copyright © 2015 Mary Pletsch

"The Red Unicorn Candy Store"
Copyright © 2015 Katie Cross

"Vengeance for Dinner"
Copyright © 2015 Emily Godhand and J.S. Bennett

"The Trade"
Copyright © 2015 Raphyel M. Jordan

"His Most Violent Friend"
Copyright © 2015 Gregory D. Little

"Laura's Magic Clock"
Copyright © 2015 Robert J. McCarter

"Correlation Effect"
Copyright © 2015 Falcon's Fables LLC

"Feeding the Feral Children"
Copyright © 2015 David Wolverton/aka David Farland

IF YOU LIKED ...

If you liked *A Game of Horns*, you might also enjoy:

One Horn to Rule Them All

ABOUT THE EDITOR

Lisa Mangum has worked in the publishing industry since 1997 and is currently the Managing Editor of Shadow Mountain Publishing in Utah. She is also the author of four award-winning young adult novels (The Hourglass Door trilogy and *After Hello*) as well as several novellas and short stories. She lives in Utah with her husband, Tracy.

OTHER WORDFIRE PRESS TITLES

Our list of other WordFire Press authors and titles is always growing. To find out more and to see our selection of titles, visit us at:

wordfirepress.com